D0278653

Val McDermid is the author of twenty-four bestselling novels, which have been translated into more than thirty languages, and have sold over ten million copies. She has won many awards internationally, including the CWA Gold Dagger for best crime novel of the year and the *LA Times* Book of the Year Award. She was inducted into the ITV3 Crime Thriller Awards Hall of Fame in 2009 and was the recipient of the CWA Cartier Diamond Dagger for 2010. In 2011 she received the Lambda Literary Foundation Pioneer Award. She has a son and a dog, and lives with her wife in the north of England.

Also by Val McDermid

A Place of Execution
Killing the Shadows
The Distant Echo
The Grave Tattoo
A Darker Domain
Trick of the Dark

TONY HILL NOVELS

The Mermaids Singing
The Wire in the Blood
The Last Temptation
The Torment of Others
Beneath the Bleeding
Fever of the Bone

KATE BRANNIGAN NOVELS

Dead Beat
Kick Back
Crack Down
Clean Break
Blue Genes
Star Struck

LINDSAY GORDON NOVELS

Report for Murder
Common Murder
Final Edition
Union Jack
Booked for Murder
Hostage to Murder

SHORT STORY COLLECTIONS

The Writing on the Wall
Stranded

NON-FICTION

A Suitable Job for a Woman

THE
RETRIBUTION

VAL McDERMID

LITTLE, BROWN

First published in Great Britain in 2011 by Little, Brown
Reprinted 2011

A CIP catalogue record for this book
is available from the British Library.

Hardback ISBN 978-1-4087-0319-9
Trade Paperback ISBN 978-1-4087-0320-5

Typeset in Meridien by M Rules
Printed and bound in Great Britain by
Clays Ltd, St Ives plc

Papers used by Little, Brown are from well-managed forests
and other responsible sources.

MIX
Paper from
responsible sources
FSC
www.fsc.org   FSC® C104740

Little, Brown
An imprint of
Little, Brown Book Group
100 Victoria Embankment
London EC4Y 0DY

An Hachette UK Company
www.hachette.co.uk

www.littlebrown.co.uk

For Mr David: for reminding me how much fun this is, for shaking up my ideas and for showing faith.

Acknowledgements

This is my twenty-fifth novel. And still I have to go around picking people's brains to make it all work. As usual, there are those who prefer to remain anonymous. Their willingness to share their experience never ceases to impress me, and I am grateful for the insight into their worlds.

Carolyn Ryan was generous with her contacts; thanks also to her and Paul for putting up with me on the caffeine-free dog walks. Professor Sue Black and Dave Barclay gave me the benefit of their forensic knowledge, and Dr Gwen Adshead talked more sense about abnormal psychology than anyone else I've ever heard.

I just write the books. It takes a small army of dedicated people to get them into the hands of readers. Thanks as always to everyone at Gregory & Co; to my support team at Little, Brown; to the peerless Anne O'Brien and to Caroline Brown who could make the trains run on time if she put her mind to it.

And finally, thanks to my friends and family whose love is really all I need. In particular to Kelly and Cameron, the best companions a woman could ask for.

Nemesis is lame; but she is of colossal stature, like the gods, and sometimes, while her sword is not yet unsheathed, she stretches out her huge left arm and grasps her victim. The mighty hand is invisible, but the victim totters under the dire clutch.

George Eliot *Scenes of Clerical Life*

1

Escapology was like magic. The secret lay in misdirection. Some escapes were accomplished by creating an illusion through careful planning; others were genuine feats of strength, daring and flexibility, both mental and physical; and some were mixtures of both. But whatever the methods, the element of misdirection always played a crucial role. And when it came to misdirection, he called no man his master.

Best of all was the misdirection that the onlooker didn't even know was happening. To accomplish that you had to make your diversion blend into the spectrum of normal.

Some settings made that harder than others. Take an office where everything ran like clockwork. You'd struggle to camouflage a distraction there because anything out of the ordinary would stand out and stick in people's minds. But in prison there were so many unpredictable variables – volatile individuals; complex power structures; trivial disputes that could go nuclear in a matter of moments; and pent-up frustrations never far from bursting like a ripe zit. Almost anything could go off at any time, and who could say whether it was a calculated event or just one of a hundred little local difficulties getting out of hand? The very existence of those variables made some people uneasy. But not him. For him, every alternate scenario provided a fresh opportunity, another option to scrutinise till finally he hit on the perfect combination of circumstances and characters.

He'd considered faking it. Paying a couple of the lads to get into a ruck on the wing. But there were too many downsides to that. For one thing, the more people who knew about his plans, the more prospects there were for betrayal. For another, most of the people inside were there because their previous attempts at dissimulation had failed dismally. Probably not the best people to entrust with putting on a convincing performance, then. And you could never rule out plain stupidity, of course. So faking it was out.

However, the beauty of prison was that there was never a shortage of levers to pull. Men trapped on the inside were always prey to fears of what might be going down on the outside. They had lovers, wives, kids and parents who were vulnerable to violence or temptation. Or just the threat of those things.

So he'd watched and waited, gathering data and evaluating it, figuring out where the possibilities offered the best chance of success. It helped that he didn't have to rely on his own observations. His support system beyond the walls had provided the intelligence that plugged most of the gaps in his own knowledge. It really hadn't taken long to find the perfect pressure point.

And now he was ready. Tonight he would make his move. Tomorrow night, he'd be sleeping in a wide, comfortable bed with feather pillows. The perfect end to a perfect evening. A rare steak with a pile of garlic mushrooms and rösti potatoes, perfectly complemented by a bottle of claret that would have only improved in the dozen years he'd been away. A plate of crisp Bath Olivers and a Long Clawson stilton to take away the bad taste of what passed for cheese in prison. Then a long hot bath, a glass of cognac and a Cuban Cohiba. He'd savour every gradation on the spectrum of the senses.

A jagged cacophony of raised voices penetrated his visualisation, a routine argument about football crashing back and forth across the landing. An officer roared at them to keep the noise down and it subsided a little. The distant mutter of a radio filled the gaps between the insults and it occurred to him that even better than the steak, the booze and the cigar would be the freedom from other people's noise.

That was the one thing people never mentioned when they sounded off about how awful it must be to be in prison. They talked about the discomfort, the lack of freedom, the fear of your fellow inmates, the loss of your personal comforts. But even the most imaginative never commented on the nightmare of losing silence.

Tomorrow, that nightmare would be over. He could be as quiet or as loud as he chose. But it would be his noise.

Well, mostly his. There would be other noises. Ones that he was looking forward to. Ones he liked to imagine when he needed a spur to keep going. Ones he'd been dreaming about even longer than he'd been figuring out his escape route. The screams, the sobs, the stammering pleas for mercy that would never come. The soundtrack of payback.

Jacko Vance, killer of seventeen teenage girls, murderer of a serving police officer and a man once voted the sexiest man on British TV, could hardly wait.

2

The big man put two brimming pints of copper-coloured ale on the table. 'Piddle in the Hole,' he said, settling his broad frame on a stool that disappeared from sight beneath his thighs.

Dr Tony Hill raised his eyebrows. 'A challenge? Or is that what passes for wit in Worcester?'

Detective Sergeant Alvin Ambrose raised his glass in a salute. 'Neither. The brewery's in a village called Wyre Piddle, so they think they're entitled.'

Tony took a long draught of his beer, then gave it a considering look. 'Fair enough,' he said. 'It's a decent pint.'

Both men gave the beer a moment's respectful silence, then Ambrose spoke. 'She's pissed my guv'nor off royally, your Carol Jordan.'

Even after all these years, Tony still struggled to keep a poker face when Carol Jordan was mentioned. It was a struggle worth maintaining, though. For one thing, he believed in never giving hostages to fortune. But more importantly, he'd always found it impossible to define what Carol meant to him and he wasn't inclined to give others the chance to jump to mistaken conclusions. 'She's not *my* Carol Jordan,' he said mildly. 'She's not anyone's Carol Jordan, truth be told.'

'You said she'd be sharing your house down here, if she got the job,' Ambrose said, not hiding the reproach in his voice.

A revelation Tony wished now he'd never made. It had slipped out during one of the late-night conversations that had cemented this unlikely friendship between two wary men with little in common. Tony trusted Ambrose, but that still didn't mean he wanted to admit him into the labyrinth of contradictions and complications of what passed for his emotional life. 'She already rents my basement flat. It's not so different. It's a big house,' he said, his voice non-committal but his hand rigid on the glass.

Ambrose's eyes tightened at the corners, the rest of his face impassive. Tony reckoned the instinctive copper in him was wondering whether it was worth pursuing. 'And she's a very attractive woman,' Ambrose said at last.

'She is.' Tony tipped his glass towards Ambrose in acknowledgement. 'So why is DI Patterson so pissed off with her?'

Ambrose raised one beefy shoulder in a shrug that strained the seam of his jacket. His brown eyes lost their watchfulness as he relaxed into safe territory. 'The usual kind of thing. He's served all his career in West Mercia, most of it here in Worcester. He thought when the DCI's job came up, his feet were already tucked under the desk. Then your— then DCI Jordan made it known that she was interested in a move from Bradfield.' His smile was as twisted as the lemon peel on the rim of a cocktail glass. 'And how could West Mercia say no to her?'

Tony shook his head. 'You tell me.'

'Track record like hers? First the Met, then something mysterious with Europol, then heading up her own major crimes unit in the fourth biggest force in the country and beating the counter-terrorism twats at their own game ... There's only a handful of coppers in the whole country with her experience who still want to be at the sharp end, rather than flying a desk.

Patterson knew the minute the grapevine rustled that he was dead in the water.'

'Not necessarily,' Tony said. 'Some bosses might see Carol as a threat. The woman who knew too much. They might see her as the fox in the henhouse.'

Ambrose chuckled, a deep subterranean rumble. 'Not here. They think they're the bee's knees here. They look at those mucky bastards next door in West Midlands and strut like peacocks. They'd see DCI Jordan like a prize pigeon coming home to the loft where she belongs.'

'Very poetic.' Tony sipped his beer, savouring the bitter edge of the hops. 'But that's not how your DI Patterson sees it?'

Ambrose demolished most of his pint while he worked out his response. Tony was accustomed to waiting. It was a technique that worked equally well at work or at play. He'd never figured out why the people he dealt with were called 'patients' when he was the one who had to exert all the patience. Nobody who wanted to be a competent clinical psychologist could afford to show too much eagerness when it came to seeking answers.

'It's hard for him,' Ambrose said at last. 'It's harsh, knowing you've been passed over because you're second best. So he has to come up with something that makes him feel better about himself.'

'And what's he come up with?'

Ambrose lowered his head. In the dim light of the pub, his dark skin turned him into a pool of shadow. 'He's mouthing off about her motives for moving. Like, she doesn't give a toss about West Mercia. She's just following you now you've inherited your big house and decided to shake the dust of Bradfield from your heels ...'

It wasn't his place to defend Carol Jordan's choices, but saying nothing wasn't an option either. Silence would reinforce Patterson's bitter analysis. The least Tony could do was to give Ambrose an alternative to put forward in the canteen and the squad room. 'Maybe. But I'm not the reason she's leaving Bradfield. That's office politics, nothing to do with me. She got a new boss and he didn't think her team was good value for money. She had three months to prove him wrong.' Tony shook his head, a rueful smile on his face. 'Hard to see what more she could have done. Nailed a serial killer, cleared up two cold-case murders and busted a people-trafficking operation that was bringing in kids for the sex trade.'

'I'd call that a serious clear-up rate,' Ambrose said.

'Not serious enough for James Blake. The three months is up and he's announced that he's breaking up the unit at the end of the month and scattering them through the general CID. She'd already decided she didn't want to be deployed like that. So, she knew she was leaving Bradfield. She just didn't know where she was headed. Then this West Mercia job came up, and she didn't even have to change landlords.'

Ambrose gave him an amused look and drained his glass. 'You ready for another?'

'I'm still working on this one. But it's my shout,' Tony protested as Ambrose headed back to the bar. He caught the glance the young barmaid threw in their direction, a faint frown on her soft features. He imagined they made an odd couple, him and Ambrose. A burly black man with a shaven head and a face like a heavyweight boxer, tie loosened, black suit tight over heavy muscles, Ambrose's formidable presence would have fitted most people's idea of a serious bodyguard. Whereas Tony reckoned he didn't even look capable of guarding his own body, never mind anyone else's. Medium height; slight of build; wirier than he deserved to be, given that his principal exercise came from playing Rayman's Raving Rabbids on his Wii; leather jacket, hooded sweatshirt, black jeans. Over the years, he'd learned that the only thing people remembered about him were his eyes, a startling sparkling blue, shocking against the paleness of his skin. Ambrose's eyes were memorable too, but only because they hinted at a gentleness apparent nowhere else in his demeanour. Most people missed that, Tony thought. Too taken up with the superficial image. He wondered if the barmaid had noticed.

Ambrose returned with a fresh pint. 'You off your ale tonight?'

Tony shook his head. 'I'm heading back to Bradfield.'

Ambrose looked at his watch. 'At this time? It's already gone ten o'clock.'

'I know. But there's no traffic this time of night. I can be home in less than two hours. I've got patients tomorrow at Bradfield Moor. Last appointments before I hand them over to someone I hope will treat them like the damaged messes they are. Going at night's a lot less stressful. Late-night music and empty roads.'

Ambrose chuckled. 'Sounds like a country music song.'

'I sometimes feel like my whole life is a country music song,' Tony grumbled. 'And not one of the upbeat ones.' As he spoke, his phone began to ring. He frantically patted his pockets, finally tracking it down in the front pocket of his jeans. He didn't recognise the mobile number on the screen, but gave it the benefit of the doubt. If the staff at Bradfield Moor were having problems with one of his nutters, they sometimes used their own phones to call him. 'Hello?' he said, cautious.

'Is that Dr Hill? Dr Tony Hill?' It was a woman's voice, tickling at the edge of his memory but not quite falling into place.

'Who is this?'

'It's Penny Burgess, Dr Hill. From the *Evening Sentinel Times*. We've spoken before.'

Penny Burgess. He recalled a woman in a trench coat, collar turned up against the rain, face arranged in a tough expression, long dark hair escaping from its confines. He also recalled how he'd been variously transformed in the stories under her

8

byline, from omniscient sage to idiot scapegoat. 'Rather less than you'd have your readers believe,' he said.

'Just doing my job, Dr Hill.' Her voice was a lot warmer than their history merited. 'There's been another woman murdered in Bradfield,' she continued. She was about as good at small talk as he was, Tony thought, trying to avoid the wider implications of her words. When he failed to respond, she said, 'A sex worker. Like the two last month.'

'I'm sorry to hear that,' Tony said, choosing his words like steps in a minefield.

'Why I'm ringing you ... My source tells me this one has the same signature as the previous two. I'm wondering what you make of that?'

'I've no idea what you're talking about. I've currently got no operational involvement with Bradfield CID.'

Penny Burgess made a low sound in her throat, almost a chuckle but not quite. 'I'm sure your sources are at least as good as mine,' she said. 'I can't believe DCI Jordan is out of the loop on this one, and if she knows, you know.'

'You've got a very strange notion of my world,' Tony said firmly. 'I have no idea what you're talking about.'

'I'm talking about a serial killer, Dr Hill. And when it comes to serial killers, you're the man.'

Abruptly, Tony ended the call, shoving his phone back in his pocket. He raised his eyes to meet Ambrose's assessing gaze. 'Hack,' he said. He swallowed a mouthful of beer. 'Actually, no. She's better than that. Carol's crew have left her with egg all over her face more than once, but she just acts like that's an occupational hazard.'

'All the same ...' Ambrose said.

Tony nodded. 'Right. You can respect them without being willing to give them anything.'

'What was she after?'

'She was fishing. We've had two street prostitutes killed in

Bradfield over the last few weeks. Now there's a third. As far as I was aware, there was no reason to connect the first two – completely different MO.' He shrugged. 'Well, I say that, but I know nothing officially. Not Carol's cases, and even if they were, she doesn't share.'

'But your hack's saying something different?'

'She says there's a signature connection. But it's still nothing to do with me. Even if they decide they need a profile, it won't be me they come to.'

'Stupid bastards. You're the best there is.'

Tony finished his drink. 'That may well be true. But as far as James Blake is concerned, staying in-house is cheaper and it means he keeps control.' A wry smile. 'I can see his point. If I was him, I probably wouldn't employ me either. More trouble than it's worth.' He pushed back from the table and stood up. 'And on that cheerful note, I'm off up the motorway.'

'Is there not a part of you that wishes you were out there at that crime scene?' Ambrose drained his second pint and got to his feet, deliberately standing back so he didn't loom over his friend.

Tony considered. 'I won't deny that the people who do this kind of thing fascinate me. The more disturbed they are, the more I want to figure out what makes them tick. And how I can help them to make the mechanism function a bit better.' He sighed. 'But I am weary of looking at the end results. Tonight, Alvin, I'm going home to bed, and believe me, there's nowhere I'd rather be.'

3

The safest place to hide anything was in plain sight. People only ever see what they expect to see. Those were some of the truths he'd learned a long time before his life had been shrunk by prison walls. But he was smart and he was determined, so he hadn't stopped learning just because his physical environment had become constrained.

Some people closed down as soon as they found themselves behind bars. They were seduced by a life less chaotic, consoled by predictability. One of the lesser-known aspects of prison life was the high incidence of obsessive-compulsive disorder. Jails were full of men and women who found a comfort in repetitive behaviour that had never occurred to them on the outside. Right from the start, Jacko Vance had steeled himself against the seduction of routine.

Not that he'd had much routine to start with. There's nothing prisoners love more than fucking up a celebrity inmate. When George Michael was banged up, the entire wing kept him awake all night roaring tuneless renderings of his greatest hits, altering the words to suit their mood as the night wore on. With Vance, as soon as they were locked in for the night, they'd whistled the theme tune from his TV show, on and on like a track on repeat. Once *Vance's Visits* had worn down their patience, they'd started on football-style chants about his wife and her girlfriend. It had been an ugly introduction, but it hadn't upset him. He'd walked on to the landing in the morning as composed and calm as he'd been the night before.

There was a reason for his composure. Right from the start, he'd been determined he was going to get out. He knew it would take years and he had forced himself to accept that. He had legal avenues to explore, but he wasn't convinced they would work. So he needed to get Plan B in place as quickly as possible to give him something to focus on. Something to aim for.

The composure was the first step on the journey. He had to prove that he deserved respect without making it look like he was trying to step on someone else's territory, particularly since they all knew he'd killed teenage girls, which made him a borderline nonce. None of it had been easy, and there had been occasional false steps along the way. But Vance still had contacts on the outside who clung on to their belief in his innocence. And he was perfectly willing to exploit those contacts to the full. Keeping sweet the alpha males inside was often a matter of oiling the wheels outside. Vance still had plenty of grease where it counted.

Keeping his nose clean inside the system was another key element in the plan. Whatever he was up to, he had to make it look like he was sticking to the rules. Good behaviour, that's what he wanted the prison staff to see. Put up with the shit and be a good boy, Jacko. But that was as much of an act as anything else.

Years ago he'd been watching the TV magazine show his ex-wife used to host when she'd interviewed the governor of a prison where there had been a terrifying riot, with the prisoners effectively taking control of the jail for three days. The governor had had a world-weary air to him, and Vance could still summon up his image when he recalled his words: 'Whatever you put in place, they'll find a way round it.' At the time, Vance had been intrigued, wondering if it might be a hook for a TV programme for him and his team. Now, he embraced what it really meant.

Of course, in prison your options were limited when it came to finding a way round anything. You were thrown back on your own resources. That gave Vance a head start over most of his fellow inmates, who didn't have much to draw on. But the attributes that had made him the most popular male presenter on British TV were perfectly suited to prison. He was charismatic, handsome, charming. And because he'd been a world-class sportsman before the accident that had ultimately led him to his TV career, he could lay claim to being a man's man. And then there was the George Cross, awarded for risking his life to save small children after a fogbound multiple-vehicle accident on the motorway. Or maybe it was supposed to be a consolation for losing his arm in the failed attempt to get a trapped trucker out of his crushed cab. Either way, he didn't think there was another jailbird in the country who had been awarded the highest honour for civilian heroism. It all stacked up in the plus column.

At the heart of his plan had been one simple element – befriend the people who had the power to change his world. The top guns who run the inmates; the officers who choose who gets the perks; the psychologist who decides how you serve your time. And all the while, he'd be alert for the key player he'd need to make it all come together.

Brick by brick, he'd built the foundations for his escape. The electric razor, for example. He'd deliberately sprained his wrist so he could plead the impossibility of a one-armed man shaving any other way. Then there had been the convenience of the Human Rights Act, which had ensured his access to state-of-the-art prosthetics. Because the money he'd made before he'd been revealed as a serial killer of adolescent girls had not been the proceeds of crime, the authorities couldn't touch it. So his artificial limb was the very best that money could buy, allowing him intuitive control and individual finger movements. The synthetic skin was so good, people who didn't know any better wouldn't believe it wasn't real. If you weren't looking for fake, you wouldn't see it. An eye for detail, that was what counted.

There had been a moment when he'd thought all his work had been wasted. But wasted in a good way. To the surprise of most people, the appeal court had eventually overturned the verdict against him. For a glorious moment, he'd thought he'd be walking out into the world a free man. But those bastard cops had slammed him with another murder charge before he could even get out of the dock. And that one had stuck like glue, as he'd always feared it might. And so it was back to the cell and back to the drawing board.

Being patient, sticking with the plan had been hard. Years had trickled by with little to show. But he'd toughed things out before. Recovering from the terrible accident that had robbed him of his Olympic medal dreams and the woman he loved had given him reserves of willpower that few people had access to. Years of training to reach the pinnacle of his sport had taught him the value of perseverance. Tonight, all that would pay off. Within a few hours, it would all have been worth it. Now he just had to make the final preparations.

And then he would teach some people a lesson they would never forget.

4

It was hard to see the victim clearly because of the white-suited forensic technicians working the crime scene. As far as Detective Superintendent Pete Reekie was concerned, that was no bad thing. It wasn't that he was squeamish. He'd seen enough blood over the years to be pretty much immune to its stomach-churning potential. He could take any amount of straightforward violence. But when he was confronted by the perverse, he'd do all he could to avoid the kind of eye contact with the dead that would leave their broken and profaned bodies etched on his memory. DS Reekie didn't like sick minds having access to his head.

It was bad enough that he'd already had to listen to his DI run through it on the phone. Reekie had been having a perfectly pleasant evening in front of his giant plasma screen, a can of Stella in one hand, cigar in the other, watching Manchester United cling on to a single goal lead against more stylish opposition in the European Championship, when his mobile had rung.

'It's DI Spencer,' his caller announced. 'I'm sorry to disturb you, sir, but we've got a bad one out here and I thought you might want to be informed.'

Ever since he'd taken over Bradfield's Northern Divisional CID, Reekie had made it clear to his minions that he didn't ever want to be blindsided by some case that the media decided to turn into an audience-grabbing crusade. This was the downside, being dragged away from a key match with fifteen minutes still to play. 'Will it not wait till morning?' Reekie demanded, knowing the answer before the question was finished.

'I think you'll want to be out here,' Spencer said. 'It's another prostitute murder, same tattoo on the wrist, according to the doc.'

'Are you saying we're looking at a serial killer?' Reekie made no attempt to hide his incredulity. Ever since Hannibal Lecter, every bloody detective wanted to jump on the serial-killer bandwagon.

'Hard to say, sir. I never saw the first two, but the doc says it looks the same. Only ...'

'Spit it out, Spencer.' Already, Reekie had regretfully dumped his can on the table by his chair and stubbed out his cigar.

'The MO ... well, it's pretty radical, compared to the other two.'

Reekie sighed, backing out of the room, half his mind on the languid centre-forward ambling towards a perfectly calibrated pass. 'What the fuck's that supposed to mean, Spencer? "Pretty radical"?'

'She's been crucified. Then stood upside down. Then had her throat cut. In that order, according to the doc.' Spencer's tone was clipped. Reekie wasn't sure whether it was because Spencer was shocked himself or trying to shake his boss. Either way, it had certainly done the business for Reekie. He felt acid in the back of his throat, alcohol and smoke transformed into bile.

So he'd known even before he left the house that he wouldn't want to look at this one. Now, Reekie stood with his back to the horrible tableau, listening to Spencer trying to make something substantial out of the shreds of information they had so far. As Spencer began to run out of steam, Reekie interrupted. 'You say the doc's sure it's the third of three?'

'As far as we know. I mean, there could be more.'

'Exactly. A bloody nightmare. Not to mention what it'll do to the budget.' Reekie straightened his shoulders. 'No disrespect, DI Spencer, but I think this is one for the specialists.'

He saw the dawning light of comprehension in Spencer's eyes. There was a way the DI could dodge endless hours of unpaid overtime, the perpetual weight of the media monkey on his back and the emotional drain on his officers. Spencer wasn't a shirker, but everybody knew how souls were shrivelled by cases like this. And there was no need for it, not when there were people with an appetite for this sort of shit. And protocols that demanded certain kinds of case should be shunted sideways. Spencer nodded. 'As you say, sir. I know my limitations.'

Reekie nodded, stepping away from the bright lights and the soft rustle of movement that marked the crime scene. He knew just who to call.

5

Detective Chief Inspector Carol Jordan grasped the handle of the bottom drawer on the left side of her desk. This was the price she had to pay for deciding to leave Bradfield. At the end of the month, her seasoned team of experts would be disbanded and she would be on her way. By then, every desk drawer, every filing cabinet, every cupboard in her office would have to be filleted. There would be personal stuff she'd want to take with her – photographs, cards, notes from colleagues, cartoons torn from magazines and newspapers that had made Carol and her colleagues smile. There would be professional material that needed to be filed somewhere within the confines of Bradfield Metropolitan Police. There would be scribbled notes that made no sense out of the context of their particular investigation. And there would be plenty of fodder for the shredder – all those bits of paper that nobody else would ever need to see. That's why she'd stayed behind to make a start on it after the rest of the team had called it a day.

But glumness set in as soon as she yanked the drawer open. It was stuffed full, case papers layered like geological strata. Cases that had been shocking, terrifying, heartbreaking and mystifying. Cases she'd probably never see the like of again. It wasn't something she should have to attack unfortified. Carol swivelled in her chair and reached for the middle filing cabinet drawer with its more familiar contents. She helped herself to one of the miniature bottles of vodka she'd collected from hotel mini bars, train buffets and business flights. She tipped the dregs of a mug of coffee into the bin, wiped it out with a tissue and poured the vodka. It didn't look much. She grabbed a second bottle and added it. It still barely looked like a drink. She knocked it back and thought it barely felt like a drink either. She tipped another two miniatures into the mug and set it on the desk.

'For sipping,' Carol said out loud. She did not have a drink problem. Whatever Tony Hill might think, she was in control of the alcohol. Not the other way round. There were points in her past when it had been a close thing, but they were behind her. Enjoying the fact that a couple of drinks took the edge off did not constitute a problem. It didn't interfere with the standard of her work. It didn't interfere with her personal relationships. 'Whatever those are,' she muttered, dragging a bundle of files from the drawer.

She'd worked her way through enough of the stack for a ringing phone to feel like rescue. The screen of her phone showed a police-issue mobile but she didn't recognise the specific number. 'DCI Jordan,' she said, reaching for the mug, surprised to find it empty.

'Detective Superintendent Reekie from Northern Division,' a gruff voice said.

Carol didn't know Reekie, but it had to be important if someone that far up the pecking order was working so late into the evening. 'How can I help you, sir?'

'We've got something here that I think is right up your team's street,' Reekie said. 'I thought it best to bring you into it soon as. While the crime scene's still fresh.'

19

'That's how we like them,' Carol said. 'But my squad's winding up, you know.'

'I'd heard you were working out your notice,' Reekie said. 'But you're still in harness, right? Thought you might want to get your teeth into one last special one.'

They weren't the words she'd have chosen, but she understood what he meant. They all knew the difference between the run-of-the-mill domestics and criminal infighting that made up most homicides, and murders that signalled a warped mind at work. Cases where there was any element of mystery at all were relatively rare. So she supposed that 'special' wasn't such a strange word to assign to a murder. 'Text me the location and I'll be there as soon as I can,' she said, replacing the unexamined files and kicking the drawer shut.

Her eye caught the empty mug. Technically she was over the limit. She felt perfectly competent to drive, a line she'd heard from dozens of protesting drunks in custody suites throughout her career. On the other hand, she preferred not to turn up single-handed at a crime scene. If they were going to take a case, there were actions that needed to be initiated then and there, and that wasn't the best use of her time or skills. She mentally flicked through her squad. Of her two sergeants, Chris Devine had had too many late nights recently preparing a case for a major trial; and Kevin Matthews was out celebrating his wedding anniversary. Reekie hadn't sounded too worried, so this probably wasn't worth messing up a rare night out. That left her constables. Stacey Chen was always happier with machines than people; Carol still thought Sam Evans cared more for his own career than the victims they were there for; which left Paula McIntyre. As she dialled Paula's number, Carol acknowledged to herself that it was always going to be Paula.

*

Some things never change, Paula thought. Driving to a murder scene accompanied by the rising burn of adrenaline. Every time, she felt the thrill in her blood.

'Sorry to drag you out,' Carol said.

She didn't really mean it, Paula thought. But Carol had always been good at making sure her team never felt taken for granted. Paula's eyes didn't leave the road. She drove well over the speed limit, but within her capabilities. Nobody wanted to be remembered as one of those cops who mowed down an innocent member of the public in their haste to reach the dead. 'Not a problem, chief,' she said. 'Elinor's on call, so we were just having a quiet night in. A game of Scrabble and a takeaway.' Carol wasn't the only one who wanted to keep everybody sweet.

'All the same . . .'

Paula grinned. 'I was losing anyway. What have we got?'

'Reekie was on an open line, so we didn't talk detail. All I know is that he thinks it's right up our street.'

'Not for much longer,' Paula said, aware of the bitterness and regret in her voice.

'It was happening regardless of whether I stayed or not.'

Paula was startled. 'I wasn't blaming you, chief. I know whose fault it is.' She flashed a quick glance at Carol. 'I was wondering . . .'

'Of course I'll put in a good word for you.'

'Actually, I was hoping for a bit more than that.' Paula took a deep breath. She'd been trying to find the right moment for days, but there had always been something in the way. If she didn't take advantage of having Carol to herself now, who knew when the opportunity would arise again? 'If I was to apply, would there be a job for me in West Mercia?'

Carol was caught on the back foot. 'I don't know. It never occurred to me that anybody would . . .' She shifted in her seat, the better to study Paula. 'It won't be like it is here, you

21

know. Their homicide rate's negligible compared with Bradfield. It'll be much more like routine CID work.'

Paula quirked a smile. 'I could live with that. I think I've done my fair share at the sharp end of fucked-up.'

'Can't argue with that. If it's what you want, I'd do my best to make it happen,' Carol said. 'But I thought you were pretty settled here. With Elinor?'

'Elinor's not the issue. Well, not like you're suggesting. The thing is, she needs to climb up the next step on her medical career. She heard there's a good job coming up in Birmingham. And Bradfield to Birmingham is not a commute any sane person would want to do. So . . . ' Paula slowed for a junction, scanning the road in both directions before she whipped through. 'If she's going to go for that, I need to consider my options. And if you're going to West Mercia, I thought I might as well trade on my connections.' She glanced at Carol and grinned.

'I'll see what I can do,' Carol said. 'There's nobody I'd rather have on my team,' she added, meaning it.

'I got on really well with that sergeant we worked with on the RigMarole killings,' Paula said, pressing her point. 'Alvin Ambrose. I'd be happy to work with him again.'

Carol groaned. 'I hear you, Paula. There's no need to push it. And it may not be down to me, in the end. You know how it is right now, the way the cuts are biting into front-line officers.'

'I know. Sorry, chief.' She frowned at the satnav then made a tentative left turn into a small industrial estate, prefabricated warehouses with their shallow-pitched roofs lining the curving road. They rounded the final bend and Paula knew she was in the right place. A scatter of police and crime-scene vehicles clustered round the last warehouse on the site, flashing blue lights turned off in a bid to avoid attention. But there was no mistaking the fluttering festoons of crime-scene tape staking out the building. Paula pulled up, turned off the engine and squared her shoulders. 'This'll be us, then.'

These were the occasions when Carol understood that, no matter how good a cop she was, it would never be enough. Always arriving after the fact grew harder to bear the longer she did this job. She wished Tony was with her, and not just because he would read the scene differently from her. He understood her desire to prevent episodes like this, events that shredded people's lives and left them with gaping holes in the fabric of the day-to-day. Justice was what Carol craved, but these days she felt it seldom showed up.

DS Reekie hadn't said much and she was glad of that. Some things went beyond words, and too many cops tried to keep the horror at bay with chatter. But nothing could keep a sight like this at arm's length.

The woman was naked. Carol could see several thin superficial cuts on her skin and wondered if the killer had cut her clothes off her. She'd ask the CSI photographer to make a point of getting them in his shots so they could make comparisons if the clothes turned up.

The woman's body had been fixed to a cross with sturdy six-inch nails through her wrists and ankles. Carol tried not to wince at the thought of what that must have sounded like; the crack of hammer on nails, the crunch of bones, the cry of agony echoing off the metal walls. Then the cross had been propped up against the wall upside down so that her dyed blonde hair skimmed the gritty cement floor, her roots a dark line across her forehead.

It hadn't been crucifixion that had killed her, though. Carol supposed you'd have to classify the savage slash to the throat as a kind of mercy, but it was a kind she hoped she'd never need. The cut had been deep enough to sever major blood vessels. Under arterial pressure, the blood had travelled an impressive distance, the spray visible on the floor all around except for one patch. 'He was standing there,' she said, half to herself. 'He must have been saturated.'

'He must be bloody strong,' Paula said. 'To shift a wooden cross with a body on it, that's hard work. I don't think I could do it.'

The white-suited figure working closest to the body turned to face them. His words were slightly muffled by his mask, but Carol could hear them clearly enough. She recognised the Canadian accent of the Home Office pathologist, Grisha Shatalov. 'The wood's only two by six. And there's nothing of her. I'd say classic addict physiology, except there's no sign that she was injecting. I bet you could lift and drag her into place without too much effort, DC McIntyre.'

'How long has she been dead, Grisha?' Carol said.

'You never ask the questions I can answer,' he said, weary humour in his tone. 'My best guess at this point is that she's been dead for around twenty-four hours.'

'The unit's been empty for about four months,' Reekie said. 'The security guard didn't notice the back door had been forced.' There was no mistaking his contempt.

'So how did we find her?' Carol asked.

'The usual. Man walking his dog last thing. The dog made a beeline for the back door. It must have smelled the blood.' Reekie wrinkled his nose. 'Hardly surprising. According to the owner, the dog charged the door, the door swung open, the dog vanished inside and wouldn't come when called. So he went in, torch on. Took one look and called us.' He gave a mirthless laugh. 'At least he had the good sense to grab the dog before it completely fucked up the crime scene.'

'But Dr Shatalov reckons she was killed last night. How come the dog didn't find her then?'

Reekie looked over his shoulder, where his DI was riding point. He'd been silent and still up to that point but knew what was expected of him. 'They didn't go that way last night, according to the owner. Obviously, we'll be checking that out.'

'Never trust the body finder,' Reekie said.

Like we didn't know that. Carol stared at the body, clocking every detail, wondering about the sequence of events that had led this young woman here. 'Any ID?' she said.

'Not so far,' Spencer said. 'We've got a bit of a street prostitution problem out towards the airport. Eastern Europeans, mostly. She'll likely be from there.'

'Unless he brought her out from the city. From Temple Fields,' Paula said.

'The first two were local,' Reekie said.

'Well, let's hope Grisha can get her looking human enough to ID via a photo,' Carol said. 'You said, "the first two", sir. You're sure this is a series?'

Reekie turned back to the body. 'Show her, doc.'

Grisha pointed to what looked like a tattoo on the inside of the woman's wrist. It was partially covered with blood, but Carol could still make out the letters. MINE. A message that was repulsive, sick and insolent. And yet, in the back of Carol's head, a devil whispered, 'Make the most of this. If you go to West Mercia, you'll never see a crime scene as interesting as this again.'

6

Against all odds, years of apparently model behaviour had earned Vance a place in the Therapeutic Community Wing at HMP Oakworth in the depths of the Worcestershire countryside. There was no set lights-out time on this wing, separated as it was from the rest of the prison; inmates could turn the light off when they wanted to. And the tiny en suite bathroom gave him a degree of privacy he'd almost forgotten existed. Vance turned out the light, leaving the TV on so he wasn't working in complete darkness. He spread a newspaper out on the table then painstakingly chopped off his hair with a razor blade. Once it was short enough, he ran the electric razor back and forth till his skull was as smooth as he could get it. Thanks to his prison pallor, there would be no difference in skin colour between the newly shaven skin and his face. Next, he shaved off the full beard he'd been cultivating over the past few weeks, leaving only a goatee and moustache behind. Over the past couple of years, he'd been varying his facial hair dramatically – from full beard to clean-shaven, from chin strap to Zapata moustache – so that nobody would pay attention when he cultivated the look that counted.

The key part of the transformation still lay ahead of him. He reached up to the bookshelf above the table and took down a large-format book, a limited edition collection of lithographs by modern Russian artists. Neither Vance nor the usual inmate of the cell had any interest in the art; what made this book valuable was the heavy paper stock it was printed on, paper so heavy the pages could be slit open and used to hide thin plastic sheets of tattoo transfers.

The transfers had been painstakingly created from photographs Vance had taken on his contraband smartphone. They replicated in exact detail the elaborate and garish body art that covered the arms and neck of Jason Collins, the man who was currently sleeping in Vance's bed. For Vance was not in his own cell tonight. The distraction he'd created had worked perfectly.

A photograph of Damon Todd's wife leaning into Cash Costello's brother at some nightclub bar had been all the currency he'd needed. Vance had casually dropped it on the ping-pong table as he'd walked past during the association period that evening. Inevitably, just as he had planned, someone had picked it up and homed in on its significance straight away. Catcalling and taunts followed and, inevitably, Todd had lost his temper and thrown himself on Costello. That would be the end of their spell on the Therapeutic Community Wing, all good behaviour undone in one uncontrollable flash of temper. Not that Vance cared. He'd never been bothered by collateral damage.

What mattered was that the ruckus had diverted the attention of the wing officers just long enough for Vance and Collins to make their way back to the wrong cells. By the time things had settled down and the screws were making the final round of the cells, both men had their lights out, pretending to be fast asleep. No reason to doubt each was where he was supposed to be.

Vance got up and ran cold water into the basin. He tore out

the first prearranged page and peeled the two sheets of paper away from the plastic. He immersed the thin plastic film in the basin, then, when the tattoo transfer began to shift, he applied it meticulously to his prosthesis. It was a slow process, but nothing like as awkward as applying it to his other arm. Yes, the new artificial limb was remarkable. But what it could do was still a distance away from the fine motor control of a living arm. And everything depended on getting the details right.

By the time he'd finished, his head was sweating and fine trickles of perspiration ran down his back and sides. He'd done the best he could manage. Put him side by side with Collins and it would be easy to tell the real tatts from the fake, but unless things went horribly wrong, that wasn't going to happen. Vance picked up the copies his helper on the outside had had made of Collins' glasses and slipped them on. The world tilted and blurred, but not too much for him to cope with. The lenses were far less powerful than Collins' own ones, but a cursory check would demonstrate that they weren't plain glass. Details, it all came down to details.

He closed his eyes and summoned up the sound of Collins' nasal Midlands accent. For Vance, that was the hardest part of the impersonation. He'd never had much of a gift for imitation. He'd always found himself sufficient. But for once, he was going to have to lose himself in someone else's voice. He'd try to keep the chat to a minimum, but he had to be ready to avoid a response in his own warm generic tones. He recalled the scene in *The Great Escape* where Gordon Jackson's character gives himself away with an automatic response when he's addressed in English. Vance would have to be better than that. He couldn't afford to relax, not for a moment. Not until he was free and clear.

It had taken years to get this far. First, to be admitted to the

Therapeutic Community at all. Then to find someone roughly the same height and build who also had a powerful need for what Vance could provide. Jason Collins had been in his crosshairs from the first day the creepy little firebug had walked into group therapy. Collins had been a hired gun, firing businesses for cash. But Vance didn't need the psychologist to tell him that Collins' motives had been darker and deeper than that. That he was in the group at all was the proof.

Vance had befriended Collins, uncovered his chagrin at losing his family life, and started to sow the seeds of possibility. What Vance's money could do for Collins' three kids, for his wife. For a long time, Vance had felt he was treading water. The crucial stumbling block was that assisting Vance would pile more years on top of Collins' existing sentence.

Then Collins got a different kind of sentence. Leukaemia. The kind where you have only a forty per cent chance of still being alive five years after the initial diagnosis. Meaning he'd probably never have a second chance to provide a future for his kids or his wife. Even if he got maximum time off his sentence, Collins felt like he'd only be going home to die. 'They'd let you go home anyway if you were that close to dying,' Vance had pointed out. 'Look what happened to the Lockerbie bomber.' It seemed like a perverse version of having your cake and eating it. Collins could help Vance escape and it wouldn't matter – they'd still let him out when he was sick enough. Either way, he'd be spending the end of his life with his family. And if they did it Vance's way, his wife and kids would never have to worry about money again.

It had taken all Vance's powers of persuasion and more patience than he knew he possessed to draw Collins round to his way of thinking. 'You all grow unaccustomed to nice,' his psychologist had once remarked. That had given Vance a powerful tool, and finally he'd cracked it. Collins' elder son was about to become a pupil at the best independent school in Warwickshire and Jacko Vance was about to walk out of jail.

Vance tidied up, tearing the soggy paper into fragments and flushing it, along with hair wrapped in thin wads of toilet paper. He scrunched the plastic film into little balls and squeezed it between the table and the wall. When he could think of nothing more, he finally lay down on the narrow bed. The air chilled the sweat on his body and, shivering, he pulled the duvet over him.

It was all going to be all right. Tomorrow, the screw would come for Jason Collins to take him for his first day of Release on Temporary Licence. ROTL was what every prisoner in the Therapeutic Community dreamed of – the day they would emerge from the prison gates and spend a day in a factory or an office. How bloody pitiful, Vance thought. Therapy that so reduced a man's horizons that a day of mundane drudgery was something to aspire to. It had taken every ounce of his skills in dissimulation to hide his contempt for the regime. But he'd managed it because he knew this was the key to his return to a life outside walls.

Because not everyone in the Therapeutic Community would be allowed outside. For Vance and a handful of others, there would always be too high a risk involved in that. No matter that he'd convinced that stupid bitch of a psychologist that he was a different man from the one who'd committed the deeply disturbing murder he'd been convicted of. Not to mention all those other teenage girls that he was technically innocent of killing, since he'd never been found guilty of their murders. Still, no Home Secretary wanted to be branded the person who released Jacko Vance. It didn't matter what his tariff from the judge said. Vance knew there would never be an official return to society for him. He had to admit, if he was in charge, he wouldn't let him out either. But then, he knew exactly what he was capable of. The authorities could only guess.

Vance smiled in the darkness. Very soon he planned to take the guesswork out of the equation.

7

The liveried police car made a slow turn at Carol's direction. 'Third house on the left,' she said, her voice a weary sigh. She'd left Paula at the crime scene, making sure things were done the way the Major Incident Team preferred. Carol had no problem with delegation, not with a hand-picked squad like this one. She wondered whether she'd have that same luxury in Worcester.

'Ma'am?' The driver, a stolid twenty-something traffic officer, sounded cautious.

Carol roused herself to attention. 'Yes? What is it?'

'There's a man sitting in a parked car outside the third house on the left. It looks like his head's leaning on the steering wheel,' he said. 'Do you want me to PNC the index number?'

As they drew level, Carol looked out of the window, surprised but not shocked to see Tony, as the PC had said, leaning on his arms on the steering wheel. 'No need to trouble the computer,' she said. 'I know who he is.'

'Do you need me to have a word?'

Carol smiled. 'Thanks, but that won't be necessary. He's entirely harmless.' That wasn't strictly true, but in the narrow terms of reference of a traffic cop, it was as close as damn it.

'Your call,' he said, drawing in front of Tony's car and coming to a halt. 'Night, ma'am.'

'Good night. No need to wait, I'm fine.' Carol got out of the car and walked back to Tony's car. She hung on till the police car drove off, then opened the passenger door and got in. At the sound of the lock clicking shut, Tony's head jerked back and he gasped as if he'd been struck.

'What the fuck,' he said, his voice frightened and disorientated. His head jerked from side to side as he tried to make sense of his surroundings. 'Carol? What the ...?'

She patted his arm. 'You're outside the house in Bradfield. You were asleep. I came home from work and saw you. I thought you might not have intended to spend the whole night spark out in the car.'

He rubbed his hands over his face as if splashing himself with water, then turned to her, wide-eyed and startled. 'I was listening to a podcast. The fabulous Dr Gwen Adshead from Broadmoor talking about dealing with the disasters that are our patients. I got home and she was still talking and I wanted to hear the end of it. I can't believe I fell asleep, she was talking more sense than anybody I've heard in a long time.' He yawned and shook himself. 'What time is it?'

'Just after three.'

'God. I got back not long after midnight.' He shivered. 'I'm really cold.'

'I'm not surprised.' Carol opened the door. 'I don't know about you, but I'm going indoors.'

Tony scurried out of his side and met her at the gate to the house. 'Why are you only coming home just after three? Do you want a drink? I'm wide awake now.'

He could be so like a small child, she thought. Out of nowhere, all eagerness and curiosity. 'I'll come in for a nightcap,' she said, following him to the front door rather than to the side door that led to her self-contained basement flat.

Inside, the house had the still cold air of a space that's been empty for more than a few hours. 'Put the fire on in my office, it warms up faster than the living room,' Tony said, heading for the kitchen. 'Wine or vodka?'

He knew her well enough not to bother offering anything else. 'Vodka,' she called as she squatted down to struggle with the ignition of the gas fire. She'd lost count of the number of times she'd suggested he have the fire serviced so it wouldn't be a wrestling match to get it going. It didn't matter now. Within a couple of weeks, the sale of this house and her flat within it would be completed and he'd have the problems of a whole new house to ignore. But then, the problems wouldn't have the chance to turn into nagging irritations. Because she'd be living there, and she didn't tolerate infuriating shit like that.

The fire finally caught as Tony returned with a bottle of Russian vodka, a bottle of Calvados and a pair of tumblers that looked as if he'd collected them free with petrol sometime in the 1980s. 'I packed the nice glasses already,' he said.

'Both of them?' Carol reached for the bottle, flinching at the cold. It had obviously been in the freezer and the spirit slid down the bottle in sluggish sobs as she poured it.

'So why are you coming home after three? You don't look like it was a party.'

'Superintendent Reekie at Northern wants me to go out in a blaze of glory,' she said drily.

'That would be a budget buster, then?' Tony raised his glass in a cynical toast. 'You'd think it came out of a different pot altogether, not just a different department in the same organisation. It's amazing how many cases have had "Major Incident Team" stamped on them since the Chief Constable's austerity drive.'

'Even more so since the word got around that I'm leaving.' Carol sighed. 'This one, though ... in less frugal times, we'd have been fighting Northern for it anyway.'

'A bad one?'

Carol swallowed a mouthful of vodka and topped up her glass. 'The worst kind. Your kind. Somebody nailed a prostitute to a cross. Upside down. Then he cut her throat.' She took a deep breath and let it out slowly. 'Northern think he's done it before. Not like that, obviously. We would have heard before now if he had. But they've had two dead sex workers recently. Different methods. One strangled, one drowned.'

Tony was leaning forward in his chair, elbows on knees, eyes as far from sleep as could be. 'I had a call from Penny Burgess earlier. I think it might have been about this.'

'Really? What did she have to say?'

'I don't know, I wasn't listening. But she seemed to think I should be involved. That there's something serial going on.'

'She could be right. All three of the victims have what looks like a tattoo on the inside of their wrist. "MINE", it says.'

'They didn't connect the first two?' Tony sounded incredulous.

'To be fair, they only got the chance to make the connection yesterday. The one who was drowned, she wasn't in the best condition. Grisha's not had the body long, and it took a bit of time for them to be sure what they were looking for.' Carol shrugged, running her fingers through her shaggy blonde hair. 'It was hard to pick up any significance on the first body – she had other tatts on her arms and torso, no reason to think MINE had any greater significance than the tramp stamp that said BECKHAM.'

'And this latest one? She's got MINE on her wrist too? Interesting.'

'It looks like it. There's a lot of blood and swelling, because he nailed her to the wood through her wrist—' Carol shuddered. 'But there's definitely something there. So Reekie called me and handed it off to us. They'll do the footslogging.'

'But it'll still come out of your budget. Make you look the

extravagant one, not Reekie. The women, the victims – were they local to Northern? Or were they working somewhere like Temple Fields and just got killed outside the city centre?'

'Both local. Small time, on the street, not indoor workers.'

'Young? Older?'

'Young. Drug users, not surprisingly. And of course, because of the way they earned their money, we can't be sure if they were sexually assaulted.' She held up a hand. 'I know, I know. Chances are, sex will come into it somewhere.'

'Just not always in the obvious way.' Tony sniffed his glass and made a face. 'It's always better where you buy it, isn't it? This stuff smelled wonderful in Brittany. Now it's like lighter fluid.' He took a tentative sip. 'Tastes better than it smells. So will you be looking at using a profiler?'

'It would be the obvious port of call. But Blake won't want to pay for you, and I don't want to work with the homegrown products of the national academy.' She rolled her eyes. 'You remember the idiot they sent us on the RigMarole killings? All the emotional intelligence of a brick wall. I promised the team I'd never go down that road again. Better to do without than let the Chief Constable foist another one of those on us.'

'Would you like me?' Tony said. His raised eyebrows promised the faintest possibility of double entendre, but Carol wasn't buying.

'It's the sensible option, if we want to get a result sooner rather than later.' She reached for the bottle and topped up her glass. 'But there's no way I'll be allowed to spend that kind of money.'

'What if it didn't cost you anything?'

Carol frowned. 'I've told you before. I refuse to take advantage of our personal relationship—'

'Whatever it is . . .'

'Whatever it is. You're a professional. When we use expertise from outside the police service, we should pay for it.'

'The labourer is worthy of his hire,' he said, softening the darkness of his tone with a lopsided smile. 'We've had this out before, and neither of us is going to shift our ground. You say tomato and I say potato.' He waved one hand as if he was batting away an insect. 'I think there's a way of doing this that means I get paid and you get my expertise.'

Carol frowned. 'How do you work that out?'

Tony tapped the side of his nose. 'I need to talk to someone at the Home Office.'

'Tony, it may have escaped your notice, but we have a new government. There is no money. Not for essentials, never mind luxuries like psychological profilers.' Frustrated, Carol sighed.

'I know you think I live on another planet, Carol, but I did know that.' He pulled a sad clown face that emphasised the lines his job had carved there. 'But my go-to guy at the Home Office is above the political fray. And I think he owes me.' Tony paused for a moment, his eyes drifting to the top left corner of the room. 'Yes, he does.' He shifted in his seat and stared directly at Carol. 'All those years ago, we started something in this city. Reekie's right. You should go out in a blaze of glory. And I should be there at your side, just like I was that first time.'

8

Dawn came and he had not slept. But Jacko Vance was wired, not tired. He listened to the small noises of the wing coming to life, happy in the thought that this would be the last time he was forced to start his day in the company of so many. He checked Collins' watch every few minutes, waiting for the right moment to rise and start the day. He'd had to calculate another man's mentality in all of this. Collins would be eager, but not too eager. Vance had always had a good sense of timing. It was one of the elements that had made him so successful an athlete. But today, much more depended on that timing than a mere medal.

When he judged the moment was perfect, he got out of bed and headed for the toilet. He passed the electric razor over his head and his chin again, then dressed in Collins' ratty jeans and baggy polo shirt. The tattoos looked spot on, Vance thought. And people saw what they expected to see. A man with Collins' tattoos and clothes must, in the absence of any contradictory features, be Collins.

The minutes crawled by. At last, a fist banged his door and a voice called out. 'Collins? Get yourself in gear, time to make a move.'

By the time the door opened, the officer was already distracted, paying more attention to an argument further down the corridor about the previous evening's football results than he was to the man who emerged from the cell. Vance knew the officer – Jarvis, one of the regular day-shift crew, chippy and irritable, but not someone who had ever taken any personal interest in any of his charges. So far, so good. The screw cast a cursory glance over his shoulder then led the way down the hall. Vance stood back while the first door was unlocked remotely, enjoying the solid clunk of the metal tongue sliding open. Then he followed the officer into the sally port and tried to breathe normally while one door closed and the other opened.

And then they were off the wing, moving through the main administrative section of the jail towards the exit. Trying to calm himself with distraction, Vance wondered why anyone would choose a working environment with sickly yellow walls and metalwork painted battleship grey. To spend your days here without descending into deep depression, you'd have to have no visual taste whatsoever.

Another sally port, then the final hurdle. A couple of bored-looking officers sat behind thick glass windows like bank counters, with gaps where documents could be passed through. Jarvis nodded to the nearest, a skinny young man with a crew cut and bad skin. 'Is the social worker here for Collins?' he said.

Not likely, Vance thought. Not if things had gone to plan. Not many women would turn up for work after they'd been wakened in the night by someone trying to smash into their house. Especially since the putative burglar/rapist had taken the precaution of slashing all four tyres on her car and cutting her phone line. She'd been lucky. If he'd been doing the job himself instead of having to delegate it, he'd have slashed her dog's throat and nailed it to the front door. Some things you couldn't outsource. Hopefully, what he had managed to arrange would be enough. Unfortunate for poor Jason really. He would have to set off for his Release on Temporary Licence day without the support of someone who knew him.

'No,' the man on the desk said. 'She's not coming in today.'

'What?' Jarvis moaned. 'What do you mean, she's not coming in today?'

'Personal issues.'

'So what am I supposed to do with him?' He jerked his head towards Vance.

'There's a taxi here.'

'He's going off in a taxi? Without an escort?' Jarvis shook his head, mugging incredulity for his audience.

'What's the odds? He'll have all day on the ROTL without an escort, regardless. Just means it starts a bit earlier, that's all.'

'What about orientation? Isn't he supposed to have some sort of orientation with the social worker?'

Crew cut picked a spot, examined his fingernail and shrugged again. 'Not our problem, is it? We ran it past the Assistant Governor and he said it was OK. He said Collins presented no cause for concern.' He looked at Vance. 'You all right with that, Collins? Otherwise the ROTL gets cancelled.'

Vance shrugged right back at him. 'I might as well go since I'm here now.' He was quite pleased with the way it came out. He thought it was a decent representation of how Collins spoke. More importantly, he didn't sound at all like himself. He thrust his hands into his pockets as he'd seen Collins do a thousand times, hunching his shoulders slightly.

'I want it on the record that I'm not happy with this, no matter what the AG says,' Jarvis grumbled as he led Vance through the high baffle gate that led to the outside world. He pushed open the door and Vance followed him on to a paved area flanked by a roadway. A tired-looking Skoda saloon sat by the kerb, its diesel engine rumbling. Vance smelled the dirty exhaust, a cloying note in the fresh morning air. It was a combination he hadn't experienced in a long time.

Jarvis pulled open the passenger door and leaned in. 'You take him to Evesham Fabrications, right? Nowhere else. I don't care if he says he's having a bloody heart attack and needs to go to the hospital, or he's going to shit himself if he doesn't get to a toilet pronto. Do not pass go. Do not collect £200. Evesham Fabrications.'

The driver looked baffled. 'You need to chill, mate,' he said. 'You'll give yourself a stroke. I know my job.' He craned his head so he could see past Jarvis. 'In you get, mate.'

'In the front, so the driver can keep an eye on you.' Jarvis stepped back, allowing Vance to slide into the passenger seat. He reached for the seat belt with his prosthesis, hoping any clumsiness would be put down to the length of time since he'd last been in a car. 'I don't want to hear you've caused any trouble, Collins,' Jarvis said, slamming the door shut. The car smelled of synthetic pine air freshener overlaid with coffee.

The cabbie, a shambolic-looking Asian man in his midthirties, chuckled as he pulled away. 'He's in a good mood.'

'It's not a mood, it's his permanent state,' Vance said. His heart was racing. He could feel sweat in the small of his back. He couldn't quite believe it. He'd made it out of the front door. And with every passing minute, he was further from HMP Oakworth and closer to his dream of freedom. OK, there were still plenty of obstacles between him and that steak dinner, but the hardest part was behind him. He reminded himself that he'd always believed he led a charmed life. The years in jail had just been an interruption of his natural state, not a termination. The dice were rolling in his favour again.

If he needed reinforcement in that conviction, it came as Vance took a closer look at his surroundings. The car was an automatic, which would make his life a lot easier. He hadn't driven since his arrest; getting behind the wheel would be a steep enough revision curve without having to deal with gear changes. Vance relaxed a fraction, smiling as he took in neat fields of spring grass with their tightly woven hedges. Fat sheep grazed, their stolid lambs mostly past the gambolling stage. They passed orchards, rows of stumpy trees covered in blossom that was beginning to look a little bedraggled. The road was barely wide enough for two cars to pass. It was a foreigner's ideal of the English countryside.

'Must make a nice change for you, getting out like this,' the cabbie said.

'You've got no idea,' Vance said. 'I'm hoping this is just the start. Rehab, that's what this has been for me. I'm a changed man.' Changed, in the sense that he was determined never to repeat the kind of mistakes that got him confined. But he was still a killer; he'd just learned how to be a better one.

Now, he was studying the landscape, matching their route to the map in his head. Seven and a half miles of quiet country roads before they hit the major artery leading towards Birmingham.

Vance had pinpointed three places where he could stage the next part of his plan. It all depended on traffic. He didn't want any witnesses, not at a stage in his escape when he had no weapon to defend himself. So far, one van had passed them, going in the opposite direction, but there was nothing in sight ahead of them as they climbed a long steep incline. He shifted in his seat so he could catch a glimpse in the rear-view mirror, making it look as if he was taking in the view. 'Bloody lovely round here,' he said. 'You forget, inside.' Then he jumped, genuinely startled. 'What the hell is that?' he demanded.

The cabbie laughed. 'How long have you been away? It's a wind farm. Giant windmills. They catch the wind and make electricity. Plenty wind up here, so there's plenty windmills too.'

'Jesus,' Vance said. 'They're bloody enormous.' And, fortuitously, their conversation had made the driver less attentive.

42

The moment was perfect. They were approaching a T-junction, the first of Vance's possible attack points. The car drifted to a halt, the driver pausing to point out more windmills on the horizon before checking for oncoming traffic.

In a split second, Vance smashed the forearm of his prosthesis into the side of the cabbie's head. The man yelped and threw his hands up to protect himself. But Vance was remorseless and his artificial arm was a weapon far more solid than the bone and muscle of a human limb. He brought it down again on the man's head, then swiped it hard against his face, smiling as the blood gushed from his nose. Vance used his other hand to release his seat belt so he could gain more leverage. He moved forward and cracked him across the head again, so hard he bounced off the window. The man was screaming now, hands clawing at Vance.

'Fuck this,' Vance hissed. He got his arm behind the driver's head and rammed him face first into the steering wheel. After the third sickening crunch, the man finally went limp. Vance unfastened the driver's belt and freed him from its constraint. Still pumped with adrenaline, he jumped out of the car and hustled round to the driver's side. When he opened the door, the driver slumped towards the road. Vance squatted down and got one shoulder under his torso. Taking a deep breath, he forced himself to his feet. All those hours in the gym had been worth it. He'd made sure to build strength and endurance rather than exaggerated muscle; he'd never seen any point in being obvious.

Vance staggered as far as the hedgerow that bordered the road. Breathing heavily, feeling his heart hammer in his chest, he dumped the driver on to the top bar of a metal field gate, then tipped him over on the far side. He grinned at the startled expressions on the faces of the nearest sheep as the cabbie tumbled to the ground, arms and legs flailing weakly.

He leaned against the gate for a moment, catching his

breath, letting himself recover from the overdose of fight-or-flight hormones. Then he returned to the car, this time to the driver's seat. He cancelled the right turn on the indicator, slipped the car into drive then turned left, the opposite direction to Evesham Fabrications. He reckoned it would take him about forty minutes to make it to the service area on the motorway and the next stage of the plan.

He couldn't help wondering how long it would take before someone noticed Jason Collins was still on the Therapeutic Community Wing. And Jacko Vance wasn't. Before they understood that one of the most notorious and prolific serial killers the UK had ever produced was on the loose. And keen to make up for lost time.

This time, his grin lasted a lot longer than a few minutes.

9

Paula shuffled her papers and stifled a yawn. 'I'm ready when you are,' she said, moving closer to the whiteboards that lined one wall of the cluttered squad room. Carol wondered whether she'd managed any sleep at all. Paula would have had to hang around at the crime scene to make sure everything was being done according to the Major Incident Team's protocols. Then she'd have had to go back to Northern HQ with their detectives and set up the programme of actions for the morning shift to carry out, again according to Carol's specifications. And now she was charged with delivering the morning briefing to this close circle of colleagues who had learned each other's ways with as much acuteness as they'd ever paid to a lover.

This was the squad Carol had hand-picked and built into the best unit she'd ever worked with. If James Blake hadn't walked into the Chief Constable's job with a personal mission to cut costs to the bone long before the idea occurred to the Prime Minister, she'd have been happy to stick with this bunch till she was ready to collect her pension. Instead, she was about to take another of her leaps into the unknown. Only this time, it felt like she was following instead of leading. Not the most reassuring prospect she'd ever faced.

'Briefing in five,' she shouted, giving them time to wind up whatever they were doing. Stacey Chen, their computer specialist, invisible behind her array of six monitors, grunted something inarticulate. Sam Evans, deep in a phone call, gave her the thumbs-up. Her two sergeants, Kevin Matthews and Chris Devine, raised their heads from the huddle they'd been forming over their cups of coffee and nodded.

'Got all you need?' Carol asked.

'I think so.' Paula reached for her coffee. 'Northern sent me everything from the first two deaths, but I've not had time to go through it in detail.'

'Do your best,' Carol said, heading for the coffee maker and fixing herself a latte with an extra shot. Another thing she'd miss. They'd clubbed together to buy the Italian machine to satisfy everyone's caffeine cravings. Apart from Stacey, who insisted on Earl Grey tea. She doubted there would be anything comparable in Worcester.

And speaking of missing, there was no sign of Tony. In spite of his bold promises, it looked as though he hadn't managed to deliver. She tried to dismiss the disappointment that threatened her; it had never been a likely outcome, after all. They'd just have to wrestle their way through the case without his help.

Carol crossed back to the whiteboards, where the rest of the team were gathering. She couldn't help admiring the exquisite cut of Stacey's suit. It was clearly bespoke, and expensively so. She was aware that the team geek had her own software business independent of her police job. Carol had never enquired too closely, believing they all had a right to a private life away from the shit they had to wade through at work. But it was clear from her wardrobe alone that Stacey had an income that dwarfed what the rest of them earned. One of these days Sam Evans was going to notice the almost imperceptible signs that Stacey was crazy about him. When Sam the superficial put

46

that together with her net worth, there would be no stopping him. But by the looks of it, Carol would be long gone before that happened. One drama she wouldn't be sorry to miss.

Paula cleared her throat and squared her shoulders. There was nothing bespoke about her creased jeans and rumpled brown sweater, the same clothes she'd been wearing when she'd picked Carol up the night before. 'We were called in last night by Northern Division. The body of an as yet unidentified female was found in an empty warehouse on the Parkway industrial estate.' She fixed two photographs to a whiteboard, one of the whole crime scene with the crucified body at the heart of it, the other of the woman's face. 'As you can see, she was nailed to a wooden cross then propped up against the wall. Upside down. Gruesome, but probably not enough to involve us on its own.'

She stuck three more photographs on the board. Two were identifiably tattooed human wrists; the other could have been any scrap of material with letters written on it. In each case, the letters spelled 'MINE'. Paula turned back to face her colleagues. 'What makes it one of ours is that it's apparently number three. What links them is the tatt on the wrist. That and the fact that they've all been found on Northern's patch, which isn't necessarily where you'd expect to find dead sex workers.'

'Why not?' Chris Devine was the team member least familiar with the nuances of Bradfield's social geography, having originally moved up from the Met.

'Most of the street life happens around Temple Fields in the city centre. Also most of the inside trade,' Kevin said. 'There's a couple of pockets on the main arteries out of town, but Northern's pretty clean on the whole.'

'My liaison at Northern's a DS called Franny Riley,' Paula said. 'He told me they've had a hotspot lately round the new hospital building site. Half a dozen or so women working the area where the labourers park up. He thinks they've mostly been East Europeans, probably trafficked. But our first two victims were both local women, so maybe not connected to that.' Another photo, this time of a worn-out face with sunken eyes, prominent cheekbones and lips tightly pressed together. Nobody ever looked good in a mugshot, but this woman looked particularly pissed off. 'The first victim, Kylie Mitchell. Aged twenty-three. Crackhead. Five convictions for soliciting, one for minor possession. She mostly worked on the edges of Temple Fields, but she grew up in the high flats out at Skenby – which is bang in the middle of Northern's patch, Chris. She was strangled and dumped under the ring-road overpass three weeks ago.' Paula nodded to Stacey. 'Stacey's setting up the files on our network.'

Stacey flashed a smile so quick anyone who blinked would have missed it. 'They'll be available at the end of the briefing,' she said.

'Kylie's the usual depressing story. Dropped out of school with no qualifications and a taste for partying. Soon graduated to sex for drugs, then moved on to working the streets to support her crack habit. She had a kid when she was twenty, taken straight into care, adopted six months later.' Paula shook her head and sighed. 'As far as the sex trade is concerned, Kylie was a bottom feeder. She'd got to the point of no return. No fixed abode, no pimp looking out for her. Easy meat for someone looking for the worst kind of thrill.'

'How many times have we heard this story?' Sam sounded as bored as he looked.

'Too many times. Believe me, Sam, no one would be happier than me if we never had to hear it again,' Carol said. The rebuke was clear. 'What do we know about her last movements, Paula?'

'Not a lot. She didn't even have any of the other girls looking out for her. She was notorious for taking no care of herself.

She was up for anything, didn't care about using a condom. The other girls had given up on her. Or she'd given up on them, it's not entirely clear which way round it was. The night of the murder, she was seen around nine o'clock on Campion Way, right on the edge of Temple Fields. We think a couple of the regulars there warned her off their pitch. And that's it. Nothing, till she turns up under the overpass.'

'What about forensics?' Kevin asked.

'Traces of semen from four different sources. None of them on the database, so that's only going to have any value once we've got someone in the frame. Other than that, all we've got is the tattoo. Done post-mortem, that's why there's no inflammation.'

'Does that mean we're looking for a tattoo artist? Someone with professional skills?' Chris asked.

'We need to get some expert opinion on that,' Carol said. 'And we need to find out how easy it is to get hold of a tattoo machine. Talk to suppliers, see if we can get a list of recent purchases.'

Sam got up to study the tattoo photos more closely. 'It doesn't look that skilled to me. But then, that in itself could be deliberate.'

'Too soon to speculate,' Carol said. 'Who found her, Paula?'

'Couple of teenagers. DS Riley reckons they were looking for a quiet spot to neck a bottle of cider. There's an old stripped-out Transit van down there, the nearest the local kids have to a youth club. She was shoved in the front end. Where the engine would be if there was an engine left. No real attempt to hide her. Northern already did a door-to-door locally, but the nearest houses are a good fifty metres away, and it's their back sides that face the crime scene. No joy at all.'

'Let's do it again,' Carol said. 'She wasn't beamed down from outer space. Paula, sort it with DS Riley.'

'Will do.' Paula pinned another mugshot to the board. 'This

is Suzanne Black, known as Suze. Aged twenty-seven. Half a dozen convictions for soliciting. Not quite as far down the scale as Kylie. Suze shared a flat in one of the Skenby tower blocks with another sex worker, a rent boy called Nicky Reid. According to Nicky, she used to pick up her tricks in the Flyer—'

'What's the Flyer?' Carol interrupted.

'It's a pub round the back of the airport, near the cargo area. An old-fashioned roadhouse kind of place. It dates back to when the airport was just Brackley Field aerodrome in the war,' Kevin said. 'It's not a place you'd take the wife and kids for Sunday lunch, but it's a couple of steps up from a dive.'

'Nicky says she had a few regulars,' Paula continued. 'Cargo handlers at the airport, mostly. Like Kylie, she had a habit, though her drug of choice was heroin. Nicky says she'd been using for years, that she functioned pretty well. Also like Kylie, she didn't have a pimp. He says she had a long-standing arrangement with her drug supplier – any trouble with anybody trying to muscle in on her business, he'd sort them. She was a good customer.' A wry twist lifted one corner of Paula's mouth. 'And she put other custom his way too.'

'When did Nicky last see her?' Carol again.

'Two weeks ago. They left the flat together. He went into Temple Fields, she was heading for the Flyer. Next day when he got up, she wasn't there. No sign that she'd been back. He left it a couple of days, in case she was off with one of her mates or her regulars, though that would have been unusual for her.' Paula shook her head, faintly bemused. 'The way Nicky describes it, they had this really domesticated set-up.'

'Who knew?' Sam sounded contemptuous.

'So on the third day, Nicky tried to report Suze missing. His nearest police station happens to be Northern Divisional HQ. To say they were not interested would be a profound understatement. Nicky had a come-apart in reception and nearly got arrested himself. But no action was taken. The body turned up four days ago in the Brade Canal in the course of an angling competition. According to the pathologist, she'd been drowned, but not in the Brade.'

Paula clicked a button on the pointer in her hand and a video window sprang to life on the whiteboard. Dr Grisha Shatalov, the pathologist, smiled out at them in his scrubs. His warm voice with its soft Canadian accent was stripped to tinny-ness by the cheap speakers. 'When we have an apparent drowning, the first thing we look for is whether it really is a drowning. Especially if the victim is, like this one, a drug user. Because sometimes a drug overdose can look like a drowning, the way the lungs fill up with fluid. But I can tell you for sure that, although Suzanne Black was a heroin user, this was not a drug overdose.

'So now we have to figure out if she was drowned where she was found. Have I told you about diatoms before? Doesn't matter if I have, I'm going to tell you again. Diatoms are microscopic creatures, a bit like plankton. They've got shells made of silicate, and they live in open water. Fresh water, salt water. Lakes and rivers. Every body of water has different diatoms. They're like a fingerprint, and they also vary accord-ing to the time of year.' His smile grew wider. 'You guys are fascinated, right? OK, I'll cut to the chase. When you drown, the diatoms make their way into your tissues. Lungs, kidneys, bone marrow, that kind of thing. We dissolve the tissue in acid and what's left is proof of what river or lake you drowned in.

'Well, we did the analysis and there are no diatoms in Suzanne Black's body. That means one thing and one thing only. She did not die in the canal. She died in tap water. Or fil-tered water, maybe. We ran some tests on her lungs and we found traces of soap, which to my mind narrows it down to a bath or a deep sink. I hope this little lecture has been helpful.'

Carol shook her head. 'Smooth-talking bastard. One of

these days I'm going to get the prosecution to play one of his cheery little vids to the jury. However, this is really useful information. We're not looking for a struggle by the canal, we're looking for wherever he took her for a bath.'

'Maybe he took her home with him,' Kevin suggested.

'He seems to be careful,' Carol said. 'I don't know that he'd have risked that. We need to find out where she took her punters. OK, on you go, Paula.'

'She was fully dressed when she was found,' Paula said. 'She wasn't weighted down, but the body had snagged on the usual canal debris, so she'd been in the water a while. They didn't catch the tattoo at first because the skin was so degraded.'

Carol winced at the word. No matter that it would have been used by Grisha himself; it still felt like an adjective that had no place being applied to a human body. 'But there's no doubt about it?'

Paula shook her head. 'Dr Shatalov is clear. It's a post-mortem tattoo and it looks very similar to the ones on Kylie and our Jane Doe.'

'If she drowned in a bath, there's a chance someone saw her with her killer. He had to take her somewhere with a bath. A house, a hotel or something,' Chris said.

'That's right. We need to get her photo on the local news, see what that brings out of the woodwork. Kevin, talk to the flatmate, Nicky. See if he has any photos of her.' Carol frowned, considering. 'Let's keep a lid on the connection for now, if we can. Penny Burgess has been sniffing round, but Dr Hill sent her off with a flea in her ear. She talks to any of you, do the same.' She gave Kevin a direct look, but he was ostentatiously scribbling in his notebook. 'We'll get DS Reekie to do the press call, keep MIT out of the picture for now, let the media think this is his. If our killer thinks he's not caught our attention, it might provoke him into breaking cover.'

'Or killing again,' Paula said, shoulders slumped. 'Because, right now, we've got almost nothing you could call a lead.'

'Any chance we could get Tony to take a look at this?' Everyone froze at Kevin's query. Sam stopped fidgeting, Chris stopped taking notes, Stacey stopped tapping on her smartphone and Paula's expression was fixed at incredulity.

Carol's mouth tightened as she shook her head. 'You know as well as I do, we don't have the budget.' Her voice was harsher than they were accustomed to.

Kevin flushed, his freckles fading against the scarlet. 'I just thought ... since they're winding us up anyway, why not? You know? You're leaving us. What have you got to lose?'

Before Carol could respond to this uncharacteristic defiance, the door to the squad room burst open. On the threshold, hair awry, one shirt tail hanging out, jacket collar askew, stood Tony Hill. He looked around wildly before his gaze settled on Carol. He gulped air, then said, 'Carol, we need to talk.'

There was no affectionate indulgence in Carol's glare. 'I'm in the middle of a murder briefing, Tony,' she said, her tone chilly.

'That can wait,' he said, continuing into the room and letting the door sigh shut behind him. 'What I have to say can't.'

10

An hour earlier, Tony Hill had been sitting in his favourite armchair, his games console controller in his hands, thumbs dancing over buttons as he whiled away the time until it was reasonable to expect Piers Lambert to be at his Home Office desk. The warbling trill of his phone broke into his concentration and his car spun off the road in a scream of brakes and a screech of tyres. He scowled at the handset on the table beside him. The best chance he'd had in ages to breach the final set of levels and now it was gone. He dropped the controller and grabbed the phone, noticing as he did so that it was late enough to call Piers. Just as soon as he'd dealt with whoever was on the phone.

'Hello?' There was no welcome in his greeting.

'Is that you, Tony?' The voice sounded like a Tory cabinet minister – posh with the edges deliberately rubbed off. A man more superstitious than Tony would have freaked out. Tony simply held the phone a few inches from his face and frowned before returning it to his ear.

'Piers? Is that really you?'

'Well spotted, Tony. You don't usually cotton on so quickly.'

'That's because you're not usually in the forefront of my mind, Piers.'

'And I am today? I'd take that as a compliment if I knew less about the way your mind works. Why am I on your mind?'

There was no specific reason why being on the receiving end of a call from Piers Lambert should have unsettled Tony. But in his experience, when senior mandarins made their own phone calls, it was never the harbinger of joy. 'You first,' he said. 'It's your phone bill.'

'I'm afraid I have some rather troubling news,' Lambert said.

Uh-oh. When men like Lambert used words like 'rather troubling', most people would reach straight for 'nightmarish', 'devastating', or 'hellish'. 'What's that, then?'

'It's to do with Jacko Vance.'

Tony hadn't heard the name for years, but still it held the power to make him feel ill. Jacko Vance was a psychopathic charmer without a trace of conscience. That made him far from unique in Tony's experience of the dark side of human behaviour. But Vance's destructiveness had ripped through promise that Tony had known at first hand. Vance had shattered trust in ways that few people could have imagined before his terrible damage became known. Compassion and empathy were the principles Tony had always tried to apply to his professional life. But among the many predators whose activities had threatened to strip those qualities from him, Jacko Vance had come closest. As far as Vance was concerned, the only news Tony wanted to hear was an obituary. 'What's happened?' he said, his voice rough with anxiety.

'It appears he's escaped from custody.' Piers sounded apologetic. Tony could picture his pained smile, his apprehensive eyes and the way he would touch the knot of his tie for reassurance. In that instant, he wanted to grab that tie and pull it very hard.

'Escaped? How the fuck could that happen?' Anger overtook him, nought to ninety in seconds.

'He took the place of another prisoner who had qualified for Release on Temporary Licence. He was due to spend the day at a local factory. The social worker who should have accompanied him wasn't at work and it appears Vance attacked the driver of the taxi taking him to the factory assignment, then made off in the taxi.'

'Jesus Christ,' Tony shouted. 'What in the name of God was he doing anywhere near the category of prisoner who could qualify for Release on Temporary Licence? How could that happen?'

Lambert cleared his throat. 'He's been on the Therapeutic Community Wing at Oakworth for a couple of months now. A model prisoner, by all accounts. Has been for years.'

Tony opened and closed his mouth a couple of times, reaching for the right words and failing to find them.

'There was no indication that Vance had anything planned,' Lambert continued, his voice smooth and unruffled.

Tony found his voice. 'Piers, can you explain what the hell Vance was doing on a Therapeutic Community Wing? He's on a whole-life tariff, for crying out loud. Why's he occupying a space in a rehab programme designed for people who have come to terms with their crimes? People who are working towards release? People who have a future that isn't behind bars? Answer me, damn it! Who put him in a place he could exploit? A place he could manipulate for his own ends? The perfect bloody place for someone like him to take advantage of?'

Lambert sighed heavily. 'There will, of course, be an inquiry. The psychologist who was assigned to him made the case for him to move to the Therapeutic Community Wing. He's been Category C for a couple of years now, you know.'

'Cat C?' Tony exploded. 'After what he's done? God knows how many teenage girls mutilated and murdered, and he's downgraded from Cat A to Cat C?'

56

'Technically, he's serving a single life sentence for a single murder—'

'Not to mention the murder of a police officer,' Tony continued, ignoring Lambert's response. 'A police officer who was trying to make sure no more girls died.'

'Nevertheless, we can only punish what we can prove. And the Court of Appeal found the conviction in respect of Detective Constable Bowman to be unsafe. As I said, Vance was a model prisoner. The governor of his previous prison held out as long as he could, but there were no grounds on which the authorities could refuse to reduce his threat category.' Tony picked up a note of frustration in Lambert's voice. It was good to feel that he wasn't alone in his outrage at what he was hearing. 'His lawyer threatened us with the Human Rights Act, and we both know how that would have gone. So Vance was reduced to Cat C and transferred to Oakworth.'

'This psychologist – was it a woman?'

'Yes, as it happens.' Lambert sounded startled. 'But entirely competent.'

'And entirely susceptible to Jacko Vance's charisma,' Tony said sadly. 'If anyone had asked me, I would have insisted that no female staff come into direct contact with Vance. He's clever, he's charming and he's got the knack of making men and women, but women in particular, feel like they're the only person in the world. He'll have made all the right noises about remorse and the need to atone, and what harm could it do to move him to a prison community where he could deal with his issues from the past? Even if he was never going to be returned to society, the system owed him that small kindness.' Tony made a sharp noise of disgust. 'I could write the script, Piers.'

'I'm sure you could, Tony. Unfortunately, there's no mechanism for allowing those involved in tracking down a criminal to have input into what happens to them once they fall within the remit of the prison system.'

Tony jumped out of his chair and began pacing the room. 'And he managed to impersonate another prisoner well enough to get out of Oakworth? How the hell did he manage that? I mean, Vance is the original one-armed man. He's got a bloody prosthetic arm. Not to mention the fact that he used to be on prime-time TV. Millions of people could pick him out of a line-up. How come the duty officers didn't recognise Jacko bloody Vance?'

'You are out of the loop, aren't you? Don't you remember, Vance brought a case under the Human Rights Act against the Home Office—'

'Yes, he said he was being discriminated against because he wasn't being fitted with the latest prosthetics. And the court upheld his position. But it's still a prosthesis, Piers. It's not an arm like you and I have got.'

'You don't know much about state-of-the-art prosthetics, do you, Tony? We're not talking about some bog-standard NHS artificial limb here. What Vance has got now is almost indistinguishable from what you and I have got. According to the brief I've got, he had surgery to reroute nerves, which in turn send messages to the electronics in the arm and the hand. He can move the fingers and thumb independent of each other. Over the top of it, he's got a bespoke cosmesis, which apparently is fake skin, complete with freckles, veins, tendons, the lot. The whole kit and caboodle cost thousands of pounds.'

'And we paid for that?'

'No. He went private.'

'This beggars belief,' Tony said. 'He's a convicted killer and he gets to have private medical care?'

'He was legitimately a multi-millionaire. He could afford it and the courts said he had the right to the best treatment available. I know it sounds insane, but that's the law for you.'

'You're right. It does sound insane.' Tony reached the far wall again and slapped his hand hard against it. 'I thought the families of his victims sued him? How come he's still awash with cash?'

'Because he was clever with it.' At last, a tinge of anger had crept into Lambert's voice. 'As soon as he was arrested, Vance made arrangements to take his money offshore. It's all tied up in trusts abroad, the kind of jurisdictions where we have no way of discovering who the trustees are or who the beneficiaries of the trusts are. The civil court judgements against Vance can't be enforced against an offshore trust. But when he needed funds for surgery, the money was made available. It's hugely offensive, but there's nothing we can legally do to prevent it.'

'Unbelievable.' Tony shook his head. 'But even if the arm wasn't obvious, how did he manage to fool everybody?'

Lambert groaned. 'God knows. What I'm hearing is that the prisoner in question has a shaved head, glasses and distinctive tattoos on his arms and neck. All of which Vance had copied. Someone obviously brought in custom-made tattoo sleeves or transfers with the appropriate designs. The person most likely to realise it was the wrong man was the social worker, and she wasn't in work today.'

Tony gave a sarcastic laugh. 'Don't tell me. Let me guess. Something completely unpredictable happened to her. Her boyfriend was kidnapped or her house blew up or something.'

'I have no idea, Tony. All I know is that she wasn't there, so in their infinite wisdom the officers sent him off in a taxi to his work placement. I'm told it's standard operating procedure in cases like this. Don't forget, the prisoners who get sent on these placements are on a trajectory towards release. It's in their interests not to mess up.'

'This is the most terrifying news I've heard in a long time, you know that? There's going to be bodies, Piers.' An involuntary shudder rippled across Tony's shoulders. 'How's the taxi driver? Is he still alive?'

'He has head injuries, but I'm told they're not life-threatening.' Lambert sounded dismissive. 'What concerns me most is that we recapture Vance as swiftly as possible. And that's where you come in.'

'Me? I haven't spoken to Vance since before his first trial. I've no idea where his head's at these days. You've got a prison psych who apparently knew him well enough to put him in a Therapeutic Community – talk to her.' Tony let out a sharp breath of exasperation.

'We will, of course. But I have huge respect for your abilities, Tony. I was very much on the sidelines when you put a stop to Vance all those years ago, but I remember the impact your work had on the Home Office attitude towards profiling. I want to send you the files on Vance and I want you to provide us with as detailed an assessment as possible of what he's likely to do and where he's likely to go.' Lambert had recovered his poise. His request had all the force of insistence without being obvious.

'It'd be guesswork at best.' When it came to the big beasts of officialdom, Tony knew better than to offer any shred of hope that could be used later as a stick to beat him with.

'Your guesswork is better by far than the considered opinion of most of your colleagues.'

When all else fails, Tony thought, wheel out the flattery. 'One thing I will say, even without the benefit of the files . . .'

'What's that?'

'I don't know where Micky Morgan is these days, but you need to track her down and tell her Vance is on the loose. In Vance's world view, she'll still be his wife. It doesn't matter that it was never a marriage in the first place, or that she had it annulled. As far as he's concerned, she let him down. He doesn't like being thwarted.' Tony stopped pacing and leaned his forehead against the door. 'As we all found out to our cost the last time. He's a killer, Piers. Anyone who's ever crossed him is at serious risk.'

There was a moment's silence. When Lambert spoke again, there was a gentleness in his voice that Tony had never heard before. 'Doesn't that apply to you too, Tony? You and DCI Jordan? You're the ones who brought him down. You and your team of baby profilers. If you think he's going after the people he blames for his incarceration, surely you're at the top of the list?'

It was a measure of Tony's lack of narcissism that Lambert's concern had genuinely not occurred to him. Years of clinical practice had taught him to bury his own vulnerability so deep he'd almost lost sight of it himself. And although he knew plenty about the chinks in Carol Jordan's armour, he was so accustomed to thinking of her as her own worst enemy that he'd all but forgotten there were other threats out there, threats that could undermine her far more comprehensively than her own weaknesses. 'I hadn't thought of that,' he said now, shaking his head, not wanting to believe himself a possible target. Because once he admitted that, everything he did would be tainted and skewed by the fear of who Vance might destroy next.

'I think you ought to be aware of the possibility,' Lambert said. 'I'll have the files uploaded and send you the codes to access them. As soon as we hear anything from the police in North Yorkshire, I'll be in touch.'

'I never said—'

'But you will, Tony. You know you will. We'll talk soon.'

And he was gone. For a split second, Tony thought about phoning Carol. But news like this was always better delivered face-to-face. He grabbed his car keys and jacket and headed for the door. He was halfway to Bradfield Police HQ when he remembered he'd had his own reasons for talking to Piers Lambert. But even though he thought he truly believed that no individual life was worth more than another, he had to acknowledge that, when it came to it, saving Carol Jordan was always going to trump anything else.

It wasn't an entirely comfortable conclusion, but it was inescapable.

11

Tony advanced into the room, his eyes fixed on Carol. 'I'm sorry,' he said. 'But I have to speak to you now. In private.'

Seeing how serious he was, Carol's expression shifted from annoyed to perplexed. Tony had never cried wolf in all the years she'd known him. Whatever the issue was, this was clearly no frivolous interruption. 'My office,' she said, gesturing with her head towards the open door. Tony didn't even break stride. Carol sighed and spread her hands wide in a gesture of helplessness towards her officers. Her team was well used to Tony's eccentricities, but it was still infuriating to have him walk in as if he owned the place. And whatever happened in it. 'As I said already: Kevin, talk to Suze Black's flatmate. Take Paula with you, I think. Sam, talk to Dr Shatalov about a photo we can use to ID her. Chris, work with Stacey to get the whiteboards up to speed with the files. And don't forget the tattooing machines.' She glanced over her shoulder and saw Tony was already pacing. 'I shall return,' she said wearily.

Carol shut the office door behind her but didn't bother to close the blinds. She wasn't expecting the conversation to go anywhere that needed that kind of privacy. 'This had better be good, Tony,' she said, dropping heavily into her chair. 'I've got three murders on the board. I don't have time for anything less than life or death.'

Tony stopped pacing and leaned his hands on her desk, facing her. 'I think this more than qualifies,' he said. 'Jacko Vance escaped from prison earlier this morning.'

Carol's face blanked with shock. 'What?' It was an automatic response. Tony didn't bother repeating himself. She stared at him for a long moment then said, 'How could they let that happen?'

Tony made a dismissive noise. 'Because Vance is smarter than anybody else in a Cat C prison.'

'Cat C? How could he be in Cat C? He's a convicted killer.'

'And the perfect prisoner, according to the Home Office. He hasn't put a foot out of place all the years he's been inside. Or rather, he's covered his tracks so well, that's what it looks like.' There was anger in his voice, but he couldn't be bothered trying to suppress it. If he couldn't show some emotion with Carol, then there was nowhere in his life he could open a door on what lay within. 'Not only was he Cat C, he's been on a Therapeutic Community Wing. Can you believe it? Free association, cells like hotel rooms, group therapy that he can stage-manage like the master manipulator he is.' He pushed off from the desk and threw himself into a chair. 'I could lay my head on your desk and weep.'

'So did someone help him? Did he go over the wall?'

'Obviously he's had a lot of help, inside and out. He impersonated another prisoner who was due to go out on a day release. One of those temporary licence things where they're supposed to learn how to adjust to the outside world.' He slapped his hands on his thighs. 'The other prisoner must have been in on it. You remember what Vance is like with vulnerability. He teases it out, then he homes in on it, makes people feel like he's the heaven-sent answer to whatever ails them. He'll have had something to offer that this other bloke needs.' He jumped up again and started pacing. Carol couldn't remember the last time she'd seen him so physically worked up. Then it came to her. An apartment in Berlin. Where her personal safety had been on the line. It dawned on her that this agitation might have its roots in the same cause.

'You're worried about me,' she said. 'You think he might come after me.'

Tony stopped in his tracks. 'Of course I'm worried about you. I remember what you told me. What he said to you the night you arrested him.'

Carol felt a cold thrill at the back of her neck. Vance's low angry words had chilled her at the time; they'd come back to her in dark and twisted dreams for months afterwards. Sometimes her gift for being able to remember precisely whatever she heard felt more like a curse. 'You are going to regret this night,' he'd said. Danger had come off him like a smell, leaving her feeling corrupted and afraid. Suddenly dry-mouthed, she tried to swallow. 'Surely he's not going to hang around taking revenge?' she said, trying to convince herself most of all. 'He's going to have a bolthole lined up. Somewhere he can feel in charge of his life. That's not going to be in this country, never mind anywhere near me.'

'I wouldn't bank on it,' Tony said. 'Remember what he did to Shaz Bowman.'

Recalling what Vance had done reminded Carol of the young cop who had been training as a profiler with Tony. Blazing blue eyes, brilliant analyst, impulsive servant of justice. Shaz had uncovered a cluster of potential serial killer victims, which had pleased her bosses. She'd also identified sporting hero and TV star Jacko Vance as the impossibly improbable suspect. Lacking the support of her colleagues, she'd gone her own sweet way, confronting Vance with her suspicions. And he had killed her in the most brutal and dehumanising manner. 'She was a threat to his security. To his liberty,' Carol said, knowing it was a weak response.

Tony shook his head, an angry twist to his expression. 'Nobody was listening to Shaz. Not even me, to my eternal shame. Nothing she had would have convinced a senior officer to investigate Vance, never mind arrest him. He was the big beast in the jungle, and she was a mosquito. He killed her because she'd pissed him off. The irony is that that's why he ended up in jail in the first place. If he'd left Shaz alone, she'd have been written off as a silly woman with a bee in her bonnet. Killing her was what electrified the lot of us.'

Carol nodded agreement, her shoulders slumping. 'And he's not stupid. He must understand that now, even if he didn't get it at the time. He's clearly been preparing this escape for years. So why would he risk being recaptured just to get his own back?' She glanced out of the window at the busy office outside. She badly wanted a drink, but she wouldn't let her team see her drink on duty. She wished she'd closed the blinds, but it was too late now. 'Surely he's not going to stick around just for revenge? All this time in the planning, he must have an escape hatch set up. And surely that's bound to be abroad? Somewhere without an extradition treaty?' Trying to convince herself, to keep the fear at bay.

'He doesn't look at the world the way we do, Carol. Vance is a psychopath. For years, abducting and raping and torturing and killing young girls was what gave his life meaning. And we took that away from him. That's been eating away at him ever since. Believe me, making us suffer in return is right up there at the top of his list. I know Vance. I've sat across a table from him and seen the wheels go round. He's going to want retribution – and you are going to be in the crosshairs.' Tony sat down abruptly, hands gripping the arms of the chair.

Carol frowned. 'Not only me, Tony. I just arrested him. You were the one who analysed his crimes, his behaviour. If he's got a list, you're up near the top too. And not just you. What about those baby profilers who stood shoulder to shoulder to avenge their colleague? They're in the frame too. Leon, Simon and Kay.' Fresh realisation dawned and Carol waved at the room beyond the glass. 'And Chris. I always forget that's when I first met Chris, because we were working opposite ends of the investigation. Chris will be on his list too. There was nobody more passionate about nailing Vance for Shaz's murder than Chris. She's a target. They're all targets. And they need to be warned.' Sudden anger surged in Carol's chest. 'Why have I not heard about this officially? Why am I hearing it from you?'

Tony shrugged. 'I don't know the answer to that. Maybe because I haven't delivered my risk assessment yet. But you're possibly right. I'm not convinced they played a significant enough role in Vance's eyes to be in the crosshairs now. But they do need to be told.'

'And his ex-wife,' Carol said. 'Jesus. Tell me they've informed Micky Morgan.'

'I told them straight off they should warn her,' Tony said. 'He'll perceive what she did as a betrayal. Not only did she fail to stand by him, she chose to humiliate him. That's how he'll see it. Rather than divorce him, she went for annulment. You and me, we understand why Vance wanted a marriage of convenience, but as far as your average prison inmate is concerned, not consummating your marriage means only one thing.' He gave Carol a wry look. 'That you're a sad sack of shit who can't get it up.'

Carol saw the pain in his eyes and felt the twist of the knife. It wasn't just his impotence that had come between them over the years, but it sure as hell hadn't helped. 'You're not a sad sack of shit,' she said briskly. 'Stop feeling sorry for yourself. I hear what you're saying about Micky – the way she went about getting rid of Vance set him up for ridicule, at best.'

'He'll have seen that as deliberate,' Tony said. 'But I don't think she'll be the one he goes for first. What she did was after the fact, if you like. The real villains are the ones who took his life away from him.'

'Which would be us,' Carol said. Anxiety was beginning to climb closer to alarm. She really needed that drink now.

'I think we've got a small window of opportunity before he makes a move,' Tony said. 'Vance was never one to take risks. He'll want to be rested and he'll want to be certain the plans he put in place from prison will work in practice. That gives all of us time to get our lives in order and go into hiding.'

Carol looked bemused. The notion of giving into the fear was anathema. 'Go into hiding? Are you crazy? We need to be out there, working with the search team.'

'No,' Tony said. 'That's the last place you want to be. You want to be where he won't be looking. Halfway up a Welsh mountain, or on a crowded London street. But certainly not with the search team, the very people he'll be doing his best to keep tabs on. Carol, I want us all to survive this. And the best way is to take ourselves out of harm's way till they catch Vance and put him back where he belongs.'

Carol glared at him. 'And what if they don't catch him? How long do we stay off the radar? How long do we put our lives on hold till it's safe to come out?'

'They'll catch him. He's not Superman. He's got no sense of the surveillance society that's sprung up since he was sent down.'

Carol snorted. 'You think? The hard evidence that put him away came from the early versions of what we've got now. I think he'll be very conscious of what's out there. If he was on a Therapeutic Community Wing, he'll have had a TV, a radio. Maybe even limited Internet access. Tony, Vance will know exactly what he's up against and he'll have made his plans with that in mind.'

'All the more reason to lie low,' Tony said stubbornly. He slammed his hands down on the arm of his chair. 'Damn it, Carol, I don't want to lose anybody else to that sick bastard.' His face was stripped of defences and she was reminded of how personal Shaz Bowman's death had felt to him. The blame he'd loaded on his own shoulders had weighed him down for years, not least because the courts had allowed Vance to escape the consequences of that particularly brutal act.

'You won't,' she said, her voice soft and warm. 'It's not going to be like last time. But cops like us don't hide from animals like Jacko Vance. We go out after them.' She held up a hand to stop him as he opened his mouth to speak. 'And I don't say that in the spirit of gung-ho stupidity. I say it because I believe it. If I start letting the fear take control, I might as well quit right now. Never mind a new start. The only thing I should be looking at is early retirement.'

Tony sighed, knowing when he was defeated. 'I can't make you,' he said.

'No, you can't. And unless the others have changed a hell of a lot in the past dozen or so years, you can't make them either. We need to be out there, looking for him.'

Tony screwed up his face in a pained expression. 'Please don't do that, Carol. Please. Warn the others, by all means. But just do your normal work. Leave the manhunt to people he's got no interest in killing.'

'And you? Is that what you'll be doing?'

Tony found he couldn't meet her eyes, even though he didn't feel he had anything to be ashamed of. 'I'm going to be a long way away from the front line, preparing a risk assessment. Suggestions about what Vance will want to do. Where he will want to go. I was going to hide halfway up a Welsh mountain with you so I could pick your brains, but that's not going to happen, is it?' Again, he was aware of anger creeping into his voice. This time, he clamped down on it, forcing himself to sound genial. 'So I'll probably get somebody else to deal with my appointments at Bradfield Moor today and drive back to Worcester so I can work there in peace.'

It wasn't an option that pleased Carol. She wanted him where she could keep tabs on him. 'I'd rather you stayed here,' she said. 'If we're not going into hiding, the least we should do is stay close to each other. Avoid giving Vance any opportunity for attack.'

Tony looked dubious. 'You're in the middle of a serial-killer inquiry and I'm not supposed to be working with you. If your beloved Chief Constable sees me hanging around in here, he'll have an aneurysm.'

'Tough. Anyway, I thought you'd figured out a way round that?'

Tony continued to avoid her eyes. 'I didn't get round to it. This other business put it out of my mind. And now I've got to work on this Vance assessment. I tell you what: I'll work in your office with the blinds drawn, then, when I deliver to the Home Office, I'll get it sorted out. OK?'

Carol surprised herself by laughing. 'You're hopeless, you know that?'

'But you have to promise me something in return . . .'

'What's that?'

'If he comes anywhere near any of us, you'll take cover.'

'I am not hiding up a mountain in the middle of Wales.' Carol's mouth set in a firm line.

'No, I see that. But I've still got the narrowboat moored up in the basin in Worcester. We could set sail like the owl and the pussycat. It'd take our minds off Vance.'

Carol frowned. This wasn't the Tony Hill she'd known all these years. Yes, he'd recently claimed he'd been changed profoundly by discovering the identity of his biological father, understanding the reasons why the man had played no role in

70

his life, and coming to terms with his legacy. But she'd been doubtful, seeing little evidence of any change beyond the superficial decision to leave Bradfield and move into the splendid Edwardian house in Worcester. OK, that had also meant jacking in his job at Bradfield Moor secure mental hospital, but Carol was convinced that giving up work wouldn't last for more than a few weeks. Tony identified himself too closely with the exploration of damaged minds to abandon it for long. There would be another secure hospital, another set of messy heads. She had no doubt of that.

However, the idea of taking off on an unplanned excursion to anywhere on a narrowboat was entirely out of character, a genuine marker of change. She couldn't remember the last time he'd even taken his annual leave, never mind actually going on holiday. Maybe he too was feeling the fear gnawing at his heart. 'We'll sail under that bridge when we come to it,' she muttered, getting up and heading for the door. 'But the first thing I need to do is break the bad news to Chris. Then we have to get cracking on tracking down the others and telling them.'

Tony got to his feet.

'No, you're staying right here,' Carol said, reaching past him and closing the blinds.

'I need to go home for my laptop,' he protested.

'No, you don't. You can use my computer.'

'It doesn't have my boilerplate.'

Carol gave a grim smile. 'If you mean your standard intro, just use one of your old profiles. You'll find them in the directory conveniently entitled "profiles". Sorry, Tony. If this is as serious as you made out, you have to take as much care of yourself as you would like to take of me.'

There was, she thought as she marched into the main squad room, absolutely nothing he could say to that.

12

Vance had found a Boston Red Sox baseball cap in the taxi driver's glove box. It wasn't exactly a disguise, but if there was already a description of him out there, the hat wouldn't be part of it. It was probably enough to give him a few moments' grace. He was pleasantly surprised by the new service area on the motorway. Back when he'd gone inside, a motorway service area was a depressing necessity, trapped in a 1960s time warp. Now this one at least had apparently been transformed into an attractive open-plan diner with an M&S food store, a coffee shop with twenty varieties of hot drink, and a motel. Who cared about ripping up the countryside? This was a huge improvement.

Vance drove to a quiet section of the car park, as far as he could get from the motel. He checked out the CCTV cameras and made sure he was parked in a position where the number plate couldn't be seen. Any time he could buy himself was an advantage at this point.

Out of curiosity, he opened the boot. Tucked in a corner at the back was some clothing. He reached in and shook out the folds of a lightweight rain jacket. Perfect. It was a bit tight on the shoulders, but it covered his tattooed arms, which was the most noticeable aspect of his current look. All the better for getting in and out of the motel.

Leaving the keys in the ignition in the hope that someone would steal the taxi, he walked briskly up the paved path to the motel, keeping his face tucked down into the upturned collar of the jacket. As he walked, he could feel the tension in his body. It wasn't fear; there were no grounds for fear yet. It was a mixture of apprehension and anticipation, he thought. It was a heightened awareness that would keep him safe. Not just for the moment, but for as long as he needed to carry out his plans.

He turned down the last lane of parked cars, studying them as he passed. Halfway down he saw the dark blue Mercedes estate car that he was looking for. Propped on the dashboard was a piece of paper with a number on it. The last three digits were 314.

Vance peeled away and made straight for the motel. He pushed the door open and walked confidently across the lobby to the lifts. None of the people chatting on sofas or drinking coffee at the functional tables so much as glanced at him. The receptionist, busy with another arrival, barely looked his way. Everything was exactly as he expected. Terry had done a good job of setting this up and reporting the salient details during his visits. Vance hit the call button and stepped aboard as soon as the doors opened. On the third floor, he turned left down a corridor that had the sharp chemical tang of artificial fragrance. He walked along the corridor till he came to the door marked 314. He knocked three times then stepped away from the door, ready to run if that proved necessary.

But there was no need to worry. The door swung silently open to reveal the wiry frame and monkey face of Terry Gates, the true believer who had done Vance's bidding in every particular since the day he'd been arrested. It had been Terry whose lying testimony had cast doubt on his first murder convictions, Terry who had never questioned what had been asked of him, Terry who had never wavered in his belief in Vance's innocence. For a moment he looked uncertain. Then their eyes met and his face crinkled in a toothy grin. He spread his arms wide, stepping backwards. 'Come away in, man,' he said, his Geordie accent obvious even in that short greeting.

Vance quickly crossed the threshold and closed the door behind him. He let out a long whoosh of breath and grinned right back at Terry. 'It's great to see you, Terry,' he said, relaxing back into his own honeyed tones.

Terry couldn't stop smiling. 'It's champion, Jacko. Champion. It's been so depressing all these years, only ever seeing you in them places.' He waved an arm at the room. 'How nice is this?'

It was, in truth, a lot better than Vance had expected for this stopping point on his journey back to the luxury and comfort he craved as his right. The room was clean with no stale notes of cigarettes or booze. The decor was simple – white walls and bedding, dark wood panelling behind the bed and the table that doubled as a desk. The curtains were tobacco brown. The only rich colours came from the carpet and the bedspread. 'You did well, Terry,' he said, pulling off the hat and shrugging out of the jacket.

'How did it go? Can I make you a brew? Is there anything you need? I've got all your paperwork and ID here in the briefcase. And I got some nice salads and sandwiches from M&S,' Terry gabbled.

'It went like clockwork,' Vance said, stretching luxuriously. 'Not a hitch.' He clapped Terry on the shoulder. 'Thanks. But first things first. What I need now is a shower.' He looked at his arms with distaste. 'I want to get rid of these eyesores. Why anyone would do that to themselves is a mystery to me.' He headed towards the bathroom.

'Just as well Jason did, though,' Terry said. 'With tattoos like that, nobody's looking too closely at your face, are they?'

'Exactly. Have you got a razor, Terry? I want to get rid of the goatee.'

'It's all in there, Jacko. Everything you asked for, all your regular toiletries.' Terry flashed him a smile again, ever anxious to please.

Vance closed the bathroom door and set the shower running. Terry was like a pet dog. Whatever Vance asked for, it would be there, on the double. No matter how many demands Vance made, it seemed that Terry still felt like he was the one who owed the debt. It all rested on one simple thing. Back when he'd been a national hero, Vance had spent hours by the bedside of Terry's twin sister Phyllis as she lay dying from the cancer that had rampaged through her body. Terry had thought Vance was acting out of compassion. He'd never understood that Vance sat by the beds of the dying because he liked to watch their lives leaking away. He enjoyed watching the humanity leach out of them till they were nothing more than a shell. Luckily for him, that had never even occurred to Terry as a possible motive for what he'd seen as an act of profound kindness. Phyllis had always loved *Vance's Visits*; having the real thing at her bedside had been the one light in her life as it had wasted away.

Vance removed his prosthesis and stepped into the shower, luxuriating in an endless flow of water whose temperature was entirely under his control. It was bliss. He washed himself from head to toe with an expensive shower gel that smelled of real lime and cinnamon. He scrubbed the tattoo off his neck then shaved the goatee off, leaving the moustache. He stood under the water for a long time, savouring the sense of being master of his own destiny again. Eventually, the tattoo transfer began to slip, slithering down his arm like a Dalí print. Vance rubbed his arm against his chest and stomach, helping it to dissolve into a gluey puddle then to disappear down the drain, flushing away all traces of Jason's body art.

He stepped out of the shower and wrapped himself in a thick towel. It felt impossibly soft against his skin. Next, he covered the artificial skin of his prosthesis in shower gel and eased the tattoo sleeve off, again letting it dissolve and slip away, leaving no sign of what had happened there. As he dried himself, Vance's thoughts slipped back to Terry. He'd perjured himself for Vance. Who knew how many criminal offences he'd committed in the past year on Vance's behalf – everything from obtaining false ID to money laundering. He'd set up the practicalities of Vance's escape. There had never been even a hint that he might betray the man he still hero-worshipped. And yet . . .

The fact that Terry was the man who knew too much was inescapable. He'd kept the faith for so long because he'd managed to convince himself that Vance was innocent. It was impossible for him to believe that the man who had made his sister's last weeks bearable could also be a killer. But this time, it would be different. Vance had plans. Hellish plans. And when the terror started, when the full revelation of his revenge became clear, there would be no wriggle room for doubts. Not even Terry could fly in the face of that coming storm. Terry would have to accept some personal responsibility for the havoc Vance planned to wreak. It would be a terrible moment for him. But there was no escaping the fact that Terry was a man who had the courage of his convictions. Having stood four square behind Vance for so long, the realisation of his error would send Terry straight into the arms of the police. He wouldn't be able to help himself.

THE RETRIBUTION

Which incontrovertibly made Terry the man who knew too much. For him to reveal what he had done, to lay out the knowledge he possessed would be the end of everything. That was something Vance couldn't allow to happen.

13

D etective Sergeant Alvin Ambrose tried not to fret too much as he endured the security checks he had to go through to get into Oakworth Prison. Body scans, metal detectors, give up your phones, hand over your radio ... If they took as much care with the people they let out, he wouldn't be here right now.

Not that he should be here, by rights. True, Oakworth was on West Mercia's patch and close enough to Worcester to make the escape the indisputable responsibility of the city's CID. That meant, Ambrose thought, that this assignment should have been handled by his boss. But ever since Carol Jordan's appointment to the job he'd wanted had been announced, it seemed like DI Stuart Patterson had gone on strike. Everything he could shunt Ambrose's way was dumped on the sergeant's desk. And so it was with this. Any hope Ambrose had had of seeing his boss take charge had vanished as soon as the identity of the escaped prisoner was revealed. That Carol Jordan had been involved in his initial arrest had simply cemented what was becoming standard operating procedure in their office.

As far as the head of CID was concerned, Patterson was handling the case. The reality was that Ambrose was fronting it up. Never mind that the prison governor would expect a higher rank than sergeant to be leading the hunt for a dangerous escapee like Vance. Ambrose was just going to have to lump it and rely on his formidable presence to get him through. At least he might be able to call on Carol Jordan's expertise ahead of her arrival in Worcester. When he'd worked with her before, he'd been impressed. It wasn't easy to impress Alvin Ambrose.

At last, he was through the checks and through the sally port and trailing down a corridor to an office where a surprisingly young man was sitting behind a cluttered desk. He jumped up, holding his swinging jacket front down with one hand, sticking out the other to greet Ambrose. He was tall and rangy, full of bounce. As Ambrose drew near enough to shake his hand, he could see that his skin was criss-crossed with dozens of fine lines. He was older than he appeared. 'John Greening,' he said, his handshake as vigorous as his appearance. 'Deputy Governor. The boss has gone London, talking to the Home Office.' He widened his eyes and raised his eyebrows. He reminded Ambrose of David Tennant's rendition of Doctor Who. The very thought made him tired. Greening gestured towards a seat, but Ambrose remained standing.

'Hardly surprising,' Ambrose said. 'In the circumstances.'

'Nobody is more embarrassed than us about Jacko Vance's escape.'

Embarrassed seemed a woefully inadequate word to Ambrose. A serial killer had walked out the front door of this man's jail. In his shoes, Ambrose would have been paralysed with shame. 'Yeah. Well, obviously there'll be an inquiry into a screw-up of this magnitude, but that's not what I'm here for right now.'

Greening looked peeved. Not angry or ashamed, Ambrose thought. Peeved. Like someone had criticised his tie. Which frankly would have deserved all it got. 'I can assure you there's no indication of corruption among our staff,' he said.

79

Ambrose snorted. 'That's almost worse, don't you think? Corruption might have got you off the hook with less pain than incompetence. Anyway, I'm here now because I need to talk to Jason Collins.'

Greening nodded stiffly. 'The interview room's set up for you. Audio and video streams. We're all very surprised at Jason's involvement. He's been doing so well on the Therapeutic Community Wing.'

Ambrose shook his head in disbelief. 'A prize student, obviously.'

Greening nodded towards the officer who had escorted him in. 'Officer Ashmall will show you to the interview room.'

Dismissed, Ambrose followed the officer back into the corridor, through another sally port and further into the labyrinth of the prison. 'Did you know Vance?' Ambrose asked.

'I knew who he was. But I never had direct contact with him.'

That closed down that conversation. Another right-angle turn, then they stopped outside a door. The officer unlocked it with a swipe card and held the door open for him. Ambrose stood just inside the doorway for a long moment, taking in the man sitting at the table that was bolted to the floor. Shaved head, goatee, tattoos. As reported. Collins raised his head to meet Ambrose's eyes with a flat contemptuous stare. 'What are you looking at?' Ambrose had experienced that kind of challenge so often in his years on the force that it bounced off without leaving a mark.

He said nothing. He looked around the room, as if sizing up its grey walls, strip lighting and tiled floor for an estate agent's brochure. The room smelled of stale bodies and farts. It almost made Ambrose nostalgic for the days of cigarette smoke. Two strides took him to the empty chair opposite Collins and the prison officer left them to it, pointing out the button Ambrose should press when he was done.

'Jason, I'm Detective Sergeant Alvin Ambrose from West Mercia police and I'm here to talk to you about your involvement in Jacko Vance's escape.'

'I know what you're here for,' Jason said, his voice sullen and heavy. 'All I know is that he asked me to swap cells last night.'

Ambrose burst out laughing, a deep hearty roar that filled the room. Collins looked startled and afraid. 'Do me a favour,' Ambrose said once he'd recovered himself. 'Cut the crap and tell me what you know.'

'I don't know nothing. Look, it was supposed to be a joke. He reckoned he could pass for me, I reckoned he couldn't. I never thought it would get as far as it did.' Collins smirked, as if to say, 'Prove me a liar.'

'It must have taken a lot of planning, for a joke,' Ambrose said sarcastically.

Collins shrugged. 'That wasn't my worry. He was the one who reckoned he could get away with it. He was the one had to make it work.' He gave a thumbs-up sign with both hands. 'Fucking good on him.'

'I don't believe you.'

Collins shrugged again. 'Believe what you like. I couldn't give a shit.'

'You know your days on this wing are over, right? You're going back to Cat A. No privileges. No comfy duvet or private bathroom. No touchy-feely therapy sessions. No prospect of a cushy day out of jail. Not till you're an old man. Unless you've got some information that can cut you a break.'

Collins' mouth curled in a sneer. 'Better than information. I've got cancer, fat man. I'll be on hospital wings. I'll be going home to die, just like the Lockerbie bomber. Nothing you can threaten me with comes close to that shit. So you might as well piss off.'

He wasn't wrong, Ambrose thought as he pushed the chair

back and walked to the door. As it opened to release him from the interview, he turned back and smiled at Collins. 'I hope the cancer treats you as kindly as Vance treated his victims.'

Collins sneered. 'You ain't seen nothing yet, copper. According to Jacko, he's got plans that'll make the past look like *Jackanory*.'

14

C hris Devine felt a dark flush of anger rise up her neck. She had always considered herself well tough enough for the Job. Emotional fragility had never threatened her equanimity. For a long time she'd thought she was unshockable. Then Shaz Bowman had died at the hands of Jacko Vance and Chris discovered she could be as devastated as anyone else. But she hadn't fallen apart. She wouldn't give him the satisfaction. Instead she'd used that pain as an impetus to take the fight to Shaz's killer and join the impromptu team Tony and Carol had assembled to bring Vance down. Nothing had given her more satisfaction in her entire career.

In the half-dozen years she'd spent on the MIT in Bradfield, Chris had thought about Shaz almost every working day. They'd worked together when Shaz had first made it into CID and they'd been a good team then. At this level, they'd have been unstoppable. This was the kind of work Shaz had dreamed of doing and she'd have been good at it.

Mixed with Chris's regret was an inescapable element of guilt. Even though she wasn't Shaz's boss by then, she still blamed herself for not paying close enough attention to what Shaz had been doing; if she hadn't been so wrapped up in her own concerns, she might have provided back-up and kept the young detective safe. But she hadn't and it was a failing she lived with daily. Ironically, it had made her a better colleague, a stronger team player.

Even now there was no shred of forgiveness in her heart for Jacko Vance. His very name still had the power to provoke a surge of anger in her, an anger she suspected would only ever be stilled by direct physical violence. Now, listening to Carol Jordan's news, Chris could feel that familiar rage burn inside her again. Pointless to engage in recrimination. What mattered was putting Vance back where he belonged and making sure he stayed there. 'How's the hunt being organised?' she said, ramming the lid down on her anger.

'I don't have any information,' Carol said. 'Nobody's bothered to tell me officially what's going on. I only know because the Home Office asked Tony for a risk assessment. And he thinks all of us who put Vance away need to watch our backs.'

Chris frowned. She understood the gravity of Tony's opinion. She wasn't sure she agreed, though. 'Makes sense. He couldn't stand being crossed,' she said slowly. 'That's why he killed Shaz. Even though she was no threat to him. Not really. He had all the power. But she had the bottle to go up against him and he couldn't tolerate that.'

'Exactly.'

'All the same . . . I can see why he thinks you and him might be in the firing line. But the rest of us? I don't think we made it on to Vance's radar. We were just the little people, and guys like Vance don't have to pay attention to the little people. There's no spectacle in the little people like us.'

Carol gave a dry laugh. 'Funny, I never think of you as one of the little people, Chris. I appreciate what you're saying, but I still want to cover the bases. What I need you to do is to track down the other three who worked with us and warn them that Vance is on the loose and could be a risk to their safety.'

Chris looked up at the corner of the room and cast back into her memory. 'Leon Jackson, Simon McNeill and Kay ... what was Kay's surname?'

Sam Evans, on his way out of the room, overheard Chris's last comment and couldn't help himself. 'Not like you to forget one of the laydeez, Chris,' he teased.

'Some people are just—' she shrugged. 'Forgettable, Bill.'

'Ha, ha,' he said sarcastically as he let the door swing closed behind him.

'She was forgettable, though,' Carol said. 'I think she did it deliberately. Melting into the background so people would forget she was there and say something they didn't intend to.'

Chris nodded. 'She was a good interviewer. Different to Paula, but maybe just as good. But what was her surname?'

'Hallam. Kay Hallam.'

'That's it, now I remember. It's funny, isn't it? You'd think after an experience like that, we'd all have stayed in touch. Kept an eye on each other's careers. But soon as the first court case was over, they all scattered to the four winds. It was like they didn't want any contact to make it easier to erase the whole thing from the memory banks. Then when we all met up for the appeal and the second trial, it was like a bunch of embarrassed strangers.'

Carol nodded. 'Like when you run into people at a wedding or a funeral that you were once close to, but it's been so long it's too awkward. You can't recover the way you were but you both know it used to be different and there's something painful and sad about it.'

It was hard to say who was more surprised by Carol's comments. They had worked together for long enough for Chris to know just how rare it was to hear Carol Jordan speak so clearly from the heart. Both women guarded their privacy, deliberately avoiding intimacy. Close as this team was, they didn't socialise together. Wherever they opened their hearts, it wasn't in the office.

Carol cleared her throat. 'Kay sent me Christmas cards for three or four years, but I think that had more to do with wanting to be sure I would give her a good reference than a desire to stay in touch. I've no idea where she is now, or even if she's still a copper.'

Chris tapped the names into her smartphone. 'I'll get on to it. Maybe the Federation can help. At least they should be able to tell me if they're still serving officers.'

'Will they give out information like that?' Carol said.

Chris shrugged. 'They're supposed to be our union. You'd think they'd want to protect us.' She gave a wicked grin. 'Besides, I have my little ways. They might not be as pretty as Paula's, but they get results.'

Carol threw up her hands in surrender as Chris swung round and started hammering the keys of her computer with the force of someone who had learned her skills on a typewriter. 'I don't want to know any more,' she said. 'Talk to me and Tony when you're done. And Chris ...?'

Chris looked up from the screen. 'What?'

'Don't get so wrapped up in this that you forget to watch your own back. If Vance has got a list, you're on it too.' Carol stood up and made for the door.

'So, with all due respect, guv, where exactly are you going all on your lonesome?' Chris called after her.

Carol half-turned, a wry smile crinkling the skin round her eyes. 'I'm going to Northern Divisional HQ. I think I'll be safe there.'

'I wouldn't bank on it,' Chris muttered darkly as the door closed behind Carol.

*

It was unusual for Vanessa Hill to be at a loose end at lunchtime. Just because food was a necessity, there was no reason not to use eating time purposefully. So working lunches were a perennial feature of her calendar. Either out with clients or in the office with key personnel, planning campaign strategies and assessing potential markets. She'd been running her own HR consultancy for thirty years now and she hadn't become one of the leading headhunters in the country by accident.

But today she was stranded. The insurance broker she was supposed to meet for lunch had cancelled at the last minute – some nonsense about his daughter breaking her arm in an accident at school – leaving her in the centre of Manchester with nothing to occupy her until her two o'clock appointment.

She couldn't be bothered sitting in the pre-booked restaurant alone, so she stopped outside a sandwich bar and picked up a coffee and a filled roll. She remembered passing a carwash with valet on her way to the restaurant. It was about time the car had a good going over. There was a time when she did that sort of thing herself on the grounds that nobody else would do it as thoroughly, but these days she preferred to pay. Not that it represented any compromise on standards. If they didn't do it well enough, she simply insisted they do it again.

Vanessa drove into the valeting bay, issued her instructions and settled down in the waiting room, where a TV high on the wall provided a rolling news channel for its customers. Heaven forbid that anyone should be thrown on their own resources, Vanessa thought. She unwrapped her sandwich, aware of being studied by the fifty-something bloke in the off-the-peg suit that hadn't been pressed this week. She'd already dismissed him as pointless in a single sweep of her eyes when she walked in. She was practised at sizing people up more swiftly than clients often believed possible. It was a knack she'd always had. And as with all of nature's gifts, Vanessa had learned to maximise it.

She knew she wasn't the most beautiful of women. Her nose was too sharp, her face too angular. But she'd always dressed and groomed to make the most of what she had, and it was gratifying that men still gave her the once-over. Not that she was remotely interested in any of them. It had been years since she'd expended any time or energy on anything that went beyond flattery or flirting. Her own company was more than adequate for her.

As she ate, Vanessa kept half an eye on the screen. Lately, the news had felt like a daily retread. Middle East unrest, African unrest, government squabbling and the latest natural disaster. One of her employees had been making everyone laugh round the water cooler the other morning, doing an impression of an overly religious neighbour delivering doom, gloom and the four horsemen of the apocalypse over the dustbins. You could see her point, though.

Now the newsreader seemed to perk up. 'News just in,' she said, her eyebrows dancing like drawbridges on fast forward. 'Convicted murderer Jacko Vance has escaped from Oakworth Prison near Worcester. Vance, who was convicted of the murder of a teenage girl but is believed to have killed many more, disguised himself as a prisoner who was booked on a day's work experience outside the prison.'

Vanessa harrumphed. What did they expect? Treat prisoners like it's a hostel and they'll take advantage. 'Prison officials have declined to comment at this stage, but it's understood that former TV presenter and Olympic athlete Vance hijacked a taxi that had been hired to take the other prisoner to his workplace. Over now to local MP, Cathy Cottison.'

A plain woman in an unflattering neckline appeared on St Stephen's Green outside Westminster. 'There are many questions to be answered here,' she said in a strong Black

Country accent that Vanessa struggled with. 'Jacko Vance is a former TV star. He's only got one arm. How on earth did he fool the prison staff enough to get out in the first place? And how is a prisoner like Vance anywhere near the sort of prisoner who goes out on day release? And how come a prisoner gets in a taxi by himself, without an escort? And how does a one-armed man hijack a taxi without a weapon? I will be putting these questions to the Home Secretary at the first opportunity.'

Vanessa was paying serious attention now. Heads would roll over this. And where heads rolled, recruitment opportunities were not far behind. To her disappointment, the news angle was left behind as they segued into the back story of Vance the athlete, Vance the TV personality and Vance the killer. Her focus began to drift away, then suddenly, a familiar figure appeared on the screen. 'Psychological profiler Dr Tony Hill, seen here with a police colleague, was instrumental in exposing Vance's crimes and bringing him to justice.'

Of course. It had completely slipped her mind that Tony had been involved in the Jacko Vance case. Most mothers would have been proud to see their only son featuring so positively in a national news story. Vanessa Hill was not most mothers. Her son had been an inconvenience since even before he'd been born and she'd managed to sidestep anything approaching a maternal response to him. She had set her face against him from the beginning and nothing he had done had changed her position. She despised him and scorned what he did for a living. He wasn't a stupid man, she knew that much. He had the same knack for insight that she possessed. He could have turned his gifts to good use, made a success of himself.

Instead, he'd chosen to spend his days with killers and rapists and the scum of the earth. What was the point of that? Honestly. Remembering he'd been thwarted by her bastard son almost made her feel like rooting for Jacko Vance. She turned away in disgust and took out her phone to check her emails. Anything had to be better than watching that rubbish on the telly.

15

There was something desperately sad about the flat that Nicky Reid had shared with Suze Black. The worn-out furniture had clearly been culled from the meanest of second-hand shops. The scenic photographs on the walls looked as if they'd been cut out of magazines and slotted into cheap IKEA frames. The carpet was threadbare, its colour lost in the mists of time. But it was both cleaner and tidier than Paula had expected. It felt like a room put together by a pair of kids playing at keeping house.

Nicky caught her observant eye and said, 'We're not scum, you know. We try to live a decent life. Tried.' He pointed to a bowl of oranges, apples and bananas on a side table. 'Fruit and stuff. Proper food. And we pay the rent.' He crossed one skinny denim-clad leg over the other and folded his hands over his knee. The campness of the posture undercut his attempt at dignity and Paula felt even more sad for him.

'I'm sorry about Suze,' she said. 'What happened to her is unforgivable.'

'If you lot had listened when I reported her missing ... If you'd taken me seriously ...' The accusation hung in the air.

Paula sighed. Her tone was tender. 'I understand why you

feel so angry, Nicky. But even if we'd gone on red alert when you reported Suze missing, we'd have been too late. I'm sorry, but the truth is, she'd been dead for some time before even you knew she was gone. I know you feel guilty, Nicky, but there's nothing you could have done different that would have made any odds to the outcome.'

Nicky sniffed loudly, his eyes bright. Paula couldn't decide if it was cocaine or grief; judging by Kevin's body language, he'd already made his mind up.

'She was great – Suze,' Nicky said, a wobble in his voice. 'I've known her for years. We were at school together. We used to bunk off and go down the video arcade, hang around smoking and playing bingo with the pensioners.'

'You both had problems with school, then?'

He gave a scornful little laugh. 'School. Home. Other kids. You name it, me and Suze managed to get in it up to our fucking necks. She's the only person who's still in my life from back then. Everybody else fucked me over then fucked off. But not Suze. We took care of each other.'

Paula reckoned he was relaxed enough now for a harder question. 'You're both working the street, right?'

Nicky nodded. 'Rent.' He looked up at the cracked ceiling, blinking back tears from big blue eyes that were the stand-out feature in his narrow bony face with its thin lips and chipped teeth. 'We couldn't do anything else. Suze tried working in the corner shop, but the pay was crap.' He gave a little shrug. 'I don't know how people manage.'

'Most people don't have an expensive drug habit,' Kevin said, not unkindly.

Nicky flicked at a tear with the tip of his fingers. 'So fucking sue me.'

'Suze was doing heroin, am I right?' Paula said, trying to get back on track.

Nicky nodded and began picking at the skin round his

thumbnail. 'She's been using for years.' He flashed a quick look at Paula. 'She wasn't, like, off her tits. Just nice and steady, like. She could cope. On heroin, she could cope. Off heroin?' He sighed. 'Look, I know you think we're shit, but we were doing OK.' He reached for his cigarettes and lit one. As an afterthought, he offered one to Paula, who managed to refuse.

'I can see that,' Paula said. 'I can see how hard you've been trying. I'm not here to give you a bad time for any of it. I just need to be sure whether Suze died because of something in her life or because she was in the wrong place at the wrong time.'

Nicky straightened up, uncrossing his legs and gripping the seat of the chair. 'There was nobody in her life who would want to do Suze a bad turn. I know you think I'm bigging her up because she's dead, but that's not how it was. Look, she was a hooker and a heroin addict, but she wasn't a bad person. She never had a pimp. She just had a dealer who looked after her.'

'Who was her dealer?'

He shook his head. 'I'm not going to name names. That would be stupid and I'm not stupid. Whatever you might think. Look, she was a good customer. And she brought other customers to him, so he took care that nobody gave her a bad time. Nobody poached on her pitch. Everybody knew the score. When those fucking East European bitches turned up at the building site, they thought they could work the Flyer when the weather turned shitty.' Nicky smirked. 'That didn't last long. Those Russian fuckers think they're hard, but they're not hard like Bradfield hard.'

'How long had Suze been working the Flyer?' Kevin asked. He knew Paula didn't like her flow being interrupted, but he hated feeling like a spare part.

Nicky scratched his head, crossing his legs again. Paula

wished she had Tony Hill's ability to read a person's body language. She'd recently been on an interrogation course that
had devoted some time to the subject but still she felt as if she
was only skating over the surface. 'I don't remember,' he said.
'It feels like forever, you know?'

'Did she have regulars?' Paula asked. 'Or was it mostly air-
crew passing through?'

'Both.' He inhaled deeply and let the smoke flow from his
nostrils. 'Some of her regulars were crew that fly the same
route all the time. Like, if it's Tuesday it must be the Dubai lot.
She had a few Arab regulars, coming in and out from the Gulf.
Some locals who work the cargo terminal.' He sighed. 'I don't
know names or anything like that. I never really paid attention. I wasn't that interested in her punters, if you must know.'

'Did she have a place where she took them? A hotel room,
a bedsit, somewhere like that?' *Drowned in a bath*, Paula
thought.

Nicky gave a small splutter of laughter. 'Are you kidding?
She was a street-level prostitute. She never worked in a
brothel or a sauna. She worked the streets. She fucked them
round the back of the Flyer. In their car, if they had one.' He
laughed again, a terrible choked sound. 'It's not *Pretty Woman*,
our lives.'

'What about where these guys were staying? The out-of-
towners must have had hotel rooms. Did she go back with
them?'

Nicky shook his head. 'Like I said, Suze was street. She
wasn't going to get past any hotel receptionist with a pulse.
Why are you asking about this?'

'We think she wasn't killed where she was found,' Paula
said.

'They said she was drowned. And they found her in the
canal. Why would you think she wasn't killed there?'

'They found the wrong water in her lungs,' Paula said. 'It

wasn't canal water. Wherever she drowned, it wasn't in the canal.' She waited while he processed that information. 'Any idea where that might have been?'

'No fucking idea at all.'

'Did she ever mention feeling threatened?'

'The only time there was ever any bother was with the East Europeans. And like I say, that got sorted out. It was months ago, anyway. If there had been any blowback off that, it would have hit a long time ago. Whoever killed her, I don't think it was personal. Anybody could have picked her up. Once the Flyer shut its doors, she worked on the street. It's not like anybody had her back. Out there, she was on her own. It wasn't like in Temple Fields where I work. We're team-handed there. Somebody pays attention who I go with. I do the same for them.' He shook his head. 'I told her she should find somebody to work with. But she said there wasn't enough work to go round. I can't blame her. She was right. Fucking recession.'

'What? People cutting back on paying for it?' Kevin said, a hint of sarcasm obvious to Paula.

'No, copper,' Nicky said angrily. 'More people out on the street selling it. We've been noticing that, me and Suze. A lot of new faces.'

That was interesting, Paula thought. She wasn't quite sure why, but anything out of the ordinary couldn't be disregarded in a murder inquiry. 'Any trouble from the new faces?'

Nicky ground out his cigarette in an African ceramic ashtray, then lifted the top and dropped the stub neatly below. No overflowing saucers here, Paula noted. 'There's been some rucks down Temple Fields,' he said at last. 'But not out the arse end of Brackley Field.' He picked up his cigarette packet and tapped it on the arm of the chair. 'When will they let me have her body?'

The question came out of nowhere. 'Are you her next of kin?' Paula said, playing for time.

'I'm all she's got. Her mum's dead. She hasn't seen her dad or her two brothers since she was nine. She was in care, same as me. We look after each other. She needs a proper funeral and no other fucker will do it for her. So when do I get to sort it out?'

'You need to talk to the coroner's officer,' Paula said, feeling bad about sidestepping a question that had no easy answer. 'But they won't release her right away. With her being a murder victim, we need to hold on to her for a while.'

'Why? I knew there had to be a post-mortem. I mean, I watch TV, right? I understand that. But now that's been done, surely I can have her back?'

'It's not that simple,' Kevin said. 'If we arrest someone—'

'*If?* Don't you mean when?' Nicky jumped to his feet and began to prowl up and down the room, lighting a cigarette as he moved. 'Or is she not important enough to qualify for "when"?'

Paula could sense Kevin tensing alongside her. 'Here's how it goes. *When* we arrest someone, he has the right to ask for a second post-mortem. Just in case our pathologist got it wrong. It's particularly important when there's some question about cause of death. Or, like in this case, a forensic issue relating to the body.'

'Fuck,' Nicky spat. 'The rate you lot work at, we could all be dead before you arrest someone.' He stopped, leaning his head on the wall. In silhouette, he looked like an artist's rendition of despair. 'What happens if this twat gets away with it? How long before you decide to give her back to me?' He was getting worked up now. There would be nothing more of value from Nicky today, Paula realised.

'Talk to the coroner's officer, Nicky,' she said, calm but not condescending. 'He can answer your questions.' She stood up and crossed the room to where he stood and put her hand on his arm. Through his long-sleeved top, she could feel hard bone and quivering muscle. 'I'm sorry about your loss. I promise you, I don't take any murder lightly.' She handed him her card. 'If you think of anything that might be helpful, call me.' She gave him a thin smile. 'Or if you just want to talk about her, call me.'

16

C arol glared at Penny Burgess, the crime correspondent of
the *Bradfield Evening Sentinel Times*. It was probably as well
for the reporter that Carol was watching the press conference
on CCTV and not in the same room. From her earliest days in
Bradfield, the reporter had alienated Carol, in spite of her
appeals to sisterhood and justice. It infuriated Carol that someone who claimed to espouse the beliefs closest to her own
heart could deny them so effectively in her actions. What was
almost more irritating was that the woman seemed to be bul-
letproof. No matter that her career regularly seemed to hit the
rocks – there she was, still getting those front-page bylines and
showing up in the press room looking as expensively turned
out as a London fashion journalist. She'd nearly destroyed
Kevin Matthews' career and his marriage when she'd seduced
him into an affair and a series of operational indiscretions, but
still she sat there in the front row at police press conferences as
if she were made of stainless steel.

Today, she was being as tenacious as ever. Once she got an
idea into her head, she was like a serial killer with a victim in her
power. She wouldn't give up until she'd exhausted the possibilities of her prey then finished it off. It was an admirable trait,

Carol supposed. Provided you had the judgement to know when the idea was actually worth the pursuit. She'd been driven to the point of public rage by Penny herself; she knew exactly what Pete Reekie was experiencing now. It didn't help that Penny was actually on to something Reekie wanted to keep under the radar. There was a dull flush across his prominent cheekbones and his brows were drawn down low. 'As I said right at the start of this press call, the aim of this morning's exercise is to identify an unknown murder victim. Somewhere out there is a family who are unaware of what has happened to their daughter, their sister, maybe even their mother. That's the number one priority,' he said, biting his words as if they were a stick of celery.

Penny Burgess didn't wait for an invitation that surely wouldn't have come. She was straight in there, coming back at the point she'd introduced some time earlier. 'Surely the number one priority is to catch a killer? To stop the death toll rising any further?'

Flustered, Reekie looked around for help. But there was none. 'That goes without saying,' he said. 'But our first step is to identify the victim. We need to know where she encountered her killer.'

'She encountered him on the streets of Bradfield,' Penny interrupted. 'Just like his first two victims, Kylie Mitchell and Suzanne Black. Superintendent, do you have a warning to issue to the city's street prostitutes while this serial killer is at large?'

'Miss Burgess, I have already said there is no reason to believe these murders are the work of one man. The women were all killed in markedly different ways and locations—'

'My source tells me there's a link between all three crimes,' Penny Burgess cut in. 'The killer leaves a signature. Would you care to comment on that?'

Take it back to her, Carol urged mentally. *She's short on details, that's why she hasn't run the story.*

The same truth had finally dawned on Reekie. 'Can you elaborate?' he snapped. 'Because I don't think you have any idea what you're talking about. I think you're just looking for a sensationalist angle. Because that's the only way you can get your editor interested in the murder of a street sex worker. It's only got value for you if you can spin it into something that sounds like an episode from a TV series.'

There was a shocked silence in the room. Then a cacophony of voices began shouting questions. *You've gone too far*, Carol thought. *You've really pissed her off now.*

The police press officer managed to bring some calm to the half-dozen reporters in the room. Then Penny Burgess's voice rang out again:

'Will you be inviting DCI Jordan's Major Incident Team to contribute to the inquiry?'

Reekie glowered at her. 'I've no intention of discussing operational matters in this forum,' he said. 'I'm going to say this one more time, and then this press conference is over.' He half-turned and gestured towards the cleaned-up image Grisha Shatalov had managed to produce. The woman still looked dead, but at least now she wouldn't give most people night-mares. 'We are concerned to identify the victim of a brutal murder that occurred in Bradfield some time between Tuesday evening and Wednesday morning. Someone must know this woman. We urge you to come forward in strictest confidence with any information about her identity or her movements prior to her death. Thank you for your cooperation.' Reekie turned on his heel and marched out, ignoring the questions still coming from the reporters.

A few moments later, he burst into his office and threw his papers on a small table by the door. Carol swung round in the swivel chair and pasted a sympathetic look on her face. 'Bit of a nightmare, Penny Burgess,' she said.

Reekie glared at her as he subsided into the comfortable

chair behind his desk. 'I still don't see why I had to deal with her. What's the point in trying to pretend we've not got a serial killer on the rampage? Why can't we just front up about it? Reveal your team's on the case?' He picked up a pen and began tapping it end to end on his desk. She noticed a faint indentation on his finger where a wedding ring should have been. 'That would reassure people.'

Carol swivelled to face him. Reekie needed his feathers smoothed down; yet another of the political games she hated having to play. 'But as you pointed out in there, it would get a lot more media attention. Which is a problem on two counts. One: it's always harder to run an investigation with the world's press breathing down your neck, and these days the faintest whiff of a serial killer generates the kind of media shit-storm that makes life impossible for investigating officers. Greedy media on a twenty-four-hour cycle means a level of scrutiny that none of us wants to operate under. And two: this kind of killer revels in publicity. He wants to be a star. He wants to be the centre of attention. Take that away from him, and you put him under stress. And stress leads to mistakes. And mistakes are how we catch them.'

'That's easy for you to say. You didn't have to stand up there and lie.' He kept up the annoying thing with the pen. Carol wanted to snatch it from him, to play the martinet teacher to his sulky small boy. She resisted the urge with some difficulty.

'You didn't have to lie. Just not reveal the whole story. The one thing that was a relief to me from that display was that her source isn't at the heart of the investigation.'

Reekie nodded. 'I suppose so. If he was, she'd have known about the tattoo instead of having to go all coy about the "signature".'

'So we're in the clear for now.' Carol stood up. Reekie made no move to shake hands or get to his feet. Clearly he still felt bruised from his close encounter with Penny Burgess.

'Let me know if your guys on the ground get anything on the ID.'

'As soon as we hear anything, you'll know. Let's stay in close touch on this one, Carol. We don't want it to get away from us.'

Carol turned and made for the door. They always had to have the last word, to remind her who was the ranking officer. At moments like this, she knew exactly why she appreciated Tony Hill.

17

Tony Hill was well aware that his responses were not the same as those of other people. Take memory, for example. Even though he'd been drinking coffee with Carol Jordan for more years than he cared to consider, he still found himself standing at the counter in coffee shops or in his kitchen, having to pause while he sorted through the database in his head to recall whether she drank espresso or cappuccino. But he was no absent-minded professor. He could remember the signature behaviour of every serial offender he'd ever encountered, both as a profiler and a clinician. All memory was selective, he knew that. It was just that the principles that governed his memory were unusual.

So it came as a surprise to him when he sat down to write a risk assessment of Jacko Vance that he had no recollection of ever having formally profiled him. After Carol had left, he'd closed his eyes and tried to summon up a mental image of his report. When nothing materialised, his eyes had snapped open as he realised that his pursuit of Vance had been so out of the ordinary that he'd written nothing down at the time it was happening. Of course, the hunt for Vance had been unusual, in that it hadn't originated with a police investigation. It had been the result of a training exercise for the aspiring profilers Tony had been working with on a Home Office task force. And once things had started moving, there had been no time to sit back and analyse Vance's crimes in those terms.

To buy himself some time while he considered what he knew about Vance, Tony found one of his previous profiles on Carol's laptop and copied his standard introductory paragraphs.

The following offender profile is for guidance only and shouldn't be regarded as an identikit portrait. The offender is unlikely to match the profile in every detail, though I would expect there to be a high degree of congruence between the characteristics outlined below and the reality. All of the statements in the profile express probabilities and possibilities, not hard facts.

A serial killer produces signals and indicators in the commission of his crimes. Everything he does is intended, consciously or not, as part of a pattern. Discovering the underlying pattern reveals the killer's logic. It may not appear logical to us, but to him it is crucial. Because his logic is so idiosyncratic, straightforward traps will not capture him. As he is unique, so must be the means of catching him, interviewing him and reconstructing his acts.

It didn't really fit the bill. That was because Lambert wanted a risk assessment, not a crime-based profile. He could keep the second paragraph, he supposed. But the first would have to change. He created a new file and began.

The following risk assessment is based on limited direct acquaintance with Jacko Vance. I saw Vance in public on several occasions and I interviewed him twice: once in his home when he may have realised he was the object of investigation; and a second time after he had been arrested on suspicion of murder. However, I am familiar with the detail of his crimes and have sufficient knowledge of his background to feel confident in preparing an assessment of how he is likely to respond to being on the run, having successfully outwitted the system and escaped from prison.

'What's going through your head, Jacko?' Tony said softly, leaning back in the chair and locking his fingers behind his head. 'Why this? Why now?'

A sharp knock at the door interrupted his conversation with himself. Paula stuck her head in, a determined look on her face. 'You got a minute?' Before he could reply, she was through the door and shutting it behind her.

'What if I said no?'

Paula gave him a tired smile. 'I'd say, "tough shit".'

'I thought as much.' Tony took off his reading glasses and studied Paula. There was history between them, a stained and complicated web of connections that had spread out over the years till it had become a sort of friendship. He'd led her through the labyrinth of grief after the death of a colleague who had also been a friend; she'd pushed him into doing the right things for the wrong reasons; he'd made her break the rules then stood in the firing line when Carol had turned her sights on her. Respect was the keystone of their relationship. Just as well, Tony thought, otherwise he might have found it hard to forgive Paula the happiness she'd found with Dr Elinor Blessing, a happiness he doubted he had the capacity for. 'I don't suppose this is a social visit?'

'Can I ask what you're working on?' Paula clearly wasn't in the mood for small talk. Carol must be expected back soon, then.

'I'm doing a risk assessment for the Home Office. I don't know if Carol said anything to you guys, but it'll be public knowledge before too long. Some things you can't keep quiet. Jacko Vance escaped from Oakworth this morning. Because I was involved in putting him away, they want me to stare into my crystal ball and tell them where he's going to go and what he's going to do.' Tony's sardonic stare matched his tone.

'So you're not working on our case?'

'You know how it is, Paula. Blake won't pay for me and DCI Jordan refuses to let me work without being paid. I thought I might be able to call in a favour via the Home Office, but they won't agree, not now. They'll want me totally focused on Jacko. No distractions.'

'It's just stupid, not making the most of your skills,' Paula said. 'You know what we're working on?'

'A string of murders that looks like a serial. I don't know much more than that,' he said. 'She tries to keep me out of temptation's way.'

'Well, consider me the temptress. Tony, this is right up your street. He's the kind of killer you understand, the sort of mind you can map like nobody else. And this is MIT's last tango. We want to go out on a high note. I want to leave Blake with a sour taste in his mouth when the chief goes off to West Mercia. I want him to understand the class of the operation he's flushing down the toilet. So we've got to come up with the right answer, and fast.' Her eyes were pleading, a contrast with the fierceness of her words.

Tony wanted to resist the draw of Paula's words. But in his heart, he agreed with everything she'd said. There was no rational explanation for what Blake was doing except that it would save some money to close the specialist unit. His conviction that spreading MIT's skills more thinly would produce more effective outcomes was, in Tony's opinion, a crackpot idea that would produce the opposite result. 'Why are you telling me this?' he said, a last-ditch bid to still the interest quickening in him.

Paula rolled her eyes and tutted. 'I thought you were supposed to be the smart one? Because we need your help, Tony. We need you to profile the killer so we can make some progress instead of getting bogged down in the mountain of crap this kind of inquiry produces.'

'She won't have it. Like I said: there's no budget to pay me and she won't exploit me.' He opened his hands as he shrugged, going for the deliberately cute smile. 'I've begged her, but she won't take advantage.'

Paula groaned. 'Spare me the single entendres. Listen, it's simple. It doesn't matter what she wants. Because she's not going to know. Because it's going to be our little secret.'

Tony groaned. 'Why am I getting that sinking feeling? Whenever you and I go off on our own initiative, it always ends in tears.'

Paula grinned, her eyes sparkling with mischief. 'Yeah, but you can't argue with our results. Every time we've gone behind her back, it's moved the investigation forward.'

'And she's ripped us a new one,' Tony said with feeling. 'It's all right for you, you get to go home to Elinor. But I'm supposed to be living with her in Worcester—' The words were out before he could stop them.

Paula's face couldn't make its mind up between astonishment and delight. 'What? You mean, like now? She'll have her own flat, like she has now, in the basement?'

Tony closed his eyes and put his fists to his temples. 'Shit, shit, shit. I wasn't supposed to say anything.' He dropped his hands to the desk and sighed. 'It's not like it sounds. Sharing the house, that would be a better description. Look, Paula, we didn't— *she* didn't want the team to know. Because you'd all jump to conclusions and then the sideways looks and the cheesy sentimental crap would start and she'd have to kill you all.' He ran a hand through his hair, leaving it standing up in spikes.

Paula just smiled. 'It's OK. I won't say anything. It's nobody's business. Frankly, I can't think of anyone else who'd put up with either of you. And I mean as housemates,' she added hastily as he opened his mouth to contradict her.

'You're probably right,' he said.

'So will you help?' Paula said, closing the subject and getting back to what she really wanted.

'She'll kill me,' he said.

'Yeah, but not nailing this one will kill her,' Paula said. 'You know how she is about unfinished business. Justice not being served ...'

Tony leaned back in the chair and stared at the ceiling. 'I am going to live to regret this. OK, Paula. Get Stacey to send me the usual package. I make no promises, but I'll take a look at it after I've done the Jacko Vance assessment.' He straightened up abruptly. 'And let's try to keep it a secret for once. Please?'

18

By the time she made it back to the squad room, Carol was ready for some good news. She'd had to fend off a call from the Chief Constable on the drive back from Northern HQ, during which James Blake had shown considerably more concern for the state of his budget than the lives of the women whose circumstances pushed them on to the streets to sell the one commodity of value they had left. Given his passion for cuts, she wondered how long it would be before some bright spark in government headhunted him.

She stuck her head into her office, where Tony was staring into her computer. A small stack of paper sat to one side, a pen on top of it. She could see scribbled notes, complete with asterisks and underlinings. Tony barely acknowledged her arrival, settling for an inarticulate grunt.

'Any news on Vance?' she said. She'd managed to put thoughts of the escaped prisoner to one side while she'd been out of the office, but there was no avoiding it now Tony had squatter's rights over her office.

He shook his head without looking up. 'Nothing. I rang Lambert a while back. The cameras picked up the taxi when he joined the M5 heading north and they're tracking forward from that. But you know how hard it is to do that stuff in real time. You just need one crap camera and you're stuck with a load of options to track.'

'Do you know who's coordinating the search?'

'I thought you'd be up to speed on that. Oakworth's on West Mercia's patch, after all.'

'I'll make some calls,' Carol said, leaving him to it and returning to her team to check on their progress. Paula was on the phone at the nearest desk, so Carol pulled up a chair to wait for her to finish.

Paula covered the mouthpiece and said quietly, 'I'm just talking to my contact at Northern – Franny Riley. I'll put him on speakerphone so you can listen in.'

Paula pressed a button and a deep Mancunian growl emerged from the tinny speaker. '. . . and that's why we're so short-handed.'

'All the same, Sarge, I'm going to need more bodies than that to do a proper door-to-door *and* get the photos out on the street.'

'Paula, I know. Tell me about it.' In the background, Carol could hear another voice. 'Hang on a minute, let me put you on hold, my DI's just come over.'

Whatever Franny had intended, what he actually did was to put his phone on speaker too. Carol immediately recognised the other voice. DI Spencer, the SIO from Northern that she'd replaced as head of the investigation.

'Are you tied up, Franny?' Spencer asked. 'Only, I need you to take a look at the witness statements on that aggravated burglary.'

'I'm on to MIT, trying to get the door-to-door sorted,' Riley said.

'For fuck's sake,' Spencer said, disgusted. 'I thought bringing them in was supposed to take the load off us? Ever since they came on board, it's been do this, sort that, check the other.

MIT, what does that stand for again?' Before Franny could respond, Spencer gave his own answer. 'I'll tell you what it stands for: Minorities Integration Team,' he said, guffawing at his own wit. 'A pair of lezzas, a jungle bunny, a Chink and a ginger. All led by a gash.'

Carol recoiled in shock. It had been a long time since she'd heard that kind of abuse from a colleague. It was the language of prejudice that was supposed to be history in modern polic- ing. She'd always suspected the canteen cowboys were still riding the range, but they were generally too savvy to show their true colours in front of anybody who might disagree. Apparently it wasn't just media hype that the old sexist and racist conditioning still existed beneath the surface.

Paula reached for the phone to cut off the call, her face revealing that Carol wasn't the only one who was horrified. But Carol pushed her hand away and leaned forward. 'DI Spencer. This is Detective Chief Inspector Jordan. Thanks to the wonders of modern technology, your offensive attitudes have been broadcast to my entire team. My office, now.'

There was a long silence. Then the high-pitched tone of a line gone dead. Carol sat back, feeling faintly queasy. She looked around at her team, who had all stopped what they were doing when Spencer's words had sunk in. 'DI Spencer will be here shortly to apologise. If any of you experience any obstruction whatsoever from Northern, I want to know about it. No covering anybody's backs. We're not going to be stopped from doing our jobs. Now let's get cracking. We've got three murders to solve.'

Stacey delivered one of her rare smiles. 'And I've got some- thing here that might just help.'

19

There was added urgency to Tony's risk assessment now. As if it wasn't enough to have Vance on the loose, he needed to free himself up so he could approach his new undercover project with a clear head. And he was going to have to find somewhere else to work. It would be hard to keep his progress secret from the person whose office he had taken over, especially when that person was as acute as Carol Jordan.

I believe Vance suffers from Narcissistic Personality Disorder. The key to any understanding of Vance is his need to be in control. He wants an environment where he is in charge. It's always all about him. He needs to manipulate the individuals around him and to be in charge of the way events unfold. Some controlling personalities use threats and fear to keep people in line; Vance uses charisma to blind them to what he is really about. That's not just because it's easier to maintain – it's also because he needs their adoration. He needs to have people look up to him. It's what his whole life was about before he went to prison and I imagine it shaped his life behind bars.

THE RETRIBUTION

He has enormous self-discipline, which dates back to his adolescence. He was desperate to carve a niche for himself where people would respect and admire him. His mother largely ignored him and his father treated him with contempt. He didn't like the way they made him feel and he was determined to make the world take notice of him. Probably the only thing that kept him from violent criminality in his teenage years was the discovery of his athletic talent. Once that had been identified, it offered him an avenue to the sort of adulation he wanted to experience.

But to realise that goal, he had to acquire self-discipline. He had to train and he had to find a way to organise himself mentally as well as physically. That he had such a phenomenally successful athletic career is testament to how well he succeeded. He was only months away from an almost certain Olympic gold in javelin when he had the accident that cost him the lower half of his throwing arm. At least one psychologist who has interviewed Vance has identified the accident and its aftermath as being a transformative moment, as if Vance had been a mentally healthy individual up to that point. The evidence cited in support of this position is that the destruction of his arm came about as a result of a heroic act.

It's my contention that Vance has always been mentally disordered. The amputation was a stress point in his life that tipped him over the edge. We have anecdotal evidence of sadistic sexual behaviour before the accident and also of violent cruelty to animals. The level of sadistic torture he exhibited towards his victims demonstrated no learning curve – he was already at a place mentally where this was what he wanted.

Vance has always been very good at hiding his deviant behaviour behind the appearance of candour and charm. That he is physically attractive has always been a significant factor in his ability to convince others that he is not the problem. In the years when he was a leading TV personality, it was often said that women wanted to sleep with him and men wanted to be him. I do not imagine he has lost the power to command that sort of response. I recommend a review of his time in prison and a reassessment of any questionable incidents in his contact circle, particularly any violent or suspicious deaths.

I don't know the details of his escape from Oakworth, but I would be very surprised if they did not involve collaboration from inside and outside the prison. Although it is more than twelve years since he was sent to prison, he still has a cohort of the faithful on the outside. There is a Facebook group called *Jacko Vance is Innocent*. As of this morning, 3,754 people 'like' this. One of those people – and I use the number advisedly, because Vance doesn't take chances and having more than one person knowingly involved is taking a chance – has helped him. I recommend checking the logs of his visitors. It would be helpful to know who he has spoken to on the phone, but he will almost certainly have had a contraband mobile for any crucial communications.

Do not rule out any of the professionals with whom he has had contact in prison. Remember Myra Hindley and the prison officer who became her lover. They hatched an escape plan that never got off the ground. Vance is undoubtedly a smarter operator than Hindley ever was. We know that he managed to persuade a prison psychologist that he was a fit and proper person

114

to occupy a place on a Therapeutic Community Wing. Personally, if the only way to keep Jacko Vance off a TCW was to burn down the prison, I'd be there with a can of petrol.

Tony paused and read the last sentence again. It was harsh, no doubt about that. And he hadn't built his career on slagging off his colleagues. On the other hand, someone who was supposed to be immune to manipulative bastards like Vance had been lulled into putting him where he absolutely shouldn't have been. Psychologists were trained to understand damage and how it avenges itself; someone had been woefully lacking here and he didn't feel like covering her back. Not now Jacko Vance was out there and in all probability looking for revenge. Especially since he himself might be one of the targets of his vengeful rage. So he let the words stand, stark in their informality.

There was supposed to be a prison social worker accompanying him to the work placement. It is possible that this individual is also implicated in his escape. If there is a genuine reason for the social worker's absence, it may also have been engineered by Vance from inside the prison. If, for example, the social worker's family was under threat of some kind.

Nevertheless, prison professionals must not be above suspicion, both in what has happened and what may happen. Vance has certainly been given support from outside and it is extremely likely that he's going to continue in that mode.

He pushed his glasses up and rubbed the bridge of his nose. 'So much for the straightforward stuff,' he muttered. Everything he'd written so far should be self-evident to

115

anyone with half a brain. But he'd learned over the years that there was a game to be played here. You had to include the obvious so that those who read the report could congratulate themselves on being as perspicacious as the professional. Then they didn't feel so aggrieved when you hit them with something they hadn't expected. Never mind that that was what they paid you for. Deep down, everybody thought what he did was little more than applied common sense.

Some days, he thought they were right. But not today.

Tony rolled his shoulders and laid his fingers on the keys. He took a deep breath, like a pianist waiting for the conductor's baton, then started typing furiously.

Vance is a planner. He has a bolthole which has been organised by whoever has been working on his behalf on the outside. He will stay clear of his old stamping grounds because he knows that's where we will look. He will not be in London or Northumberland. Where he chooses to base himself will be dependent on what he plans to do.

This is going to be a temporary base. He will stay here only for as long as it takes to do what he plans to do. He will already have arranged a further destination where he will go to ground and rebuild a life for himself. He would be foolish to try to do this in the UK; I suspect he will have chosen a destination abroad. He has a substantial amount of money at his disposal, so he has a lot of options. It's tempting to assume he will go for somewhere that doesn't have an extradition treaty with the UK, but he's arrogant enough to think he's not going to be found. There's nothing in the records to suggest he speaks another language. He needs to be able to communicate in order to control, so he'll go some place where English is the primary language. The USA is hard to get into, but once you're there it's easy to lose yourself, particularly if, like Vance, you've got plenty of money and therefore no need to trouble the social security system. He'll also want to be somewhere he can have access to the best in prosthetics with no questions asked, so again that points to the USA. And, unlike Australia or New Zealand, they tend not to show UK TV programmes, so there's little chance of anyone spotting him from reruns of *Vance's Visits*. There are also possibilities offered by some of the Gulf states, where privacy is highly prized and where English is widely spoken. Normally I'd say follow the money, except that guys like Vance know people who know how to make the money disappear without a trail.

So the big question is what he has planned before he leaves for his ultimate destination. Based on how he behaved towards Shaz Bowman when he thought there was a possibility of her thwarting him, I believe Vance intends to avenge himself on the people he holds responsible for his incarceration.

His prime target will be the police officer who was responsible for tracking him down and arresting him: Carol Jordan, currently a DCI with Bradfield Metropolitan Police. There were other officers involved in the unofficial investigation: Chris Devine, currently a DS in the same force; Leon Jackson, who was a DC with the Metropolitan Police; Kay Hallam, who was a DC with Hampshire; and Simon McNeill, who was a DC with Strathclyde. Given the relatively high profile of my own involvement in the process, I would expect also to be on his list of targets.

Seeing it on the screen in black and white made it seem less real somehow. Just words on a page, nothing to lie awake worrying and wondering about. Really, what were the chances of Vance coming after him like an avenging angel? 'Whistling in the dark,' he muttered. 'And out of tune, at that.'

He carried on typing.

> The other main targets will be his ex-wife, Micky Morgan, and her partner Betsy Thorne. In Vance's world view, they failed to keep their end of the bargain. Micky betrayed him by revealing that their marriage was a sham. She refused to support him in court and never came near him in prison. When she had the marriage annulled because it had never been consummated, she made him a figure of derision and contempt. She became the enemy. Wherever she is, Vance will show up sooner rather than later. Staking out these potential targets may well be the most effective way of snaring Vance.

All of which was very bloodless, very academic. Nothing to do with the screaming in the back of Tony's brain when the image of Shaz Bowman's destruction flashed unbidden before his eyes. He didn't want Piers Lambert to think he was hysterical, but he wanted to make damn sure he paid attention.

> Jacko Vance is probably the most efficient and focused killer I have ever encountered. He is vicious and without remorse or compassion. I suspect he has no limits. He does not kill for pleasure. He kills because that's what his victims deserve, according to his self-righteous view of the world. He has committed a highly organised escape from jail. I don't think there's

anything significant in the timing. I think it's simply taken him this long to get everything perfectly in place. And now, unless we take decisive action, the killing will start.

20

Stacey wasn't the only one who knew how to get information out of a computer, Kevin told himself. He had a twelve-year-old son who used his home computer like an extension of himself. It had been a steep learning curve, but Kevin was determined to keep abreast of his son. Back when he was a boy, his dad had shared his knowledge of what went on under a car's bonnet and that had been the single thing that had kept them on speaking terms during Kevin's own adolescence. It seemed to Kevin that the twenty-first-century equivalent of messing about in lock-ups with motors was being able to play World of Warcraft online with your kid. Beyond that, he'd learned how to do slide presentations, how to typeset a poster and how to refine his Google searches. He kept quiet about it in the office, though. He had no desire to tread on Stacey's toes or to have the limits of his capabilities cruelly exposed.

Ten minutes with Google and another metasearch engine revealed that there was no shortage of businesses that could supply a tattooing machine. Even given the current obsession with body art, Kevin found it hard to believe they could all make a living. He had no tattoos himself; he reckoned they'd look weird on his freckled skin. His wife had a scarlet lily on her shoulder and he'd always admired it, but she'd never fancied another and he hadn't loved it enough to try to persuade her otherwise.

His searches had thrown up too many listings for there to be any point in trying to track down a recent purchase in the Bradfield area, even supposing the vendors were cooperative. Since many of those who practised body art liked to think of themselves as being mavericks and enemies of the system, he suspected most of them would be reluctant to help.

After scrolling through a dozen screens, Kevin came up with three suppliers with local addresses. Two were tattoo parlours, the third a business that seemed to cover everything from hairdressing sundries to jewellery for piercings. He copied their details and made an action file, suggesting officers should visit all three businesses and ask about recent sales, both online and in person. It was the sort of tedious inquiry that Northern Division could handle. And if it produced something worth chasing, then office politics would be satisfied as well as the inquiry.

He smiled as he hit the 'send' button. It felt good to delegate the drudgery. Too often, Kevin was convinced he got the boring routine work in MIT. It was the chip on his shoulder. Maybe that would change when they were scattered throughout the force. He wouldn't mind a bit. It was about time he got to show the flair that might earn him promotion.

It never occurred to him that Carol Jordan passed routine inquiries his way because his thoroughness was exemplary. In a world where most officers did as little as they could get away with, Kevin was notable for his attention to detail, his finicky insistence on having everything nailed down. He didn't realise it, but he was the reason Carol Jordan's blood pressure was as low as it was. And she knew it.

Vance dressed in the clothes Terry had left neatly folded on the toilet cistern. New underwear and socks, chinos and a

121

long-sleeved blue twill shirt with a neat button-down collar. At the bottom of the pile was a wig – a thick mop of mid-brown threaded with silver. Vance put it on. The hair fell naturally into a parting on the opposite side to his own hair. Although the style was similar to the old Jacko Vance from the days of TV glory, he somehow looked distinctively different. The final touch was a pair of clear glasses with stylish black oblong frames. The man in the mirror looked nothing like Jason Collins. Not much like the old Jacko Vance either, he thought with a trace of regret. There were lines where none had been before, a little sagging along the jaw, a few broken veins in the cheeks. Prison had aged him faster than life on the outside would have. He'd lay money that his ex-wife was wearing better. Still, he'd put a few more lines on her face before he was done with her.

When he emerged, Vance was gratified by the look of delighted surprise on Terry's face. 'You look great,' he said.

'You did a good job,' Vance said, patting Terry's shoulder. 'Everything's perfect. Now, I'm starving. What have you got for me?'

While he ate, Vance checked the contents of the briefcase Terry had brought with him. It contained two counterfeit passports with matching driving licences – one set British, the other Irish; a thick wad of twenty-pound notes; a list of bank accounts in names matching the passports with the accompanying pin numbers; several credit cards; a set of utility bills for a house on the outskirts of Leeds; and four pay-as-you-go mobile phones. Tucked into a pocket were sets of car keys and house keys. 'Everything else you need is at the house,' Terry said. 'Laptop, landline, satellite TV . . . '

'Brilliant,' Vance said, finishing the last forkful of salad with tuna and edamame beans. 'Half of this food, I've no idea what it is. But it tastes bloody good.'

'I stocked the fridge at the house yesterday,' Terry said eagerly. 'I hope you like what I got.'

'I'm sure it'll be fine.' Vance wiped his mouth on a paper napkin, then scooped the detritus of their picnic into a bin. 'It's time we made a move,' he said. He stood up, then turned back to the bed where Terry had been sitting. He pulled down the covers and punched the pillow to create an indentation. 'Now it looks like someone slept here. When the maid comes in, there won't be anything untoward for her to remember if the police come asking questions.'

Vance let Terry lead the way to the car, saying simply, 'You drive,' when they reached the Mercedes. He didn't doubt his ability to drive; Terry had done as he was told and bought an automatic with cruise control. And something called satnav; that was an innovation since he'd last driven a car. Nevertheless, he'd rather make his first attempt away from potential witnesses, just in case.

As Terry pulled out of the parking space, Vance relaxed into his seat, letting his head lean on the contoured rest. His eyelids flickered. The adrenaline had finally died down, leaving him tired and depleted. There would be no harm in sleeping while Terry drove him to his new home. Because there were still plenty of things to deal with before he could properly rest.

The jolt of driving over a speed-control bump in the road roused Vance. He woke with a jerk, momentarily disorientated. 'What the—? Where are we?' he gasped as he came to, looking wildly around. They were passing what looked like a security gatehouse, but it appeared to be empty. Just beyond the gatehouse was a pair of brick pillars. Gateposts without gates or walls, Vance thought irrelevantly.

'Welcome to Vinton Woods,' Terry said proudly. 'Just what you asked for. A private estate set out on its own; detached houses with a bit of garden to separate you from the houses next door. The kind of place where nobody knows their neighbours and everybody minds their own business. You're eight miles from the motorway, six miles from the centre of Leeds, seventeen miles from Bradfield.' He followed a curving road lined with substantial houses with brick and half-timbered facades. 'This is the Queen Anne section,' Terry said. At a junction, he turned left. 'If you go right, you come to the Georgian bit, but we're in the Victorian part of the estate.' These houses had stone facades and twice-mocked Gothic turrets. They were scaled-down versions of the mansions mill owners built in salubrious suburbs after the coming of the railways meant they didn't have to live on top of their factories. Vance thought these modern replicas were ugly and pitiful. But one of these fakeries would be perfect for now.

Terry turned off the main drag into a cul-de-sac of six substantial houses set back from the street. He drove towards one of the pair at the head of the street, slowing and steering towards the triple garage that extended out on one side. He took a remote control from the door pocket and pointed it at the garage. One door rose before them and he drove in, making sure the door was closed before he turned off the engine and got out.

Vance stepped out of the car and looked around. Terry's van occupied the third bay of the garage. The signwriting advertised his market stall, where he sold a mind-boggling range of tools, both new and second-hand. He'd clearly used it to deliver his personal gift to Vance.

The garage had a workbench running down one wall. Above it, tools hung in a gleaming array. Two sturdy vices were fitted at opposite ends of the bench. If anyone other than Terry had been responsible, Vance would have been enraged. But he knew there was no hidden meaning here. After all, Terry didn't believe the prosecution's story of the terrible things Vance had done to young girls with the last vice he'd owned. He took a step towards the workbench, imagining the feel of firm flesh in his hands. 'I took the liberty of kitting out your workshop,' Terry said. 'I know how you like to work in wood.'

'Thank you,' Vance said. Later, he told himself. Much later. He reached for his most charming smile and said, 'You've thought of everything. This is perfect.'

'You haven't seen the house yet. I think you'll like it.'

All Vance wanted to see right now was the kitchen. He followed Terry through a side door into a utility room furnished with a washing machine and a tumble drier and onwards into a kitchen that was a gleaming monument to modernity. Granite, chrome and tiles were all buffed to a mirror sheen. It took Vance a moment or two to pick out what he was looking for. But there it was, exactly what he needed. A wooden knife block, set to one side of the granite-topped island in the middle of the room.

Vance drifted over to the island, exclaiming all the while at the very perfection of his magnificent new kitchen. 'Is that one of those American fridges that dispense ice and chilled water?' he asked, knowing Terry would be impelled to demonstrate its powers. As soon as Terry's back was turned, Vance slid a medium-sized knife from the block, slipping the handle inside his shirt cuff, holding his arm loosely at his side.

As Terry turned back with a brimming glass of water, ice cubes bumping against the sides, Vance raised his prosthetic arm and appeared to draw him into an embrace of delighted gratitude. Then his other hand came up and plunged the knife into Terry's chest. Up and under, avoiding the ribs, making for the heart.

The glass of water tumbled to the floor, soaking Vance's shirt. He flinched as the cold water hit his skin, but didn't stop what he was doing. Terry made a terrible strangled grunting sound, his face a shocked accusation. Vance pulled the knife back and stabbed again. Now there was blood between them, spreading its tell-tale stain across the front of their clothes. It raced across Vance's shirt, following the path the water had already made. Its progress over Terry's sweatshirt was slower, the colour more intense.

Vance pulled the knife free and stepped back, letting Terry fall to the floor. His top lip curled in disgust as Terry twitched and moaned, hands clutching his chest, eyes rolling back in his head. Vance took no pleasure in the killing itself; he never had. It had always been secondary to the pleasures of inflicting pain and terror. Death was the unfortunate by-product of the things he really enjoyed. He wished Terry would hurry up and get it over with.

All at once exhaustion hit him like a physical blow. He staggered slightly and had to grip on to the granite worktop. He had been running on adrenaline for hours and now he'd run out of fuel. His legs felt shaky and weak, his mouth dry and sour. But he couldn't stop now.

Vance crossed to the kitchen sink and opened the cupboard underneath. As he'd expected, Terry had supplied him with a full battery of cleaning equipment. Right at the front was a roll of extra-strong rubbish bags. On the shelf beside them, a bag of plastic ties. Just what he needed. As soon as Terry was done with dying, he could bag him up, truss the bag and dump him in the back of his own van. He'd work out what to do with the van and its owner at some later stage. Right now, he was too tired to think straight.

All he wanted was to clean up then crawl into bed and sleep for twelve hours or so. His anticipated celebration dinner could wait till tomorrow, when the rest of his fun would begin.

He glanced across at Terry, whose breath was now a faint gasp that brought bubbles of pink froth with each exhalation. What the fuck was taking him so long? Some people had absolutely no consideration.

21

Detective Inspector Rob Spencer looked more like a car salesman than a detective. Everything about him was polished, from his teeth to his shoes. Sam, who liked to think of himself as a pretty smooth operator, had to concede to himself that Spencer probably edged it. Still, Sam wasn't the one who was about to suffer gender reassignment without benefit of anaesthetic at Carol Jordan's hands.

When he arrived, Carol was hidden behind the phalanx of monitors Stacey used to keep the inconvenient real world at bay. Stacey had been running the limited data they had on the three murders through the algorithms of the geographic-profiling software that she'd tweaked to her own specifications. She was pointing out the hotspots they'd already identified. 'Chances are he lives or works somewhere in the purple zones,' Stacey said, outlining them with a neat laser pointer. 'Skenby. Obviously. We didn't need the program to tell us that. But more data will narrow it down.'

Spencer peered around the room, looking a little lost. Paula thought he was trying to find a match for himself and, failing that, the next best thing. He fixed on Sam, but as he approached, Sam picked up his phone and pointedly turned away to make a call.

'Can I help you?' Paula said, in a tone that promised the opposite.

'I'm looking for DCI Jordan's office.' Spencer sounded gruff, as if he was trying to assert his right to be there.

Paula gestured with her thumb at the closed blinds that marked off Carol's territory. 'That's her office. But she's not in it.'

'I'll wait for her there,' Spencer said, taking a couple of steps towards the door.

'I'm afraid that won't be possible,' Paula said.

'I'll decide what's possible, Constable,' Spencer said. Paula had to give him marks for bravado. She'd never have dared to make an incursion on Carol Jordan's turf and attempt to occupy the high ground.

That was when Carol chose to step out from behind the barrier of screens. 'Not in my squad room, you won't,' she said. 'My office is occupied right now.' She came closer, leaving less than half a metre between them. Although she was a good twenty centimetres shorter than him, her presence was by far the more impressive. The look in her eyes would have stripped the gloss off a shinier surface than his. Spencer looked like a man who had come face-to-face with his most embarrassing adolescent memory. 'Normally, I wouldn't dream of conducting this conversation in front of junior officers,' she said, her voice sharp as an icicle. 'But then I don't normally have to deal with someone who has managed to insult every one of those officers. In the circumstances, it only seems fair to share.'

'I'm sorry, ma'am,' Spencer said. 'Obviously I had no idea my remarks were being broadcast.'

'I'd say that was the least of your worries,' Carol said. 'I've been an officer in BMP for the best part of seven years now, and I've mostly been proud of that. What I heard from you today made me feel glad for the first time that I'm leaving. These are probably the best detectives you will ever work with. And all you can offer them is ill-informed prejudice.'

Spencer flinched. 'It was meant to be a joke.'

Carol rolled her eyes, irritation and incredulity sharing the billing. 'Do I look stupid? Do I strike you as the kind of person who's going to go, "Oh well, that's all right then"? How exactly is it a joke to demonstrate ignorance and bigotry in front of junior officers? To make it seem acceptable to denigrate your fellow officers for their skin colour or sexual orientation?'

Spencer fixed his gaze somewhere above her head, as if that would help him escape her disgust. 'I was wrong, ma'am. I'm sorry.'

'When this case is over, you're going to have a lot of time to figure out just how sorry. I'm going to talk to HR and make sure you are sent on every available equal ops and multicultural education course for as long as it takes you to understand why your behaviour is unacceptable anywhere in 2011. And to set the ball rolling, you are going to make a personal apology to every member of this squad before you leave here today.'

Spencer was shocked into meeting her eye. 'Ma'am—'

'It's Detective Chief Inspector Jordan to you, Spencer. I'm not the bloody queen. Now, you've got a lot of credibility to recover with my team. You can make your apologies before you leave. But meantime, we've got some information that should move things along. We've ID'd the third victim.' She turned on her heel. 'Stacey?'

Stacey walked her chair out from behind the monitors, a tablet computer in her hand. 'Leanne Considine. She was arrested in Cannes for soliciting.'

'In Cannes? You mean, like Cannes in France?' Spencer looked and sounded bemused.

'The only one I know of,' Stacey said.

'But how do you know that? How did you find that out?'

Stacey gave Carol an enquiring glance. 'Go ahead,' Carol said.

'One of the things we've done at MIT is build informal relationships with our counterparts abroad,' Stacey said. 'I've got contacts in seventeen European jurisdictions who will run prints for me. It's got no evidential value, because it's unofficial, but sometimes it's useful for showing us where to look. Her prints and her DNA were a no-show on our database, so I tried my contacts. She turned up in France. Four years ago, though, so not the most current info.' Stacey pinned Spencer with a look and gave a grim smile. 'Not bad for a Chink.'

Spencer's lips thinned to a tight line and he breathed heavily through his nose. Carol's smile was almost as thin. 'We do have more,' she said.

'Leanne's address at the time was a student hall of residence here in Bradfield. That gave me a lot of options for back-door searching,' Stacey said.

'That's another thing we do a lot of round here,' Sam said. 'Back-door searching. We like to be a bit more subtle than kicking people's front doors in.'

'Ideally, we prefer them not to even notice we've been in,' Stacey said drily. 'Bottom line is, Leanne is from Manchester. She has an undergraduate degree in French and Spanish from Bradfield University. She is currently studying for a PhD on "Inventions of self in the works of Miguel Cervantes". Whatever that means. And, as it appears, funding her studies by selling sex on the streets of Bradfield.'

'Some people will do anything to avoid taking out a student loan,' Kevin said sourly.

'We can't all be successful capitalists,' Stacey said. 'I've got an address for her parents in Manchester. And an address for her here in Bradfield.'

Paula's mobile vibrated and she checked it out, only half-listening to what was going on around her.

'Excellent,' Carol said. 'Sam, Kevin – once DI Spencer has finished with you, get yourself over to her place and see if she's got flatmates. Let's start building up a picture of her life.' She turned back to Spencer. 'I'd like you to arrange a Family Liaison Officer for her parents, and take personal charge of breaking the news. They deserve a ranking officer, they've lost a daughter. Paula, take yourself off to the university, find who-ever was supervising her and talk to them. We need to know where she intersected with her killer, and that means filling in the blanks. Leanne Considine encountered a man who bru-talised her and killed her. We need to find him before he finds another victim. And one more thing – so far, we've stopped this becoming a media circus. Let's get it done and dusted before we've got the Penny Burgesses of this world crawling all over us.'

22

Kevin thought it was ironic that the student house where Leanne Considine had lived was a scummy shit-tip compared to the home Nicky Reid had shared with Suze Black. In his world, there was something topsy-turvy about a pair of hookers living in a place that was clean and tidy while four graduate students shared what could only be described as squalor. The kitchen worktops were cluttered with dirty mugs and glasses, takeaway food containers and empty wine bottles. Back in the mists of history, someone had thought it was a good idea to put carpet tiles on the floor. Now they were stained and shiny with use. The thought of coming down barefoot in the morning to make a cup of coffee made Kevin shudder inside.

Only Siobhan Carey had been at home when they'd arrived. Kevin had broken the news of Leanne's death and confirmed the identification with the photo Grisha had supplied them with. He'd expected her to fall apart. Young women mostly did, in his experience. But in spite of clearly being shocked and saddened, Siobhan had stayed calm. No hysteria, no floods of tears, no throwing things at the walls. Instead, she'd texted her housemates, who had made it back inside a quarter of an hour. 'We were lucky to get this house,' Siobhan had said while she rinsed mugs and made tea for the detectives. 'It's only a ten-minute bike ride from the university library. That's where we all mostly work. It saves on the heating bills in the winter.'

It was the perfect lead-in. Behind her back, Kevin gave Sam the nod. This was one for him. Siobhan had the air of a young woman who was trying a little too hard. There was something about the artful arrangement of her Primark layers, the care she'd taken with her hair and her make-up, that said she understood she wasn't going to be the first pick on anybody's list. Her nose was a little too long, her eyes a little too narrow, her body a little too plump. She'd be grateful for some one-on-one attention from a good-looking bloke like Sam. And Sam knew just how to charm the birds out of the trees. Definitely time for Kevin to take a back seat.

'It seems to get tougher every year, being a student,' Sam said, his voice like hot chocolate on a cold day. 'They hike up your fees, they raise your rents, they cane you for having an overdraft . . .'

'Tell me about it,' Siobhan said.

'I don't know how you all manage, especially doing the postgraduate stuff.' Sam sounded like his heart was bleeding for her.

Siobhan turned to face him, leaning against the counter while the kettle boiled. Her thin cardigan had slipped off one shoulder, revealing a not particularly expert tattoo of a bluebird. 'I work four nights a week stacking supermarket shelves,' she said. 'Friday afternoon, I deliver the local free paper. And every month I end up having to ask my dad for an extra fifty quid to cover the rent.'

'You're lucky to have a dad who can afford an extra fifty quid a month. A lot of people can't find that much to spare these days,' Sam said.

'He's great, my dad. One day I hope I can pay him back.'

When he's old and sick and needs someone to feed him and change him, Kevin thought. *That's when he'll be looking for payback. Bet you're not so keen then, Siobhan.* But he said nothing, leaving it to Sam.

'What about Leanne?' Sam said. 'What did she do to make ends meet?'

Siobhan turned away abruptly, saved from answering by the boiling of the kettle. 'How do you have your tea?' she said brightly.

'We both have milk, no sugar,' Sam said, not sure about Kevin but not really caring. What he wanted was to keep the flow of conversation going, especially since Siobhan clearly didn't. 'So – Leanne. Did she have a part-time job too? Or did her family subsidise her?'

Siobhan made a big number out of draining the teabags and pouring the milk. She put the mugs down in front of the two detectives with a little flourish. 'There you are, guys. Freshly brewed Yorkshire tea. You can't beat it.' Her smile was considerably weaker than the tea.

'How long had you known Leanne?' Sam said, moving away from what had turned out to be a difficult question. He'd circle back to it, but for now, let her think she'd won.

'Just over a year and a half. We're both attached to the Modern Languages department. She was Spanish, I'm Italian. With her doing her undergraduate degree here in Bradfield, she'd already snagged this house and she was looking for people to share. She wanted other postgrads, not undergrads.' Siobhan sipped from her mug and looked at Sam over the rim. 'Undergrads just want to drink and party. Postgrads are more serious. We're spending all this money because we're really serious about what we're doing. My first term at Exeter, one of the Hooray Henrys in my hall of residence actually threw up over my laptop. Then he called me a stupid working-class tart when I complained. Frankly, you want to be as far away from wankers like that as possible.'

She was talking too much now, trying to fill the space so Sam couldn't get back to the hard questions. 'Totally,' he said. 'So you and Leanne got on well?'

Siobhan's face puckered in consideration. 'I wouldn't say we were friends. We didn't really have much in common. But we got along all right. Obviously. I mean, here we are, second year in the same house.'

'What about the other two? Have they been here as long as you?'

'Jamie and Tara? Well, Tara moved in when I did. Then, about six months later, she asked if Jamie could come and live with her. They've been together about three years, and he didn't like the people he was living with. Plus, let's face it, splitting the bills four ways instead of three made sense. Obviously they have to share a bedroom, but Jamie has first dibs on the living room when he needs somewhere to work.'

'And he doesn't mind being the only bloke in a house full of women?'

Siobhan snorted. 'What's to mind?'

Sam produced his most silky smile. 'I imagine there's a lot more pluses than minuses.'

Before Siobhan could respond to his flirtatiousness, the front door banged shut. There was a clatter of bikes in the hall, then two people in cycling Lycra and rain jackets stormed in, still unfastening their helmets. They were both talking at once as they entered, focused entirely on Siobhan, barely a glance at the two strange men sitting at their kitchen table. 'Sweetie, this is awful,' in a woman's voice, 'Are you sure it's Leanne?' in a man's voice. Both southern accents, sounding like presenters on BBC Radio 4. They all hugged and murmured, then the new arrivals turned to face Kevin and Sam.

Even with their helmets off, Jamie and Tara were eerily

similar. Both tall, broad in the shoulder and narrow in the hips, blonde hair tousled and shining, long narrow faces and pointed chins. At first glance, they looked more like brother and sister than lovers. It took closer inspection to reveal key differences. Tara had brown eyes, Jamie blue. Her hair was longer and finer, her cheekbones higher and broader, her mouth wider and fuller. Siobhan introduced everyone, and they all crammed round the small kitchen table. Jamie seemed more concerned for Tara than devastated by the news about Leanne. Of the three of them, Tara seemed most affected. Her eyes were sparkling with tears, and she kept raising her hand to her mouth and biting down on her knuckle as Kevin shared as little information as possible about Leanne's death.

Once everyone was settled, this time Kevin took the lead. 'Obviously in a murder investigation, the first thing we need to establish is the movements of the victim. We believe Leanne died the evening before last. So, can you remember when you saw her last on Tuesday?'

They looked at each other for inspiration. It was hard to say whether they were struggling to remember or making some kind of tacit agreement. But what they had to say showed little sign of collusion. Siobhan had seen Leanne at lunchtime – they'd shared a special-fried rice past its sell-by date that Siobhan had brought home from work. Siobhan had spent the afternoon teaching a seminar. Then she'd gone to work till 11 p.m. Jamie had been working at home before leaving at half past five to walk to the local pub, where he'd been working till midnight. Leanne had still been in the house then. Struggling to keep her tears at bay, Tara explained that she'd spent the afternoon working in the local call centre, where she did six shifts a week. By the time she'd returned at seven, Leanne had left the house. Three friends had come round with pizza just after eight and the four of them had played bridge until Jamie came home. Perfectly shaped alibis that would all have to be checked, but which contained nothing even slightly suspicious. No shifty eye movements, no bad body language, no hesitation in providing names and contact numbers.

So that wasn't what Siobhan was uneasy about.

'I'm amazed you find time to study,' Kevin said conversationally. 'I see my kids growing up, and it scares me, how hard it's going to be for them to get through university.'

Jamie gave a one-shouldered shrug. 'It's a complete nightmare. But what can you do? Like my father says, "Life's a bitch." Our generation's learning that lesson a bit earlier, that's all.'

Kevin leaned forward, trying to draw them into a conspiratorial huddle. 'So what did Leanne do to make ends meet?'

Sam hadn't been wrong in thinking Siobhan didn't want to go there. Now it appeared that the other two housemates were equally reluctant. 'I'm not sure,' Jamie said, his eyes on his tea.

'We didn't really discuss it,' Tara said, her voice shaky and her expression hopeful. There was clearly something more significant than regret going on now.

Sam pushed his chair back, deliberately disrupting the group. 'That's the biggest load of bollocks I've heard in a long time. And believe me, I spend my life listening to criminals shooting me a line.' Seeing their shocked expressions, he pressed on. 'You live in a shared house with a woman for a year and a half, and you don't know what she does to pay the bills? That is crap.'

Jamie straightened his shoulders. 'You've got no right to talk to us like that. We've just lost a very dear friend and we're in shock. If my father—'

'Spare me,' Sam said sarcastically. 'Your friend has just been murdered. Brutally murdered. I didn't know her, but I saw what he did to her and I am bloody determined to catch him and put him away. Now, if that doesn't matter to you, just say.' He twisted his mouth in a 'please yourself' expression. 'Cases like this, the media love to find someone to beat up while they're waiting for us to make an arrest.'

'You wouldn't dare,' Jamie said, trying to sound tough and failing.

'We're only trying to protect her memory,' Siobhan blurted. The other two glared at her. 'It's going to come out sooner or later, guys,' she said, shooting for pathos and hitting the bulls-eye. 'It's better if we just tell them and get it over with.'

'She did exotic dancing,' Tara said flatly.

'And the rest,' Jamie added. His attempt to appear a man of the world didn't even get out of the starting blocks.

'How do you know that, Jamie?' Kevin said pleasantly. 'Were you a customer?'

'Don't be disgusting,' Tara said. 'We all know because she told us. We knew she was working in a lap-dancing club up near the airport. At first, she tried to make out she was just working behind the bar, but it was obvious that she had a lot more cash than you earn pulling pints. We were all a bit pissed one night and I asked her straight out if she was ... you know, taking her clothes off for men. She said she did lap dancing and admitted that she had sex with some of the men. Off the premises, she said. She'd meet them after work and do them in their cars.' Tara's lip curled involuntarily at the thought.

'That must have been a shock for you all,' Kevin said gently.

Jamie breathed heavily, puffing out his lips. 'No kidding! Nobody imagines ending up sharing a house with a hooker.'

'Sex worker,' Siobhan corrected him primly. 'It was Leanne's choice – and you could never accuse her of bringing her work home. If she hadn't told us the kind of bar she was working in, we'd never have known, not from anything she said or did round the house. After the shock passed, we all kind of ignored it. It just didn't come up. It's like I said. We all got along together but we weren't really close. We had our own lives, our own friends.'

Sam was watching Jamie to see if there was any sign of a different response. But both of the others seemed comfortable with Siobhan's account. 'Did she have a boyfriend?'

'She once said she never met any men,' Siobhan said. 'I know that sounds weird, but she said the men at work were losers and tossers. We were talking about how hard it is to find the time to meet anyone, never mind invest in a relationship, and she said she couldn't remember the last time she'd met a bloke she even wanted to have a drink with.'

Another dead end. 'What was the name of the club where she worked?' Kevin asked.

They all looked nonplussed. 'I never asked,' Tara said. 'It's not like we were going to turn up for a drink.'

'What about you, Jamie? It's the sort of thing a bloke might be more interested in,' Sam said.

'Don't judge me by your standards,' Jamie said, a sneer on his face and in his voice.

A low chuckle from Sam. 'I wasn't. That's why I thought you might know. Tara, you said it was up by the airport. Can you remember how you know that?'

Tara frowned and rubbed the side of her cheek with her finger. After a few moments when everyone waited expectantly, she said, 'She asked me if I knew whether there was any bike parking at the airport. She'd got a cheap flight to Madrid, but it was a really early check-in. She said she'd be as well going from work, because it would only take her fifteen minutes to cycle there.' When she smiled, Sam could see what Jamie saw in her. Her whole face lightened and she gave the first indication so far that she might be fun. 'So she must only have been a couple of miles away, tops.'

'Thank you, we'll check that out. Is there anyone else you can think of that Leanne was particularly friendly with? One of her fellow Spanish postgrads? Any of the lecturers?'

They exchanged looks again. 'She was sociable enough, but

she didn't have much free time. Like all of us,' Tara said rue-fully. 'I can't think of anyone in particular, but she did a lot of Facebooking. She had a lot of mates in Spain.'

'I know her password,' Siobhan said. 'One time when she was in Spain, she couldn't get online and she texted me to post something on her Facebook page. It was LCQuixote.'

'Can you write that down for me?' Sam slipped his note-book across the table. 'We could do with some photos too, if you've got any?'

Jamie stood up. 'I've got some on the computer. I could print you off a few?' He returned a few minutes later with a handful of prints on A4 paper. One showed Leanne in a strappy sparkly top raising a glass to the camera, head back and laughing. The ruck of people in the background looked like a party in full swing. Jamie pointed to it. 'I had a birthday party last year, here in the house.' There were a couple obvi-ously taken in the kitchen where she was wearing a baggy T-shirt and jeans, leaning against the fridge. In one of them, she was sticking her tongue out at the photographer. The last one showed her standing by her bike, helmet in hand, hair loose, grinning. 'This one was taken a couple of weeks ago,' he said. 'She'd just got back from the library. I was trying out the camera on my new phone. Will these do?'

Kevin nodded. 'It would be helpful if you could email them to us.' He was pretty sure they'd got as much as they were going to get from the housemates, so he took out his cards and handed them round. 'My email address is on there. We're probably going to have to talk to you again,' he said. 'But in the meantime, if anything occurs to you, call us.' He wasn't going to hold his breath.

Outside, as they walked back to the car, Sam chuckled. 'What's so funny?' Kevin said.

'Just thinking how well DI Spencer's bunch of wankers would have handled that interview. Anything out of the mainstream, like a PhD student hooker, and they're going to be totally flummoxed.'

Kevin scowled. 'He's a complete twat.'

Sam shrugged. 'He just said out loud what a lot of people think. In a way, I'd rather deal with the likes of Spencer. Better to know where you stand than have to deal with the hypocrites who pretend it makes no odds to them. But deep down, they despise you. You know how I love to dance?'

Kevin knew. It was one of the more surprising things about Sam. It sat awkwardly alongside ruthless ambition and a loyalty that barely went beyond self, but there was no doubting it. 'Yeah,' he said, unlocking the car and getting behind the wheel.

Sam settled into the passenger seat, hitching up his trousers to avoid bagging the knees. 'Occasionally, when I ask a woman to dance, a white woman, she'll just look me up and down and come straight out with it – "I don't dance with black guys." It knocks you back on your heels a bit, because most people just don't say that kind of thing any more. But that's fair enough, you know. What pisses me off much more than that is when I ask a white woman to dance and she makes some excuse, like she's too hot or she's too tired or she's waiting for a drink. And then five minutes later, I see her on the floor with some complete muppet. That makes me want to go over and say something so cutting she'll cry all the way home.'

'So you're saying you don't mind what that bell-end Spencer said?'

Sam stroked his goatee. 'I mind, but I'm not going to lose sleep over it. And neither should you. Me and my ginger homie, we are going to show them how a murder investigation is run. And that is the best revenge, my friend.'

23

'**I**'m a serving police officer,' Carol said calmly. Underneath the surface, Tony could hear tightly controlled anger. 'I don't go anywhere without a police escort. It's called my team.'

A long silence. A tightening of lips and shoulders. 'No, of course they don't come home with me. But I'm presuming you will be providing cover for Dr Hill? ... His house is divided into two flats. He lives upstairs and I live downstairs.' Tony could imagine how much it was costing Carol to reveal details of her private life to Piers Lambert. 'Surely the same team is capable of watching two doors in the same building? I thought this was a time of austerity?' More silence. Carol drummed her fingers on the desk and closed her eyes. 'Thank you, Mr Lambert.' And the call was over. 'Bloody bureaucrats,' Carol said.

'Tell me you've accepted protection,' Tony said.

'I could tell you that, but it would be a lie. Move over, let me get to my filing cabinet,' Carol said. Tony obediently wheeled himself to one side so she could reach the drawer with the secret stash of vodka. Carol took out a miniature and sloshed it into the cup of coffee she'd walked in with. She sat down on the visitor's chair and glared at him. 'What? You heard what I said. Look out there.' She gestured at the squad room beyond the blinds. 'The place is awash with coppers. Vance is not going to get near me while I'm at work.'

'He got out of a prison without anybody stopping him. And now he seems to have disappeared into thin air. Pretty good for a man with a recognisable face and an artificial arm.'

'For God's sake, Tony. Vance is not going to walk in here and murder me. And when I'm at home, the team that are watching you can keep an eye on me too. Now, can we just stop talking about this?'

Tony shrugged. 'If that's what you want.'

'It's what I want.'

'OK.' He stared at the computer, closing down the windows he'd already minimised when Carol had walked in to take Lambert's call. The last thing he needed was for her to see what he was working on. 'I'm going home, then. Piers told me my guardian angels are waiting for me downstairs in reception. So I don't have to hang around here any longer.'

'I won't be much longer, if you want to hang on and come back with me?'

He shook his head, getting to his feet. 'My car's here. Plus I've got stuff to be getting on with.' *Stuff which will really piss you off.*

Taken aback, Carol said, 'Oh. I thought we could have a chat about the move. My move. I need to figure out what to do about the excess furniture. Because your house is fully furnished and I've got one or two things I want to bring with me. My bed, mainly. Because I love that bed.'

Tony smiled. 'So bring your bed. The one in your room's a bit of a monstrosity anyway. I can sell it, or give it away, or put it in the garage so there's something to put back when you've had enough of living with me and need to be on your own again.' He gave her a nervy, anxious look, seeking reassurance.

She ran a hand through her hair, turning shaggy into spiky.

'I don't think that's going to happen.' Her smile was uncertain too. 'We've spent years taking very small steps towards each other. We never do anything in relation to each other unless we're belt-and-braces sure of it. I can't believe this is going to end in disaster.'

He stood up and moved round the desk to put a hand on her shoulder. 'We won't let it. I'll get someone from the antiques centre round to value the bed. And now, I'm going home. It's ten o'clock and I'm knackered. I'll talk to you tomorrow, OK?'

She covered his hand with hers. 'OK.'

'I know you think I'm overreacting,' he said, drawing away and moving to the door. 'But I know what men like Vance are capable of. And it's taken us so long to get this far, I couldn't stand to lose you now.'

Then he was gone.

Vance woke up with a start, heart racing, all his senses on full alert. For a moment, he had no idea where he was, thrashing around in the big bed and getting tangled in the unfamiliar duvet. Then the silence sank in and he remembered. He was not where he expected to be. He was miles away from his confined cell in HMP Oakworth. He was in Vinton Woods, in a house owned by a Cayman Islands corporation whose sole director was Patrick Gordon, the name in one of the passports in the briefcase Terry had given him.

He rolled over and snapped on the bedside lamp. Its white glass shade cast a soft light over part of the room. That was novel in itself. The light in his cell at Oakworth had illuminated every corner, exposing its limits and its limitations. But this glow left things to the imagination. Vance liked that.

The bedding, though, was lamentable. That would have to go. Terry had been working class to the core. He really believed that black satin sheets meant you'd arrived.

Vance looked at his watch and was surprised to see it was barely ten o'clock. He'd been asleep for about six hours, but now he was in that peculiar state of still being tired and yet alert. Something had woken him up, some anxiety that had invaded his dreams, and now he couldn't quite grasp it. He got out of bed, enjoying the feel of soft, rich carpeting beneath his feet. He had a piss, realised he felt hungry, and padded downstairs to the kitchen. Another freedom to luxuriate in.

He switched on the lights, pleased to notice there was no obvious sign of his earlier violence. He wasn't naïve enough to think he'd destroyed all the forensic traces of what had taken place, but he wasn't anticipating any forensic scientists examining the place. To the casual observer, to the estate agent who would soon be selling the place, there was nothing amiss.

Vance opened the fridge and laughed out loud. Terry had clearly done a commando raid on Marks and Spencer. Ready meals, fresh meat and veg, fruit, milk, champagne and freshly squeezed orange juice. He pulled out the fizz and popped the cork one-handed while he decided what to eat. He settled on some Chinese appetisers, but struggled to make sense of the oven controls. Eventually he worked it out, but the edge had gone from his good mood.

As he poured a second glass of champagne, he recalled what lay behind the spike of anxiety that had awoken him. He hadn't checked the camera feeds. That was mostly because he hadn't actually explored the house before exhaustion had knocked the feet from under him. If he'd seen a computer, it would have reminded him.

He prowled through the darkened house, not wanting to draw attention by snapping lights on and off. He found a dining room, a TV room, a sitting room and finally, tucked away at the back of the house, a study. The soft moonlight from outside was enough to navigate by and he crossed to the desk, turning on a lamp that cast a pool of light over the dark

145

wooden desk. Terry had clearly run out of imagination by the time he'd got to the study. A big desk, an extravagantly padded leather chair and a credenza were the sole furnishings. A laptop sat on the desk, a printer on the credenza. Vance assumed the oblong box on the window sill that flashed a trembling array of blue lights at him was the wireless router. He'd seen pictures of routers on the Internet, but never the real thing until now.

He flipped open the laptop. Terry had wanted to get an Apple. He said it was better for what Vance wanted. But he knew his learning curve was going to be steep as it was – the computers he'd been able to access in Oakworth had been old and slow, the access to the Internet severely restricted. He couldn't help laughing. What the fuck were they thinking, letting someone like him loose on computers? If he'd been in charge, he would never have allowed inmates access to mobiles or the net. If you wanted to stop prisoners communicating with the outside world, then ban mobile-phone coverage from the prison. Never mind inconveniencing the staff, if you were serious about keeping a grip on your prisoners, you had to do shit like that. He'd bet you couldn't get a mobile signal in a gulag.

He could hardly believe how quickly the machine booted up. It was a thing of beauty compared to what he'd grown used to. He went back to the kitchen to fetch the briefcase and opened it on the desk beside the laptop. Vance took out a small address book and thumbed it open at 'U' and directed the web browser to the first of a list of urls on the page. It opened an anonymous-looking website that asked for a password. Then he went to the letter 'C' and typed in the first string of letters and numbers on the page. 'C is for camera,' he said aloud as he waited for the page to open. Seconds later, he was looking at a screen divided into quarters. One quarter was in complete darkness. One showed a brightly lit kitchen;

146

beyond that, a dining area; beyond that still a sitting area with a vast inglenook fireplace. It looked like a barn conversion, judging by the scale and the hammer beams in the ceiling. Another showed the same open-plan space but from the other end. A man was sprawled on a long leather sofa. Greying blond hair, indistinct features, a T-shirt with a logo Vance didn't recognise, and a pair of boxer shorts. Over to one side, a woman was sitting at a desk, tapping on a laptop. Beside her was a glass of red wine. The fourth quadrant showed the top of an open staircase leading to a gallery bedroom. It was hard to make out much detail, but it looked as if there was a bathroom and a dressing room behind the main area.

Vance watched, fascinated, a self-satisfied smile on his face, as nothing much happened. So many private investigators, so few scruples. Ask around and you could find one who would do more or less anything, as long as you could find a way of dressing it up in some guise that made it sound remotely legitimate. It hadn't been cheap to get the cameras in place, but it had been worth every penny. He wanted to be sure exactly how the land lay before he took on this act of revenge.

He closed down the window and repeated the process with another access code. This time, the views were external. They showed a large Edwardian house set in a good-sized garden. The cameras showed the approach to the front door, a view of the living room from the outside, a wide shot of the back of the house and the driveway. In the light from nearby street lamps, the house appeared to be empty. The curtains were open, the windows dark. Vance nodded, still smiling. 'It's not going to be dark forever,' he said, moving on to the third access code.

Again, four camera angles. A gravel drive leading to a long, low farmhouse covered in some kind of creeper. Very English. He could see what looked like a stable block in the distance, lit by floodlights. Next, the block itself. He'd seen places like this all over the country; the brick and wooden frontages of stable yards where horses occupied the stalls, paid for by the largesse of rich men and women and tended by ill-paid workers who loved the beasts more than most of their owners ever would. A figure passed across the yard, his movements jagged. A beam of light arced out from one hand. He shone the light jerkily on each door in turn before disappearing from sight. The third quadrant showed the rear of the house, while the fourth was a long shot of the approach to the drive. Parked across the entrance was a horsebox, making it impossible for a vehicle to pass. Vance's smile grew broader. Anticipation was so sweet.

Reassured by what he had seen, he closed the computer down. There were other sets of cameras waiting to be activated, but now wasn't the time. If his cameras were picked up on one of his early hits, he imagined the police would sweep all the other possible locations for hidden surveillance. If there was no electronic signal, they would be almost impossible to find. Or so Terry had told him. It would be nice to keep tabs on all his targets all the time, but he was willing to hold back in the interests of keeping ahead of the game.

This time, he took the precaution of carrying the briefcase upstairs with him. Now he had satisfied his curiosity, he was feeling sleepy again. The spy cameras were every bit as good as he had been promised. If he'd had any doubts about whether he could carry out his mission, they were all dispelled. Tomorrow, the next phase would begin.

Tomorrow there would be blood.

The Toyota didn't look red under the sodium street lights. That was just as well, since the number plates belonged to a tan Nissan. All very confusing for a witness, or even someone trying to analyse a CCTV tape. Not that the driver expected

148

them to be running surveillance of the sex workers' beats. All that bleating about front-line cuts and budgets – what little money the cops had at their disposal these days was going where the taxpayers could see it. Neighbourhood patrols, turning up at burglaries instead of giving out a crime number over the phone, anti-social behaviour. Orders from on high to make it look good, keep the government on the right side of the voters.

It was total jackpot time for anyone below the *Daily Mail* parapet – people traffickers, white-collar fraudsters, prostitute killers. Most criminals were probably happy about that. But the Toyota's driver was pissed off. He wanted to be paid attention to. If his exploits weren't all over the papers and the TV, what was the point? He might as well not bother.

How could the cops not notice what was going on? Maybe he should start taking photos of his victims with his trademark front and centre. The media would be all over it soon enough if that sort of thing started landing on their desks. Then the cops would have to sit up and pay attention.

Fletcher drove slowly through Temple Fields, Bradfield's main red-light district. The Vice squad had cleaned it up a lot in recent years, the gay community had annexed whole streets, and there was a lot less sex for sale out in the open than there used to be. The brasses worked inside, in saunas and massage parlours or out-and-out brothels. Or else they'd moved out to other parts of town, like the dual carriageway near the airport and round the back of the hospital building site.

The traffic on Campion Way was heavy, which suited him. It wasn't usually this clogged so late at night. But some of the cars had yellow scarves hanging from the windows and Fletcher reckoned Bradfield Victoria must have had an evening kick-off. He vaguely remembered they were in the Europa League, which the guys down the pub derisively referred to as, 'Thursday night, Channel 5. Not football as such.' He didn't understand the comment, but he grasped the fact that it was derogatory. He often didn't really get what the guys in the pub or at work were on about, but he knew the best way to hide his true self was to conceal his bewilderment and act like he was one of the quiet ones who didn't say much but took it all in. It had served him well over the years. Well enough to fool Margo for long enough to make her his. And once that had stopped working, well, he'd managed to deal with that without it coming back to haunt him, and never had to explain it away because nobody expected him to.

As the cars crawled up the dual carriageway, Fletcher studied every woman he passed who might be working the street. His search wasn't random; he knew exactly what he was looking for. In his heart, he didn't expect to get lucky here on the fringes of Temple Fields. He'd thought he would have to cast his net wider tonight.

But just when the traffic began to pick up speed, he saw what he was looking for. It was impossible to stop, so he took the next turning on the left, found a mildly illegal parking spot and doubled back. He wanted so badly to run it was like the pain you get when you need to pee. But the last thing he wanted was to draw attention to himself. So he walked briskly, hoping she would still be in sight when he rounded the corner.

And yes, there she was. Unmistakable, even though he was approaching her from behind. She was clearly working. He could tell by the way she walked; the swivel in the hips, the languid half-turn towards the traffic, the ridiculous heels that bunched her calves into tight knots.

He could feel the blood pounding in his head. His vision seemed to blur at the periphery, leaving her as the only clear element. He longed for her. He ached to take her away from the filth and the depravity that she was wallowing in. Didn't she know how dangerous it was out on these streets?

'Mine,' he murmured softly as he slowed down to match his pace to hers. 'Mine.'

24

Alvin Ambrose skimmed yet another report that took the search for Jacko Vance no further forward. DI Stuart Patterson dropped into the chair opposite and sighed. His expression reminded Ambrose of his younger daughter, Ariel, a child who appeared to be working up to taking 'sulking' as her specialist subject on *Mastermind*. 'This is going bloody nowhere,' Patterson said. 'Why can't you find him?'

You, Ambrose noted. Not *we*. Apparently even the tangential involvement of Carol Jordan in the case had increased his boss's disengagement from what was going on with his team. 'I've got twenty officers chasing down reported sightings on our patch alone. Other forces all over the country are doing the same. I've got another team going through CCTV footage, trying to track the taxi he escaped in. Plus officers talking to the prison staff. The Home Office has dispatched a specialist team to protect the ex-wife. We're doing everything we can. If there's anything you think we've not got covered, then tell me and I'll action it.'

Patterson ignored the request. 'We're going to look like bloody bumpkins. Can't even catch a one-armed man as familiar to half the country as Simon Cowell. Carol Jordan's going to be laughing up her sleeve at us.'

Ambrose was shocked. He was used to a different Patterson, a man who wore his Christianity with subtlety, a man who wasn't afraid of showing compassion. His bitterness at being passed over had stripped away all his admirable qualities. 'Carol Jordan had a front-row seat the last time Vance went on the rampage. She's not going to be doing any kind of laughing any time soon,' he growled. He wasn't even going to dignify his comment with the usual, 'With respect, sir.'

Patterson glared at him. 'I know that, Sergeant. All the more reason she'll be on our case.'

Ambrose was spared having to reply by the arrival at his desk of a weary-looking uniformed constable clutching a bundle of paper. 'I've got something on the taxi,' he said, too tired for enthusiasm.

Patterson sat upright and beckoned the constable. 'Let's see it, then.'

'We've found it here in the city,' he said. 'It's turned up in the Crowngate car park.'

'Good work,' Patterson said. 'Alvin, get a forensics team over there to give it the once-over.'

'That's already been actioned,' the constable said, flushing at Patterson's glare. 'The chief super was in the control room when the report came in. He actioned it, sir.'

'Typical,' Patterson muttered. 'The one chance we get to look like we're doing something and the brass nick it.'

'As long as somebody's chasing it up,' Ambrose muttered.

'We've been back-tracking it on the cameras,' the constable carried on uncertainly. 'We found it entering the parking structure at 9.43 p.m. So we worked back through the road and traffic-light cams. We think whoever drove it into the city nicked it from the car park on the M42 services. Because, see, we checked back on their cameras, and it was parked there mid-morning. It's hard to see much of the driver, but it could be Vance with a baseball cap on. You can see he's got tattoos on his arms ... ' As he spoke, he splayed camera stills over the desk. 'Then he puts on a jacket and walks away. Hours later, a completely different bloke comes down the line of cars. See? It's hard to be sure, but it looks like he's trying the doors. And he's a completely different height and build to the guy who parked it.'

'Lovely,' Ambrose said. 'Cracking job. Can we see where Vance went after he parked the car?'

'Not so far. He either went to another car, or inside the services building or to the motel. That's his only choices. We're working on all the footage right now. Everybody's being really helpful for once.'

'Nobody likes a serial killer,' Ambrose said. Re-energised by the new information, he jumped to his feet. 'I'm going out there right now with a team. Print me out a sheaf of those shots. And keep me posted with whatever you find out about Vance.' He looked a question at Patterson, who shook his head.

'Just send a team, Sergeant. You need to be here, keeping an eye on things.'

'But sir—'

'You're wasted out there. That's a job for foot soldiers, not for anybody who wants to make a good impression on the new regime.'

Ambrose felt the urge to punch Patterson on the nose, to knock some sense into a man who had taught him much of what he understood about being a good detective. If this was what thwarted ambition did to a man, God spare him from that particular lust. Deflated, he sat down again. 'Good job,' he said to the constable. 'Keep me in the loop.' Then he reached for the phone. 'I'd better get a team organised, then.'

'You better had,' Patterson said, getting to his feet. 'I'll be in the canteen.'

There were two lap-dancing clubs within easy cycling distance of Bradfield International Airport. Both denied ever having employed Leanne Considine. Both managers were stony-faced, clearly well-practised in the art of giving nothing away to law enforcement. After the second knock-back, Sam and Kevin sat in the car grumbling at each other, neither coming up with anything more constructive than waiting in the car park till the girls started coming out. 'They won't talk to us,' Sam said gloomily. 'We're going to be sat here for hours, all for nothing.'

'That's even supposing it was this club she worked at. We could be totally wasting our time here. There's a burger van about a mile down the road. We could fuel up to keep us going while we wait.'

Sam sighed. It wasn't his idea of a good time, but anything was better than sitting here doing nothing. Kevin started the engine and headed for the exit. Sam kept his eye on the club and just as they were about to turn on to the main road, he yelped, 'Wait! Back up!'

Kevin jammed on the brakes, throwing them both against their seat belts. 'What the fuck?'

'Just back up, slowly.'

'What is it?' Kevin said, easing the car back towards a parking slot.

'We're idiots,' Sam said, flicking through the photos Jamie had printed for them.

'Speak for yourself.'

'Her bike,' Sam said, pulling out the shot of Leanne with her bike. 'She rode her bike to work. Remember what Tara said?'

'So?'

'So the bike should still be where she left it. And I'm sure I saw a bike in the headlights as you turned. I'm going for a closer look.'

'Please yourself,' Kevin said. 'Give me a shout if you're right.'

Sam scrambled out of the car and ran across to the back of

the club. The building was a U-shaped single-storey brick structure with all the imagination of a five-year-old's Lego construction. A wooden fence linked the two arms of the U, forming an enclosed back yard where industrial skips for bottles and rubbish were stowed. The gate stood ajar, and it was through the gap that Sam thought he'd glimpsed a bike.

He slipped inside and saw at once he'd been right. The car headlights had caught the reflective fixtures on the back wheel and mudguard; the bike itself was tucked in behind one of the skips, chained to the fence with a heavy-duty chain. Sam compared it to the one in the photo. It was hard to be sure in the limited light, but he thought they matched. He was about to walk back to the car with the news when he heard a door sigh open then click closed nearby. He heard the snap and flare of a cigarette lighter and risked a peek round the edge of the skip.

In the glow of the cigarette, he could see the hard-faced bitch who'd given him and Kevin their marching orders. Sam glanced back to the car. Kevin was leaning against the head rest. He looked like he was taking a nap. It was just Sam and the woman. He considered for a moment. Sam was always driven by what would produce the best result for Sam. Normally, that didn't include monstering a witness, because there were usually other people around to testify to his bad behaviour. But out here in the dark, behind a dodgy club, it would be his word against hers. And who was the credible one here? She'd already lied to him and Kevin, so he reckoned he was on solid ground.

Light on his feet, he edged round the skips so that he came up behind the woman. He was close enough to smell the heavy musk of her perfume, cut with the cigarette smoke, and still she was oblivious. Swift and sure, he snaked his arm round her throat and jerked her backwards. She stumbled into him, he shifted his hand over her mouth and with his other hand ripped her cigarette from her fingers. No nasty little burns for him.

She was wriggling and struggling, so he wrapped his other arm round her. 'See how easy it is?' he hissed into her ear. 'You come out for a smoke, and there's an evil fucker waiting for you. That's what happened to Leanne. Or something very like that.' He pushed her away, using a perversion of a dance move to swing her around facing him. His other arm pinned her to the wall.

'Fucking copper.' She spat at him but he was fast enough to avoid the gob of spit.

'You lied to me, bitch,' he said. 'I could really hurt you, and nobody would believe you. But that's not what I want. I just want the truth. I don't want the bastard who killed Leanne to do the same thing to another woman. I've just shown you how easy it is. How very, very vulnerable you are. So what happened on Tuesday night?'

'You wouldn't dare lay a finger on me,' she said. 'I'll have you for assault, attempted rape, the lot.'

Sam laughed. 'Like anyone would believe a slag like you.' He shifted his weight, straightened his fingers and jabbed his stiff hand under her ribs. She gasped with pain and shock. Sam remembered the secret thrill of being bad and tried not to let it ride him too hard. 'I don't want to hurt you – but I will. Tell me about Tuesday night.'

'It was just like any night. Leanne came on about nine and did a few dances. She left around midnight. That's all I know.'

'Not good enough.' Sam jabbed under the ribs again. 'There's more than that. What about the CCTV? You've got cameras on the car park. You've got cameras all over the club.'

She gave a triumphant sneer. 'They're wiped. One of the barmen came in this morning and said the filth were showing photos of Leanne all over town, that she'd been murdered. The owner was in and he told me to wipe the tapes. He didn't want a murdered tart connected to his nice clean business.' It sounded like her contempt for her boss was on a par with her contempt for the police.

'Did you look at the tapes before you wiped them?'

She looked away. A guilty look, Sam thought.

'What your barman didn't know, because we haven't told anybody yet, is that the bastard who killed Leanne wasn't a beginner. He's done this before. More than once. And if we don't get him, you can bet he'll do it again. And since you're showing him what easy pickings he can get around here, chances are it'll be one of your girls.' Sam gave a jeering smile. 'Or maybe even you.'

The look she gave him was loaded with hate. 'I took a quick look at the car park tapes around the time she left. I was curious. If one of our clients had anything to do with it, I wanted to know who it was. For safety's sake. Whatever you might think, I don't want my girls hurt.'

Sam eased the pressure on her. 'And what did you see?'

'I saw Leanne walk out the back door and across the car park to the far corner. She got into a car and the car drove off.'

Sam wanted to punch the air. Or failing that, punch this bitch for the casual way she'd fucked over the investigation into Leanne's death. 'What kind of car? What colour was it?'

'How the fuck do I know what kind of car? Do I look like Jeremy fucking Clarkson? And the CCTV's black-and-white. So all I can tell you about the colour is that it wasn't black and it wasn't white.'

Now he really wanted to go to town on her. 'I don't suppose you saw the driver either?'

'A white blob. That's all I saw.'

'Fucking great.' Sam didn't bother hiding his disgust. 'I don't suppose you took a note of the number either?' He stepped away. 'Thanks for your help. I'll have a uniform swing by for your statement tomorrow.'

Now for the first time she looked genuinely worried. 'No

way,' she said. 'Look, I've told you what I know. Don't fuck it up for me with my boss.'

Sam gave her a considering look. 'You're the licensee, right?'

'Right. So you've got my name and address. It's not like I can do one.'

'Come in under your own steam tomorrow. BMP HQ, not Northern Division. Ask for MIT. Have you got that?'

She nodded. 'MIT.'

'If you're a no-show, I'll be here tomorrow night, mob-handed. Whether you're here or not, your boss will know all about how helpful you've been to the police. Are we clear on that?'

She glared at him, eyes sparkling with frustration. 'I'll stick to my end, you stick to yours.'

He heard her swear at him as he walked back to the car, but he didn't care. She might have wiped the tapes in the club, but her boss didn't control all the road cameras. Sam was pretty sure that, whatever direction Leanne's killer had taken, he would be picked up. This killer's days were numbered and it was all thanks to Sam Evans. Jordan would have to acknowledge this piece of work. She might be on her way out, but Sam was on his way up.

25

A watery sun infiltrated Tony's kitchen, giving everything a slightly surreal cast. While the coffee brewed, he browsed the news online. Vance's escape was the headline everywhere, an excuse for a rehash of his crimes and trials. Tony featured in most of the stories, Carol in a few. The media had tried to get to Micky Morgan, Vance's ex-wife, but they'd arrived at the stud where she and her partner bred racehorses to find a horsebox across the drive and hard-faced stable lads patrolling the perimeter. Nobody had even seen Micky, never mind managed to get a quote. Instead they'd settled for interviewing an assortment of nobodies who had once worked alongside Vance. The prison authorities hadn't come out of it well either, which was as predictable as morning following night.

There wasn't much coverage of Leanne Considine's murder, mostly because as far as the media was concerned she was still identity unknown. Once they discovered who she was and that she had a secret double life, there would be a feeding frenzy. Her housemates would be under siege till they cracked and revealed – or invented – her lurid life. If they had any sense, they'd screw enough money out of the media to pay their university fees.

But for now, she was just a down-page filler for the nationals. Even Penny Burgess had to be content with eight paragraphs. Carol had told him about the press conference, but Penny hadn't had the nerve to go against what Reekie had said. She'd be furious when she found out the truth, he thought, picking up his espresso and going through to his study. He glanced out of the window, gratified to see the surveillance van still parked on the other side of the street.

The downside of Carol's refusal to have her own protection was that he was stuck in Bradfield until Vance was either behind bars or deemed not to be a risk. If he went down to the house he'd fallen in love with in Worcester, his protection would come with him. Which would mean leaving Carol exposed and vulnerable here at night. And that was definitely thinking the unthinkable.

The other great unthinkable was what was going to happen between him and Carol. For years, they'd danced a strange quadrille, drawing closer, then being driven apart by events and their own histories. They were like those bar magnets kids used in experiments at school; one moment, the attraction was irresistible, then you switched poles and the force between them made it impossible for them to get close. In the few months since her acceptance of his offer of a home in the house he'd inherited, they'd typically managed to avoid any real discussion of what that might mean beyond the fact. The only thing that was clear was that she would have her own space – a bedroom, a bathroom and a room that would double as a sitting room and home office. Whether this change in geographical circumstance would mean a different kind of change was something neither of them seemed able to broach.

Tony was almost convinced he was ready to try to move forward. Well, moving forward was what pop psychology would call it. He was well aware that what passed for forward motion was often a way of heralding a different kind of change. He didn't want to damage the quality of his connection with Carol and part of him was still concerned that climbing into bed together would do just that. He'd never had much success with the business of sex. Mostly, he'd been impotent. He could become aroused, though probably a lot less than most men seemed to. But as soon as he got naked with a woman, his penis clocked off. He'd tried Viagra, which had cured the physical symptoms but messed with his head. On the other hand, maybe that had been more to do with the fact that the woman he'd been with was not Carol. Tony let out a deep, heartfelt sigh. It was all so complicated. Maybe they should just leave things be. OK, it wasn't perfect. But what was?

Meanwhile, the best he could do for Carol was to work behind the scenes to help her team ensure that their last hurrah ended in glory. But before he got stuck into that, he needed to find out what was happening in the hunt for Vance.

He didn't want to put Ambrose in an awkward spot with his boss, so rather than call him, he sent a text. Tony felt quite proud of himself as he hit the 'send' button. When it came to passing for human, he knew he still had plenty to learn. But maybe he was finally picking up a few pointers in the tact-and-diplomacy department.

He'd barely begun to download the files Stacey had left in the Cloud for him when Ambrose called back. 'Hiya, mate,' Ambrose said in his low rumble. No names; he was always careful not to compromise himself.

'Thanks for getting back to me.' That was one he'd learned by heart; apparently, unless you were a teenage boy, you didn't just grunt when somebody returned a call. 'Any news on Vance?'

'He's still in the wind. And we're under siege from the world's media,' Ambrose said. 'We found the taxi he nicked.

162

He left it round the back of the northbound services on the M42. But no sign of the man himself. We've got officers going through the CCTV cameras as we speak, but don't hold your breath. The best definition pictures are from inside the services building. If Vance didn't go in there, we're probably fucked.'

'I suppose it was too much to hope for.'

'I'm only just beginning to realise what a clever bastard he is. I never paid much attention to the case at the time, I had too much going on in my own neck of the woods. Have you got any tips?'

'He's not on your patch any more. I'd put money on it. Whatever his plans are, I'm pretty sure they don't involve hanging around Oakworth. And he will have plans,' Tony said heavily.

'Obviously. You don't go to those lengths to get out and not be sorted on the outside. Does the name Terry Gates mean anything to you, by the way?'

'Oh shit,' Tony groaned. 'Sometimes I am too stupid to live.' Even as he spoke, he hoped that wouldn't turn out to be a prediction.

A humourless laugh came down the phone. 'I'll take that as a yes.'

'Fuck. Ambrose, I'm sorry. I should have remembered Terry Gates.' As he spoke, Tony could see Gates in his mind's eye. Arms with cables of muscle under the skin, big brown eyes like a trusting animal, an open face that broke into a grin whenever he looked at Vance. Tony recalled watching Gates work his market stall. He knew when to be technical with the blokes, when to jolly the women along to buy tools they'd never known they needed. He was shrewd with the public and yet he was completely blind where Vance was concerned. 'Why are you asking?'

'He was Vance's only regular visitor. He showed up every

163

month, never missed, according to the records. We asked the local lads to give him a knock. And guess what? He's not where he should be. Nobody's seen hide nor hair of him since the morning before Vance broke out. So what's the score there, Tony?'

Tony closed his eyes and rested his forehead on his hand. 'Terry had a twin sister, Phyllis, who developed terminal cancer. Back in the day, Vance used to do these hospital visits. It was supposedly his big charity work. At the time, people bought the line that he was giving comfort to the sick. The real reason was a lot creepier. He liked watching the dying. It was as if he fed off the notion that they had no control over anything any more. But like most of the relatives of the patients Vance sat with, Terry never believed there was anything sinister going on. He saw Vance as an angel of mercy who had eased his sister's passing.' He straightened up, the flow of his story energising him.

'He was so locked into that conviction, it was impossible for him to believe Vance was guilty of the crimes he stood accused of. One of the murder charges hinged on a tool-mark. Vance had a bench-mounted vice in his secret hideaway that had a very distinctive defect on one face. And the prosecution had an arm preserved from a murder victim fourteen years before – it had the matching tool-mark in the bone. The obvious inference, taken with all the other circumstantial evidence, was that Vance was the killer. And then along came Terry Gates, who went into the witness box and swore he had sold the vice second-hand to Vance less than five years before. That whoever had owned that vice previously was the killer, not Vance. That undermined the case against Vance on that earlier murder, which made proving he was a serial killer almost impossible, given how little evidence we had.'

'So Gates actually perjured himself for Vance?'

'It's hard to put any other interpretation on it,' Tony said.

'He must have really loved his sister.'

'Too much, I suspect. And after she died, Vance became a kind of surrogate. If he didn't keep Vance safe, he was letting his sister down.'

Ambrose made a dark, grumbling sound. 'I don't get that. The guy's a serial killer and you perjure yourself to keep him out of jail because he was nice to your sister? People make my head hurt, doc.'

'Mine too, Alvin.' He knocked back his espresso in one, blinking and shuddering as the caffeine hit. 'So Gates still thinks he owes Vance.'

'Looks like it.'

'You need to get a warrant for Gates's house and go through everything. If he's been Vance's eyes and ears and hands and legs on the outside, there must be a trail. Vance is smart, but Gates isn't. He'll have left tracks. Vance will have told him to destroy everything, but he won't have. That's the only place you'll find a clue.'

'Sounds like a plan. Thanks,' Ambrose said. 'You don't think Gates will turn up?'

All of his professional instincts told Tony with absolute certainty that Terry Gates would never walk through his front door again. 'Gates is dead, Alvin. Or as good as. He knows too much.'

'But why would Vance turn on him when Gates has always been the one on his side?' Ambrose's voice was reasonable, not critical.

'Gates managed to stay in Vance's corner because he could always convince himself Vance was the persecuted innocent. But whatever Vance has up his sleeve, it's not going to be pretty. And Gates won't be able to avoid understanding his involvement. I think when he's confronted with incontrovertible proof that his hero is a villain, Gates will turn. And Vance is acute enough to get that.' Tony opened the top desk drawer and poked around the detritus inside, looking for something to crunch. 'He'll kill him rather than take the risk. I know it might not look that way, but he's not a risk-taker. Everything is calculated.'

'Have you got a team on you?'

Tony glanced out of the window again. 'There's a surveillance van outside the house. I'm not planning on going anywhere complicated today. If I go out at all, it will be to Bradfield Moor, which is a bloody sight more secure than Oakworth turned out to be.' Right at the back, he found an old packet of cinnamon-flavoured Lifesavers. He hadn't been across the Atlantic for at least two years, but he didn't think boiled sweets could go off. One-handed, he ripped the packet open and popped one in his mouth. The outside had gone a bit soft, but the heart of the sweet was hard, resistant to his teeth. Tony crunched down on it, letting sugar and spice fill his mouth, making him feel inexplicably calmer.

'Are you eating something?' Ambrose said.

'Will you keep me posted?'

'I'll do what I can. Look after yourself.'

The line went dead and Tony stared at a list of files on his screen, taking nothing in. How could he not have taken Terry Gates into account? The oversight shook his faith in himself, making him wonder what else he might have missed. Had he let his concern for Carol interfere with the process of analysis that he so depended on? Without that clarity, he was no use to an investigation. No, scratch that. Without that clarity, he was a liability.

Tony pinched the bridge of his nose, screwing his eyes tightly closed. He visualised a white cube and placed himself at the heart of it. He breathed deeply and regularly, forcing everything else from the front of his mind. When all he was conscious of was white space, he opened his eyes and placed his hands flat on the desk on either side of the keyboard. 'You kill women who sell sex,' he said to the empty room. He reached for his glasses and began the long process of crawling into the labyrinth of a killer's damaged mind.

26

Carol was working her way through the overnight reports when she came upon Sam's write-up of his interview with Natasha Jones, manager and licensee of Dances With Foxes. The information was useful – a witness to Leanne leaving the club in someone else's car could be a crucial brick in the wall of evidence that would put a killer away. And the action Sam had suggested was spot-on: 'Recommend requisition of traffic-camera data on Brackley Road in both directions from club. Time frame 11 p.m. – 1 a.m. on Tuesday night/Wednesday morning. Aim: ID car carrying Leanne Considine away from Dances With Foxes lap-dancing club at 673 Brackley Road.' But there was something off-kilter about the interview report. For one thing, Sam had been out with Kevin but there was no mention of Sam's sergeant. All in all, it felt evasive and Carol knew Sam well enough to realise that when he was being evasive, there was usually something to evade.

She looked out into the squad room, where Kevin and Paula were on the phone. There was no sign of Sam, so she scribbled a note. 'My office when you're done.' She left it in front of Kevin, who gave her a look of pained resignation. He was in her visitor's chair inside two minutes.

'Nice work last night,' Carol said, leaning back in her chair and resting her feet on her open bottom drawer.

'Thanks,' Kevin said cautiously.

'I've seen Sam's report. You seem strangely absent.'

Kevin crossed his legs, propping his left ankle on his right knee. He drummed his fingers on his left knee. He was as relaxed as an exam candidate. 'It was Sam's show. The manager tried to blag us into believing Leanne never worked there. When we were leaving, Sam spotted Leanne's bike. So he went back to confront the manager.'

'Where were you?' Still keeping it light, not quite sure what she was looking for.

'I was in the car.'

'What? You couldn't be bothered following up?'

Kevin pursed his lips. His fingers stopped dancing and clutched his knee. 'That's not actually how it went.'

'So how did it go?'

'Does it matter? Sam got what we needed. It doesn't bother me that he followed his nose and came up trumps.' He shifted in his chair, trying for nonchalant and missing spectacularly.

Carol sized him up. Now she had a clearer idea of what had gone on. Sam had left Kevin in the lurch and chased his own gut instinct. Stupid behaviour at any time, but especially when there was a killer on the loose. 'You know you should always work in pairs when you're dealing with people who understand the power of screaming "foul" at every opportunity. Sam left himself exposed, and you shouldn't have let that happen.' By Carol's standards, it was the mildest of reprimands, but it was enough to make Kevin's milky skin flush dark red.

'I understand,' Kevin said, his expression mutinous. 'I didn't realise he was going to conduct the interview there and then.'

Carol shook her head, a wry smile on her face. 'And how long have you been working with Sam?'

Kevin stood up. 'I take your point.'

Carol followed him into the room, looking for Paula. But while she'd been talking to Kevin, Paula had disappeared. 'It's like the bridge of the *Marie Celeste* in here,' she said aloud.

'I'm still here.' Stacey's voice came from behind the monitors. 'I'm looking at footage from traffic cameras.'

'Shouldn't some uniform from traffic be doing that?'

'The truth? I don't trust them to do it properly. They get bored too easily.'

Carol walked back to her office, unable to keep from smiling. Her bloody-minded, arrogant specialists were never going to be conventional team players. God help the commanding officers who ended up with the members of her squad. It almost made her want to stay, just to see the fun and games.

Vance had only been on the loose for a matter of hours, but that had been long enough for Maggie O'Toul to get her defences in order. So far, the media hadn't discovered that she was responsible for advocating Vance's transfer to the Therapeutic Community Wing, but she clearly realised that was going to happen. When Ambrose turned up for their appointment at the Probation Service offices where she was based when she wasn't at Oakworth, the receptionist acted as if she'd never heard the name. He'd had to produce his ID before she would even acknowledge the existence of Dr O'Toul. It didn't help his mood.

Maggie O'Toul's office was a cubicle on the second floor with a view across the street to a former cinema turned carpet warehouse. When Ambrose entered in response to her, 'Come in,' she had her back to the door, staring out the window as if something remarkable was happening in the world of carpets. The office was crammed with books, files and papers, yet they were organised in such a way that the overall impression was one of neatness. It wasn't much like any space where Tony Hill was working.

170

'Dr O'Toul?' Ambrose said.

Slowly, apparently reluctantly, she swung round to face him. She had one of those weakly pretty faces marked by anxiety that always made Ambrose feel like he had the upper hand. He thought her looks were the kind that used to be called 'elfin' when Audrey Hepburn was a star. Her face was framed by artificially dark hair in a gamine cut which emphasised the fact that she wasn't going to revisit fifty. 'You must be Sergeant Ambrose,' she said, her voice weary, her mouth turning down at the corners. Her lipstick seemed the wrong sort of colour for her complexion. He didn't know much about that sort of thing, but he'd always had a good eye for what looked well on a woman. He never thought twice about choosing a gift of clothes or jewellery for his wife, and she always seemed happy to wear what he'd bought. Maggie O'Toul did not look like a happy woman.

Christ, who did he think he was? Tony Hill? 'I need to talk to you—'

'About Jacko Vance,' she interrupted, finishing his sentence for him. 'Am I to be the scapegoat? The blood sacrifice? The person to stand in the pillory of the *Daily Mail*?'

'Spare me the histrionics,' he said roughly. 'If you know your job at all, you must know that Vance is a dangerous man. All I care about is getting him back behind bars before he starts killing again.'

She gave a dry little laugh and ran her fingers through her hair. Her nail polish was the same wrong colour as her lipstick, making her fingers look oddly mutilated. 'I rather think I'm better qualified than you to form an accurate impression of what Jacko Vance is capable of these days. I know it's hard for you to grasp, but even people who have committed dreadful crimes like Jacko are capable of finding a route to redemption.'

The phrase smacked of a soundbite from a platform presentation. 'He's already put one person in hospital today,'

Ambrose said. 'What I'm looking for from you is not a lecture about how rehabilitated Vance is. Clearly, he's not. How you square that in your professional world is up to you. But I don't have the luxury of breast-beating right now. What I need is a sense of how he will behave, where he will go, what he will do.'

She was smart enough to know she'd been thwarted. 'I sincerely think he is no threat,' she said. 'Like all of us, he will lash out if he's cornered or frightened.'

'The man he battered senseless was a taxi driver,' Ambrose said flatly. 'I can't readily see how a thirty-four-year-old taxi driver made him feel cornered or frightened. No matter how crap his driving was.'

'There's no need to be facetious,' she said primly. 'Look, hear me out. I'm not stupid, Sergeant. I've been doing this job a long time and I am no pushover. I recommended Jacko for the Therapeutic Wing because in our sessions together he was remorseful and insightful about his past crimes. He fulfilled all the criteria for the community, except for the fact that he would never be eligible for release. But why should someone be denied the best chance to recover from the disaster that is their life simply because they can't gain a hundred per cent of the benefit from that opportunity?'

Another soundbite, Ambrose thought. He wondered how much of her career Maggie O'Toul had planned to build on redeeming Vance. 'Tell me, how did his remorse manifest itself?'

'I'm not sure what you mean. He expressed regret and he unpicked the chain of circumstances that drove him to commit his crimes.'

'What about atonement? Did he talk about that at all? About the people whose lives he'd destroyed?'

She looked momentarily annoyed, as if she'd missed a trick. 'Of course he did. He wanted to meet his victim's relatives and apologise in person. He wanted to make amends to his ex-wife for all the grief he'd brought her.'

'Can you remember which victims he mentioned?'

'Of course. Donna Doyle's family, that's who he wanted to speak to.'

'Just them?'

She drummed her fingers quietly on the arm of her chair. 'She was his victim, Sergeant.'

Ambrose cracked a half-smile. 'The only one he was tried and convicted for. What about the other girls he abducted and killed? Did he give up their names at all? Did he express any regrets for their deaths?'

'As you well know, he has always denied those accusations and he was never charged with any other murders.'

'He was actually charged with one other, but he got off because his pal Terry Gates perjured himself. And he was convicted of killing Shaz Bowman till the Appeal Court threw it out. Did Vance mention them among his sins?'

Dr O'Toul exhaled heavily. 'I am not engaging in a point-scoring competition with you, Sergeant. I know my competence. I suggest you stick to yours. I'll say it again: I think Jacko is no threat. I'm disappointed that he has hatched this plot to escape, but I imagine he simply found prison finally intolerable. My guess would be that he will leave the country for somewhere he feels safe.' She smiled, her cheeks subsiding into an array of concentric curved lines. 'And I do believe he will live a rehabilitated life.'

Ambrose shook his head in disbelief. 'You really believe all that, don't you?' He stood up. 'This is pointless. Unless you have a specific notion of where he might be – maybe some place he mentioned, some person he was close to – there's no point in continuing this interview.'

'I have no idea where he might go. Nor who he knows on the outside. I do think this is a tremendous waste of manpower,' she added. 'I wouldn't have recommended Jacko for this community if I hadn't known he was a changed man.'

Ambrose headed for the door, pausing as he prepared to step into the corridor. 'I hope you're right. I really hope you're right. I would love to be proved wrong on this.' He rubbed the back of his thick neck, trying to loosen the tight muscles. 'And I think you are right about one thing. There are people out there that Vance has unfinished business with. But I don't think he wants to atone for what he's done. I think his plan is to make them pay through the nose for what they've done to him.' Ambrose didn't wait for a reply. He didn't even close the door behind him. Maggie O'Toul didn't deserve the satisfaction of a slammed door.

27

Paula had not gone far. When she'd seen Carol Jordan heading her way, she'd almost panicked, wondering if her boss had by some sixth sense detected that she was speaking to Tony. But Kevin had been the focus of her attention and Paula had wound up the conversation with, 'If you're that near, meet me in the Costa Coffee on Bellwether Street. Five minutes.' And she'd shot off before anyone could ask where she was going.

Now she was sitting with the largest skinny latte the coffee shop could provide, waiting for her partner in crime. He didn't keep her long, plonking himself down at the table opposite her. 'You not getting a coffee?' she asked, half-rising.

He shook his head. 'Some days, it's just too hard to choose.' He frowned. 'I think the politicians have got it wrong. It's not more choice we need, it's less. Too much choice is too stressful. There have been experiments, you know. Rats live longer and healthier lives when they have fewer choices, all other things being equal.'

Sometimes Paula wondered how Carol Jordan coped with any kind of social relationship with him. His capacity for tangential conversation was beguiling, but hard to handle when you wanted to get straight to the point. 'Did you get all the files?' she said.

He produced a quirky little smile. 'I assume so. But that's one of the unanswerable questions, isn't it? Because I won't know about the files I didn't get. It's like when you're doing a lecture and you ask if everyone can hear you. Because obviously, if they can't hear you, they can't answer the question, so you're none the wiser.'

'Tony!'

'Sorry. I'm in a funny mood at the moment.'

Paula scowled at him. 'We all know you and the chief are watching your back in case Jacko Vance comes after you. Hell, so does anyone who can read. So I will cut you a bit more slack than usual.'

Tony ran a hand through his hair. 'I'm not used to people knowing stuff about me,' he said. 'I've had all these phone calls from journalists wanting me to write profiles of Vance. I don't think they have any idea how dull a profile is. Even if I was interested enough to return their calls, I couldn't turn what I do into tabloid fodder. Or even *Guardian* fodder. I only came out of the house because the phone was doing my head in. And then Penny bloody Burgess turned up on my doorstep.' He shuddered. 'You'd have to be some sort of masochist to want to be a celebrity.'

'Is anybody keeping an eye on you?' Paula asked, suddenly anxious. Tony might be on the far side of odd, but she'd grown fond of him over the years. She'd lost one friend in the course of duty and she knew enough about that kind of grief. Tony had reached out a hand to her then, a hand that had stopped her falling, and she still felt she owed him. There were some debts that could never be paid.

Tony nodded. 'So I'm told. There's been a surveillance van outside the house since before I got home yesterday and there's a very polite young man who's keeping tabs on me on foot.' He made a face. 'It's reassuring, I suppose. But I don't think Vance is coming after me. Simple revenge isn't his style. He's much more twisted than that. But how precisely the twist will manifest itself, I don't know. So it's been quite good for me to have your case to think about. It keeps me from fretting.' He peered at her, blinking like an owl in the light. 'Tell me – what's your take on Carol? How's she coping?'

'You'd never know there was anything else going on except for these murders. She's got her work face on and that's that.' She gave a sad little smile. 'It would kill her to show vulnerability to the likes of us. She needs us to believe in her so she can convince herself she's indomitable.'

Tony's eyebrows twitched up and back again. 'Have you ever thought of a career in psychology?'

'What? And end up like you?' Paula laughed out loud.

'They're not all like me.' He mugged at her. 'Just the good ones. You could do this, you know. You're better than you know.'

'Enough, already. What do you make of it? Is it the same killer, do you think?'

'I don't think there's much room for doubt. It's the same person, Paula. The tattoo is post-mortem. It's signature behaviour. But that's about all that fits the typology.' He pulled a spiral-bound notebook from his battered leather briefcase. 'There's no clear evidence of him having sex with his victims. Kylie had unprotected sex with four men, we don't know about Suze because of her immersion in the canal, and Leanne's body has no traces of semen. There isn't any at the site either.

'Then there's the victims themselves. There's common ground, obviously. They were all selling sex. They were all, in effect, street hookers. I know Leanne was working in the lap-dancing club, but her acts of prostitution were not controlled by a pimp or in a brothel. So from that perspective, she was in the same category as the other two. But here's the thing about his victims. It's like he's moving up the social scale of prostitutes. Kylie was as low down the pecking order as you can go. Suze had dragged herself off the bottom of the heap. And Leanne – well, Leanne was as near as you can get to a respectable woman. Now, I know there's a rule of thumb in this kind of crime that says an offender starts with the most vulnerable of victims and grows in confidence with each kill. But in my experience, that confidence doesn't generally grow so far or so fast. Leanne is a big jump from Kylie. And that's odd.'

'Maybe he's just more emotionally mature than some of the killers you've dealt with.'

Tony shrugged. 'It's certainly possible. But my gut reaction would be that, if he's that emotionally mature, he wouldn't need to be doing this.' He spread his hands. 'But what do I know? I just missed a major trick doing a risk assessment of Vance, so I'm not feeling very bloody infallible today.'

'So is there anything you can tell me that might point us towards the killer?'

Tony looked disconsolate. 'The only thing—' He stopped himself, scowling at the table.

'The only thing . . .?'

He tutted. 'I shouldn't say this. Because it's based on nothing more than a feeling.'

'As I recall, your "feelings" have worked out well for us more than once. Come on, Tony. Don't hold out on me.'

'It's as if he's throwing down a gauntlet. Like, "None of you are safe. It's not just the bottom feeders, it's all of you." Like nobody's safe on the streets with him around. Peter Sutcliffe, the Yorkshire Ripper, he talked about cleansing the streets. It's as if this one has a similar ambition. He wants to scare them off the streets.' He absently picked up Paula's coffee and took a drink. 'I don't know. And there's something else that's really bugging me and I don't know what it is. There's something about the crime scenes, the murders themselves. It's bothering me and I don't understand why.'

'Well, he's doing something different every time. That's unusual, isn't it?' Paula took her coffee back.

'Yes, to the degree he's doing it. But that's not what's bugging me. I'm aware of the degree of difference, that's all filed away under "unusual but explicable". There's something else and I can't put my finger on it and it's bloody annoying.'

'Leave it alone. It'll come to you when you're in the thick of something else.'

Tony grunted, unconvinced. 'It's weird. I've almost got déjà vu about it. Like I've seen it all before. But I know I haven't. I can't even think of a case in the literature where the killer tattoos his victims post-mortem. I wish I could shake the feeling, but it's bugging the hell out of me. Have you made any progress with the investigation?'

Paula told him about Sam's discovery the night before. 'Stacey's working on it. If there's anything to be got, she'll get it.'

'You might want to ask her to see if she can find any courtyard-style motels between the Flyer and Dances With Foxes. This is clearly territory he's familiar with. And they do like to stick to where they know. Suzanne Black was drowned somewhere he didn't have to take her past a receptionist. I don't think he took her home to his place. He doesn't take chances like that. But one of those motels where you check in at an office and the rooms are like apartments that open off the car park – that would fit the bill.'

'Good idea. Thanks.' She drained her coffee and pushed her chair back. 'I'm going to miss them all. We're all going to be tossed to the four winds by Blake. I'll never get another berth like this again. It's like the end of an era.'

'Blake's an idiot,' Tony said. Just then, his phone beeped. He patted his pockets till he found it. 'Message from Carol,' he said. 'She wants me to come in so Chris can debrief us.'

'What's she been up to? I haven't seen her since yesterday lunchtime.'

'She's been tracking down the other three cops who worked with me and Carol on putting Vance away. They needed to be warned personally, not left to hear about it all on the news.' He stood up. 'I'd better get over there.'

'I'll give you a ten-minute start,' Paula said. 'The last time we went behind her back, she made me feel like a toddler on a tear. And not in a good way. Let's not give her any reason to start paying attention to us.'

As soon as he walked in the door, Tony realised he was the one who should have stayed behind in the coffee shop. Carol was sitting by Chris's desk and she looked up when he walked in. 'That was quick,' she said. 'I thought you were planning to stay at home all day?'

'I was,' he said. 'But Penny Burgess came knocking so I thought I'd come in here and hide.' He nearly elaborated, but stopped just in time. The best lies are the ones with the most truth, he reminded himself.

Chris had dark smudges under her eyes and her hair looked like it had been slept on. Her usually jaunty air was subdued, like a dog that's been walked to exhaustion. She covered a yawn with her hand and barely raised her eyebrows in greeting. 'What's up, doc?' she managed, in a pale reflection of her normal style.

'We're all dancing the Jacko Vance tango,' he said ruefully, pulling up a chair and joining the two women. 'He must be rubbing his hands in glee at the thought of us all running around chasing our tails, wondering where he is and what he's doing.'

'I just spoke to West Mercia,' Carol said. 'They're coordinating the search. They've had even more than the usual spate of so-called sightings everywhere from Aberdeen to Plymouth. But not a single confirmed sighting.'

'One of the problems is we've got no idea what he looks like,' Tony said. 'We can be certain he doesn't look like a caricature of an England football supporter any more. He'll be wearing a wig, he'll have different facial hair and different-shaped glasses.'

'He's still the one-armed man,' Chris said. 'He can't hide that.'

'The prosthesis he's got isn't immediately obvious. After I spoke to my Home Office contact, I checked it out online. The cosmetic covers they have now are amazing. You'd have to look closely to realise they're not real skin, and most of us don't look closely at anything much. And what Vance has got is the best that money can buy.'

'Thanks to the European Court of Human Rights,' Carol muttered. 'So what we know is that we don't know much. Vance could actually be anywhere from Aberdeen to Plymouth. So how did you get on, Chris?'

Chris straightened up in her chair and glanced at her notebook. 'OK. Leon's still with the Met. He's done well for himself. He's exactly what the brass want – graduate, black, smart and presentable. And demonstrably not corrupt.' She grinned at Carol. 'He's a DCI now, with SO19.'

Tony snorted with laughter. 'Leon's in Diplomatic Protection? Leon, who used to be about as diplomatic as me?'

'According to my old muckers on the Met, he's learned to keep his mouth shut and play the game. But he's got respect, up and down. So I got hold of him on the phone and marked his card.'

'What did he say?' Tony said, remembering Leon with his sharp suits and swagger. He'd been smart enough to accommodate lazy, getting by on his wits rather than his work. To have climbed so far, he must have learned to buckle down.

He'd have liked to have seen that, a Leon honed by work and responsibility.

'He laughed it off. But then, he would.'

'What's his domestic set-up?' Carol asked.

'He's got an ex-wife and two kids in Hornsey, and he lives with his current partner in Docklands. I tried to persuade him to move them for now, but he won't have it.' Chris pulled a face. 'He said, "If I read an obit for Carol Jordan and Tony Hill, I'll head for the hills. But right now, I can't say I'm too worried." I couldn't budge him on that.'

'He does have a point,' Tony said. 'Leon's not near the top in terms of seniority or alphabetical order or geographical order. And given that none of us has a clue how long this is going to go on, he's probably right not to turn his life on its head just yet.'

'Unless of course the rest of us make ourselves so hard to hit Vance ends up taking out Leon by default,' Carol said, acid in her tone. 'You might want to mention that, Chris.'

Chris looked less than thrilled at the prospect. 'Simon McNeill isn't a cop any more. He stayed with Strathclyde for a couple of years after Shaz Bowman's murder, then he quit to take up a job teaching criminology at Strathclyde University.'

Tony remembered Simon's unruly black hair, his intensity and his infatuation with Shaz Bowman. Tony had heard on the grapevine that he'd had a breakdown, been diagnosed with Post Traumatic Stress Disorder and been gently eased out of the job. 'Poor sod,' he said absently. He realised both women were looking at him oddly. 'I mean, because he was besotted with Shaz, not because he ended up teaching at Strathclyde. Obviously.'

Chris looked amused as she continued. 'He's got a long-term partner and four kids. They live out in the country about an hour's drive out of Glasgow. He seemed quite unnerved by the news. He's going to talk to his local law enforcement about increased patrols. But he said where they live is at the end of a track – one way in and out. And they have shotguns. He's taking it seriously, but it sounds like he was already prepared for a siege. He told me that Western capitalism was headed for a cataclysm and then crime would skyrocket. Every man for himself. But he's made his arrangements.'

It sounded like the PTSD wasn't entirely a thing of the past. 'Christ, I hope Vance doesn't show up there,' Tony said. 'There'd be a bloodbath and chances are Vance would be the only one who'd walk away from it.'

'So that's two we can't do much about,' Carol said. 'Tell me Kay Hallam isn't gung-ho or running her own Home Counties militia.'

'Kay Hallam is why I look like a woman who's slept in her car. Because I am that woman. I had a job trying to track her down. I struggled to pick up the trail because she left to get married. Mr Right turned out to be an accountant with a practice in the Cayman Islands. The kind of bastard who helps all those loaded gits to avoid paying their taxes like the rest of us.'

Carol whistled. 'Quiet little Kay. Who'd have thought it?'

'I'm not surprised,' Tony said. 'She had that knack of watching and waiting till she was sure of her ground then she'd mirror your attitudes and position. Everybody always thought Kay was on their side and she always ran into problems with the kind of exercise where you have to nail your colours to the mast and defend your position. When Mr Right swam into her orbit, she'll have watched and waited, then swum up alongside him and made him feel he'd finally met the one person who really understood him.' He watched the two women consider his words then nod in agreement. 'It was what made her such a good interviewer. Paula has the same chameleon knack, but Paula's also got a personality of her own that she slips straight back into. I never had any idea who the real Kay Hallam was.'

183

'She's a tough cookie under that diffident exterior,' Chris said. 'She's in the UK at the moment. They've got a house near Winchester. Her boys are at boarding school there, she's back for a parental visit. She got the point as soon as I told her what was going on. And she just railroaded me. She wouldn't take no for an answer. Threatened me with everything from the *Daily Mail* to the Police Complaints Commission. In the end, I had to drive down there and brief the local nick and the two security guards she'd hired from God knows what agency. I don't know about Vance, but they scared the living shit out of me.' Chris shook her head in disbelief. 'Can you believe that I did that?'

'Not only can I believe it, but if I had her resources, I'd probably do the same thing in her shoes,' Tony said. 'Vance is seriously scary.' He frowned. 'Chris – didn't some hack write a book about Vance after the first trial?'

'That rings a faint bell. Didn't they have to withdraw it after he won his appeal?'

'That's right,' Carol said. 'They said it was libellous now Vance had been cleared. It might be worth tracking down the author and seeing if he's got anything to say. He might have information we don't have about associates and other properties Vance may have owned.'

'I'll get on to it,' Chris said.

Before Carol could respond, Paula walked into the squad room with the evening paper. 'Secret's out,' she said, brandishing the front page, where a banner headline read, SERIAL KILLER TARGETS BRADFIELD.

28

It was a beautiful day, Vance thought. Never mind that the sky was grey and there was a promise of rain in the air. He was out of jail, driving through the Yorkshire Dales, master of his own fate. By definition, that made it a beautiful day. The car was easy to drive, it had a digital radio that made it amazingly easy to switch between stations, and the GPS navigation meant he couldn't get lost among the drystone walls and sheep folds. He'd slept well, breakfasted well in front of the laptop, enjoying the coverage of his escape on the Internet. He almost felt sorry for the hapless Governor, nailed by the media like a moth on a pin. The hacks were portraying him as an incompetent fool who'd fallen for Vance's lies about rehabilitation. The truth, as usual, was more complex. The Governor was at heart a good man, clinging to the last shred of idealism. He desperately wanted to believe it was possible for a man like Vance to redeem himself. Which made him an easy mark for a manipulator as skilled as Vance.

The Governor wasn't crap. He'd just come face-to-face with a far superior creature.

After breakfast, he'd checked his cameras. This morning, he – or rather, Terry – had had an email from the PI saying

185

he'd finally managed to get the last set of cameras installed. When Vance had used the code, he'd been able to activate them and spy on another location, a late addition to his list, tagged on as a result of the most recent research Terry had carried out for him. It was the perfect little extra to complete phase one of his plans.

But that lay in the future. Now he had to concentrate on the business in hand. Today he was Patrick Gordon, complete with a thick head of chestnut hair and a few artfully applied freckles across his cheeks. The moustache and horn-rimmed glasses completed the job. He was dressed like a posh country dweller – brown brogues, corduroy trousers, Tattersall check shirt and a mustard V-necked sweater. Stockbroker turned Yorkshire gentleman. All he needed was a Labrador to complete the picture.

Just after noon, he pulled into the forecourt of a smart country pub that advertised food and traditional ales. Terry, being the thorough sort, had researched pleasant places to eat and drink near all of Vance's targets. It was as if he imagined Vance was going on some sort of grand tour, taking lunch and tea with old acquaintances. At first, Vance had thought it a crazy eccentricity, but the more he thought about it, the more appealing it seemed to flaunt himself under the noses of the neighbours.

Only a couple of tables were occupied, one by a middle-aged couple dressed for a walk in the dales, the other by a pair of men in suits. Vance studied the range of real ales, all of whose names seemed based on bad puns or fake dialect, and settled for one called Bar T'at. The barman didn't give him a second glance when he ordered his pint. He asked for a steak-and-ale pie and settled in a quiet corner where he could look at his tablet computer without being overlooked. The tablet was amazing. He'd found it in the desk drawer this morning and he'd been entranced by what it seemed capable of. It was an awkward size, really – too big for a pocket – but it was much more portable than a laptop. While he was waiting for his food, he tuned in to the cameras that were trained on the barn conversion.

Now it was daylight, Vance could see much more clearly. The area that had been blacked out in the night was revealed as a separate unit within the barn – a sort of self-contained guest flat with a tiny kitchen and bathroom of its own. A door led outside and, on the opposite wall, another presumably led into the main living area of the barn. At any rate, there was a door in a corresponding position there.

But that wasn't the most interesting element in the quadrant. So close to the camera that it was only possible to see the top of his tousled grey-blond head and one shoulder, a man sat at a long desk. The camera angle wasn't very helpful, but Vance could just make out the corner of a keyboard and the top edge of a computer monitor. Further along the desk was another keyboard, set in front of a pair of large monitors. It was impossible to make out any detail on the screens, but Vance thought it was probably computer program code. The man wasn't moving much; in all likelihood he was doing something on the computer.

There was no sign of life anywhere else in the barn. The duvet had been thrown untidily over the bed, and the linen basket was overflowing, a T-shirt hanging over the edge. So the woman wasn't around. Never mind, Vance thought. He had plenty of time. He closed the window as his food arrived and put the tablet to one side while he tucked in. After years of prison food, any meal would have seemed a treat, but this was a genuine delight. He took his time, then indulged himself with a bowl of apple crumble and thick custard.

By the time he left, the pub had filled with customers. Nobody looked twice at him as he weaved through the throng at the bar and back out to the car park. About half of the men looked like they belonged to the same sartorial club as him. He relaxed into the car, admitting to himself that he had been a little tense on this first public outing. But it had all gone perfectly.

Twenty minutes later, he drove past the converted barn that was the focus of his interest. About half a mile beyond it, he parked on a grass verge rutted with tyre tracks. He took out the tablet and waited for the page to load and refresh. In the short time since he'd left the pub, everything had changed. The man was standing by the kitchen range stirring a pan on the stove, moving rhythmically as if to music. Vance wished he had a sound feed. By the time it had occurred to him, it had been too late to set it up.

Then the bathroom door opened and the woman emerged, dressed in the black and white of a barrister who's just spent the morning in court. She ran a hand over her head, pulling off some sort of clip and letting her hair tumble over her shoulders. She shrugged out of her jacket and threw it over the banister. She kicked off her low heels and sashayed over to the man, keeping the same beat in her movements. She came up behind him and put her arms round his waist, snuggling into his back. He reached up over his shoulder with his free hand and rumpled her hair.

The woman stepped away and took a loaf out of the bread bin. Knife from the block, wooden board from a recess, basket from a deep drawer. A few strokes of the blade and she placed a basket of bread on the table as the man fetched bowls from a cupboard and ladled a chunky soup into them. They sat down and set about their lunch.

Vance reclined the car seat a little. He needed to wait for the right moment, and that might take a while. But that was OK. He'd waited years for this. He was good at waiting.

Carol took her time reading the *Bradfield Evening Sentinel Times'* splash. Sometimes when a story leaked, it staggered into the paper with the wobbly support of rumour and innuendo. This had marched on to the front page with all guns blazing. Penny Burgess had the key elements for a strong story, and she hadn't put a foot wrong. Well, not unless you counted exploiting the deaths of three women to sell newspapers. But why would it matter, this final exploitation of women whose lives had, in their different ways, been exemplars of the way lives could be so cheaply used? Carol tried not to give in to a familiar disgust and failed.

'Someone's leaked,' Carol said. 'Comprehensively.'

'Yeah, and we all know who,' Paula said bitterly. 'First they slag us off, then when you call them on it, some resentful little shit decides to try and shaft us like this.' She stabbed a finger at the paper. 'Never mind that we wanted it kept close for solid operational reasons. Getting a dig in at the Minorities Integration Team obviously matters more than catching a serial killer.'

Tony took the paper from her and read carefully. 'She doesn't even make the assumption that these are sexual homicides,' he said. 'That's interesting. Looks like she was satisfied with what she got from her source without implying there's more to it.'

'Fucking Penny Burgess,' Chris said.

'Isn't that what Kevin used to do?' Sam asked of nobody in particular.

'Shut up,' Paula snapped.

'Yes, Sam. If you can't be helpful, be silent,' Carol said. 'This means that we can't actually trust Northern with any leads we're developing. We can still get their uniforms to do the grunt work – door-to-door, showing photos around, that sort of thing. But anything else, we play very close to our chests.'

Stacey emerged from behind her screens with a glossy print in her hands. 'Does that mean we keep stuff off the whiteboards?' she said.

'What sort of stuff are we talking about here?' Carol could feel the dull beat of a headache starting behind her eyes. Too many decisions, too much pressure, too many balls to juggle; West Mercia was acquiring more of a gloss with every passing day. She did not expect to crave a stiff drink before noon in her office in Worcester. That was not the least of her reasons for moving.

Stacey turned the print round so they could all see it. 'Traffic-light camera two hundred metres from Dances With Foxes,' she said. 'Heading away from town.' The colour print showed a Toyota that could have been red or maroon, the number plate clear enough to read. The passenger looked like a woman, long hair evident. The driver's face was half-hidden beneath a baseball cap; what was visible wasn't clear enough for ID.

'Is this our guy?'

'It's the right time frame. This particular car does not feature on the traffic cam before Dances With Foxes, but it pops up here. So it either came from the club, the carpet superstore next door, or the sunbed-and-nail salon beyond that. I don't think either of them is open at that time of night. So it's almost certain that this car came from Dances With Foxes. Two other cars have the same movement pattern in the time window, but neither of them has a passenger. I would say the weight of probability is that this is the car of the man who drove Leanne Considine from the lap-dancing club.'

Stacey always delivered her reports as if she was in the witness box. Carol loved the clarity, though she would sometimes have preferred more adamantine certainty. 'Great job, Stacey,' she said. 'Anything from the plates?'

'They're fakes,' Stacey said succinctly. 'They belong to a Nissan that was scrapped six months ago.'

'What about enhancing the driver's face?'

'I don't think there's enough visible to make it worthwhile.

Certainly not for something we could release and hope to get a result from.'

Sam slammed the flat of his hand on the desk. 'So it doesn't get us anywhere.'

'It tells us that the man in the car is almost certainly the killer,' Tony said. 'If he was just a punter, he wouldn't go to all the bother of fitting fake plates to his car. That speaks to forward planning.'

Stacey turned to Sam and bestowed one of her rare smiles on him. 'Actually, Sam, I don't think it's a dead end. We need to come at it laterally, that's all. Like everywhere else in the UK, Bradfield has an extensive Automatic Number Plate Recognition CCTV network. These days, traffic cops and the security services track car movements on main roads all round the country. On A-roads, they can latch on to any car and follow it in real time. Or as near as damn it. And here's the killer: all those detailed vehicle movements are stored for five years in the National ANPR Data Centre so they can be analysed for intelligence. Or used as evidence. All we have to do is ask for any records for that plate number after the date the Nissan was scrapped. That could practically lead us to his front door. Or at least give us a good enough likeness for somebody who knows him to recognise him and come forward.' Her smile broadened. 'Isn't that beautiful?'

'Beautiful? It's better than beautiful,' Carol said. 'Can you contact them, Stacey? Impress them with the urgency. Life at stake, all the usual. We need this yesterday.' The headache was in retreat. As always in this job, a little good news went a very long way. 'We're on to something, guys. And this time, it stays inside these four walls.'

29

After the soup, the cheese and biscuits and fruit. Waste of time, all that healthy eating, Vance thought. They were going to be dead soon, regardless of the quality of their diet. He shifted in his seat, trying to get more comfortable. If they both went back to work, it would be a while before he had the chance to take them by surprise. It could be hours. But that was OK. He was from the last generation to believe in deferred pleasure. He knew that all good things come to those who wait. It sounded like one of those mnemonics schoolkids learned – Every Good Boy Deserves Favour, or Richard Of York Gave Battle In Vain. For him, it had become a mantra.

But this time, he'd guessed wrong. When they finished eating, they loaded their plates into the dishwasher. Then the woman turned to the man and ran her hand over the front of his cargo pants, stepping into him as she did so. His head tipped back and his hands found her breasts, gently moving his palms over them like a mime pretending to meet a window. She kissed his throat and he pulled her close in a tight embrace, pulling her blouse out of her skirt and running one hand up to find skin, caressing her backside with the other. She took a couple of steps forward, making him back up towards the stairs.

They let go of each other. She pulled his T-shirt over his head and dropped it to the floor. In turn, he unzipped her skirt and she stepped clear of it. 'Oh my,' Jacko breathed, seeing her stockings and suspenders. Sex had been the last thing on his mind, but he was already growing hard at the unwitting show the couple were staging for him.

He struggled upright in his seat, realising this could be his best opportunity. If they were fucking each other's brains out, they wouldn't be paying much attention to anything else. He grabbed a small holdall from the passenger footwell then got out of the car, still clutching the tablet, and set off on foot towards the barn. There was a path from the road to the main door. He'd seen it on Google Earth. Half his attention was on the screen, the other half on the terrain.

By the time he'd found the path, Vance had had to change screen views because they had made it upstairs to the gallery, a trail of clothing left behind. She was still wearing her stockings and suspender belt, he was down to one sock. Vance stumbled onwards, unable to stop watching as she kneeled on the bed and took his erect cock in her mouth. His hands were in her hair, then he was gently pushing her away, rolling her on to her stomach and entering her from behind, hands on her breasts, mouth biting her shoulder.

Vance broke into an awkward run. This was too good a chance to miss. The door, of course, was unlocked. This was the countryside, in the middle of the day. Nobody locked their doors. He opened it silently then kicked off his shoes. He stepped inside and suddenly the screen had a soundtrack of groans and grunts and half-swallowed words. Vance put down the tablet then took a pair of latex gloves out of the holdall and put them on. Next he took out the same knife that had worked so well on Terry. Noiselessly he mounted the stairs.

When his head cleared the stairway, he could see there was no need for silence. They were fucking like their lives depended on it, and Vance could feel his cock pressing hard against his clothes. Jesus, it had been so long since he had fucked a woman. For a mad moment, he thought about killing the man and taking his place. That would be the fuck of a lifetime. Then caution tripped in. Too many risks, too many chances for things to go horribly wrong. Hard enough to restrain a terrified woman with two strong arms, never mind one.

He climbed the remaining stairs, moving with ease and confidence. He was always at his best in situations where he'd planned ahead. But this was working out even better than he'd expected. He came up behind the couple just as the man moved into the final stages, his buttocks pumping, his breath coming in gasps. She was yelling too, pushing against him, her hand between her legs as she worked to bring their orgasms together.

Vance allowed himself to fall forward on top of them, his good arm snaking round under the woman's throat. He ripped the blade from one side to the other before either of his victims had even realised what was happening. Blood began to gush from her throat as Vance grabbed the man's hair with his prosthetic hand and pulled his head back. The man was panicking now, trying to buck Vance off. But the elements of surprise and control were against him. Vance dragged the knife across his throat and at once there was blood everywhere. He stepped back and flipped the man on to his back. The blood foamed and sprayed and fountained from the carotid arteries, driven higher and faster by the increased blood pressure provoked by the vigorous sex. His eyes rolled in panic, then dulled in seconds.

Vance rolled the woman over. She was already beyond help but the blood still spewed out of her neck, her skin visibly paling as he watched. He quickly stripped off his blood-soaked clothes and stood over her, hard and ready. He knew she was dying or dead, but life was so close, this wouldn't be some weird perversion. Because he wasn't a pervert. He was very clear about that. He didn't enjoy killing and he certainly had no interest in necrophilia.

But still. The blood was amazing. And it wasn't the killing that had aroused him, after all. She'd been responsible for that while she was alive. And yet . . . He didn't want to look at that wound and the almost severed head. Her boyfriend had had the right idea. Vance turned her back on her stomach, then, slick with the blood of both his victims, he lowered himself on top of her.

30

Tony followed Carol into her office and hovered in the door-way. 'I'll head off home, then,' he said. 'Now Penny Burgess has her story, I don't suppose she'll be bugging me any more.'

Carol gave him a shrewd look as she sat down. 'You seemed to be unsurprised by anything in Penny's story,' she said. 'Or by what Stacey was working on.'

Tony's smile betrayed his nervousness. He knew he should have kept his mouth shut. 'I guess I'm getting better at keeping my reactions hidden.'

'Or else you knew everything already.'

He shrugged, trying to look casual. 'Most of these investigations follow the same basic patterns. You know that better than me.'

'I suppose,' she said, without conviction. A movement in the squad room caught her eye and she said, 'Oh, shit. It's Blake. And you're not supposed to be here.'

'I'm here to talk about Vance,' Tony said indignantly. 'That's Home Office business. Nothing to do with him.' But he knew that wouldn't matter if Carol's boss had come looking for a fight.

Blake was headed straight for them, his expression serious, his pink-and-white skin flushed around the eyes. Carol stood up as he reached the threshold. The Chief Constable nodded at Tony. 'Dr Hill. I wasn't expecting to see you.' There was a surprising lack of hostility in his attitude.

'I'm working with the Home Office on the Jacko Vance escape. I needed to talk to DCI Jordan. But I'll be off now,' Tony said, easing round Blake, hoping to get out before the trouble started.

Blake's eyes wrinkled in a pained expression. 'Actually, Dr Hill, I'd rather you stayed.'

Tony and Carol shared a quick glance of bafflement. He couldn't remember Blake ever welcoming his presence, even when he'd been unequivocally on the side of the angels. Tony edged back into the room.

'Could you close the door, please?'

Now Tony was seriously worried. Blake was behaving like a man on a grave mission. If that mission involved Tony as well as Carol, the overwhelming chances were that somebody was dead. He closed the door and moved round to lean against the filing cabinet, his arms folded across his chest.

Blake smoothed his perfectly barbered hair in a nervous gesture. 'I'm afraid I have some rather bad news,' he said, the West Country burr in his voice more noticeable than usual.

Carol's eyes flitted to the squad room. Tony could see her checking. All present and correct, apart from Kevin. 'Has something happened to DS Matthews?' she said, formality disguising fear.

Blake looked momentarily wrong-footed. 'DS Matthews?' He clearly had no idea who she was talking about. 'No, nothing to do with any of your officers. Carol, I'm afraid there's been an ... incident.'

'What do you mean, an incident? Where? What's happened?' Now agitation was slipping out from behind Carol's professional mask. Tony straightened up. He could see an ominous sheen of sweat on Blake's upper lip.

'Your brother and his partner – there's been an incursion in their home. A violent incursion.'

Tony felt the shock in his chest, knew it must be worse for Carol. She was on her feet now, eyes wide, mouth moving without a sound issuing from it.

'Are they alive?' Tony said, crossing to Carol and putting his arm round her shoulders. It didn't come naturally to him, but he knew how people were supposed to behave in a crisis. He felt more for Carol than any other human being; the least he could do was what was expected of someone who cared.

Blake looked hangdog. He shook his head. 'I'm terribly sorry, Carol. They're both dead.'

Carol slumped against Tony, shivering like a wet dog. 'No,' she said. 'No, no, no.' The pitch and volume decreased with each word till she was virtually growling the last 'no'. He could feel the terrible tension vibrating in her as he held her close. She caught her breath, teetering on the edge of a sob, but somehow dragged herself back from the edge.

'What happened?' Tony asked, driven towards the story as he always was.

Blake signalled with his eyes that he didn't want to answer.

'Tell me what happened,' Carol cried, turning back to face the Chief Constable. 'You have no right to keep this from me.'

Blake wrung his hands. Tony had heard the expression, but he'd never seen so vivid a representation of it. 'The facts I have are very sketchy. Your brother and his partner—'

'Michael and Lucy,' Carol said. 'They have names. Michael and Lucy.'

Blake had a hunted look about him now. 'I apologise. Michael and Lucy were surprised by an intruder who attacked them both with a knife. It appears to have been very sudden.'

'This happened at the barn? During the night?' Tony said. He'd been there for dinner three or four times with Carol. He couldn't picture it as a crime scene. He certainly couldn't imagine anyone approaching in broad daylight without being spotted.

'As I said, I have very few details. But the officers at the scene believe the crime took place within the last couple of hours.'

'Who found them?' Carol said, attempting to cling to composure. She was defending herself now, building a wall of ice between herself and the rest of the world. Tony had seen her bulldoze her way through an extreme personal crisis before. He had also seen the aftermath, when the wheels well and truly came off.

'I don't know, Carol. I'm sorry. I thought it better to share what little I know as soon as possible rather than wait for more details.' Blake looked at Tony, seeking help. But Tony was as much at a loss as he was. He couldn't make sense of what he was hearing. He felt numb, but he knew the impact would hit him before long. Two people he had known were dead. Murdered. And it was hard to resist believing that he knew the culprit.

Carol drew away from Tony and collected her coat from its peg. 'I need to go there.'

'I don't think that's a good idea,' Blake said, trying to exert authority.

'I don't care what you think,' she said. 'My brother, my choice.' Her voice cracked on the words. She returned to her filing cabinet and took two miniatures of vodka from the drawer. One after the other, she swallowed them without pausing. As the alcohol hit, she clenched her jaw, blinking hard. Then she visibly collected herself and said, 'Tony, I need you to drive me.'

'If you're determined to go, I can have an officer drive you,' Blake said.

'I want to be with someone I know,' Carol said. 'Tony, will you drive me? Or shall I get Paula to do it?'

It was the last thing he felt like doing. But choice didn't come into it. 'I'll drive you,' he said.

'Obviously, you must take whatever time you need,' Blake said as Carol pulled her coat on and started past him. She moved gingerly, as if recovering from a bad tackle on the sports field. Tony hovered behind her, not sure whether to put his arm around her or to leave her alone. Paula, Chris and Sam stared openly, bemused at what news could have so diminished their boss.

'Tell them,' Tony said over his shoulder to Blake as they reached the door. 'They need to know.' He nodded towards Chris. If he was right about what had happened to Michael and Lucy, she needed to be aware. 'Especially Chris.' He saw the shock on her face, but had no time to deal with it. Carol was the person who mattered now.

31

Every regular pairing has its own codified car behaviour. One always drives, the other is invariably the passenger, or the driving is shared along prearranged demarcation lines, or one drives except when they've been drinking. The passenger navigates or stays out of it; the passenger criticises the driving either directly, or indirectly, by drawing their breath in sharply whenever there is the faintest risk of disaster; the passenger falls asleep. Whatever the pattern, it takes a deep crisis to alter it.

Carol passively handing over her car keys and allowing Tony to drive was a measure of how stricken she was. Where she was a confident, assured and fast driver, he was nervous, hesitant and inconsistent. It had never become second nature to him. He still had to think about his manoeuvres and, given how easily he was distracted by thoughts of patients and killers, Carol always complained she felt like she was taking her life in her hands when she had to be his passenger. Today, her life was the least of her concerns.

He programmed the satnav and set off through the late afternoon traffic. Even though the recession had cleared some of the blockages in the city's rush-hour arteries, their progress was slow. Normally, Carol would have sworn at the traffic and found some route through the back doubles that might not have saved time but had the merit of movement. That afternoon, she simply stared out of the window, eyes blank. She had closed down, like an animal hibernating through the worst of the winter, building up its strength for when it mattered.

Once before he had seen her like this. She'd been raped and brutalised, battered and bruised, beaten but not quite defeated. She'd protected herself with an inward retreat just like this. She'd locked herself away for months, denying herself any comfort that didn't come out of a bottle, keeping friends and family beyond the curtain wall. Even Tony, with all the skills at his disposal, had barely been able to stay in touch. Just when he'd feared she was slipping away completely, the Job had saved her. It had given her something to live for that he hadn't been able to provide. It was just another instance of his many failings, he thought, never stopping to ask whether she believed that too.

They'd barely cleared Bradfield when her phone rang. She declined the call without even looking at the screen. 'I can't talk to anyone,' she said.

'Not even me?' He glanced away from the road to check her expression.

She'd given him a look he couldn't fathom. There was nothing related to affection and plenty of ice. She said nothing, simply curling closer into herself. Tony focused on the driving, trying to put himself in her shoes and failing. He had no siblings. He could only imagine what it must be like to have that pool of shared memories at the heart of your childhood. Something like that could fortify you against the world. It could also be the first step on a lifetime journey of distorted relationships and twisted personalities. But everything Carol had said about her brother put them in the former camp.

When he'd first worked with Carol, all those years ago when profiling was in its early stages and she was one of his first champions, she and Michael had shared a loft apartment in a converted warehouse at the heart of the city. Very nineties. Tony remembered how Michael had helped them, offering his expertise in software development. He also remembered the unsettling period when he'd wondered whether Michael himself might be the killer. Luckily, he'd been quite wrong about that. And later, when he'd got to know Michael better, he'd felt embarrassed to have entertained so absurd a thought. Then he recalled how many killers had confounded their nearest and dearest and he felt less bad about his suspicions.

He remembered the first time he'd met Lucy. He'd come back to Bradfield after a brief and ill-fitting excursion into academic life; Carol had returned after the trauma that had nearly destroyed her. She'd moved back into the loft apartment which Michael had been sharing with Lucy. Five minutes in their company and Tony could understand why Carol had only ever seen that as a temporary solution. Some couples fitted so well together, it was impossible to imagine what could possibly drive a wedge between them. After an evening with Michael and Lucy, it was easy to picture them forty years ahead, still together, still delighting in each other's company, still teasing each other.

And so Carol had moved into the self-contained basement flat in Tony's house and eventually Michael and Lucy had cashed in on the twenty-first-century property boom and translated the loft into their breathtaking barn conversion on the edge of the Yorkshire Dales. One of the reasons for the move had been their desire to start a family away from the pressures of city life. Tony had suspected there would be a lot more pressures, bringing up kids in the middle of nowhere, when every activity from school to play would involve a drive.

But nobody had asked him. And now they were dead. The dream of children had died with them.

The smug voice of the satnav told him to take the next turn on the right. To his surprise, they were almost there. He had no recollection of most of the drive and wondered whether that had improved his driving.

They rounded the next bend and the world changed. Instead of a rural landscape where a dozen greens shaded into grey drystone walls, they'd arrived at a destination that seemed all too urban. An assortment of liveried police vehicles, the mortuary van and several unmarked cars lined the road. A white tent extended from the rear of the house, where Tony remembered the main door was. Paradoxically, it seemed more bleak than the surrounding landscape. He braked hard to avoid hitting the nearest car and pulled in abruptly behind it.

It had taken less than an hour from BMP headquarters to the barn, but Carol looked years older. Her skin had lost its bloom, the incipient lines on her face had deepened and grown firm. A soft moan escaped from her lips. 'I so wanted to believe Blake got it wrong,' she said.

'Do you want me to go and find the SIO?' Tony said, anxious to help but not being sure how to. All the years he'd known her and now she needed him most of all, he was all at sea.

Carol drew in a deep breath and let it out slowly. 'I need to see this for myself,' she said, opening the door to a blast of chill wind.

They'd barely got out of the car when a uniformed officer with a clipboard bore down on them. 'This is a restricted area,' he said. 'You can't park here.'

Tony stepped forward. 'This is DCI Jordan. And I'm Dr Tony Hill from the Home Office. Where will we find the SIO?'

The young PC looked perplexed. Then his face cleared as he worked out the solution to his dilemma. 'ID?' he said hopefully.

Carol leaned against the car and closed her eyes. Tony took the PC by the elbow and steered him away. 'That's her brother in there. She's a DCI with Bradfield. She's entitled to every bit of courtesy you can find right now. You're not going to get into trouble for taking us to the SIO, but I will personally do my level best to make your life a fucking misery if you don't.' There was nothing conciliatory in his smile.

Before the situation could develop into a conflict, a tall cadaverous man with a prominent eyebrow ridge and a beaky prow of a nose emerged from the tent and caught sight of them. He waved and shouted, 'PC Grimshaw? Bring DCI Jordan over here.'

The weight of the world removed from his shoulders, the PC led them past the cars and into Michael and Lucy's drive. The tall man strode towards them. 'You know him?' Tony asked.

'DCI John Franklin,' Carol said. 'We worked together, sort of, on the RigMarole murders. One of the bodies was on his patch. He didn't like me. Nobody from West Yorkshire likes me. Or you either, come to that. Not after we made them look like fuckwits over Shaz Bowman.'

Franklin reached them, his trench coat flapping with the speed of his approach. 'DCI Jordan,' he said awkwardly. He had one of those Yorkshire accents that made every word feel like a bludgeon to the head. However hard he tried, sympathy was always going to elude him. 'I'm very sorry.' He looked Tony up and down. 'We've not met,' he said.

'I'm Dr Tony Hill. From the Home Office.'

Franklin's bushy eyebrows rose. 'The profiler. Whose idea was it to bring you in?'

'I'm not here in an official capacity,' Tony said. 'I'm here as a personal friend of DCI Jordan. I also knew the victims. So, if there's anything I can do to help ...'

Franklin's expression was sceptical. A scatter of rain blew across the bare grass surrounding the barn and Carol shivered.

'We've got a mobile incident room coming, but for now ... We can talk in my car.'

'I want to see them,' Carol said.

Franklin looked worried. 'I don't think that's a great idea. It's not the way you'd want to remember anybody you cared about.'

She seemed physically to gather herself together. 'I'm not a child, Mr Franklin. I've seen crime scenes that would make most officers lose their appetite for days. I've got expertise here. And I know the ground. I've got more chance of spotting something that's out of kilter than any of your officers.' She indicated Tony with a nod of her head. 'And he reads a crime scene like you read a newspaper.'

Franklin rubbed his jaw. 'You're an interested party, though. The defence would make hay with that.'

'Do you have any idea what happened here?' Tony said abruptly.

Franklin bridled. 'An intruder walked in on the couple. They were in bed, apparently having sex—'

'Making love,' Carol butted in. 'With those two, it was making love. You have no idea how much they cared about each other.' Her expression was fierce.

Franklin took a moment to rein himself in. 'As you say. He attacked them from behind and cut both of their throats.' He raised his eyes to the hills. Tony reckoned he wanted to look anywhere except at Carol. 'There's a huge amount of blood. They pretty much bled out.'

Carol turned to Tony and gripped his arm. 'It's him, isn't it?'

'I think so,' he said. 'I've thought so ever since Blake broke the news. I hoped I was wrong.'

'But you're not wrong. You're too bloody late with it, but you're not wrong.'

Franklin gave an exasperated sigh. 'Do you mind telling me what the pair of you are talking about?'

'Jacko Vance,' Carol said. 'That's who you're looking for.'

Franklin tried to keep his incredulity under control. 'Jacko Vance? He only busted out of prison down in the Midlands yesterday. How's he going to be up here? And why would Jacko Vance murder your brother and his girlfriend?'

'Because he thinks we're the reason he spent twelve years in jail,' Tony said. 'He's not big on acknowledging responsibility for his crimes. I thought he would take reprisals against the team who put him away, and his ex-wife.' He gave Carol a pleading look. 'I didn't think he would take his revenge like this.'

Franklin pulled out a pack of cigarettes and bought time by firing one up. 'So you've no evidence as such?'

'Presumably the SOCOs will find something,' Carol said. 'Now, will you let me see the scene?'

Franklin shrugged. 'I think you're barking up the wrong tree. Likely this is just a horrible coincidence.' He turned his collar up against a more brutal squall of rain. 'Come into the tent, we'll get you suited up.' He chivvied them ahead of him into the tent, shouting past them, 'Somebody find suits for the DCI and the profiler.'

As they went through the awkward scramble to get into the white paper suits, Tony tried to speak to Carol. 'Are you sure you're up to this?' he said.

'I don't want to talk about it.' She turned her back to him, pulling on a pair of bootees.

'I really don't think it's a good idea. You wouldn't let a victim's family see the body of someone they loved actually at the crime scene.'

'I'm a cop. I'm used to this.' She snapped the elastic over her foot and stood up, easing her arms into sleeves.

'You're not used to seeing someone you love like this. Let me go first, at least.'

'What – you're saying you don't care enough for it to matter to you?'

'No, of course that's not what I'm saying. This is going to give you nightmares, Carol.'

She paused and gave him a level stare. 'And what kind of nightmares do you think it will give me if I don't see it for myself? It's precisely because I know what these scenes look like that I have to see it for myself. Otherwise my imagination will fill in the blanks. And how much sleep do you think I'll get then?'

He had no answer to that. She was ready before him and she didn't wait, walking straight across the raised metal plates that indicated the route into the crime scene. Tony scrambled to catch up with her, only succeeding in falling over as he struggled with the suit. By the time he made it past the front door, she was already out of sight.

The main area of the barn looked uncannily normal. Lucy's jacket hung over the balustrade, her shoes kicked off nearby. There was a T-shirt in a crumpled heap near the table and a skirt pooled by the bottom of the stairs. Apart from the metallic and meaty stink of blood, there was no sign of violence down here.

Tony looked up the stairs and gasped at the sight. The ceiling above the gallery was splashed and streaked and puddled with bright scarlet. It looked as if someone had thrown a bucket of red paint at the roof. 'You slashed the carotids,' he said softly. He climbed the stairs, careful to stand only on the protective plates.

The scene that met him at the top of the stairs was grotesque. Michael lay on his back on a bed soaked crimson. Lucy was face down next to him, her hair a web of clotted dark red. There was a dried white streak of sperm across her lower back. Blood stained the walls, the floor and the ceiling. Carol stood at the foot of the bed, colour flooding up her neck to her face. He wanted to weep – not for Michael and Lucy, but for Carol.

'There's a photograph missing,' she said bluntly to the SOCO who was working one side of the room. 'On the wall, there. You can see the outline in the blood. It was a family photo. Michael and Lucy and me. And my mum and dad. It was taken two years ago at my cousin's wedding. Michael said it was the best photo of all of us that he'd ever seen. He got prints made for me and our parents, and he hung his copy up here where it caught the morning light.'

She turned and looked directly at Tony. Because of the mask she was wearing all he could see were her eyes, their grey-blue sparkling with unshed tears. 'Now that bastard Vance has my family photo. He's taken my brother and he's taken the picture to gloat. Either that or to make targeting my parents easier.' Her voice was rising, fury taking over from the shock that had cradled her since Blake had broken the news.

'This is your fault,' she raged at him. 'You dragged me into this in the first place. It was your fight, you and your baby pro-filers. But you dragged me into it, put me on the front line when it came to nailing Jacko Vance.'

The assault was shocking. Carol had never attacked him like this in all the years they'd known each other. They'd argued on occasion, but it had never gone nuclear like this. They'd always drawn back from the brink. Tony had always believed it was because they both understood the power they had to hurt each other. But all those barriers were gone now, torn down in the wake of what Vance had done here. 'You wanted to be involved,' he said weakly, knowing as he spoke that truth was no defence here.

'And you never tried to stop me, did you? You never thought there might be consequences for me. You never have. All the times I've ended up risking everything for you. Because you needed me.' Now the rage had a mocking edge. 'And now this. You sat there and did your fucking risk assessment yes-terday and you never once suggested that Vance might go after the people I love. Why, Tony? Did you not think I would want to know something like that? Or did it just not occur to you?'

He'd known physical pain. He'd been trussed up naked and left for dead on a concrete floor. He'd faced a killer with a pistol. But none of it hurt as much as Carol's accusations. 'It didn't—'

'Look at you. Finally, you look upset. Is that what's bothering you now?' She stepped close to him and pushed him hard in the chest, making him stumble backwards. 'The fact that you didn't predict this? Didn't work it out? That you're not as smart as you thought you were? The great Tony Hill fucked up and now my brother's dead?' She pushed him again and he had to twist away to avoid falling down the stairs. 'Because that's what's happened. You're supposed to be the one who can figure out what bastards like Vance are going to do next. But you failed.' She waved an arm at the scene on the bed. 'Look at it, Tony. Look at it till you can't close your fucking eyes without seeing it. You did that, Tony. Just as much as Jacko Vance.' Her hands balled into fists and he flinched.

'Pitiful,' she snarled at him. And turned on her heel, almost running down the stairs. Tony looked down and saw Franklin shaking his head at him. He realised everybody in the barn had stopped what they were doing to stare at him and Carol.

'Can I ask where you're going?' Franklin said, putting out a hand to slow Carol as she drew level with him.

'Somebody needs to tell my parents,' she said. 'And somebody needs to be with them to make sure Vance doesn't destroy them too.'

'Can you leave the address with Sergeant Moran over there?' He pointed to a table set up in a corner of the tent where a woman in a puffa jacket and baseball cap sat at a laptop. 'We'll ask the local lads to sit outside till you get there.'

'Thanks,' she said. 'You need to be liaising with West Mercia about the hunt for Vance too. I'll give the details of the investigating officers to Sergeant Moran.'

Tony forced himself out of his frozen state of shock and called down to her. 'Carol – wait for me.'

'You're not coming with me,' she said. Her voice was like the slam of a door. And he was on the wrong side.

32

The office was a good place not to be. The shadow of what had happened to Carol hung over them all like a pall, Chris thought as she drove down the spine of the Pennines and into Derbyshire. She sipped coffee as she drove. It had cooled to a point where anyone sampling it would have been hard pressed to say whether it was warmed-up iced coffee or left-over hot coffee. She didn't care. All she wanted it for was its capacity to keep her awake. She was beginning to feel welded into the car seat after yesterday's excursion to Kay Hallam's mansion.

In an ideal world, she'd have got her hands on a copy of Geoff Whittle's banned book about Vance the cop killer and hunkered down in a corner of the office to read it before she went head-to-head with its author. But this seemed to be one of those rare cases where 'banned and pulped' meant what it said. There was no readily available copy of *Sporting Kill*, and even if there had been, there was no time for that kind of homework. Not now that the killing had started. Nobody was blaming Vance publicly yet for the double murder of Michael Jordan and his girlfriend, but everyone in the MIT squad room knew exactly who to hold responsible.

It had taken Stacey approximately six minutes to come up with a current address and phone number for Geoff Whittle, and the information that he seldom left his Derbyshire cottage these days because he was on the waiting list for a hip replacement. Given long enough, Chris suspected Stacey could have found a version of the text online somewhere. But long enough was what she didn't have.

All these years later and still it felt personal, this pursuit of Vance. Shaz Bowman's death had changed so much about how Chris viewed herself. It had stripped away the lightness from her, turning her into a more sober and more serious person. She'd stopped looking for love in all the wrong places and made conscious decisions about how she wanted to live, rather than drifting into the next vaguely interesting thing. Working with MIT in Bradfield had offered her the chance to be the kind of copper she'd always imagined she could be. She had no idea how she was going to live up to that now.

The dull browns and greens of the Dark Peak gave way to the broken light grey and silver of the White Peak. Late lambs staggered around, coming right up to the edge of the road that curled down Winnats Pass before skittering away as the car approached. When the sun shone out here it felt like an act of God.

Castleton was a village for tourists and walkers. Chris and her partner came out this way occasionally in the winter with the dogs, enjoying the landscape when it was emptier. Already in late spring, the streets were busy with strolling visitors, stepping off the narrow pavements into the road. Chris took a right in the centre of the village and drove out along the hillside till she came to a huddle of four cottages clinging to the slope. According to Stacey, Whittle lived in the furthest.

Chris parked the car on a grassy verge already churned by tyres and walked back to the house. It was a single-storey cottage built in the local limestone. She reckoned three rooms plus kitchen and bathroom, and not a lot of light. Out here, you could make a small fortune renting out a place like this as a holiday cottage. But as a place to live full-time, Chris reckoned it had major downsides, especially if you weren't able to get about. Obviously Geoff Whittle's excursion into true crime hadn't been as profitable as he'd hoped.

On closer inspection, the cottage was less prepossessing. The paint on the window frames was flaking, weeds were sprouting between the flagstones on the path and the net curtains at the window sagged precariously. Chris raised a heavy black iron knocker and let it crash back into place.

'Coming,' a voice from inside called out. There was a long pause, some shuffling and banging, then the door inched open, the aperture limited by a heavy chain. A head topped with wiry white hair appeared in the gap, peering up through grimy glasses. 'Who are you?' the man asked in a surprisingly strong voice.

Chris flipped open her ID. 'Detective Sergeant Devine. Mr Whittle, is it?'

'Are you my police protection?' He seemed indignant. 'What's taken you so long? He's been out on the streets since yesterday and I've not had a moment's rest since I saw it on the news. And how come I heard it on the news and not from one of your lot?'

'You think Vance is after you?' Chris tried not to sound as baffled as she felt.

'Well, of course he is. My book told the truth about him for the first time. He managed to suppress it after the fact, but he swore at the time he'd get his own back on me.' He almost closed the door so he could release the chain. 'You'd better come in.'

'I'm not here to protect you,' Chris said as she followed him into a dim and cluttered kitchen that seemed to double as an office.

He stopped his lopsided slo-mo shuffle and turned to face her. 'What do you mean? If you're not here to protect me, what the hell are you here for?'

'Information,' Chris said. 'Like you said, you told the truth about him. I'm here to pick your brains.'

He gave her a shrewd look. 'Normally that would cost you. But I can sell the story all round town and make more money that way. "Police seek author's help to track jailbreak Jacko." That'll work nicely. Stick a police-budget-cuts angle on it and I might even manage to flog it to the *Guardian*. Sit down,' he said, waving vaguely at a couple of chairs tucked under a pine table. He settled into a high wooden carver at the far end of the table. 'What did you want to know?'

'Anything that might help us find Vance,' Chris said, shifting a pile of newspapers on to the floor so she could sit down. 'Who he might turn to for help. Where he might go for shelter. That sort of thing.'

Whittle rubbed his chin. Chris could hear the rasp of stubble against his fingers. 'He was a loner, Vance. Not one for mates. He relied a lot on his producer, but he popped his clogs a few years ago. The only other person he might turn to would be a bloke called Terry Gates. He's a market trader—'

'We know about Terry Gates,' Chris said.

Whittle pulled a face. Chris could see dried saliva encrusted in the corners of his downturned mouth. 'Then it's hard to say who,' he said. 'Except maybe ... ' He gave Chris a shrewd look. 'Have you considered his ex-wife?'

'I thought there was no love lost there,' Chris said, her interest suddenly quickening.

Whittle gave a throaty chuckle full of phlegm and winked. 'That's what she'd like you to believe.'

There was still nothing on the radio about his earlier exploits, which surprised Vance. He'd thought that in a world of 24/7 rolling news, someone would have leaked the double murder to a media contact. He hoped they'd taken him seriously when he'd reported it from a public phone outside the pub where he'd had lunch. It would be ironic if it had been dismissed as a crank call.

Obviously, he hadn't hung around to see for himself. He had work to do and even though he was convinced of the effectiveness of his disguise, he wasn't about to take silly chances.

After he'd finished with lovely Lucy, Vance had bundled his bloody clothes into a plastic sack. He'd taken a long hot shower, getting rid of all the traces of his victims. He'd removed the family photo from the wall as a final act intended to freak out Carol Jordan, then dressed downstairs in the clothes he'd brought with him – the trousers of a pinstripe suit and a formal shirt. He swapped the wig he'd arrived with for one that was shorter and differently styled. A better match for Patrick Gordon's ID. He walked back along the path to his car, taking care not to appear hurried or to show any signs of the elation that was pumping through him. Live with that, Carol Jordan, for the rest of your miserable life. The way he'd had to live every day with what she'd done to him, shut up in a prison where he didn't belong, surrounded by ugliness and stupidity. Let her discover what it was like to suffer. Only she wouldn't be able to break out of the prison he'd made for her.

He'd dumped the bloody clothes in an industrial skip behind a hotel near Leeds-Bradford airport before parking the Mercedes in the long-stay car park. Like so many things, the system here had changed since he'd gone inside. Now, you had to take a ticket and hang on to it, paying at some machine somewhere else. He wondered how many dim-witted parking attendants had been made redundant, and how much it had added to the sum of human happiness not to have to deal with the surly bastards.

Vance put on the suit jacket and picked up a briefcase. Then took a bus to the terminal, but instead of making for the check-in desks, he headed towards the car-rental counters. The Mercedes could have been spotted, or picked up on traffic cameras, and he wasn't taking any chances. Using the Patrick Gordon ID, he hired an anonymous Ford saloon complete with GPS and charged it to an account that ultimately wound its way back to Grand Cayman. The ease of the transaction was something else that had changed for the better. He flirted mildly with the woman behind the counter, but not so much that she'd remember him.

Within twenty minutes, he was on his way, the necessities of vengeance transferred from one vehicle to another. If everything went according to plan, he'd have completed his second act of vengeance within hours. Maybe even his third, if he had a fair wind at his back. The only question in his mind was whether he should book into a motel later, or drive all the way back to Vinton Woods. What luxury, to have such options, he thought. For too long, he'd been trapped without anything but the most basic choices, confined within someone else's rules. He had so much lost time to make up for, thanks to Carol Jordan and Tony Hill and his bitch of an ex-wife. Still, they were all going to be condemned to a lifetime of suffering. Suffering from which there could be no escape.

Vance smiled at the thought as he pulled into a petrol station. There was true satisfaction in what he was doing. When he was safely installed in his Caribbean villa or his Arabian mansion, he'd be able to look back on this and feed off the sheer pleasure of it for the rest of his life. Knowing his victims still felt the pain would just be the icing on the cake.

33

There was no question of following Carol. Tony stood help-less at the top of the stairs, flayed and gouged by her savagery. It felt as if the bond between them had been ruth-lessly severed. He was cast adrift, not least because Carol of all people knew exactly how to cause him maximum damage. She was right, too. She'd given him all her trust, taken wild risks for him, put her life on the line for him. And he'd failed.

He should have considered the bigger picture. But he'd been so sure that he remembered all that was important about Vance. He hadn't talked to the prison psychologist because he'd dismissed her professional value on the grounds that she'd let herself be seduced by his charm. That didn't mean she didn't have something valid to say. He hadn't talked to the prisoner whose place Vance had taken on the temporary release. He'd been too cocksure to think Vance's dupe would have any useful insights. He'd left it to Ambrose to do the interviews he should have sat in on, at the very least. It wasn't arrogance to believe that he'd have got more from them, just cold hard fact. And he'd let himself be distracted by Paula's desire to have Carol walk out the door in a blaze of glory. It had been a desire he shared. He'd always wanted only the best for Carol. He suspected he'd failed more often than he'd succeeded.

He stood by the stairs, gazing at the macabre spectacle, trying to make sense of what he was looking at. It had to be Vance. Tony had never had any difficulty with the notion of coincidence, but sometimes what your brain told you was happening was exactly the way it was. For this to be random was beyond the bounds of credibility.

There was, of course, another possibility. There usually was.

'Dr Hill?' Franklin was shouting his name, calling him back to the here and now.

He turned away from the scene and went downstairs. 'This wasn't about sex,' he said to Franklin, who looked incredulous.

'What do you mean, it wasn't about sex? According to the preliminary reports, he killed them when they were having sex and then, after he'd slit her throat, he fucked a dying woman.' Franklin sounded like a man who couldn't decide between anger and sarcasm. 'Can you tell me in what sense that's not about sex?'

Tony rubbed the bridge of his nose. 'Let me put it this way. Michael and Lucy have been together for ten years or so. If you were trying to catch them having sex so you could get off on killing them while they were in the act, would you choose a Friday after lunch?' Now it was Tony's turn for sarcasm. 'Would you reckon that was the best time to find them fucking each other's brains out, Chief Inspector? Is that the way it works round here?'

Franklin scowled. 'When you put it like that ...'

Tony shrugged. 'I think he just got lucky. He came here to kill them and it turned out much easier than he expected. As for the sex – he's been banged up for a dozen years. Lucy was an attractive woman. Even in death. And he turned her over, so he wouldn't have to look at her face.' He looked at the floor. 'At what he'd done to her.'

'How do you know he turned her over? She could have been on her stomach all along.'

'The blood. If she'd been on her front, the blood couldn't have sprayed as far as it did outwards and upwards.'

'Suddenly you're a blood-spatter specialist as well as a shrink.' Franklin shook his head.

'No. But I've seen a few crime scenes in my time.' Tony turned away. 'Take it or leave it, it's not about the sex.'

'So what is it about?'

Tony blinked hard, surprised at the urge towards tears. 'It's about payback. Welcome to the wonderful world of Jacko Vance, Chief Inspector.'

Franklin looked uncertain. 'You seem bloody sure of yourself, doc.'

'Who found them?'

'There was an anonymous phone call from a box in a village about fifteen minutes' drive away. The caller was a male, nothing distinctive about his accent. A local patrol car was dispatched. The door was open, our lads came in.' The corners of his mouth turned down in sympathy. 'First time for the pair of them. I doubt they'll sleep tonight. Does that tell you anything?'

'It's Vance. The one murder he did outside his serial murders had the same element of spectacle. What he did then, he's doing again, now. He's sending a message. It's targeted at a specific group of people, just like the last time. And he wants to make sure the message comes through loud and clear. He tipped you off once he was well clear of the crime scene, because he wanted it to be fresh when you got here. He wanted Carol Jordan to see the full horror of what he'd done to the people she loved.' He felt bitterness like a taste on his tongue. He'd been so slow, so stupid.

Franklin looked unconvinced. 'You don't think you're maybe bigging this up, making yourself a bit too important?

220

Maybe it's not all about you and DCI Jordan. Maybe it is just a random psycho. Or maybe it's got something to do with Lucy Bannerman. She was a criminal defence barrister, doc. It's a job where you piss people off quite regularly.' His accent thickened, giving even more weight to his words.

'To the extent where this seems like a reasonable response?' Tony jerked a thumb upwards.

'You're the psychologist. People don't always deliver ... what is it you folk call it? "A proportionate response"? Somebody she should have got off gets sent down ...' He spread his hands. 'They order it from inside. Or some toerag on the outside decides topping the brief is a way to earn brownie points.' He moved towards the tent entrance, reaching for another cigarette. Tony followed him into the open, where a light rain obscured the nearby hills. 'Alternatively, she got some bastard off – a kiddie fiddler or rapist or something where feelings run high – and some Charles Bronson vigilante weighs in to teach the system a lesson.' Franklin cupped his hands round the cigarette and lit up, taking in a deep lungful of smoke and exhaling it with a dramatic sigh.

'In all the years I've been doing this job, I've never come across the murder of a lawyer because somebody didn't like the outcome of a case. Not outside TV shows, anyway,' Tony said. 'That's pretty lame as an alternative scenario. And so's the random psycho. Random psychos tend to be sex killers. And I just explained to you why this wasn't about sex. Saying it's about Lucy's job makes about as much sense as saying it was provoked by the violence in the computer games Michael coded.'

Franklin opened his mouth to say something but he was interrupted by one of the technicians calling from inside the barn. 'Boss? You need to see this.'

'What is it?' Franklin threw his cigarette aside with an irritated air and stomped back inside. Tony followed him, figuring any chance to pick up more information about the case was worth taking.

The techie was pointing to where one of the hammer beams of the roof met the wall. A stepladder stood nearby. 'It's almost impossible to see it. I saw a tiny flash of light when I was coming down the stairs. You wouldn't see it in normal lighting, it's just because we've got the crime-scene lamps up.'

'I still can't see what you're on about,' Franklin said, screwing up his face and peering into the roof.

'I went up and had a look. It's a tiny TV camera. We need to do a full electronic sweep. But it looks like somebody's been spying on them.'

Franklin gave Tony a scornful look over his shoulder. 'So much for your theory. Vance was banged up until yesterday morning. There's no way he could be behind this.'

'You don't think so? Talk to Sergeant Ambrose at West Mercia about Vance's contacts with the outside world.'

'If it makes you any happier, doc, I'll bear all this in mind,' Franklin said, condescending. 'But I'm not putting my next month's wages on Jacko Vance.'

'We'll see whose DNA turns up in the sperm on Lucy's back.' Frustrated and fed up, Tony turned away and began to clamber out of his paper suit. There was nothing more for him here. Franklin might pretend to have an open mind, but it was a pretence. He was convinced the answer to this crime lay in Lucy Bannerman's professional life, and that would be the thrust of his investigation until the undeniable forensics came up with something more than Tony's conviction based only on experience and instinct.

He was halfway back to the road when he realised Carol had left him stranded.

34

In a little over twenty-four hours, life had been turned on its head for Micky Morgan. News of her ex-husband's escape had arrived at her farmhouse door in the shape of half a dozen cops who looked like they'd escaped from some TV crime drama. Black outfits, forage caps, stab vests and faces like slabs of granite. Micky was accustomed to being admired and it was disconcerting to have men's eyes slide off her and show more apparent interest in the layout of her kitchen and back yard. The one in charge introduced himself as Calman. She assumed it was his surname but was too discomfited to ask.

In spite of the fact that her kitchen was big enough for a dozen stable lads to sit round the table eating breakfast, the men in black seemed to fill all the available space. 'I don't understand,' Micky said. 'How did he escape?'

'I don't have much detail,' Calman said. 'Only that he impersonated another prisoner who was due to go out on day release.'

'And he was in Oakworth? Jesus, that's no distance from here.'

'It's about forty-five miles. Which is one of the reasons why we're so concerned for your safety.'

Betsy had entered from outside just in time to hear

223

Calman's response. She pulled off her riding hat and shook her head to free her hair. Her face was flushed from riding out and she looked ridiculously fresh compared to the storm troopers mooching round their kitchen. 'What's about forty-five miles?' she said, automatically going to Micky's side and putting a hand on her partner's arm.

'Oakworth Prison. Which, apparently, is where Jacko has just escaped from.' Micky flashed a look at Betsy that signalled caution. 'These officers are here to offer us protection.'

'Do we need protection?' Betsy said. 'Why would Jacko want to hurt us?'

'My orders, Ms Thorne,' Calman said.

He knows exactly what the set-up is here, Micky thought. *He's been briefed. Someone told him about the subterfuge of marriage we concocted between Jacko and me to save my TV career from the homophobic tantrums of the tabloids. Is he here to protect us or to keep an eye on us?* 'I agree with Betsy,' Micky said.

But that had been before Calman had broken the news of a double murder in Yorkshire that his bosses believe might be Vance's handiwork. This time, the officer by his side in the kitchen had a gun, a big black affair the like of which she'd never seen outside a TV screen. It screamed incongruity. H&K just didn't go with Aga. 'I don't believe Jacko would do that,' Micky said. 'Surely there are other possibilities?'

'Possibilities?' Calman said, sounding as if he'd never heard the word spoken before. 'We like to concentrate on the likely answers. Experience shows that's usually where the truth lies. We're going to be giving you blanket coverage. Both driveways will have officers on duty and we'll have other armed officers patrolling. I know you've got your lads out walking the fields. I'll be talking to them, making sure they know what the parameters for action are. I don't want you to worry, ladies. I just want you to take care.'

They'd stamped out into the yard, leaving Micky and Betsy

to stare at each other across the table. Betsy had spoken first. 'Has he called you?' she asked.

'Don't be silly,' Micky said. 'He wouldn't be so crazy. And if he was, you think I wouldn't tell you?'

Betsy's smile was strained. 'Funny old thing, loyalty.'

Micky jumped up and rounded the end of the table. She hugged Betsy close and said, 'You are the only loyalty I have. I only married him because I wanted to be with you.'

Betsy reached up and stroked Micky's hair. 'I know. But we both knew there was something off-kilter with Jacko and we chose to look the other way. I was afraid he might expect that of us again.'

'You heard Calman. They think he's coming after us, not coming for tea.' She kissed Betsy's forehead. 'They'll keep us safe.'

She couldn't see the expression on Betsy's face, which was probably just as well. 'Officer Calman and his merry men? If you say so, sweetheart. If you say so.'

The suburban street was quiet at this time of day, parking spaces easy to come by because so many were out at work. Vance drew up a couple of doors down from his target and turned off the engine. He didn't have camera feeds on this house. He'd decided it was too risky. Carol Jordan was a worthy opponent; he wasn't going to take chances with her. But his investigator had come up with invaluable information that would make Vance's next act so much easier.

He took out the tablet computer and checked the camera feeds back at the barn. As he'd expected, Jordan and Hill were there. She was climbing down the ladder from the bed gallery, leaving him behind. It was tempting to watch, but all he needed to know was that they were far enough away for him to have time for his task. He snapped a pair of nitrile gloves over his hands and smiled.

Everything he needed was in another of the lightweight nylon holdalls Terry had obtained for him. One last look round to make sure the coast was clear. Then Vance gently lifted the bag and headed up the path to Tony Hill's house. He cut round the side of the house, past the side porch that covered the stairway down to Carol Jordan's basement flat.

At the back of the house, he carefully put down the bag then moved to a small rockery in the corner. One of the stones was fake, its hollow interior containing a key to the back door. The investigator's notes had read, 'Hill is a classic absent-minded professor. He forgot his house keys on two of the five days I observed him.' *Happy days*, Vance thought as he let himself in.

He prowled through the ground floor, allowing himself a few minutes' grace to get a feel for Tony Hill, the weird little bastard who had thought he could get one over on Vance. Billy No Mates, according to the investigator. Carol Jordan seemed to be the only friend in his life. So the more he hurt Carol Jordan, the more he would hurt both of them.

Under the stairs was the door that had to lead to the basement. There were bolts on the door, but they were undone. So too was the mortice lock. The door opened to the touch. So much for the fiction that theirs was the formal relationship of landlord and tenant. These two were in and out of each other's space, as unterritorial as a flock of sparrows.

The converse never occurred to him: that here were two people who each respected the other's privacy so much they had no need for locks to enforce it.

Vance ran lightly down the stairs to Carol's domain, almost tripping over an elderly black cat who still got up to greet new arrivals in his world. 'Fuck,' Vance yelped, staggering, desperate not to drop his burden. He managed to right himself, giving his shoulders a shake.

He placed the holdall on the floor and set off on a tour of

the premises. He found what he was looking for in the tiny utility room off the hallway. On the floor, a bowl of dried cat-food and another of water. Next to them, a plastic bin half-full of dried cat-food. Vance gave a little giggle of delight. How beautiful it was when things went according to plan.

He brought the holdall through and unzipped it, closing the door behind him to keep the cat out. First he emptied the cat-food into a carrier bag. He took out a powerful coiled metal spring, held together by a plastic clip. He placed that in the bottom of the bin, attaching the clip to a sensitive mechanism connected to its rim. He took out a pair of acid-proof gauntlets and pulled them over his gloves. Then with infinite delicacy, he opened the polystyrene container in the holdall and lifted out a glass vessel. Clear oily liquid sloshed gently against the sides as he lowered it on to the spring. He removed the lid, exposing the sulphuric acid to the air. Finally, he fixed a pho-toelectric cell to the mechanism inside the bin and closed the lid.

The next time Carol Jordan opened the cat-food bin, the spring-loaded container of acid would be catapulted upwards into her face. It probably wouldn't kill her. But the acid would burn into her skin, destroying her features, leaving her disfig-ured and scarred. She would almost certainly be blinded and in hideous pain. Just the thought of it made Vance feel excited. She would suffer. God, how she would suffer.

But Tony Hill would suffer more, knowing this time he'd failed to stop Vance in his tracks. The perfect double whammy, really.

Kevin was fed up. There were, in his opinion, far too many motels near the airport. And Stacey had apparently tracked down addresses for every last one of them. There was a wide range, both in terms of cost and of facilities. Not to mention willingness to cooperate with a pushy cop at a busy time of day. It was a bastard of a chore and it pissed him off that yet again he was assigned to the scut work. He'd made one professional mistake that had cost him his inspector's rank, but that had been years ago. It seemed that he was never going to be forgiven. Maybe leaving the MIT behind would finally be the route back to promotion.

He'd split the accommodations into three rough groups. Top of the line were the budget chains, but paradoxically, their front-desk security was often questionable. They were so accustomed to turning a blind eye to groups of students and football fans trying to save money by squeezing eight people to a room that a troupe of lap dancers could have high-kicked their way from the entrance to the lifts without anyone paying attention. The killer would have found it relatively easy to check in with Suze Black without attracting attention, but getting her out might have been more of an issue.

There was one possibility, where one of the lifts went straight down to a basement car park. Kevin thought it was a long shot – there were too many elements of risk for it to fit with the care this killer took in every other aspect of his operations. But he filed it away as somewhere to come back to if he didn't make any progress elsewhere.

At the opposite end were the places that were little more than glorified guest houses. Kevin didn't even bother ringing the doorbell of those. Suze Black wouldn't have got across the threshold alive, never mind dead.

That left a tranche in the middle – privately owned, mostly struggling to keep going in a recession, mostly willing to turn a blind eye to what was going on in their rooms. But still, Kevin reckoned they would mostly also draw the line at a man dragging a dripping corpse across the foyer and out to the car park.

He was on the point of giving up when he finally struck gold. The Sunset Strip had sunk so low beneath the horizon it was hard to imagine how it had ever been a hopeful twinkle in anyone's eye. It was a two-storey building covered in peeling terracotta stucco, an irregular quadrangle sketched around parking spaces marked out in peeling whitewash. The units were like individual apartments. On the ground floor, you could practically drive right up to your door. Perfect for stashing a dead prostitute in your boot without anybody catching sight of what you were up to.

Kevin parked by the office, which occupied the first ground-floor unit on the left. The fat kid behind the counter looked barely old enough to shave, never mind drink. He had sallow skin, bumpy with subcutaneous spots and eyebrows that bristled in five directions at once. Nondescript brown hair gelled up on the top of his head made him look like a refugee from a comedy sketch show. He barely looked up from the comic book he was reading. 'Yeah?' he grunted.

Kevin flipped open his ID. It took thirty seconds for the kid to realise there was something he was supposed to be looking at. He shifted a wad of chewing gum from one cheek to the other and assumed an expression of weary boredom. 'Yeah?' again.

This was clearly not a time for small talk. 'Were you working here on the third?'

More gum shifting, a little light chewing. A hand that looked like an inflated latex glove yanked a drawer open and took out a sheet of paper marked out in boxes. He poked a finger at the third box on the top line. KH, BD, RT. 'That's me. RT. Robbie Trehearne.'

'Do you remember anything particular about that night?'

Trehearne shook his head. 'Nope.'

'Can I see the register?'

'What about a warrant? Are you not supposed to have a warrant?'

Kevin took a gamble on Robbie Trehearne being exactly as dim as he appeared to be. 'Not if you just show it to me.'

'Oh. OK.' He put the comic book down and turned the

computer monitor on the desk so Kevin could also see it. His fingers flew over the keys with surprising dexterity and a page appeared on the screen, headed with the date. Only the rooms that were occupied appeared. Six rooms were listed, accompanied by names, addresses, car registrations and means of payment. Three of the six had paid cash.

'Do you verify the information people give you when they check in?'

'Verify it how?'

'Like, do they have to show any ID? Do you check the registration matches the car?'

Trehearne looked at him as if he was an alien. 'All I'm supposed to be bothered about is if the credit card works. If they want to lie about their names and addresses, who gives a shit?'

'Yeah, why would you want to keep accurate records?' Kevin's sarcasm was lost on the kid.

'Exactly. More trouble than it's worth.'

'Can you print me a copy anyway?' Kevin said. 'Do they fill in registration cards?'

'Yeah, but we just bin them once we've put the details on the computer.' He gave a smug little smirk. 'No DNA for you tonight, Mr Copper.'

Kevin thought this was looking increasingly like the place. Anyone who'd ever been here once would know exactly how perfect the layout was and how slack their processes were. 'I know it's going to be hard for you to cast your mind back, Robbie, but do you remember any of the staff or the customers complaining about a room being wet underfoot? Or a really wet bathroom? Unusually wet.'

'That's a very fucking strange question,' Robbie complained. 'Like, bathrooms are full of water. Baths and showers and toilets and basins. They're meant to be wet, you know?'

Kevin had children. He knew that you loved them unconditionally, whatever they did or said or turned out to be. But

230

he was struggling to believe that anyone could love Robbie Trehearne. 'I said, "unusually wet",' he said, struggling to keep a grip on his patience.

Robbie excavated his ear with his index finger then inspected it. 'I don't know what night it was, OK? But when I came on duty one teatime, Karl said did I know if anything weird had gone on in number five. Because the chambermaid said all the towels were soaking wet. Like, dripping wet. And the carpet in the room was soaked through, over by the bathroom. That what you mean?'

'Yes,' Kevin said, taking another look at the screen. Room 5 had been let that night for cash to someone called Larry Geitling. The name meant nothing to him. But it was a start, at least. 'I'll need to talk to the chambermaid.'

'She comes on at six tomorrow morning.'

'Tonight?'

Trehearne giggled: a soft, unnerving sound. 'I don't know where she lives. I don't even know her second name. Buket, that's what we call her.'

Misunderstanding, Kevin frowned in disgust. 'You call her "bucket"? What? Because she's a cleaner? You can't even be bothered to use her name?'

'Boo-ket, not bucket. It's her name. She's Turkish.' Trehearne looked delighted to get one over on Kevin. 'I don't have a mobile number for her. The only way you'll get to speak to her is if you turn up when she's working. Six till twelve, that's her hours. Or you could maybe catch her at the carpet warehouse down the road. She cleans there eight till ten some nights.'

It wasn't satisfactory, but there was nothing Kevin could do about it. 'Fine,' he said. 'I'll be back. And she better be here, Robbie. Or there'll be all sorts of trouble for you and your boss.'

231

35

Vance had made six stops at service stations between Leeds and Worcester. At each one, he'd bought a plastic five-litre container and filled it with petrol. At the last one, he'd gone inside the main concourse building and bought a packet of cigarettes and a lighter. On the outskirts of Worcester, he slipped out of the heavy early evening traffic and booked into an anonymous motel. It had been a long day, and he was tired. Tired people made mistakes, but that was something Vance couldn't tolerate in himself.

The receptionist barely glanced at him, so engrossed was she in a conversation with a colleague. 'Breakfast is half past six till ten,' she intoned automatically as she handed him a plastic oblong. 'Your key works the lights, you put it in the slot by the door.' Another novelty, Vance thought.

In the room, he drew the curtains, kicked off his shoes and undressed to his Calvin Kleins. He slipped between the sheets and turned the TV on to a news channel. The double murder made the second item on the news after the latest uprising in the Arab world. No ID yet, of course. A copper with a dense Yorkshire accent talked of tragedy and lines of inquiry. In other words, Vance thought, they had absolutely nothing on

232

him. There would be forensics, of course. He hadn't bothered to cover his trail. He didn't mind them knowing he was responsible. What mattered was staying ahead of the game so he could complete his agenda before he left the country.

His own headline came towards the tail of the bulletin. He was, apparently, still on the loose after his daring jailbreak. The police officer they'd wheeled out in front of the camera looked furious to be there. He was a big guy with a shaved skull, skin the colour of strong tea and shoulders that bulged tight under his suit. He looked like he was better suited to sorting out a closing-time brawl than solving anything that needed finesse and intelligence. If that was all he had to contend with, Vance wasn't too worried about being recaptured.

He set the alarm on his phone then closed his eyes for the nap that would leave him prepared for his next act of revenge. When he woke up, it was dark outside, the night a grimy grey with low cloud blocking the sky and greasy rain on the window. Vance took out the laptop and pulled up a set of camera views. The substantial Edwardian villa still showed no sign of life. It was what he expected. The bastard who lived there had more than enough going on to keep him busy right now. But it was always better to be careful.

He wondered what was happening back at the barn. The police investigation should be well under way by now. He'd save that for later, though. He wanted to crack on with his remaining task for the day. Vance pulled on a pair of jeans and a hooded sweatshirt, then headed for the car.

The satnav was already programmed with the address, a quiet street off the main A38 overlooking the dark blank of Gheluvelt Park. He pulled straight into the gravel driveway of the house he was interested in, amused at the notion that he was currently appearing on his own camera. It was a double-fronted house in mellow red brick with the deep bay windows and imposing doorway outlined in pale cream. Heavy curtains were visible, tied back at the margins of the windows, and the garden looked well cared-for. This was a house that many would envy, Vance thought. But not for much longer.

He swung the car round so that the bonnet faced towards the street. Then he made three trips to the back of the house, taking two containers of petrol each time. Finally he brought a bundle of free newspapers he'd picked up at one of the service areas. The rear wall was crisscrossed with wooden trellis that carried clematis vines to the upper floor. That would be one ignition point.

The unscrupulous investigator Terry had hired for Vance had provided details of the alarm system. Disappointingly, he'd failed to discover the code to disable it. That wasn't the end of the world. It would just make life a little more complicated. Vance went back to the car and returned with a backpack. He peered through the windows, making sure he had the right rooms. His first choice was a living room with plenty of flammable furnishings and wooden shelves full of vinyl and CDs that would provide plenty of fodder for the fire once it had taken hold. The other was a study lined with bookcases stuffed with hardbacks and paperbacks. Again, a perfect source of fuel for the blaze.

Vance took out a plunger with a suction cup on the end and fixed it firmly to one of the small panes of glass in the study window. Then he took a glass cutter and carefully excised the pane from its frame, holding the plunger tight with the prosthesis. He edged it free, then poured two containers of petrol through the gap. He repeated the exercise at the living-room window, then threw the remaining petrol over the trellis and the fat stems of the clematis. He bunched some sheets of newspaper together, pushing them almost all the way through the window before he ignited them with the lighter. The petrol vapour by the window whooshed into flame and it spread almost instantly across the carpet.

Vance grinned in delight. He stuffed bundles of newspaper between the trellis and the plant stems, then lit those, watching long enough to be sure that the fire was going to catch. Finally, he set light to the study, enjoying the way the flames sped along the floor in the shape of the petrol splashes.

He'd have liked to stay, but it was too dangerous. He'd go back to the motel and watch the fire take hold on the cameras. He wasn't going to phone this one in. He didn't want the fire brigade to arrive too soon, and someone was bound to spot it eventually. It would take a while – the house wasn't overlooked at the back – and that suited Vance. Nothing less than complete gutting would do.

He walked briskly back to the car and drove sedately out of Tony Hill's driveway.

After her second near-miss in half an hour, Carol admitted belatedly to herself that she probably shouldn't be driving. But she'd had no choice. This was news that had to come from her. She couldn't let her parents find out from a stranger. This was her responsibility in every sense and she had to shoulder it. She pulled off the motorway at the next services and ordered hot chocolate and a blueberry muffin to raise her blood sugars and combat the state of shock that still had her in its grip.

She stirred her drink compulsively, unable to remember ever feeling this bleak. After the rape, when she'd been convinced she couldn't be a police officer any more, she'd thought it was impossible to descend any lower. But this was far worse. Before, she'd been determined to restore the damage done to her. This time, she could be as determined as she liked, but it wouldn't bring back her brother or her friend.

Carol had never needed a wide circle of friends. She'd always been content with a small group of intimates, a handful of people she could trust with everything that mattered. Michael had always been one of those; with only a couple of years between them, they'd managed a closeness denied to many siblings. When he'd got together with Lucy, Carol had been afraid that she'd lose that straightforward sharing they'd always known. She'd been afraid that she and Lucy would become competitors for his attention. At first, it had been sticky. There were always going to be jagged edges between a senior cop and a defence brief. But the more they'd seen of each other, the clearer it became that they were kindred spirits. Their professional lives were both underpinned by a desire for justice; what divided them became less important as time passed. And so Lucy had ended up as one of that close circle. And now, in one day she had lost two of the people she loved most, and sent a third into exile.

She picked at her muffin, tearing it apart with agitated fingers. She'd never been so angry with Tony. He should have seen the possibility that Vance's revenge would take as perverse a form as his previous crimes. There had never been anything straightforward about the way his mind had expressed itself. No reason to think prison would have changed that. It was obvious to her now, but she wasn't the psychologist here. It should have been obvious to Tony from the get-go.

Carol finished her drink and got back on the road. Progress was horrendously slow. Nobody would choose to drive down the M1 on a Friday night unless they had to. The traffic congealed in unpredictable clots, then suddenly the jam would disperse and everyone would hammer the pedal to the metal till they hit the next blockage. The faces that were lit up by passing headlights were frazzled, enraged or bored. Nobody looked cheerful or happy to be there.

She'd just passed the turning for Nottingham when she remembered her poor old cat, Nelson. There was no way she'd be getting home tonight, and at seventeen, Nelson was too old to be left without fresh food and water overnight. Normally, she could have asked Tony to take care of him. But right now she never wanted to speak to Tony again. There was a spare key in her desk drawer, she thought. Paula could be relied on not to snoop if she had access to Carol's flat. Once upon a time, she probably would have. Carol was pretty sure Paula had been a little bit in love with her for a long time. But being with Elinor had damped down those feelings. Now she could trust her just to feed the cat.

Wearily, she scrolled down to Paula's number on the car's computer screen and tapped the mouse. Paula answered on the second ring. 'Chief,' she said. 'We're all so sorry.' There was no doubting her sincerity.

'I know,' Carol said. 'I need you to do something for me.'

'Anything. That goes for all of us. Anything we can do to help.'

'I'm not going to make it home tonight. There's a key to my flat in my desk drawer. I need you to feed Nelson.'

There was a momentary pause. 'Just feed him?'

'Food and water. There's some cooked chicken and rice in the fridge in a plastic box. And dried food in a plastic bin on the floor.'

'Carol . . .' Paula spoke gently. Carol was taken aback. She couldn't remember Paula ever using her name.

'What?' She sounded more abrupt than she'd intended. But she didn't think she could handle kindness right now.

'The word is that Vance might have killed Michael and Lucy.'

'That's right.'

'I don't want to seem paranoid, but . . . well, I could take Nelson back to ours. You wouldn't have to worry about him then.'

For a moment Carol couldn't speak. Her throat seemed to close in a precursor to tears. 'Thank you,' she said, not sounding like herself at all.

237

'No problem. Do you have a cat carrier?'

'The cupboard under the stairs. You don't mind?'

'I'm glad there's something I can do to help. If there's anything else you need, just say. That goes for all of us,' Paula said. 'Even Sam.'

Carol almost smiled. 'I'm on my way to tell my parents. I've no idea when I'll be back. I'll talk to you soon, Paula. Thank you.'

There was nothing more to be said and Paula was smart enough to know it. Carol drove on, turning over what she knew about Vance and his history. But nothing helpful surfaced. The last time she'd felt this powerless, she'd spent months trying to find solace in the bottom of a bottle. The one thing she did know right now was that she was determined she wasn't going there again.

By the time she left the motorway, the traffic had thinned out. Her parents had retired to an Oxfordshire village a couple of years before, hoping to indulge their twin passions for gardening and bridge. Her father enjoyed watching the village cricket team and her mother had taken to the Women's Institute with puzzling glee. They'd suddenly become caricatures of middle-class middle-Englanders. Neither Carol nor Michael had grown into adults who had anything in common with their parents, and last time she'd gone to stay, Carol had run out of things to say depressingly early in the visit.

On a Friday evening, the only sign of life in the village was light. The thatched pub was spotlit, and most of the houses round the green displayed the discreet glow of lamps from behind curtains and blinds. There were few street lights, and no huddled groups of adolescents lurking beneath them. The closest anyone here came to anti-social behaviour was making too much noise when putting the empties out for the recycle truck.

Carol turned down the narrow lane that led to her parents'

house. It was the last of three, and as she pulled up outside, her headlights caught the reflective markings of a police car tucked into a gateway a little further down the lane. Carol stilled the engine and got out, waiting for the Family Liaison Officer from the car to come and check her out.

The FLO appeared to be about Carol's age, but that was where any similarity ended. She was a dumpy woman with dark hair shot through with wiry grey strands pulled back in an unflattering bun beneath her uniform hat. Her skin showed the remains of virulent acne and her eyes were set close together on either side of a sharp nose. But when she smiled, her face softened with kindness and Carol could see why she'd ended up doing a job that few officers relished. 'DCI Jordan, is it?' she said. 'I'm PC Alice Flowers. I've been on station since half past four, and nobody's been near the house. I could see the occupants moving around, so no need to worry that any-thing happened before you arrived.' She had a faint Oxfordshire burr in her voice which was as reassuring as her smile. 'I just want to say how sorry I am about your brother.'

Carol acknowledged her words with a tip of her head. 'I've never been very good at the death knock,' she said.

'That's nothing to be ashamed of,' Alice said. 'Shall we get it over with, ma'am?'

Carol reached into the car and grabbed her coat, slipping it on and turning up the collar. She gave a sharp sigh. 'Let's do it,' she said, squaring her shoulders. Please God, she could hold it together.

They walked up the flagged path between the box hedges that her father kept clipped to precisely knee-height. A wooden porch jutted over the path and Carol led the way. Alice stayed a couple of discreet steps behind her as she rang the doorbell. Silence, then a scuffle of feet, then a light snapped on over their heads.

The door opened and Carol's mother appeared, looking like

an older and less stylish version of her daughter. The look of mild curiosity on her face gave way to astonishment. 'Carol! What a surprise. You should have phoned.' She broke into a smile. Then, as she took in the expression on Carol's face and spotted the uniformed officer behind her daughter, her face froze. Her hand flew to her mouth. 'Carol?' she said, her voice unsteady. 'Carol, what's happened?'

36

Kevin plonked himself down on a corner of Paula's desk. She didn't even look up from the report she was skimming. 'What?' she said.

'The cleaner from the motel, the one who reported the wet carpet? She cleans at the carpet warehouse in the evenings. I thought I'd take a run over there and see what she's got to say. Do you fancy coming with me?'

'No,' she said. 'I've nearly finished going through these door-to-doors, then I'm going round to the chief's flat to collect her cat. He'll be starving if I leave it much longer.'

'Aw, come on, Paula,' Kevin wheedled. 'You know you're better with women than I am.'

'In every possible sense,' Chris called over from her desk.

Kevin pretended to be offended. 'At least I'm admitting it. She's Turkish, Paula. She's probably working off the books. I'll scare her. You'll get her to talk.'

Paula groaned. 'I promised I'd pick up Nelson.'

'Is Elinor in?' Chris said.

'She should be.'

'I'll do it, then,' Chris said. 'I'm going out anyway to talk to the street girls, see if any of them have seen anybody dodgy with the dead women. I'll pick up the cat and drop him off with Elinor. I'd take him back to ours, but I don't think the dogs would be very happy.'

'Problem solved, then,' Kevin said, relieved.

'There's a key to the flat in her desk drawer,' Paula said, resigned to her fate. She reached for her jacket and followed Kevin.

The carpet warehouse was as cheerless as Christmas for one. The shutters were down over the big display windows at the front, but they eventually found a small door tucked away round the side. The light that should have illuminated it had burned out, which was probably a blessing in disguise. Kevin hammered on the locked door and eventually it was opened by a skinny woman with the blue-black skin of equatorial Africa. 'What?' she said.

'We're here to talk to Buket,' Paula said.

'Nobody here,' the black woman said, shaking her head for emphasis.

'Buket works here. She's not in any trouble. We just need to talk to her.'

The woman half-turned her head. 'Not here.'

'We're from the police,' Paula said. 'No trouble, I promise. But I need to talk to her. You have to let us in.' Little white lies, the kind that just trip from a copper's tongue after enough time in the job.

The woman stepped back suddenly and let the door swing open. 'No trouble,' she said, disappearing round an array of carpets on a giant metal frame. In the distance, they could hear the motor of a vacuum cleaner. The echoing vastness of the prefabricated metal warehouse competed with the sound absorbency of so much carpet to make it hard to figure out where the noise was coming from. They did their best to follow it and finally emerged in an open area where carpet samples mounted on boards were stacked in wooden holders.

A small plump woman with a hijab was wielding an industrial cleaner with surprising energy.

Paula walked round into her eyeline and waved at her. The woman literally jumped in surprise, then fumbled with the power switch. The motor's note died away, leaving a faint resonance. 'Are you Buket?' Paula asked.

The woman's dark eyes widened and darted to each side as if seeking an escape. Kevin let her see him and gave what he hoped was a reassuring smile. 'We're not from Immigration,' he said.

'We don't care if you're here legally or if you're being paid cash in hand,' Paula said. 'We are police officers, but there's no reason to be afraid of us. Come on, let's sit down.' She pointed to a desk with a couple of customer chairs in front of it. Buket's shoulders slumped and she let herself be led to a chair. Kevin had no idea how Paula did it, but it impressed him every time she led an unwilling witness to communication.

'Are you Buket?' Paula asked gently.

'That is my name,' the woman said.

'And you also work at the Sunset Strip motel?'

Again, the darting eyes. Her olive skin seemed paler and she bit her lower lip. 'I not want trouble.'

'We're not going to cause you trouble. We want to ask you about something that happened a little while ago at the motel. OK?'

'I don't know anything,' Buket said immediately.

Paula pressed on regardless. 'One of the rooms you clean was very wet.'

Buket's face cleared, as if she'd been given the all-clear after some hideous medical procedure. 'The room was wet, yes. This is what you want to know?'

'That's right. Can you tell me about it?'

'So much water. Towels are heavy and drip everywhere. Bathroom floor is wet, big puddles. Carpet near bathroom is so

243

wet it goes—' she made a liquid, sucking sound – 'under feet. I tell manager, I not want trouble.'

'Did it look like the bath had overflowed?'

Buket frowned. 'Over . . .?'

'Too much water from the bath?'

She nodded vigorously. 'From the bath, yes. Water is clean, not dirty. Not from toilet. Nice smell.'

'Can you remember which room it was?'

'Five. I am sure.'

'And did you see the people in room five at all? Did you perhaps see them leave in the morning?'

Buket shook her head. 'I saw nobody from five. I see other people, but not from five. I leave it till last room in case sleep late, but when I go in, nobody is there.'

Paula looked at Kevin. 'Can you think of anything else to ask Buket?'

'Just her surname and address,' he said, smiling at Buket but talking soft and fast. 'We'll need to get fingerprints and DNA to eliminate her when the forensics team get stuck in to room five. Good luck with that.'

There was something about working late on a Friday night that pissed off Detective Sergeant Alvin Ambrose more than any other. It was the end of the school week, the night when the kids could stay up a bit later. He liked to take them swimming on a Friday night. It made him feel like a normal dad, the kind of bloke who did things with his kids that didn't get interrupted because of the stupid, the addicted and the drunk.

He was even more pissed off because he was stuck on his own in the CID room. Whatever Patterson's agenda was right now, it still didn't seem to include taking responsibility for the CID team he was supposed to lead. He'd walked away mid-afternoon, telling Ambrose to get on with it. Because there was so little doing, Ambrose had sent most of the team home, but on standby. Nobody knew where Vance would be spotted next or when. They had to be ready to roll at short notice when they had something definite to go at. He had officers out talking to prison staff who had been off-duty at the time of the escape, but other than that he couldn't actually think of anything constructive to do.

The worst irony of all was that, in Ambrose's experience, nothing worth working late for had ever happened on a Friday. He'd had great results over the years, spectacular arrests backed up with genuine confessions. But never on a Friday, for some reason. So there was a double resentment for Ambrose. That was before he even added on the bitterness of being at the beck and call of a bunch of mad bloody Geordies who couldn't even speak proper English.

The reason he was chained to his desk was the trickling through of results from Northumbria Police's search of Terry Gates's house and the lock-up where he stored his market-stall gear. Ambrose had wanted to go up there himself to conduct the search, but his boss had said there was no need, that the cops in Newcastle knew how to conduct a search. Which translated to, 'I don't have the budget for you to go gallivanting.'

So here he was, waiting for the next pile of nothing from the North East. So far, Terry Gates had not lived up to Tony's promise of carelessness. All of the paperwork that Northumbria Police had scanned in and emailed down to Ambrose had been connected to Gates's own finances, either private or professional. There were two computers, however. One at the lock-up, which appeared to be solely for the business, and another, more modern machine at home which showed signs of attempts to clean up its hard disk. Both were on their way by secure courier; they would be with Ambrose in the morning. He'd tried to get hold of their local forensic computer expert,

Gary Harcup, to put him on standby for the arrival of the computers, but so far Gary hadn't got back to him. The fat twat was
probably too busy playing some online game to have bothered
checking his messages. After all, it was Friday night for geeks
too.

Ambrose was wondering whether he could reasonably call
it a day when the phone rang. 'DS Ambrose,' he sighed.

'Aye, it's Robinson Davy from Newcastle here,' a voice as
deep and sonorous as Ambrose's own announced.

'Hi, Robinson.' What kind of first name was 'Robinson'
anyway? Ambrose thought it was only Americans who
indulged in the weird habit of giving people surnames for
Christian names, but it seemed to be a feature of the North
East as well. So far today, he'd spoken to a Matthewson, a
Grey and now a Robinson. Madness. 'Have you got something
for me?'

'I think we just might have, Alvin. One of my lads found a
SIM card taped under a desk drawer in the lock-up. We fired
it up, to have a look at the call record. The funny thing was,
there was no call record. It looks like it had never been used to
make calls. But one of my lasses knows her way around this
kind of thing and what she found was he'd used the calendar.
It's full of appointments – times and dates and places, mostly
down in London. There's phone numbers too, and email
addresses.'

This was the first piece of evidence that resembled anything
like a break, and Ambrose felt that quickening of interest that
usually came before a breakthrough. 'Can you transmit this
information to me? Print it out, or whatever?'

'The lass says she can upload it to the Cloud and you can
download it from there,' Davy said doubtfully. 'I haven't a clue
what she means, but she says it's easily done.'

'That's great. Just ask her to email me with the instructions
when it's ready. Thanks, Robinson, that's great work.'

Ambrose put the phone down, grinning like an idiot. It looked like the law of Friday had finally been broken. He reckoned that deserved a celebration. Maybe he had time to nip out to the pub for a quick one before the information came through from Newcastle. It wasn't as if he'd be able to do much with it tonight.

As he stood up, a uniformed PC burst into the room. He was pink-faced and eager. For a moment, Ambrose wondered if some accidental encounter had led to Vance's capture. Too often, serial killers were unmasked by chance – the Yorkshire Ripper because he'd used false plates on his car; Dennis Nilsen because the human flesh he'd flushed down the toilet had blocked the drain; Fred West because one of his kids made a joke about their sister Heather being 'under the patio'.

'You're pals with that profiler, aren't you? The one who's moved into that big house down Gheluvelt Park?' He sounded excited.

What had Tony got himself into now, Alvin wondered. He'd already had to dig his pal out of one embarrassing situation at the house. It sounded like there might be another in the pipeline. 'Tony Hill? Yeah, I know him. What's happened?'

'It's his house. It's on fire. According to the patrol car lads, it's a total inferno.' It suddenly dawned on the young cop that his glee might not be entirely appropriate. 'I thought you'd like to know, sir,' he wound up.

Ambrose hadn't known Tony Hill for long. He couldn't claim to know the man well. But one thing he understood was that, somehow, that house on Gheluvelt Park meant far more to the strange little psychologist than mere bricks and mortar. Because he counted Tony Hill as a friend, that meant Ambrose couldn't ignore the news he'd just been given. 'Bloody Friday nights,' he muttered angrily. He reached for his coat, then stopped as a terrible thought hit him.

247

He swung round and glared at the young PC. 'Was the house empty?'

His dismay was obvious. 'I – I don't know. They didn't say.'

Ambrose grimaced. Just when you thought it couldn't get any worse, it could.

37

Although she'd always known Carol lived in a basement flat beneath Tony's house, Chris had somehow expected it to be more than it was. She was accustomed to senior officers going for the biggest mortgage they could get away with in order to buy the swankiest house they could afford. Living as Carol Jordan did here in three rooms with a tiny kitchen and a shower room felt curiously temporary, as if she hadn't quite decided whether she liked Bradfield enough to stay. Back in the day, they'd been unwitting neighbours in the Barbican complex in London. Those spacious, elegant and striking apartments were the sort of backdrop a woman like Carol Jordan should have. Not this subterranean bolthole, attractive though it was.

Scolding herself for behaving like the host of some reality TV makeover show, Chris found the cat carrier under the stairs and scooped Nelson up. Once she'd wrestled him inside, she carried him upstairs and stowed him in the back of her estate car. One more trip to get his food and then they were done.

She found the chicken and rice Paula had told her about, then went through to the utility room to pick up the dried food. 'Better check there's enough,' she said under her breath, reaching out to lift the lid.

A metallic snap, then a rush of air and liquid struck her full in the face. For a moment, all Chris knew was that her face was wet. She had long enough to wonder why there was water in the cat-food bin before the searing agony hit her. Her whole face felt on fire. Her eyes were screaming nuggets of pain within a larger hurt. She tried to scream, but her lips and her mouth stung with the same smarting sting and no sound emerged. But even in the grip of the maddening pain, something told her not to rub it with her hands.

Chris fell to her knees, struggling not to let the agony take over every part of her. She backed away, managing by good luck to make it through the doorway and away from the spreading pool of acid. Now her knees and shins were starting to smart with the burn of the corrosive liquid.

Groaning, she managed to reach for her phone. Thank God it was a BlackBerry, with keys you could feel. She pressed what she thought were three nines and through the terrible insanity of pain she managed to growl the address to the operator who answered.

She could manage no more. Unconsciousness fell like a blessing and she toppled sideways to the floor.

By the time he'd picked up his car, Tony felt like he'd stumbled into a remake of *Planes, Trains and Automobiles*. Franklin had refused to give him a lift in a police car to the nearest rail station. 'My officers are investigating a double murder, not running a taxi service,' he'd grunted, turning on his heel and walking away.

Tony didn't know the address of the barn, let alone how to give proper directions, so he couldn't call a taxi, even if he'd had a number, which left him with no option but to set off on foot. It was tiring to walk long distances these days. A while back, a patient at Bradfield Moor had gone off his meds and run amok with a fire axe. Tony had stepped in to protect other staff and had ended up with a shattered knee in exchange for lives saved. His surgeon had done her best, but he'd ended up with a limp and a refusal to undergo any more surgery for as long as he could manage without it. Now his knee was stiff every morning and ached when it rained. Not that Carol would have been thinking about that today.

After a mile or so limping in the rain, he came to a marginally less narrow road and turned left, guessing that was the direction for Leeds and, ultimately, Bradfield. He stuck his thumb out and kept walking. Ten minutes later, a Land Rover pulled up. Tony climbed in, moving a reluctant Border collie in the process. The man behind the wheel wore a flat cap and brown overalls; an archetypal Dales sheep farmer. He gave Tony a quick glance before they drove off and said, 'I can take you to the next village. You can get a bus from there.'

'Thanks,' Tony said. 'Miserable day, isn't it?'

'Only if you're out in it.'

And that was the end of the conversation. He dropped Tony at a little stone bus shelter, where the timetable informed him that there would be a bus for Leeds in twenty minutes. From Leeds, it was a forty-minute train journey to Bradfield. From the station, a ten-minute cab ride to his car.

After all that time with nothing to think about but the events of the day, Tony was tempted to go to bed and pull the covers over his head and stay there. But that was no kind of answer to what ailed him. He needed to go to Worcester, for two reasons. Worcester was the heart of the search for Vance. He could work with Ambrose, analyse whatever information came into the manhunt and do what he could to help put Vance away. For good, this time.

But Worcester was also the place where he had found peace. He couldn't explain, but the house that Edmund Arthur

Blythe had left him had settled the constant restlessness that had always eaten away at him. Nowhere had ever felt like home before. And it made no sense. OK, Blythe had been his biological father. But they'd never met. Never spoken. Never communicated directly until Blythe had died and left Tony a letter and a legacy.

At first, Tony had wanted to ignore everything to do with the man who had abandoned him and his mother before he was born. Even though he was objective enough to understand that walking out on Vanessa was always going to be a strategy that had huge appeal. He'd thought that long before he knew the circumstances surrounding Blythe's decision to walk away.

Then he'd gone to take a look at the house for himself. On the face of it, this was not a house he would have chosen. It wasn't a style of architecture that particularly appealed to him. The furnishings were comfortable and matched the house, which meant they felt old-fashioned to him. The garden was meticulously planned and beautifully executed, and thus entirely beyond the capabilities of a man who hired a gardening service to mow his own patch of lawn once a fortnight.

And yet, he'd felt this house close around him like a security blanket. At some deep level, he understood it. It made no sense and it made perfect sense at one and the same time. So tonight, when the relationship at the core of his life had fractured, he wanted to be where he'd felt most whole.

So he got behind the wheel and started driving. There was no escape from the thoughts that revolved in his head. Carol was right. He was the one who was supposed to figure these things out. It wasn't as if he was lacking data. He had the burning examples of Vance's past to work with. The root of his serial murders had not been lust, it had been revenge for his loss of control over someone else, and for the future he'd lost. And that revenge had been, as this was, indirect. When he'd finally been captured and the nature of his crimes understood, someone else had ended up carrying the weight of his guilt because she was convinced that, if she hadn't thwarted him, he would never have killed. She was wrong, of course. Vance was a psychopath; at some point the world would not have bent to his will and he would have resolved it with extreme violence.

Knowing all this, he should have understood how Vance would have designed his vengeance. As he saw it, Tony, a handful of police officers and his ex-wife had wrecked his life. He'd had to live with that. Every day in jail, he'd been confronted with the life he'd lost. So for revenge to be appropriate, his enemies would have to live with loss. An eye for an eye, a tooth for a tooth. Not a day would pass now without Carol shouldering the terrible guilt of her brother's death. Vance's equation was clear: Michael and Lucy had died because of what Carol had done to him. Her arresting him had been the first step on his journey away from the life he loved. Now the first step on his journey of revenge had destroyed the people Carol loved.

How long had Vance been planning this? It had all the hallmarks of something that had been going on for months, if not years. First, he'd had to build his record of perfect behaviour in jail. That couldn't have been easy for a prisoner with such a high profile. Cons won status by fucking with big-name prisoners. Then there was the nature of his crimes. Kidnapping, raping and murdering teenage girls was bordering on nonce behaviour. To have overcome these obstacles must have taken all of Vance's charm, not to mention substantial investment inside and out.

Of course, money had never been a problem. Vance's wealth had been accumulated by legal means, so the authorities were powerless to prevent his team of financial wonder boys from playing musical chairs with his fortune. By the time the civil lawsuits against Vance had worked their way through the courts, the bulk of his fortune was safely stashed away in some offshore haven. His only remaining asset in the UK had been the converted chapel in Northumberland where he'd held his victims hostage before leaving them to die. Eventually it had been sold to a Canadian with a taste for the ghoulish and who didn't mind its macabre history. The proceeds had gone to the relatives of the dead, but it had been a fleabite compared to the wealth Vance had salted away.

So when he'd wanted money for bribes or sweeteners, there would have been channels to get that to where it needed to be. That was the obvious solution to the question of how Vance had stayed safe in jail, how he'd bought himself time and space to play the role of the perfect prisoner. Which in turn had put him in a position where he could manipulate a psychologist into putting him on a Therapeutic Community Wing.

Tony wished somebody had taken a moment to keep him posted on Vance's adventures in jail. He'd have moved heaven and earth to have him put back in the general prison population. It was an article of faith for Tony that everyone deserved a shot at redemption. But the terms of that redemption weren't constant. They shifted according to the nature of the individual; men like Vance were simply too dangerous to be allowed to take their second chances at large.

So while all this planning had been going on inside, Vance had been making his arrangements on the outside. Maybe the way to figure out how to stop him was to work out what he would have needed to put in place ahead of his escape. As he'd discussed with Ambrose, the obvious conduit for those arrangements was Terry Gates.

For a start, Vance would need a place to stay. Terry couldn't shelter him at home or anywhere connected to his business; that would be far too obvious. So there had to be somewhere else. A house, not a flat, because Vance needed to be able to come and go with as little observation as possible. Not in a city street, because there were still too many people who watched and wondered in cities, people clued into the zeitgeist who might recognise him from his TV days. Not in a village either, where his every departure and arrival would be public property. Some suburban estate, perhaps. A dormitory community where nobody knew their neighbours or cared what was going on behind closed doors. Terry would have been the straw man who did the viewing and the buying, the front for Vance's money. So they needed to dig into Terry's activities on that front.

The next question was which part of the country Vance would opt for. His prime targets were Tony, Carol and Micky, his ex-wife. Bradfield or Herefordshire. The other cops would be the second-tier targets – Bradfield again, London, Glasgow, Winchester. Tony thought Vance would avoid London, precisely because the cops might assume he'd head for somewhere he knew well. On balance, he thought Vance would hole up in the north. Somewhere near Bradfield, but not in the city itself. Somewhere close to an airport so that when the time came to get out of the country, it would be straightforward.

Tony was in no doubt that Vance planned to get out of the country. He wasn't going to attempt to build a new life on this small crowded island where most of the population had a strong memory of what he looked like. So he'd also have at least one new identity in place. He made a mental note to Ambrose to have all airports alerted to pay special attention to anyone with a prosthetic arm. With all the electronics in his state-of-the-art prosthesis, he'd drive the metal detector crazy. Vance had gone to jail before 9/11; he would have no experience of contemporary airport security, and that might just be his Achilles heel.

But if he'd thought that through, he'd be leaving on a ferry. And the north was the less obvious ferry route out of the UK. He could get to Holland or Belgium from Hull, he could go from Holyhead or Fishguard to Ireland and from there to France or Spain. Once he was on mainland Europe, he was gone.

Or he might have a separate artificial arm with no metal components. Something that looked good enough to bypass casual inspection even if it didn't actually work. Tony groaned. There were so many possibilities when you were dealing with a smart opponent.

Maybe he should leave the practicalities to Ambrose and his colleagues and focus on what he supposedly did best. Finding a way through the labyrinth of a twisted mind was his speciality. Even if he felt he'd lost the knack, he had to try. 'What's your next target, Jacko?' he asked out loud as he moved into the middle lane of the motorway, out of the line of trucks he'd been mindlessly inhabiting for the past twenty miles.

'You've been doing your research. You've given somebody a list of names. You sent them out there to pry into our lives, to find who we love so you know who to destroy for maximum impact. You got them to plant cameras so you could keep watch on your targets and pick the best moment. That's how you killed Michael and Lucy. You didn't just chance upon them making love. You were watching and waiting for an opportunity. And that was the perfect one. You could get in without them knowing, you could creep up on them and slash their throats before they knew what was happening. Having sex with Lucy as she lay dying was just the icing on the cake. It wasn't part of the plan. You just couldn't help yourself, could you, Jacko?'

The car behind him flashed its headlights and he realised his speed had dropped back to fifty. Tony tutted and put his foot down till he was back at seventy-five. 'So your spy told you Carol loved Michael and Lucy. That she spent some of her time off walking in the Dales with them. That if you wanted to make Carol suffer, that was the best way to do it. So somebody's been poking round Michael and Lucy's lives and somebody's been in that barn planting cameras.' Another area for Ambrose to look into. Maybe he'd have more luck persuading Franklin to follow a line of inquiry that included Vance. 'Bastard,' Tony muttered.

'So then we come to me,' he said. 'Who do I love? Who have I ever loved?' His face twisted in a painful grimace. 'There's only you, isn't there, Carol?' He sighed. 'I'm not much of a success when it comes to the human stuff. I love you and I'm completely crap at doing anything about it. He's not going to kill you, though. Your job is to suffer. And maybe he means Michael and Lucy to be a double whammy. You'll suffer every day, and I'll suffer because it's hurting you. And if Vance really gets lucky, it'll be too much for us and you'll drive me away. That would do it for me. That would reduce my life to a shell.' Unexpected tears welled up in his eyes and he had to swipe the back of his hand across his face. 'If your man's done his homework, Jacko, you'll know how to hurt me. Through Carol, that's the way to go.'

That left Micky. Deep in Herefordshire with the faithful Betsy, keeping her head down and breeding racehorses. That would have been Betsy's doing, he'd have put money on it. Betsy came from thoroughbred stock herself, that English county stock where women still wore tweed and cashmere and had Labradors at their heels and wondered, really wondered what the world was coming to. Tony smiled at the memory of Betsy, brown hair with strands of silver caught back in an Alice band, cheeks like Cox's Pippins, running a TV show in exactly the same way as her mother probably ran the local village. He suspected she ran Micky Morgan too. That when Micky's world had fallen apart, when TV turned its back on employing a magazine-show host whose husband was on trial for murdering teenage girls, when her millions of fans recoiled in shock, it had been Betsy who had ignored the wreckage and moved them on to the next successful thing.

The next successful thing had been the racing stud. Tony had known nothing about it till he'd seen the stories in the media that morning. But it made perfect sense. Racing circles were a law unto themselves and they were still a haven for posh girls like Betsy. Micky would have fitted right in. Good looking enough to improve the scenery, but not inclined to be a problem with the husbands. Well-mannered, personable and good company. Let's face it, Tony thought, there were plenty of people in the racing community with chequered pasts that seemed to pass without notice. Betsy had got it right again.

All of which made Betsy the obvious target for Vance's rage. Never mind that she was the one whose clever plan had facilitated his sadistic campaign of murder all those years before. It hadn't been her intention, obviously, but the *mariage blanc* she'd concocted between her own lover and a man who wanted cover had been the perfect mask for Vance. While Micky and Betsy had blithely thought the lie was for their benefit, it had instead provided a hellish alibi for a serial killer. But Vance had gone to jail and they were still together. Tony couldn't imagine that was a state of affairs Vance would be happy about.

To his surprise, the exit for Worcester was almost upon him. He left the motorway, making a note to impress on Ambrose the importance of protecting Betsy. Her death would be satisfying in itself, but it would also destroy Micky. Double whammy again, just like the last one.

Tony yawned. It had been a long and stressful day. All he wanted was to fall into bed now, but he knew he'd have to talk to Ambrose first. Never mind. He could at least make the call from a comfortable armchair with a glass of Arthur Blythe's excellent Armagnac in his hand. He turned into his street, shocked to see a trio of fire engines blocking the road ahead. Police cars were jammed around the fire engines, making it impossible to drive further. The pavements were dotted with bystanders, craning their necks for a better view of somebody else's disaster.

With a terrible sense of foreboding, Tony got out of the car. The smell and taste of smoke hit him, acrid and dense. He walked up the middle of the road, breaking into a run as he rounded the curve and saw flames spearing the sky, jets of water rising against them. The smoke was making his eyes water, but he could still make out where the fire was. He broke into a run, tears streaming down his cheeks, yelling wordlessly.

A bulky body stepped into his path, grabbing him close and tight. 'Tony,' Ambrose said. 'I'm sorry.'

Tony bared his teeth in a primitive snarl. 'Never crossed my fucking mind,' he forced out between sobs. 'Never crossed my fucking mind.' He smashed his head into Ambrose's shoulder. 'Useless bastard,' he cried. 'No use to Carol, no use to myself, no fucking use to anyone.'

38

Paula huddled over the cup of hospital coffee, shivering with shock. Kevin was sitting on the floor in the corner of the relatives' waiting room, arms round his knees, staring intently at the coarse fibres of the carpet tiles. 'I keep thinking it should have been me,' Paula said through chattering teeth.

'No, it should have been Carol,' Kevin said, his voice low and rough. 'That's who it was meant for. Her cat, her flat. Jacko Vance strikes again. Jesus Christ.'

'I know it was meant for Carol. But it was me that should have taken the bullet for her, not Chris.'

'You think she'd have been any happier about that?' Kevin said. 'She cares about you both. She cares about all of us. Just like we care about her. The only person who's got guilt on this one is Vance.'

'We don't tell Carol, OK?'

'We can't keep something like this from her. She's bound to find out. It'll be all over the media.'

'Blake said they were putting it out as an accident right now. No mention of Vance. Carol's got enough on her plate, dealing with what happened to Michael and Lucy. She can learn about this later.'

Kevin looked doubtful. 'I don't know . . .'

'Look, we'll tell Tony. See what he says. He knows her better than anyone else. He'll know whether we should tell her or not. OK?'

'OK,' Kevin conceded.

They subsided again, each lost in their own painful thoughts. After a while, Kevin said, 'Where did you say Sinead was?'

'Brussels. She'll be on the first flight she can get. It might not be till morning, though. You should go home, Kevin. One of us needs to get some sleep.'

Before he could speak, the door opened and a tall man in scrubs walked in. His skin was the colour of a manila envelope and his eyes looked as if they'd seen even more than the two cops. 'You're Christine Devine's family?' He sounded suspicious.

'Kind of,' Kevin said, scrambling to his feet to meet the doctor on his own terms. 'We're cops. We work in the same elite unit. We're like family.'

'I shouldn't talk to anyone other than immediate family or next of kin.'

'Her partner is flying back from Brussels. We're here in her place,' Paula said bleakly. 'Please, tell us how Chris is doing.'

'Her condition is very serious,' the doctor said. 'She's had sulphuric acid thrown in her face. It's a corrosive, so she has extensive burning to the skin. What makes acid burns worse than fire burns is the degree of dehydration the acid causes. Your friend's face is very badly burned. She will be extensively and permanently scarred. She has lost the sight of both eyes.'

Paula cried out, covering her mouth with her hand. Kevin reached over and gripped her shoulder tightly.

'None of that is life-threatening,' the doctor continued. 'But she has swallowed and inhaled droplets of acid and that's a much greater cause for concern. There's a risk of fluid building up in the lungs. We'll be watching very carefully over the coming days and hours. For now, we've put her in a medically induced coma. It gives her body a chance to start the recovery process. And it keeps her from having to endure the pain.'

'How long will she be like that?' Paula asked.

'It's difficult to say. A few days at least. Possibly longer.' He sighed. 'There's nothing more I can tell you. You should probably go home and get some rest. There's unlikely to be any change soon.'

He turned to leave, then looked back at them. 'Your friend is facing a long and difficult road back to anything approaching normal life. She's going to need you then a lot more than she needs you now.' The door swung shut behind him.

'Fuck,' Kevin said. 'Did you ever see that documentary about Katie Piper, the model who had acid thrown in her face?'

'No.'

'I wouldn't recommend you watch it any time soon.' His voice cracked and suddenly the room was filled with the sound of his sobs. Paula took him in her arms and together they stood in the grim little room and cried for everything that had been lost.

It wasn't the first time Carol had broken the news of a child's death. But it was definitely the worst. There was something profoundly wrong about being the one to deliver such catastrophic grief to your own parents' door. But it was still better than having a stranger play that role, even though she knew her mother would never be able to open the door to her again without remembering that terrible moment.

At the words, 'Michael's dead,' her mother had fallen into her arms. The strength had gone from Jane Jordan's body; all her power had been routed into the terrible wailing sound that issued from her mouth. Carol's father had come running from the kitchen at the sound and stood helpless, not knowing what was going on.

'Michael's dead,' Carol said again. She wondered if she'd ever be able to say it without feeling a physical ache in her chest. David Jordan staggered, grabbing at a frail hall table which tottered under his hand. Her mother was still making that hellish sound.

Carol tried to move out of the doorway but it was hard to manoeuvre. To her surprise, Alice Flowers eased her way past them in spite of her bulk, supporting Jane from behind and allowing Carol to come in and close the door. Between them they half-dragged, half-carried Jane into the living room and laid her on a sofa.

David followed them, bemused and lost. 'I don't understand,' he said. 'How can Michael be dead? I had an email from him this morning. There must be some mistake, Carol.'

'Dad, there's no mistake.' She left Alice holding her mother on the sofa and went to her father. She put her arms around him, but he was as stiff as he'd always been in the face of any emotion from the female members of his family. David had been a great dad when it came to having fun or being stuck with your maths homework. But he'd never been the one you went to in any kind of emotional state. Yet still she clung to him, dimly aware that he'd grown thin, a pale imitation of his more vigorous self. *How did that happen without me noticing it?* An endless expanse of time seemed to pass. Finally, Carol let her father go. 'I need a drink,' she said. 'We all do.'

She went to the kitchen and returned with a bottle of whisky and three tumblers. She poured a stiff measure into each glass then emptied one in a single gulp. She refilled it, then handed one to her father, who stood looking at it as if he'd never seen a drink before.

Jane had run out of steam and was leaning against Alice, a piteous expression of misery on her face. She held a hand out for the whisky and knocked it back exactly as Carol had done. 'What happened? Was it a car accident?' she said, her voice cracked and broken. 'That stupid sports car of Lucy's. I knew it was dangerous.'

Carol sat down next to the whisky. 'It wasn't a car accident, Mum. Michael was murdered. And so was Lucy.' Her voice rose at the end of the sentence and she could feel tears at the back of her throat. She'd been holding herself together all day and now she was starting to come apart. She supposed it was something to do with being with her parents. Even though she was the one taking the adult role, she couldn't help slipping into her natural position in the emotional hierarchy.

Jane shook her head. 'That can't be right, dear. Michael didn't have an enemy in the world. You must be confused.'

'I know it's hard to take in, but Carol's right.' Alice Flowers demonstrated why she was an FLO with the gentle firmness of her tone.

'What happened?' David asked abruptly, slumping down on the nearest chair. He tried to drink his whisky but it chattered against his teeth and he lowered the glass again. 'Was it a burglar? Someone trying to break in?'

Alice Flowers took over again. 'We believe someone broke in, yes. It may have been an escaped prisoner.'

Jane struggled upright, frowning. 'The one on the TV? That terrible Vance man? Him?'

'It's possible,' Alice said. 'Officers are still examining the scene. It's early days. We will keep you informed, of course.'

'Vance?' Jane turned an accusing glare on Carol. 'You arrested that man. You sent him to prison. This isn't just some random attack, is it? This is because of you and your job.'

Here it comes. Carol put her hand to her face, fingers clawing hard at her cheek. 'It's possible,' she groaned. 'He may have been looking for me.' *Or he may just have wanted to rip my heart out and roast it on the fire.* Jane looked at her with loathing and

Carol understood why. She'd have done the same thing if it had been possible.

'This is not Carol's fault, Mrs Jordan,' Alice said. 'This is the fault of the man who attacked your son and his partner.'

'She's right, Jane,' David said, his voice dull and toneless.

'Believe me, Mum, I'd have done anything for this not to happen. I'd have taken a bullet for Michael. You know that.' Carol couldn't stop the tears now. They streamed from her eyes, running down her face and dripping from her chin.

'But he's the one that's dead.' Jane folded her arms across her chest and began rocking to and fro. 'My beautiful boy. My Michael. My beautiful, beautiful boy.'

And so it had gone. Grief, recriminations, tears and whisky had circled round each other all night. Carol had finally crawled into bed just after three, so tired she could scarcely undress. Alice Flowers had promised to remain till morning, when she'd be relieved by a colleague. She understood Carol's fear that Vance might not stop at her brother.

Carol lay stiffly under the covers of a bed she'd only slept in half a dozen times. She was afraid to close her eyes, afraid of the images her mind would project if she let down her guard. In the end, exhaustion won out and she crumpled into sleep in a matter of seconds.

She woke just after eight with a dull headache and a panicky fear of the silence in the house. She lay for a few minutes trying to pull herself into some sort of shape to face the day, then dragged herself upright. She sat on the edge of the bed, head in her hands, wondering how in the name of God she could carry on with her job, her life, her parents. Alice Flowers was wrong. Michael's death was her fault. The responsibility lay squarely at her door. She had not protected him. It was as simple as that.

Knowing that, she didn't think she could stay under her parents' roof any longer. She dressed in yesterday's clothes and

265

headed downstairs. Her parents were in the living room with Alice. They appeared not to have moved. 'I need to go,' she said.

Jane barely lifted her head. Listless, she said, 'You know best. You always do.'

'Can't you stay?' David said. 'You should be here with us. You shouldn't be among strangers, not when you're grieving. We need you here, your mum and me.'

'I'll be back,' Carol said. 'But I can't settle while the man who killed Michael is free. Finding killers is what I'm best at. I can't just sit here, I'll go mad.' She crossed to her mother and gave her an awkward hug. She smelled of whisky and sour sweat, like a stranger. 'I love you, Mum.'

Jane sighed. 'I love you too, Carol.' The words felt dragged from her lips.

Carol withdrew and crouched by her father's chair. 'Take care of Mum,' she said. He patted her shoulder, nodding. 'I love you, Dad.' Then she stood up and gestured with her head to Alice.

On the doorstep, she straightened up and reached for the familiar persona of Detective Chief Inspector Carol Jordan. It felt as if it was on a very high shelf. 'I don't want them left alone,' Carol said. 'Vance is out there, taking revenge on the team that put him away. I'm not convinced he's finished with me yet. So they need to be guarded as well as supported. Is that clear?'

Alice gave her a solemn look. 'We'll take good care of them for you. Can I ask where you'll be?'

'I'm going to Worcester. That's where the search for Vance is being coordinated. That's where I need to be.' *And God help Tony Hill if he crosses my path.*

39

The marina was shrouded in morning mist, the brightly painted cabins emerging like dream boats on silvered water. The cabin roofs stretched side by side as far as the eye could see, like an angular ploughed field of black earth. Above the band of mist, the red brickwork of old china warehouses loomed, freshly cleaned and pointed as part of the process of renovation. Saved from dereliction, they'd become the New Jerusalem of the middle classes: loft apartments offering a water view. Once this had been Diglis canal basin, a thrumming focus of industry, one of the hubs in the movement of goods and raw materials around the Midlands. Now, it was Diglis Marina, a centre of leisure and pleasure. It was prettier, there was no doubt about that. And there was still a traditional pub with a skittle alley where people could sit over their real ale and pretend they'd done an honest day's work.

Tony sat on the roof of his narrowboat nursing a mug of tea. He'd never felt so bleak. Two people were dead and one was maimed because he'd failed at the one thing he was supposed to be good at. And he'd lost the only place he'd ever felt at home. All his life, he'd wanted to find somewhere he belonged. Carol Jordan had been half of that answer; the house had miraculously been the other. And now they were both gone. Carol in righteous contempt, the house razed to a shell. It had been full of things that were fodder to a fire – books, wood, paintings, fine carpets – and now they were reduced to smouldering ash.

He'd never been given to self-pity, which he reckoned was just as well, given how much there was about his life that was so pitiful. Even now, he wasn't sorry for himself. Anger was at the heart of it, with disgust running a close second. Obviously the ultimate blame lay with Vance. He was the killer, the arsonist, the wrecker of lives. But Tony should have seen what was coming. Not once but twice he'd failed to figure out what Vance would do next. It was no excuse to point to the enormity of what Vance had done, to try to hide behind the fact that his actions were off the scale of extreme. Tony was trained and paid to have insight into men like Vance, to work out what made them tick and to stop them doing what they lived for.

Most people, when they fucked up at work, it wasn't a big deal. But when he fucked up at work, it cost people their lives. He felt physically sick at the thought of Vance out there somewhere, making his next carefully planned move in his sadistic campaign. The longer this went on, the clearer it was to Tony that he'd been right about one thing at least – Vance was working to a set schedule that had been in place well before he'd made his jailbreak.

After Ambrose had dragged him away from the fire the night before, he'd made Tony sit down and drink sweet tea in the back of an ambulance. He'd stayed with him while the firefighters subdued the blaze. He'd put an arm round Tony's shoulders when the roof timbers had collapsed with a rending crash. He hadn't raised an eyebrow when Tony had laid the crime at Vance's door. And he'd made notes when Tony finally composed himself enough to run through the thoughts that had occurred to him on the drive down to Worcester.

When they'd parted on the wrong side of midnight, Ambrose had been heading for the police station to brief his team and put the wheels in motion. But there had been nothing more for Tony to do. At least he still had *Steeler*, Arthur Blythe's perfectly groomed narrowboat. It didn't fill him with peace in the way the house had, but it was better than nothing. And he'd taken some of the photographs from the house back to Bradfield, so there were still some tangible images of the man whose genes he'd inherited. Tony tried to take some comfort from this, but it didn't work. He still felt hollowed out and violated.

Then he'd got Paula's message and understood the full scope of his failure to do his job properly. Vance seemed intent on taking from them everything that mattered. There were two paths he could go down in response to that. He could give in to the pain and the loss, walk away and spend the rest of his life unfulfilled and regretful. Or he could scream, 'Fuck you!' at the heavens and get back to stopping men like Vance. Tony reminded himself that there had been years before Carol came into his life, even more years before the house had been part of him. He'd lived well enough in that wilderness. He could do it again.

Tony drained his mug and got to his feet. Like the man said, when you ain't got nothing, you got nothing to lose.

40

Aching with tiredness, raw with anguish, Paula leaned against the car bonnet and lit a cigarette. 'Can I have one?' Kevin asked. He was even paler than usual, the skin round his eyes almost greenish in tone. He looked as if he'd slept as little as she had. Sinead had shown up just after midnight and they'd stayed with her for a couple of hours, trying to offer consolation where there was none to be found. Then Paula had gone home and lain in bed staring at the ceiling, one hand cradled between both of Elinor's.

'I thought you'd stopped,' she said, handing the packet over.

'I have. But some days . . . ' Kevin shivered. Paula knew just what he meant. Some days, the most ardent non-smokers yearned for the nicotine support. He lit up with the practised air of a man who has forgotten none of the pleasures of smoking. He inhaled greedily. His shoulders dropped an inch on the exhale. 'After yesterday . . . you think you've seen it all. And then you see that.'

'That' was the contents of a cardboard box left round the back of a freezer food shop near the tower blocks at Skenby. It had been discovered just before dawn by the member of staff detailed to open up the loading bay for an early delivery. The box was about a metre long, half a metre deep and the same wide. It was sitting in the middle of the loading bay and had once held bags of oven chips. That it held something very different now was evident from the dark stains on the cardboard and the leaking pools of reddish brown liquid. The staff member, who wasn't paid enough to think, opened it up and promptly fainted, hitting his head on the concrete and knocking himself out. The delivery driver had arrived to find him still out cold, next to a box containing a dismembered body. He'd thrown up, putting the finishing touches to the contamination of the crime scene.

The first cops on the scene had called MIT directly, mostly because the top limb in the box was an arm with the word 'MINE' tattooed just above the wrist. Paula and Kevin had arrived just as the doctor was formally pronouncing the bits in the box dead. 'What have we got?' Kevin asked.

'You'll have to wait for the pathologist to give you a definitive answer,' the doctor recited. Even he looked a little pale and pinched in the grey dawn light. 'But in the absence of any other indications, I'd say you're looking at one body that's been chopped up into its component parts. There's a torso, a head, two arms, two thighs and two lower legs.'

'Jesus,' Kevin said, looking away.

'Has it been properly dismembered or just hacked apart?' Paula couldn't seem to drag her eyes away from the gruesome sight.

'For all the use that is to us these days,' Kevin said bitterly. 'All you have to do is watch that Hugh Fearnley-Whittingstall to learn amateur butchery.'

The doctor shook his head. 'This isn't even that good. At a guess – and this is just a guess, mind, and don't tell Grisha Shatalov I said so – I'd say he used something like a circular saw. The way it's gone through the bone, you can see the cutting marks.' He pointed with his pen at the top of a femur. 'That's mechanical.'

'Jesus,' Kevin said again. 'Any idea how long she's been dead?'

The doctor shrugged. 'Not long. The blood's not oozing, hypostasis is just under way. Given the temperature ... I'd say probably not much more than a couple of hours. But don't quote me, it's not my job.'

'Any ideas on cause of death?' The doctor was moving away now and Paula followed him.

'You really will have to wait for Grisha for that,' he said, making for his car.

And so she'd ended up smoking with Kevin while the crime-scene operatives did their thing with cameras and sticky tape and chemicals and the local cops went door-to-door in a bid to find a witness. It wasn't likely round here. The single-storey arcade of shops stood alone, an island in a sea of cheap housing and people struggling to keep their heads above water. Nobody would have seen anything. Not even the ones who had.

'He's ringing the changes, this one,' Kevin said.

'I was hoping Tony would come up with something helpful. But obviously he's got more pressing things on his mind.'

'Have you spoken to the DCI again?' Kevin asked.

'Nope. I hope I don't have to either. It's always hard to keep stuff from her. I'll just have to talk about the cat being safe round at ours, curled under a radiator.'

'Is that true?'

'Yes. One of the team at the scene found him in his carrier in Chris's car. Elinor came and got him.'

'I tell you, I wouldn't like to be Vance if she gets to him ahead of the pack.'

'She won't do anything to compromise the legal process,' Paula said, convinced she understood Carol far better than Kevin. 'She's all about justice. You know that.'

'Yeah, but this is her brother,' Kevin protested. 'You wouldn't be human if you didn't want to make him suffer.'

'Think about it, Kevin. Vance did this because she's the one who put him away. He hated being in jail so much that he's killed two people to get back at the person he thinks is responsible for that. And set that hideous booby trap that was designed to get her. The terrible irony is that it got Chris, who was one of the people who helped put him away before. So don't you think sending him back to jail is the best suffering she could dish out? And don't you think the chief's smart enough to have worked that out for herself?'

He finished the cigarette and ground it out under his heel. Then he turned up the collar of his jacket. 'I suppose,' he said. 'So, have you got any bright ideas about how we're going to ID this one if her prints don't come up on the database? I don't suppose we can ask one of the uniforms to take the head round with them ...' He winked at Paula. Gallows humour was what kept them sane out on the streets. You could never explain it to an outsider.

'If I thought it would speed things up, I'd do it myself.' Paula tossed her cigarette end in the gutter and took out her phone. 'So, what do you want for breakfast? I'll get Sam to pick up some filled rolls on his way over. Bacon? Sausage? Egg?'

Kevin grinned. 'Bacon for me. And plenty of tomato sauce. I love it when it oozes out the sides ...'

'Sick fuck,' Paula said, turning away just in time to see Penny Burgess bearing down on them. 'And here comes another one.'

They exchanged looks and bolted for the crime-scene margins, where the uniformed officers would effectively manage the borders. They made it just in time, leaving Penny plaintively calling their names. Paula looked back at the furious journalist and nudged Kevin in the ribs. 'No morning's a complete bust if you get to piss off the press, is it?'

Her comment somehow broke the logjam of pain they'd

been stuck in since the night before. They were so busy gig-
gling like children they completely missed Penny's shouted
question about Tony Hill's house being burned to the ground.

Ambrose was briefing his boss when Carol Jordan walked into
his squad room stony-faced and blank-eyed. DI Stuart
Patterson barely moved his head in greeting. Carol looked like
she'd be hard pressed to care less. She ignored the other officers who all paused and turned to look at the new arrival.
'Alvin,' she said, pulling out a chair by his desk. 'Vance: what's
happening?'

Startled, Ambrose looked at Patterson for guidance. The DI
carefully avoided his sergeant's eyes, taking out a packet of
chewing gum and unwrapping a stick. 'This is my operation,
DCI Jordan.'

'Really?' Carol's voice walked the line between politeness
and insult. 'So, DI Patterson, what's happening?'

'Sergeant? Perhaps you could bring DCI Jordan up to speed,
as a courtesy to a member of another force?'

Ambrose gave him a look he normally reserved for naughty
children. 'We were all appalled by what happened to your
brother and his girlfriend,' Ambrose said. 'I couldn't be more
sorry.'

'That goes for me too,' Patterson said, momentarily shamed
out of his surliness by the reminder of what Carol had lost. 'I
thought you were on compassionate leave, supporting your
parents.'

'The best support I can give my family is to work the case. I
know DCI Franklin is keeping all his options open, but I'm
convinced Vance is behind this. Which is why I'm here.'

Ambrose could only imagine the effort it was taking for
Carol to hold herself together. Some people might have condemned her for not being with her family at a time like this,
but he understood the irresistible drive to be doing something.

He also realised that it had its price. 'We've still no positive leads on where he might be,' Ambrose said.

Patterson snorted. 'We know where he bloody was last night,' he said.

Carol's eyes brightened. 'You do? Where was he?'

'Smack bang in the middle of Worcester. Right under our noses.' Patterson looked disgusted, as if a bad smell were literally under his nose.

Carol leaned forward. 'How do you know?'

'We don't know for certain,' Ambrose said, a cautionary note in his dark rumble.

Patterson rolled his eyes. 'How many other people have got that big a grudge against Tony Hill?'

Her eyes widened in shock. 'Tony? Has something happened to Tony?'

'He's OK,' Ambrose said, wishing his boss would show Carol some of the sensitivity he prided himself on. 'Well, physically OK. He's pretty upset, though. Last night, somebody burned his house to the ground.'

Carol started as if she'd been slapped. 'His house? His beautiful house? Burned down?'

Patterson nodded. 'Arson. No question about it. Petrol as accelerant. The fire started at the back of the house where it's not overlooked. By the time anyone noticed it, the fire had properly taken hold. The fire brigade had no chance of saving it.'

'That house was full of beautiful things that would go up like a Roman candle,' Carol said. She ran her hands through her hair. 'Didn't you have anyone watching it? Christ, this has got Vance written all over it.'

'That's what we thought,' Ambrose said. 'I've got a team going through the traffic cameras now, to see if we can spot what he's driving. But if he's got any sense, he'll have dumped that car and moved on to another by now.'

275

'And he'll have changed his appearance,' Carol said. 'We've got no idea what he looks like.'

The door was shouldered open at that point by a uniformed PC cradling a computer tower in his arms. Another followed him with a similar burden. 'Where d'you want these, guv?' he called to Patterson.

Patterson looked bemused. 'What are they?'

The uniform hid his impatience badly. 'Computers. Towers for desk-top machines, complete with hard drives.'

Patterson was in no mood to take cheek from a uniform. 'I can see what they are. But what are they doing here?'

'They're from Northumbria. Urgent overnight delivery. So where do you want them?'

'They're Terry Gates's computers,' Ambrose said. 'I asked for them. Tony thinks Gates isn't smart enough to have cleaned them up properly.' He pointed to a table against the wall. 'Stick them down there, would you?'

Patterson's air of discontent deepened. 'Nobody told me about this. I suppose you'll be wanting to spend a fortune on Gary Harcup now?'

Ambrose looked mutinous. 'I will when I can get hold of him. He's the expert. And we need an expert for this.'

'The Super will blow a gasket when you blow the budget on fat Gary,' Patterson said. 'It's not like he's that fast either. Vance will be on the other side of the world before Gary gets anything off those hard drives.'

Carol cleared her throat. 'Who is Gary Harcup?'

'He's our forensic computer specialist. He costs a fucking fortune, he looks like a bear and he's about as easy to deal with as a bear,' Patterson said.

'I can do better than that,' Carol said.

'You're a computer expert? Forgive me, DCI Jordan, but you don't look much like a geek to me.' Patterson could be so bloody annoying, Ambrose thought wearily.

276

Carol ignored him. 'My computer specialist, Stacey Chen, is a genius. She can do stuff that makes other geeks weep.'

'That's all very well, but she's a BMP officer, not a West Mercian.'

'She's a cop. And an expert witness. That's all that matters,' Carol said, taking out her phone. 'I can second her to you.' Her questioning look was directed at Ambrose. 'She's the best.'

'I'm not going to say no,' Ambrose said. Patterson turned away in apparent annoyance.

Carol summoned up Stacey's mobile number. 'I'll get her on the road right now.'

'Doesn't she have other stuff on? I thought you guys were looking at a serial?' Ambrose asked.

'It's a question of priorities,' Carol said. 'And right now, my team knows exactly where their priorities lie.'

41

Putting Humpty Dumpty together again required starting somewhere. So Tony turned on his computer and made himself another brew while he waited for the latest files from Bradfield to download. He sat down and opened the latest email from Paula, sent from her phone less than an hour previously. The news of a fourth victim saddened him and fed his own sense of failure, but there was no room for his personal feelings in his work. His empathy, yes, but his emotions, no.

The presentation of the body sounded even more bizarre than the last. Dismemberment wasn't as common as people thought. Professional killers did it to hinder identification. But according to Paula, all the pieces were present and intact, so that wasn't what was going on here. If Tony had been presented with this case in isolation, he could have usefully speculated about the significance of the dismemberment. It might be about exerting the ultimate literal control over a victim. 'She can't walk away if she's got no legs,' he said. Or it might be about punishment. 'She's so evil she needs to be taken apart and put together again from scratch.'

He rubbed his scalp with his fingertips. 'But that's not what's happening here,' he said. 'What he's shown us before is totally different. Of course it's about control. Serial murder is always about control. But that's not the point of this.' He threw his hands in the air. He wanted to pace but the boat was too small. 'Face it, Tony, the dismemberment could be completely meaningless. Random. The first thing that popped into his head.'

Except that was ridiculously wrong. You didn't make careful plans to go out and kill, plans that included fake number plates and baseball caps to confound the cameras, then choose a completely arbitrary murder method on the night. There was something structured going on here, even if he couldn't work out what it was. And the harder he tried to pin it down, the further out of reach it seemed.

Tony drank his tea and stared out of the porthole at the glassy water beyond, letting his thoughts drift. Whatever had been niggling at the back of his mind since the previous murder was squirming harder now, but he still couldn't nail it. Maybe the crime-scene photographs would help.

He went back to the computer and opened the file. And was reminded that sometimes the world worked the way you wanted it to. When Tony looked at the photographs in sequence, first murder to latest, the images fell into place like a jigsaw. All at once, he understood what he was looking at. It made sense and it made no sense at one and the same time.

'*Maze Man*,' he said softly. It had been an American import back in the nineties. Late-night Channel 5, watched by Tony Hill and three other people, if the ratings were anything to go by. It was a low-budget TV series about a psychological profiler who constantly referred to 'the maze of the mind' and wittered on about criminals being lost in the maze, taking wrong turnings, giving in to the soul of the Minotaur. Tony had only watched it because if he'd had a Facebook page, insomnia would be one of the hobbies he listed. That, and because the consequent rise in his blood pressure from watching something so ludicrous reminded him he was alive.

279

The unrelenting stupidity of its plots and the illogicality of the protagonist's conclusions were probably what had limited its lifespan to a single series. Chances were, it had probably been revived on some satellite channel in the middle of the night, but it had passed Tony by. However, if he was right, it had not bypassed the man who was killing sex workers in Bradfield.

Excited now, Tony googled *Maze Man* and clicked on its IMDB entry. Twenty-four episodes made in 1996, starring Larry Geitling and Joanna Duvell. Tony barely remembered her, a cookie-cutter California blonde, but Geitling's face remained fresh in his memory, all chin and cheekbones and crinkles round the sapphire blue eyes when he went thoughtful. Which happened mostly just before the commercial breaks, as Tony recalled. Geitling's name rang a vague bell, but he couldn't put his finger on it and Google didn't help.

But he knew the name was in his head for a reason. Working on the principle that anything is worth a try, he summoned up Stacey's patent case-indexing system. It trawled every document scanned or imported into a case and created a master index. He typed in 'Larry Geitling' and nearly tipped his chair over when he got a hit immediately. Larry Geitling had been the name used by the man who had checked into room five in the Sunset Strip motel, the room whose carpet and towels had been saturated with water the night Suze Black had gone missing. This was a real connection, not just the mad profiler's hunch.

He went back to Google and tracked down an episode-by-episode chronology of the series, complete with dismally low-res screenshots, all compiled by some sad bastard in Oklahoma City who was convinced *Maze Man* was the most criminally underrated show ever produced by American TV. However, Tony was grateful to him today, for this peculiar little website confirmed what had been jittering away at the back of his mind for the past few days. Impossible as it seemed, the four murders in Bradfield corresponded exactly to the crimes in the first four episodes of *Maze Man*.

He'd been absolutely right when he'd said these killings were not about lust or sex. He didn't even think they were about power. They were about something completely different. At the heart of these murders was a man who needed to kill, but not for any of the usual reasons. He wasn't killing because he wanted to watch women die, or because he hated them. The paraphernalia of the murders didn't matter to him; he hadn't been able to come up with a coherent way of killing. It was as if he was trying on different methods to see if he could find one that worked for him. He was using the TV series as a source of templates for serial murder. Tony had never encountered anything quite like this, but it made a twisted sort of sense.

So if it wasn't about the killing itself, what was the motivation for these murders? The answer had to lie with the victims, somehow. But what could it be?

In the meantime, he had something to share. He picked up his phone and called Paula. As soon as she answered, he said, 'This is going to sound really weird.'

'I was just about to call you,' Paula said.

'Have you had a break in the case?'

'No, Tony. I was going to call you because I just heard about your house and I wanted to commiserate,' she said patiently.

Sometimes Tony ran out of road when he was passing for human. He didn't know what to say, so he said nothing.

'It's what friends do,' Paula said. 'I'm really sorry about your house.'

'So am I,' he said. 'And about Carol's brother and his partner. And about Chris. How is she, by the way? Any news?'

'No change. Which they say is a good thing.'

'I wish I could do something more positive to put him back

behind bars. But I don't seem to be able to do much with Vance, so I took a look at the stuff Stacey sent me this morning.'

'I sent it, actually. Stacey's on her way to Worcester. Play your cards right, she might buy you a coffee.'

Tony was taken aback. How had he fallen this far out of the loop? 'Stacey's coming here? Why? What's happened?'

'The DCI's ordered her down to Worcester to drill into the hard drives of a couple of crappy old computers from some geezer called Terry Gates. Apparently he—'

'I know who Terry Gates is and what we're all hoping to find on the computers. I just didn't know Stacey was involved. I thought West Mercia had their own specialist.'

'Ambrose couldn't get hold of him. Anyway, the chief decided—'

'You said that before. How is Carol involved? I thought she was at her parents' place?'

'According to Stacey, she's at West Mercia HQ, calling the shots. Sort of picking up the reins a bit early, you could say.'

The knowledge was like a weight in his chest. He knew Carol would believe she was capable of running an investigation, but he didn't think she was. She needed time and space to process what had happened and its implications. If she didn't do that, when the inevitable crash came, she would fall hard and she would fall far. He'd seen that happen to her before and he didn't know if he could bear it a second time, not when he bore a large share of the responsibility. 'Great,' he said heavily. 'I don't suppose anybody's had the bottle to tell her to back off?'

Paula snorted. 'Like that's going to happen.'

'She shouldn't be doing this.'

There was a long pause. Then Paula said, 'So, was there a reason why you were calling me?'

'Are you old enough to remember a TV series called *Maze Man*?'

'I don't know. Am I? Because I don't remember it.'

'It was on Channel 5.'

'I don't think I've ever knowingly watched Channel 5.'

Tony chuckled. 'You're such a snob. Anyway, they only made one series. It was about a profiler and a cop—'

'Sounds familiar. Was she blonde?'

'You're not funny, Paula. Anyway, it was pretty crap. But I watched most of it because it was so bad it made me feel like a profiling genius. But here's the thing. These four murders you've got – they're identical to the murder methods in the first four episodes of *Maze Man*.'

'Are you sure?'

'I'm sure. Strangulation. Drowning in a bath and dumping the body in a canal. Inverted crucifixion and throat cutting. And dismemberment and delivery in a cardboard box. And the clincher is this: He's using the name of the actor who played the hero, the psychologist. Larry Geitling. That's who he checked into the motel as, right?'

'Jesus. That's sick.'

'I'm sending you a link to a website. Some guy in Bumfuck, Nowhere USA is a *Maze Man* nut and he's catalogued every episode. Actually, now I think about it ... maybe you should talk to him, see if he's in contact with any other *Maze Man* anoraks. Because our killer has to be another *Maze Man* nut. The series has never been released on DVD or video, as far as I can make out. Our guy must have taped it back in 1997. He must still have it.'

'Or maybe his video recorder just chewed up the tapes and he's decided to recreate it for himself.'

'Have I ever told you how much I hate cop humour?' Tony said. 'Listen, Paula, this is really interesting. Serial killers do what they do because something in the process, the shape of how they do it, the act itself – something pushes their hot button. They mutilate breasts because they have issues with femininity. They rape with knives because they have issues with sexual potency. They put out eyes because they have issues with being spied on. Whatever. But this guy – he doesn't have a hot button. Or at least, he hasn't found it yet. It's like he's working his way through a list of murder methods, trying them out for size. Does this one fit? Does this give me a rush?'

'What? You mean, he wants to be a serial killer, but he doesn't know what to do to enjoy it?'

'Kind of, yes. Either that or each time he's been so disgusted he's had to find another way to do it next time.' Now he was pacing. Three steps one way, wheel, three steps the other way. 'There's a reason why he's killing. But it's not the killing itself. He's sending a message with the tattoo, he's saying, "Look at me, these are MY achievements." Paula, if he could find another way to achieve his goal, a way that didn't involve killing, he would.'

'That's a hell of a strange profile, Tony.'

'I know. And worst of all, I don't see how it takes you any further forward in terms of nailing this guy.'

'Back in the old days, you'd be right,' Paula said. 'But your suggestion that he might be in touch with the *Maze Man* geek – that's a cracking idea. Chances are, they'll have a forum or a weblist or some such nonsense. Or even a set-up that captures all the visitors to the site. Stacey's going to love this – something to get her teeth into at last, instead of just being a clearing house for Northern's data. Soon as we get her back, she can get stuck in. Tony, I knew I was right to drag you into this.'

'The way I feel this morning, it's me who should be thanking you. It's good to have a distraction to stop me from throwing myself in the canal.'

'You don't mean that,' she said awkwardly, not entirely comfortable at being in such personal territory with Tony. It wasn't the sort of area where their friendship normally went.

'Of course I don't,' he lied.

'So if you're right about *Maze Man*, what's the next murder in the sequence?'

Tony cleared his throat. 'She'll be flayed. Her face will be untouched, but her body will be flayed.'

Paula felt faintly sick. 'What I love about this job,' she said. 'Always something to look forward to.'

42

Carol knew she was being a pain in the arse to Ambrose and Patterson but she didn't care. Their opinion of her was a poor second to tracking down Vance. Ambrose had printed out the list of Terry Gates's diary appointments and given it to her. 'I've put one of my best lads on this, but we're not getting very far because it's a Saturday and nobody's answering their office phones,' he'd said. 'I thought you might like to take a look, see if it kicked up any ideas.'

She thought he was just trying to keep her out of his way, but she didn't care. She was just grateful for something to do. Carol couldn't cope with inactivity. It was that quality, rather than her inability to deal with her parents' grief and blame, that had brought her to Worcester in the first place. Now, left with time on her hands, she wouldn't be able to avoid thinking about Michael. And that would lead straight to the bottle. This time, she really didn't want to go down that route. She didn't want to become the disaster in her own life. She didn't know whether she'd be able to find her way back a second time.

So she started on the list. She soon realised it could be broken down into three separate trips to London and one to

Manchester. The first London visit consisted of three appointments. There were phone numbers, addresses and initials for
all three. Patterson had reluctantly set her up with a phone
and a computer and she started with a visit to Google, which
led her to a company that provided a directory of office tenants throughout London. Two of the addresses appeared on
the site, with full lists of the buildings' tenants, but the third
drew a blank.

Both of the companies she'd tracked immediately also had
websites. They specialised in providing off-the-shelf companies
in countries whose financial regulatory systems were less than
transparent. Carol printed out the scant information on each
and put them to one side.

She rang the number attached to the third appointment of
the day and found herself listening to the recorded message of
the City of Westminster Archives Centre. Curious now, she
accessed their website. Halfway down the list of site contents,
she saw what she thought might have been a likely target for
Gates – General Register Office Indexes. If Vance was building
new identities, he'd need ID. In the bad old days, a criminal
looking to construct a new identity only had to go to St
Catherine's House or, later, the Family History Centre in
Islington, where the records of births, marriages and deaths
were kept. There, they could find the death certificate of
someone around the same age as them, preferably one who
had died as a baby or a young child. From there, they could
backtrack to the birth certificate and then order a copy of it.

Armed with a birth certificate, other layers of genuine ID
could be built up. Driver's licence. Passport. Utility bills. Bank
accounts. Credit cards. And there was a whole new identity
that would pass muster in an airport or a ferry terminal.

But terrorism had closed many of those doors, making it all
a lot harder. The certificates were kept away from public gaze.
All that was available were skeleton details, attached to an

index number that you had to have before you could order the certificate itself. It took a lot more time and patience to set the scam in motion, and it left a paper trail. Carol quickly typed out a suggested action for Monday morning and forwarded it to Ambrose. Some lucky sod was going to have to get on to the General Register and find out whether Terry Gates had commissioned any birth, marriage or death certificates. That would at least provide a starting point for possible aliases for Vance.

Of course, these days nobody bothered with the slow patient layering of a real ID. Forgery had become so sophisticated that providing the forger with a name, a date of birth and a photograph was enough for them to come up with a whole suite of documents that looked entirely authentic. But you still had to have a genuine starting place in case anyone checked. Carol would have bet a month's salary that Terry Gates had gone to the Westminster index to find a plausible ID for Jacko Vance. Maybe even more than one.

Checking details like the ones on Terry Gates's SIM card was infinitely quicker and easier, thanks to the resources of the Internet and the databases the police could access. A few years back, what Carol achieved inside a couple of hours would have taken several detectives days of footslogging and questioning people who operated on the fringes of the law. Even though the only human being she'd managed to talk to was an old mate on the Fraud squad, she had a pretty clear idea of what Terry Gates had been doing. Company formation, ID documents, private banks, a private investigations firm that was definitely dodgy and an ex-solicitor who specialised in crawling through the Land Registry to sell property information to scummy tabloid hacks. It pointed to two distinct operations. The first was to create new IDs and set up conduits for Vance to be reconnected with his money. The second goal was clearly directed at tracing and tracking other individuals. Presumably Vance's vengeance targets. A bunch of detectives were going to be very busy indeed come Monday morning if they hadn't found Vance by then. At least by that time they would have a clearer idea of the extent of the payback Vance had planned.

She'd almost finished a detailed note for Patterson when Stacey Chen walked in. She looked like she'd stepped out of the pages of a weekend supplement with her perfectly coordinated designer leisurewear and a Henk case. Carol knew, because she'd googled it, that the sleek black carbon-fibre carry-on cost more than ten grand. There was a time when she'd wondered whether Stacey was on the take. Then she'd done a bit more digging and discovered that just one of the software applications Stacey had developed in her spare time had made her over a million a year for the past five years.

Carol had once asked Stacey why she bothered with the day job. 'What I do at work – if I did it as a private citizen, I'd be arrested. I like having a licence to dig around in other people's data,' she'd said. She'd also thrown a quick expressionless glance at Sam Evans, which was an answer of a different kind.

Stacey spotted her and headed over. 'Thanks for coming,' Carol said.

'It sounds a lot more interesting than the Bradfield cases,' Stacey said. 'So far, that's just been routine processing. Though Paula has come up with something that definitely has data-mining prospects.'

'Really?' Bradfield had slipped off Carol's radar completely in the past twenty-four hours. Stacey's comment reminded her that she had responsibilities elsewhere. 'She hasn't said anything to me.'

Stacey's face gave nothing away. 'We all thought you had enough on your plate. And it's such a weird idea, Paula wanted to check it out before she made a big deal out of it.'

'So what is it?' Anything to distract her, even if it was a case that felt a million miles away.

'There's been another body, did you know about that?'

Carol shook her head. 'Someone should have told me that, at least.'

Stacey gave Carol a quick run-down on the case. 'Because this was so distinctive, so bizarre, the connection was indisputable,' she concluded. 'There was an obscure American TV series in the late nineties called *Maze Man,* and these killings mirror the murders in the first four episodes. And there's a fan site run by a guy in Oklahoma. Paula was going to call him to see if he had any contact with other fans in the UK, but I told her he might clam up. These anoraks are often very protective of each other, they see themselves as lone heroes standing up against the tide.' She raised her eyebrows. 'Us being the tide, in this case. Weirdos. Anyway, I suggested I take a look at the site first. They might have a forum, or a visitors' book, or a Twitter feed that I can raid. I'll poke about and see what I can find.' She smiled, dissolving her sternness. 'There's always a back door.'

'Very interesting. And Paula came up with this all by herself?'

Stacey busied herself with the Henk, hefting it on to a desk and opening it. 'Apparently.'

With anyone else, Carol would have written this off as displacement activity. With Stacey, it was hard to be sure. Still, her instincts said there was something a little off in Stacey's account. 'Would I be crazy if I said it sounds a lot like the way Tony's mind works?'

Stacey gave her a look. 'Paula's a big fan, you know that. Maybe his way has rubbed off on her.'

Carol knew the brick wall of loyalty when she ran into it. 'Terry Gates's computers are over there.' She pointed to the table. 'See what you can do with them. Don't ignore the Bradfield cases either. His cycle is definitely speeding up.'

Stacey shrugged. 'I can set programs running on the Gates

hardware and work the Oklahoma stuff while I'm waiting for results. With luck, I'll have something for you later today. If not, tomorrow.'

Stacey's reassuring competence was exactly what Carol needed right then. It was good to know somebody was on top of things. But if Tony Hill was interfering with the Bradfield cases, she wanted to know. Her brother's murder had demonstrated that Tony wasn't the operator he used to be. The way she felt right now, she didn't think she could ever work with him again. And the last thing she wanted was to be blindsided by him. 'Thanks, Stacey,' she said vaguely, already looking for Ambrose and the answer to her next question. Where exactly was Tony Hill?

43

If Vance had needed any support for his conviction that his programme of retribution was the right thing, he would have pointed to his deep and dreamless sleep. No nightmares troubled him, no tossing and turning, no staring at the ceiling praying for unconsciousness. After he'd done his work at Tony's, he'd brought a Chinese takeaway back to his hotel room and surfed the news channels till he felt sleepy. It wasn't just that he was interested in seeing how his own exploits were reported; he'd been away from full access to the media for a long time, and he was interested to see how it had developed while he'd been gone.

He couldn't help feeling a twinge of regret. He'd have been a perfect fit for this multimedia universe. Twitter and Facebook and the like would have suited him much better than a lot of those idiots who basked in the public's adoration these days. Something else Carol Jordan and Tony Hill and his bitch of an ex-wife had robbed him of. Maybe he should set up a Twitter account to taunt the police with. Vanceontherun, he could call himself. It was tempting, but he'd have to pass. If he'd learned one thing behind bars, it was that everything you did in cyberspace left a trail. He had enough on his plate without the elaborate covering of his tracks that would be involved in thumbing his electronic nose at the authorities. Enough that they knew he was out there and doing his thing.

It was mid-morning when he woke, and he was gratified to find a selection of photographs of the fire on a local news website. Arson was apparently suspected. Well, duh. There was no mention of Vance, and whoever had written the report hadn't bothered to find out anything more about 'the owner, Dr Tony Hill' who wasn't available for comment. One thing made Vance's antennae twitch. In the background of one shot, he could see the distinctive head of the cop who'd been on TV talking about his escape. Polished dark skull, watchful eyes, a face that looked like it had encountered a few fists over the years. And here he was at the fire.

Someone was making the right connections. Which was fine by Vance. They could connect the dots as much as they liked, but he was always going to be one step ahead. Take right now, for example. The safest place in the country for him was Worcester. Because they'd be convinced he was long gone. This was the one place they wouldn't be keeping an eye out for him. He could have walked through the Cathedral Plaza shopping mall without raising an eyebrow. The idea made him laugh with delight.

But safe though he was here, he had no intention of hanging around. He had places to go, people to see. And none of it was going to be pretty. But first, he had to put his final preparations in place. He paid a visit to his cameras. The barn was dead; presumably the police had found a camera and swept for the others. That was why the cameras at Tony Hill's house and Micky's farm were on the outside – the police would be looking in all the wrong places. It seemed he'd been right again.

Vance checked out the suite of images from the stud farm in Herefordshire where his treacherous ex-wife and her lover had created their new lives. He'd done Micky and Petsy a huge favour when he'd married Micky. The rumour and gossip that had swirled around Micky was hindering her ascent to the very pinnacle of TV presenting. That had died a death when they'd tied the knot. Obviously she must be straight, for why would Vance marry a lesbian when he could have had his pick of beautiful, sexy women? Cynics tried to shoot the line that Vance was also gay. But nobody believed that. He had a heterosexual track record and never a whisper that he swung both ways.

Of course, the marriage had been a sham. What Micky got out of it had been clear from the start, and she'd been so keen to accept the benefits that she'd chosen not to question his excuse for wanting it. He'd spun her a line about wanting protection from the fans who stalked him, convinced her that what he liked was the no-strings contract between himself and the high-class hookers he used for sex, and promised her he would never embarrass her with some tacky encounter with a kiss-and-tell nobody. That was easier to believe than the truth – that he wanted cover for his other life as a serial abductor and killer of teenage girls. Not that he had ever shared that truth with Micky.

He'd kept to his side of the deal. He expected her to stick to her end of the arrangement in return. But as soon as things got sticky, instead of providing the alibis he needed, she'd washed her hands faster than Pilate. There was nothing that infuriated Vance more than people who didn't honour their debts. He always kept his word. The only time he'd promised and failed to deliver was when he swore to the British people that he would bring home an Olympic gold medal. But they hadn't seen it as a let-down, because the reason had been so heroic.

He wished they'd been able to understand his other actions in the same light. He'd done what he had to do. It might not have been the reaction most people would understand, but he wasn't most people. He was Jacko Vance and he was exceptional. Which meant he was an exception, outside the petty rules the rest of them had to live by. They needed the rules. They couldn't function without them. But he could. And he did.

Vance checked out the images one by one, watching them intently, zooming in where he could. The shape of the protection that was in place soon became clear. The police were staking out the road approaches to the farm in both directions. The drive was still blocked by a horse box. A police Land Rover stood at the entrance to the back drive, three officers visible inside it. Two pairs of officers in the forage caps of firearms officers patrolled the perimeter of the house itself, their Heckler and Koch automatics carried at port arms.

It looked like the yard itself was being protected by the stable hands, a group of men who appeared to have been manufactured out of pipe cleaners, wire and plasticine. A couple of them had shotguns broken over their arms. What interested Vance was that they all dressed in variations of the same outfit. Flat caps, waxed or quilted jackets, jeans and riding boots. The cops didn't look twice when one of them walked out of the house and headed for the stable block. Or vice versa.

Which would have been interesting if he'd been aiming to get inside the house. But his plans were very different. And from the looks of this set-up, eminently likely to be successful. Vance showered and dressed and checked out with half an hour to spare. Nothing to attract attention.

He left the car on a side street a short distance from the car-hire firm where Patrick Gordon had already booked today's vehicle, the kind of SUV that fitted in perfectly in the countryside. It had, as he had specified, a tow ball. He drove back to the previous car, retrieved his petrol cans, laptop bag and holdalls from the boot, and set off for Herefordshire. He had one stop to make on the way, but he had plenty of time. It was a lovely day, he realised as he left Worcester behind.

Time to make the most of it.

As usual when he was thinking, time had slipped past Tony without him noticing. He'd only realised how late it was when his stomach rumbled in protest at having missed out on breakfast and lunch. There were various tins and packets in the cupboards in the galley, but he couldn't be bothered cooking at the best of times and today didn't qualify as one of those. So he locked up and went ashore. He considered the pub but rejected the idea. He wasn't ready for other people, not even strangers.

A few redbrick streets away, he found the perfect solution in a corner chippie. He hurried back to *Steeler* with a fragrant parcel of cod and chips so hot it nipped his fingertips. The prospect of something good to eat reminded him to hold on to the idea that not everything was shit.

He turned on to the pontoon where his boat was moored and stopped in his tracks. A familiar figure was standing on *Steeler*'s stern, leaning against the cabin with arms folded, thick blonde hair ruffled by the wind. For a moment his spirits lifted, grabbing at the possibility of a reconciliation. Then he made a proper assessment of her body language and accepted Carol wasn't here to bury the hatchet and explore how they could best move forward together against Vance.

If that was the case, he had to wonder what she was here for. Standing staring wasn't going to answer that question. Warily, as if fearing a physical attack, Tony walked down the pontoon till he was level with the boat. 'There's probably enough for two,' he said.

Carol took the olive branch and snapped it across her knee. 'I'm not planning on staying long enough to share a meal,' she said.

He'd never got anywhere with Carol by being conciliatory. 'Please yourself,' he said. 'But I need to eat.' He stepped on board and glared at her till she moved to one side so he could unlock the door and clamber below. He'd left her with no option but to follow him if she wanted to talk.

He pulled a plate out of the rack and unwrapped his fish and chips, tipping them on to the plate. As she came gingerly down the steps, he backed into the main cabin and shoved his papers and laptop to one side so he could eat. He pulled a can of Coke out of his coat pocket and set it beside his plate. 'Some would say this is more my style than what I've just lost,' he said.

'I heard about the house,' Carol said. 'I'm sorry.'

'Me too. I know it's trivial compared to Michael and Lucy, but it still hurts. So I have paid a little for my stupidity.' He tried not to sound bitter. He could see from the narrowing of her eyes that he'd failed.

'I didn't come here to beat you up for letting them down.' She leaned against the galley, arms folded, her pain obvious. So many times he'd imagined her here, daring to indulge little fantasies of them going out for a run on the narrowboat like normal people did. Who was he kidding? They weren't normal, either of them. Even if they got out of this alive, they weren't going to turn into the kind of pensioners who pottered around the canal system painting kettles with castles and roses and discussing which pub on the Cheshire Ring did the best steak pies.

Tony popped a chip in his mouth and gasped as the hot potato burned his mouth. 'Wah! That's hot!' He chewed it, mouth open, till it was cool enough to swallow. 'Sorry.' Hapless grin, little shrug. Who did he think he was kidding? He'd never had the kind of charm to get out of trouble, least of all with Carol. 'So why did you come and find me?'

She took a couple of steps forward and woke the laptop

from its sleep, picking up the scribbled notes that sat beside it. The screen faded up, revealing a crime-scene photo of a cardboard box open to reveal dismembered limbs. She read aloud. '"*Maze Man*. 1996. One season on HBO. Based on novel by Canadian James Sarrono. Website www.maze-man.com. Facebook? Twitter?" And lots more of the same. What the fuck is all this about?'

He considered lying. Considered claiming he'd pressured Paula for the information because he wanted to try to make it up to Carol. But that was pitiful and one of the things he'd decided in the course of the long night was that he was going to try to do better than pitiful in future. 'Your team loves you. They don't want you to go. And the only thing they can think of to give you as a leaving present is a result. So even though they know you're opposed in principle to me working for nothing, and even though they've probably worked out by now that I have to carry the can for your brother's death – in spite of that, they asked me to help. Because they think I can help. And I think I have.' He gestured at the papers in her hand. 'I came up with *Maze Man*.'

'That's your idea of investigative help? A tenuous connection to an obscure TV series that isn't even available on DVD? What kind of use is that, even if it's real and not just wishful thinking?' Her fury burned bright. Tony didn't think it had much to do with the Bradfield killings. In normal circumstances, she'd have gone with rueful irritation and given Paula an ear-bashing later. This was anger of a different order.

He took his time, breaking off a piece of fish and eating it. 'The crime scenes are virtually identical. The killer used the name of the star to book a motel room where he probably drowned his second victim. There's a website which seems to have about a dozen people regularly posting on its forum. If one of them lives in Bradfield, he could be your killer. Or he could know your killer. It's better than nothing, which is what your team had got until I suggested this.'

Carol slammed the papers down on the table. 'How can you be bothered with this? How can you give a shit about some weird fuck killing prostitutes when Jacko Vance is out there? You're in his sights, just like I am. You should be working with Ambrose and Patterson, trying to find Vance, not fucking about here with something that is none of your business.' She was shouting now, her voice shaking with tears he knew she would do anything to avoid shedding. 'Clearly you don't care about me, but don't you care about yourself?'

Tony stared defiantly at her. 'Actually, you've got that the wrong way round. I probably don't care enough about myself, but I really do care about you. And Vance knows that. That's probably why Chris is in hospital right now.' Even as the words crossed his lips, he cursed his own stupidity.

Carol looked as if he'd slapped her. 'Chris is in hospital? This is the first I've heard about it. What the hell happened to her?'

Tony couldn't meet her eye. 'She went to fetch Nelson instead of Paula. Vance got into your flat and booby-trapped the cat-food bin. She got a face full of sulphuric acid.'

'Oh my God,' Carol said faintly. 'That was meant for me.'

'Yes. I think it was. To make you suffer more and to make me suffer too.'

'What— How is she?'

'Not good.' There was no easy way round the truth now he'd opened the door on it. 'She's lost the sight of both eyes, her face is terribly burned and they're scared about her lungs. She's in a medical coma to keep her stable and pain-free.' He reached out for her but she flinched away. 'We didn't tell you because we thought you had enough to contend with.'

'Christ,' she said. 'This just gets worse. What are you doing now? Why aren't you working on Vance?'

'I've already given Alvin all the help I can. He knows where I am if he needs me.' He felt himself choking up and cleared his throat. 'I can't work miracles, Carol.'

'I used to think you could,' she said, her face crumpling. She bit her lip and turned away from him.

Tony's mouth smiled but the rest of his face didn't follow its lead. 'You can fool some of the people some of the time ... I'm sorry, Carol. I really am. If it makes you feel any safer, I think he's going to go for hurting Micky next. That probably means Betsy's the one at risk. Alvin's done a big production number with the local police, they've got armed protection at their place.' He poked his food with his finger, appetite gone. 'I don't know what else we can do. And yes. I'm bloody terrified of what he's got planned.'

'Ironic, isn't it? We're protecting the woman who enabled Vance's criminal career all those years. Their fake marriage facilitated him abducting and imprisoning and torturing and raping and killing young women. And you and me, the ones who stopped him, we're the ones who have lost. She's going to walk away unscathed again,' Carol said, anger taking over. 'It's so unfair.' She slumped into the big leather swivel chair opposite him, running out of energy at last.

'I know. But at least you're safe here.'

'What do you mean?'

'I don't think he knows about this place. I think he's had someone investigating our lives, watching where we go and what we do and who we see. Those hidden cameras in the barn—'

'What hidden cameras? Why wasn't I told about this?' She managed to summon up her last reserves of outrage. 'And how the hell did you know?'

'The techs discovered them while I was still there. Didn't Franklin tell you?'

'Franklin tells me about as much as you do, as it turns out.'

Tony let it go. He'd never wanted to fight with her in the first place. 'Anyway, I don't think he knows about the boat. I haven't been here in ages. Saul from the pub keeps an eye on her for me. And when I came down here last night, Alvin got one of the techs to sweep it for me. No cameras, no bugs. So I think it's off Vance's radar. It's a safe house.'

'He was watching them?'

'He picked his moment. When they were least likely to notice him walking right up to them.'

'Bastard,' she said. She closed her eyes and dropped her head in her hands.

'There's a cabin up front,' Tony said. 'Nice bed. Arthur liked his comforts. You could catch a couple of hours' kip before you actually fall over.'

She shook herself, stood up and promptly sat down again. 'Whoa. Haven't got my sea legs yet. Thanks but I need to—'

'You don't need to be anywhere. Your team in Bradfield know how to run an operation. Alvin Ambrose and Stuart Patterson need some space to prove themselves to you before you're really their boss. If they do need you for anything, someone will call you.' He'd never tried harder to make her trust him. Even if it was only until she was awake again, it was worth the effort.

Carol looked around, considering. 'What about you? You look like shit. Did you sleep last night?'

'I never sleep,' he said. 'Why would one more night make any difference?' It wasn't strictly true. The terrible sleep patterns of most of his adult life had succumbed to the calm of Arthur Blythe's house. It was one of the reasons he'd loved it so much. But he'd never told anyone, and he couldn't tell her now. It would feel too much like a desperate reach for pity. 'Go and sleep, Carol. You can fall out with me all over again when you wake up.'

'That's true,' she said. But she didn't argue. He watched her walk the few feet to the fore cabin, his heart as heavy as it had ever been. He couldn't escape the conviction that there was something very final going on between them.

44

You could hire anything in coalition Britain, Vance thought. It used to be that everything was for sale. Now, it seemed, everything was for rent. If you couldn't afford to own it, you could at least pretend you could. And thanks to the Internet, you could find the person who wanted to meet your needs.

By late afternoon, he had a quad bike on a trailer attached to his SUV. From the same farm shop he'd bought a massive sack of specialist stud feed cubes. How ironic was that, a pair of lesbians running a racing stud? At least it made dressing the part easier. He'd also bought a quilted green gilet, a lambswool sweater, a tweed cap and a pair of riding boots. He was all set.

Two miles from Micky's farm, he pulled off the minor road on to a track that led through a patch of woodland. Once he was out of sight of the road, he unloaded the quad bike then unhitched the trailer and turned the SUV round, ready for a quick getaway. He changed into his disguise, trimming his moustache into a narrow toothbrush and replacing his Patrick Gordon glasses with a pair of goggles. He loaded the sack of feed nuts on to the back of the quad bike, on top of his fire kit, and started it up.

He drove down the road for about a mile then, as he'd

memorised from maps and Google Earth, he pulled into a farm gateway on the right. He bounced across a wide expanse of cropped grass, glad that there hadn't been much rain lately. On the far side was another gate, which led to a field where half a dozen horses looked up uncuriously as he skirted the edge of their pasture. Now he could see Micky's farm, the house just visible beyond the stable block and the hay barn.

Vance could feel his heart pounding as he approached. He was taking far more of a risk than he enjoyed. But he was determined to make Micky pay for what she'd done to him. He'd thought of leaving her alone for a while. Wait till the police got tired of keeping an eye on her. Let her fear and fret for months, never knowing when he'd come for her. There would be a certain satisfaction in that. But what he wanted more than that was to get away clean and free. He didn't want to have to come back to the UK once he'd left. He wanted to be done with his retribution. Pay the bills and walk away.

So here he was, motoring towards Micky's perfect bloody life. He hoped she was enjoying this last evening of peace.

As the shadows lengthened, he made his way through the final gate and drove towards the barn. One of the stable lads came round the end of the block as he approached and flagged him down. 'Micky asked me to drop off these stud nuts,' Vance said casually, his accent as upper crust as he could make it. 'What's going on? The place is bloody crawling with police.'

'You know that bloke Vance that's escaped from prison? Him that's on the run?' He sounded Irish, which was perfect. He couldn't know all the neighbouring landowners the way a local would. 'He's Micky's ex. He's threatened her with all sorts, apparently.'

Vance gave a low whistle. 'That's hard luck. Tough on Micky. And on Betsy too, poor old thing. Anyway, I better stick these in the barn like I said I would.'

The lad frowned. 'That's not our usual brand.'

'I know. I've been having awfully good results with them. Real improvements in condition. I said I'd drop them round so she could give them a try.' He gave a rueful smile. 'Promised to do it yesterday, but I've been running around like a headless chicken.' The lad moved to one side and Vance put the bike in gear and moved forward.

The hay barn was an old-fashioned wooden barn that backed on to the stable block. On one side were bales of straw, on the other, sacks and bales of fodder. Vance couldn't have been less interested. He motored down to the far end of the barn and turned the bike round before he dismounted. He pulled the feed off the bike, then started work.

Vance dragged one of the straw bales closer to the back of the barn so that it acted as a bridge between the wooden wall and the stack of bales. Then he propped it up on the wall so there was a wedge-shaped space underneath. He poured the petrol over the straw, then he packed the empty space with foam chips. Finally, he lit half a dozen cigarettes and stuck them into the foam. If the arsonist he'd cultivated in jail had told him the truth, the foam would smoulder for a while, then the petrol vapours would ignite the straw. The barn was a fire-trap, and the fire would spread into the roof of the stables, bringing the roof down on the terrified horses.

The only downside was that he wouldn't be around to see it. Hiding in plain sight was a lot harder in rural Herefordshire than it was in a city like Worcester. Vance climbed back on the bike and headed back the way he'd come. This time, nobody stopped him. The stable lad he'd spoken to before actually waved.

People were so easy to fool. The quickness of the hand deceived the eye, every time. He hadn't lost any of his magic. As Micky was about to find out.

45

Paula was sitting in Stacey's seat, having been left in nominal charge of the MIT's computer systems. Stacey had left her with dire injunctions about what not to interfere with. Paula might be willing to chance her arm by going round Carol Jordan, but she knew better than to try the same stunt with Stacey. So three of the six screens were off limits to her. They were processing information constantly but she had no idea what it was about or whether there were any results the team should know. Stacey had assured her that she would monitor the system remotely, which was fine by Paula.

But the remaining screens were her business. The investigation on the ground in Northern Division fed all its data into their computers and that was immediately shared with MIT. Of course, that presumed that Northern were uploading everything that crossed their paths and not making false assumptions about prioritising. She also hoped there weren't any numpties who thought they could make a name for themselves by hugging their interview product close to their chest so they could pursue their own leads instead of pooling them. Sam had tendencies in that direction, and the last few years had demonstrated that you could only go so far in eliminating the Lone Ranger streak.

So she'd been the one who learned that the fourth victim had been identified. This time, the killer had been a little less thorough in his precautions and he'd ditched the victim's handbag in a litter bin just round the corner from the body dump. Paula called up the images of the bag, and saw a stained, beaded pouch with a long thin strap. The contents were arranged next to it: a dozen condoms, a purse containing £77, a lipstick, and a mobile phone. A sad full stop to a life, Paula thought.

The phone was registered to Maria Demchak at an address in the Skenby area. Preliminary inquiries – whatever that meant, Paula thought sceptically – had her down as an illegal from Ukraine, probably trafficked, living in a terraced house with a dozen other young women under the protection of a former professional boxer who was married to an ex-lap dancer who happened to be Russian.

'This is interesting,' she said. Kevin Matthews, the only officer remaining in the squad room, came over for a look. 'This one seems to have had a pimp.'

'He's getting bolder,' Kevin said. 'His first three were loners. Nobody looking out for them when they were out working. But a pimp keeps an eye on his assets. This bastard thinks he's invincible. Maybe that's the way we'll bring him down.'

'I hope you're right. He's getting careless too. We didn't find any ID or handbags with the other three. Tony said he might be keeping them as souvenirs.'

'I tell you, this was a really public way to deliver the fourth victim,' Kevin said. 'Every single person who shops in that arcade is going to get the full SP on all the gory details. It's not just going to be Penny Burgess baying for blood. This is going to go national. No, never mind national. It's going to go international, like Ipswich a couple of years ago.' He chuckled. 'I was on holiday in Spain when that was going on. You should have heard the Spanish newsreaders trying to get their tongues round Ipswich. I tell you, never mind Vance. We're going to be front and centre all over the world.'

'The chief's not going to like that.'

'She's not here. She won't have a say. It'll be Pete Reekie calling the shots on the press conference for this one, and I don't think he'll hold back now. Face it, Paula, we're going to be under siege from the reptiles of Her Majesty's press tomorrow. And we have got the square root of fuck all to give them.'

Right on cue, Stacey's desk phone rang. Both reached for it but Paula was faster. 'DC McIntyre,' she said.

'It's Stacey.'

'Hi, Stacey. We've got an ID for number four—'

'I know, I told you I'd monitor the case traffic. I've got something for you from the Oklahoma website.'

Paula grinned and gave Kevin a thumbs-up. 'You are a genius, Stacey. Have you got a name for us?'

'I've got a starting point,' Stacey said repressively. 'There's nobody from the UK among the forum posters. But I found a back door into the site and managed to pull up the email archive. About a year ago, an email arrived, which is now in the system inbox on my number one screen. I'm in the process of tracking down the sender, I'll forward those details on soon as.'

'Thanks. How's it going down there? How's the chief holding up?'

'I'm too busy for this, Paula. I'll give you relevant information when I have it.' And the line went dead.

'All the social skills of a hermit crab,' Kevin said.

'I thought she was getting better, but I'm just going to have to face it: that girl is never going to hold down a seat at gossip central. Let's see what she's got for us.' Paula was already opening the email. She pulled it up to fill the screen and read, 'Hi, Maze Man man. Love your site. I am a Brit, nobody over here seems to remember the show. I have the whole set on video, but they're getting a bit worn out. Do you know any-body in England who has a set I could copy? All the best, MAZE MAN FAN.'

A note from Stacey followed. 'See reply: "Sorry, MMF, no Brits come by here. Good luck with your search." See email address: am data-mining for Kerry Fletcher on my system. More later.'

Paula turned and gave Kevin a high five. 'It's a start,' she said.

'It's more than that. It's a name. A solid lead, which we have been seriously lacking on this case so far. Let's see if we can get this whole thing wrapped up before the guv'nor comes back from Worcester.' He shook his head. 'Bloody Worcester. I'd barely heard of the place six months ago. Now I can't turn round without falling over it.'

Paula's mobile rang and she looked at the caller ID screen then pulled a face. 'I'll tell you one good thing about Worcester,' she said. 'Penny bloody Burgess doesn't work there.'

Tendrils of smoke spiralled upwards, melding into one before separating into gauzy wisps that dissolved into the ever-thickening air. Yellow and red pinpricks bloomed on individual strands of straw, blossoming into tiny flames that mostly sput-tered and died. But some survived, bursting into flame like a kernel of corn popped in a pan. They crackled and spat, trans-forming the straws into conduits of fire, carrying the blaze upwards and outwards.

The blaze grew exponentially, doubling its reach in minutes, then seconds, till the pile of bales at the back of the barn was a wall of flame, clouds of smoke trapped to thicken under the roof. Tongues of fire licked at the wooden roof beams, spread-ing along their length like water spilled on a flat surface. At that point, nobody had noticed what was happening.

It was the roof beams that were the bridge into the stable

block itself. They extended into the roof space of the stable so the two buildings could offer each other mutual support, strengthening both in the process. The fire crept along the sturdy joists, delayed but not defeated by the mortar that was supposed to seal their passage into the stable block.

The horses smelled the smoke before the humans did. Uneasy, they stamped and snorted in their stalls, heads tossing and eyes rolling. A grey mare kicked the walls of her loose box, whinnying high and loud, the whites of her eyes stark against the black rims of her eyelids. When the first spears of flame penetrated the floor of the hayloft above the horses, unease shifted closer to panic. Hooves clattered and foam flecked the corners of their mouths.

By now, the fire was moving fast, finding flammable material in its path; wood, hay and straw succumbed quickly. Terrified horses screamed and kicked the wooden doors of their stalls. Even though stable lads were out and about, patrolling in defence of their bosses, by the time anyone caught on to what was happening, the fire was in the driving seat.

The first lad on the scene, Johnny Fitzgerald, opened the nearest stable door on a scene from hell. Horses with rivers of flame running down their backs reared and screamed, their flailing hooves wild weapons against any would-be rescuer.

Johnny didn't care. Shouting, 'Fire! Fire! Call the fire brigade!' he ran towards the chestnut mare with the white mask that he'd ridden out on that very morning, pausing only to grab a rope halter coiled on a hook by the door. Falier's Friend was one of his favourites, a gentle-tempered mare who was transformed by the sight of National Hunt fences into a speeding bullet of desire to be at the front of the field. Lowering his voice, Johnny approached, talking constantly in a monotone. The horse remained on all four hooves, head swinging from side to side, eyes rolling, snorting and whistling as gouts of flame landed on her back and ran down her side to the ground, where they created fresh rivers of fire. The heat was tremendous, searing Johnny's nose and throat as he moved forward. The noise of the horses and the fire tore at his heart, fear and pity surging through him. He loved these beasts, and it felt like there was no way out of this without death putting in an appearance.

Johnny wasted no time in getting close enough to toss the halter over the horse's head and throw back the bolt on the stall door. 'Come on, my lovely girl,' Johnny said. Falier's Friend needed no encouragement. She lunged towards the opening, almost sweeping Johnny from his feet as they both headed out into the yard.

By now, there was a frenzy of activity. The fire's grip was concentrated at one end of the block, and all around, stable lads and police protection officers were doing what they could to stop it spreading and to rescue the horses. Johnny spent a few valuable seconds trying to calm the chestnut mare, then handed the rope to a cop. He pulled off his sweater and dunked it in a trough of water, then swathed his head in it before he went back in.

If it had been bad before, it was hellish now. He could barely stand the heat as he forced himself forward towards the next horse. Midnight Dancer, a black beauty whose condition was the envy of every yard in the area. Now her glossy dark flanks were dulled with smoke and ash and sweat, her screaming whinny a knife that went through Johnny's smoke-dulled brain. He burned his hand on the hook that held the nearest halter, but he managed to hold on to the rope.

Lassoing the horse was almost impossible. Tossing head, flashing teeth, twitching ears all made her a treacherous target. Johnny swore softly, trying to make his curses sound like endearments. All at once he was aware of a figure beside him. Through the dense black smoke, he made out the familiar face of Betsy Thorne, his boss and mentor. 'I've got water,' she shouted. 'I'll throw it at her, try to shock her, you get the halter on her.' It was hard to decipher her words over the crackle of flame, the clatter of hooves and the cacophony of squeals and screams, but Johnny got the gist.

Betsy threw the bucket of water at Midnight Dancer and for a split second, the horse was still. Johnny wasted no time and threw the halter. It caught on the horse's ears, then slithered down the back of her neck. As Betsy reached for the bolt on the door, there was a loud crack, then a screeching creak. They both looked up as one of the heavy oak joists came away from the roof, a massive flaming missile headed straight for them.

Without pause, Johnny dropped the halter rope and threw himself at Betsy, his slight weight enough to shove her out of the path of the falling beam. Scrambling to her feet, she turned to see Johnny and Midnight Dancer both fatally pinned beneath the still-burning rafter. At the sound of another creak overhead, Betsy swiftly clambered over the dead lad and the beam towards the pale rectangle of the door.

As she stumbled into the yard, Micky swept her into her arms. Betsy pulled away, hot vomit surging from her stomach and splattering the herringbone brick of the yard. Tears were running down her face, and not just from the smoke. As she steadied herself, one hand on the cool wall of a building not on fire, the fire brigade's engines swung into the yard, splashing blue light on the scarlet flames shooting through the roof.

Betsy panted, legs suddenly weak. So this was what it felt like when Jacko Vance came after your peace of mind. At the thought, she was sick all over again.

46

The boat rocked and Tony's heart leapt in his chest. Only the impact of a human body had that effect. He tried to scramble to his feet, but the space between the bench seat and the table was too tight. Panicked, he scrabbled for purchase with his feet then nearly wept with relief when he heard Ambrose calling, 'OK if I come down?'

'For fuck's sake,' Tony said. 'You nearly gave me a heart attack.'

Ambrose appeared, legs first. 'You need to get yourself a doorbell. Or one of those brass bells like some of them have got. Be a proper water person.' He looked around, taking in the laptop and the scattered papers. 'DCI Jordan was looking for you,' he said. 'I told her you were probably here.'

'Thanks,' Tony said. 'Did I mention she thinks her brother's murder is my fault?'

'Ah,' said Ambrose. 'She didn't say anything. I thought . . .'

'Any day before yesterday, you would have thought right.'

'So where has she gone?'

Tony gestured towards the bows with his head. 'She's having a kip.'

Ambrose smiled the weary smile of a married man who

knows how these things go. 'So you sorted things out, then?'

Tony shook his head, trying not to show how upset he was. 'Armed truce, I think you'd have to call it. Exhaustion in a points victory over rage.'

'At least she's talking to you.'

'I'm not sure that's a plus,' Tony said wryly. He was spared any further explanation by the opening of the cabin door.

Looking slightly smudged and tousled, Carol appeared. 'Does this place have— Oh, Sergeant Ambrose. I had no idea you were here.'

'Just arrived, ma'am. I hoped I'd find you here. I've got an update for you both,' he said, all serious business now his next boss was in the room.

'In a minute,' Carol said. 'Tony, what do you do for a loo here?'

'The door on the left,' he said, pointing right. Carol gave him a pissed-off look and disappeared into the head. 'It's actually a proper bathroom,' he said to Ambrose. 'She'll be impressed.'

Ambrose looked doubtful. 'If you say so.'

'This update – it's not good, is it? I can tell by the way you were avoiding looking at either of us.'

Ambrose glared at him. 'You know better than to ask.' He looked around the galley appreciatively. 'This is lovely, this. I'd love a boat. Me and the wife and the kids, we'd properly enjoy ourselves with one of these.'

'Really?' Tony tried not to sound bemused.

'Yeah. What's not to like? Your own boss, no traffic jams, take things easy, but you've still got your home comforts around you.'

'You could borrow it, you know.' Tony waved an expansive hand in the air. 'I hardly use it. You might as well.'

'You mean it?'

'Sure. Trust me, Alvin. This is not going to be my home. I'm only here right now because I realised this morning that it's safer than Bradfield.'

Carol emerged in time to hear the last phrase. She'd managed to smooth out the crumples and looked fresh and alert. 'I wish you'd thought about safety a bit sooner,' she said, before giving Ambrose the full wattage of a welcoming smile. Tony wondered how she could find the energy to keep lashing out at him. 'So, Sergeant. What have you got that's too important for a phone call?'

The corner of Ambrose's mouth quirked in something that might have been a smile. 'To be honest, I needed to get out of the building. There's a kind of energy that builds up when an inquiry isn't going the way you want. It's not a good energy, and sometimes you just got to get out of it. I need to get my mojo back. So I took the opportunity to bring you the latest news myself.' He sighed. 'It's not good, I'm afraid, though it's a lot less bad than it could have been.'

'Micky?' Tony asked. 'Has he gone for her? Is she OK? Is Betsy OK?'

Ambrose nodded. 'They're both fine.'

'What happened, Sergeant?' Carol cut in, cool and firm, back in full professional command of herself.

'Vance got through the security cordon.' He shook his head in amazement. 'He was on a quad bike with a bag of stallion stud nuts, whatever they are. Dressed like one of the local landed gentry. One of the stable lads stopped him, but he gave some convincing load of tosh about having promised Micky to drop off this special feed. Drove straight into the barn and set a slow-burning fire. Then drove off on this bloody quad bike in full view of the cops. He was out of sight by the time the barn went up.'

'Was anyone injured?'

'A stable lad died trying to save Betsy Thorne. She nearly

got hit by a falling beam. Would have, if it hadn't been for the dead lad knocking her clear. A couple of the stable lads have minor burns, apparently. They think the real target was the stable block itself. He was going for the horses.' Ambrose looked apologetic. 'Like Tony said: he's going for what matters to his victims. So they have to live with the consequences of what they did to him.'

Carol's face froze in a rigid mask.

'What happened to the horses?' Tony asked. It was the first thing that came to mind.

'Two dead, the rest were either out in the fields or else rescued by the stable lads. They were incredibly brave, according to the officers on the ground.'

'And they didn't catch him? He just drove away on his quad bike,' said Carol, exasperated and angry.

'They found the quad bike in a wood nearby. Along with a trailer. From the tyre tracks, it looks like he was driving an SUV. West Midlands have already got details of the trailer-hire place, they're hoping to find out what he's driving. But it's Saturday evening and there's nobody there, so God knows when that'll pay off.'

'He wasn't driving an SUV last night, was he?' Tony asked. 'One of your people told me one of the neighbours saw a Ford saloon in the driveway before the fire started.'

'Yeah, we've backtracked on the traffic cameras and we think that's what he was driving. No clear shots of him, though. And we lose him about a mile away from yours. He must have cut through side streets, away from the main roads.'

'So he dumped that car and hired an SUV,' Carol said. 'Have you checked all the car-hire places in the area? He had to make the swap somewhere, and he wouldn't have wanted to drive the Ford any longer than he had to. It was tainted, it had to go.'

316

Ambrose looked startled. 'I don't think we've done that yet,' he said, sounding worried. So he should, Tony thought.

Carol fixed him with a cold blue stare. 'You're really not used to this scale of operation, are you, Sergeant? Not had much experience of coordinating manhunts down here in West Mercia? Struggling with first principles, are you?'

'We only just found out about the SUV before I left the office,' Ambrose said. 'I expect it's been actioned by now. But I don't know, because I've not been there. We're not incompetent, ma'am.'

'No. I'm sure you're not.' Carol sighed. 'Is it me, or does it seem to you that Micky's got off very lightly in all of this? Compared to me, and Tony? And Chris, of course, who got what was meant for me.'

'What's your point?' Tony said, butting in before Ambrose could say something she'd flay him for.

She blinked hard, screwing up her eyes. 'She was his enabler for years. Old habits die hard. Isn't that what you're always telling us, Tony? What if this fire was just Vance throwing dust in our eyes? What if Terry Gates wasn't Vance's only helper on the outside?'

47

Even on a Saturday evening, Heathrow was still so busy that only the security staff paid any attention to the customers. Nobody wondered why a man with dark hair, brown eyes behind glasses, and a moustache might re-emerge from the men's toilets with dark blond hair in a completely different style, bright blue eyes and no facial hair. For now, Patrick Gordon was back in his box, replaced by Mark Curran, company director from Notting Hill.

He'd left the SUV in the long-stay lot and within half an hour he was behind the wheel of another Ford, a silver Focus estate this time, Bruce Springsteen's Greatest Hits blasting out of the speakers. Better days, indeed. Tonight he was going to sleep in his own bed, back in Vinton Woods. He might even take a day off tomorrow. Even the Lord rested on the seventh day. He had more acts of vengeance to perform, more spectacular deaths to orchestrate and deliver. Then it would be time to shake the dust of this old, tired country from his heels. He'd originally thought the Caribbean would fit the bill for his new life. But the Arab world was the crucible of change right now. A man of means could live very well in a city like Dubai or Jeddah. There were places in the Gulf where life was still cheap, where a man could exercise his appetites without interference, as long as the price was right. More importantly, these places had no extradition arrangements with the UK. And everyone spoke English. So he'd covered his bases and bought a property in each region.

Vance could almost feel the warmth on his skin. It was time he took what was rightfully his. He'd worked hard for his success. All those years of pretence, hiding his contempt for all the insignificant people he'd had to be nice to, acting like he was one of them. The common touch, that's what they said he had. As if. The only common touch he'd wanted was the one where he got to slap them senseless.

Prison had almost been a relief. Of course he still had to present a facade to the authorities. But there were plenty of opportunities behind bars to strip off all the false faces and let people see the real Jacko Vance in the full rawness of his power. He loved that moment when so-called hard men realised he wasn't the pushover they'd assumed; the way their eyes widened and their mouths tightened in fear when it dawned on them that they were dealing with someone who had no limits. Not in the way that they understood limits. Yes, prison had been the perfect place to hone his skills.

But now it was time to leave all that behind him and start a new life where he could focus on the good bits. As he drove through the dark he turned over to the radio news channel for the on-the-hour bulletin. The news of his attack on Micky's stud should have hit the headlines by now. The headlines bypassed him in a blur of noise: Arab street protests, coalition cuts, prostitute murder in Bradfield. Then the item he was waiting for.

'The racing stud farm of former TV star Micky Morgan was targeted in an arson attack this evening. A stable lad died in the inferno, while trying to rescue horses from the blazing stables. Two horses were also killed in the fire, which started in a hay barn. But prompt action by the stable staff meant the remaining fifteen thoroughbred racehorses were rescued. The building itself was extensively damaged. Police refused to comment on whether the attack was connected to the escape from prison this week of Ms Morgan's ex-husband, the former athlete and TV presenter Jacko Vance. But a source close to Ms Morgan said, "We've been holding our breath, waiting for that evil man to strike out at Micky. To attack defenceless horses is as low as it gets." More on this story in our next bulletin on the half-hour.'

Vance slammed his hand down on the steering wheel, making the car swerve, provoking a blare of the horn from behind. 'Two horses and a stable lad?' he shouted. 'Two fucking horses and a poxy stable lad? All that risk, all that preparation for two fucking horses and a stable lad?' It wasn't enough. It wasn't nearly enough. It wasn't even Micky who loved the horses, it was Betsy. He'd wanted the stables obliterated, Betsy's second life destroyed, Micky impotent when it came to taking the pain away. The arsonist whose information he'd relied on had got it wrong. Either that or the greasy, greedy bastard had deliberately lied to him.

Rage flooded his body, raising his temperature and making him feel caged inside the car. Vance took the first exit and parked in a lay-by. He got out of the car and started kicking the plastic rubbish bin, swearing at the night. All the tension that had kept him going during the preparation for the attack on Micky's farm exploded in a sudden rush of violence. 'Bitch, bitch, bitch,' he shouted into the sky.

Finally, he exhausted himself and staggered back against the car, a tide of angry misery still engulfing him. What he'd planned, that would have been enough. He'd have been satisfied with that. But she'd managed to get one over on

320

him yet again. He couldn't allow that to happen. Things would have to step up now. He'd complete tomorrow's mission tonight. Thanks to his fetish for contingency planning, he'd brought all he needed with him, just in case. Afterwards, he could go back to Vinton Woods and lie low for a few days. He could activate the other camera systems and figure out how to destroy the other cops. Then he could come back for a second bite of the cherry and really make Micky pay.

Anything else was not an option.

Her legion of fans would still have recognised Micky Morgan, in spite of the years that had passed since she'd last appeared on their TV screens. It didn't matter that there were silver threads running through the thick blonde hair, or that there were lines radiating from the corners of her blue eyes. The bone structure that underpinned her beauty meant she was still clearly that same woman who had smiled into their living rooms four days a week at lunchtime. The constant exercise of working with horses meant she'd kept in shape; her trademark long shapely legs still looked as good as ever they had, as Betsy frequently reassured her.

But tonight, the last thing on Micky's mind was how she looked. Betsy had come close to losing her life for her beloved horses. If it hadn't been for the quick wits and quicker hands of Johnny Fitzgerald, she'd have been the one crushed beneath a smouldering beam and Micky might have been without the only person who still made her life worth living. They'd been together for more than fifteen years now, and Micky couldn't imagine life without Betsy. It went beyond love; it was a shared set of values and pleasures, a complementary set of skills and failings. And tonight she'd nearly lost it all.

The same thoughts and fears kept circling her mind,

pushing everything else to the periphery. She knew with her head that Betsy was safe and well, soaking in the tub upstairs to get the smell of smoke out of her hair and skin. But Micky's emotions were still churning. She really wasn't paying much attention to the police officer who kept asking her questions she didn't know the answers to.

Yes, she thought this was Jacko's handiwork. No, she hadn't heard from him since he'd escaped. She hadn't actually heard from him in years, which suited her just fine. No, she didn't know where he might be. No, she didn't know who might be helping him. He'd never been big on friends. Just on using people. No, she hadn't seen or heard anything out of the ordinary that evening. She and Betsy had been playing bridge with a couple of friends from a nearby village when the alarm had gone up.

Micky shuddered at the memory. Betsy had been first to her feet, throwing her cards to the table and running for the door. The police protection officers had tried to keep them from leaving. They clearly hadn't expected to be straight-armed out of the way by a middle-aged woman who was stronger than either of them. Micky had run after her, but one of the officers had been a bit more together and he'd grabbed her round the waist and manhandled her indoors. 'It could be a tactic, the fire,' he'd shouted at her. 'He could be trying to draw you out so he can take a potshot at you.'

'He doesn't do shooting,' Micky had shouted back at him. 'You need two arms to target shoot well. And he doesn't do anything he can't do well.'

Where that had come from, she didn't know. Until the events of this week, it had been a long time since she'd thought of Jacko. But since his escape, he'd felt like a constant presence, always at her shoulder, continually watching her and telling her how she could improve. When the police had come to her door, telling her what they believed he was up to, she'd had no trouble believing she would be high on his list of those who should be punished.

If not for Betsy and the horses, she would have run. Daphne, one of the friends they'd been playing bridge with, had counselled her to go. 'Darling, he's a brute. You mustn't let yourself be a target for his spite. Betsy, tell her. She should take herself off somewhere he won't find her.'

But it wasn't an option. She couldn't leave Betsy behind. And besides, how long was she supposed to stay gone? If they caught him in a day or two, fine. She could come back. But Jacko was resourceful. He would have planned his escape and its aftermath in detail and with precision. He could be on the lam for months. For ever. And what was she to do then? No, running wasn't an option.

The policeman asked something and Micky roused herself enough to ask him to repeat it. 'I asked if you could give us a list of the people who are turning up to take your horses away.'

'I can do that,' Betsy said, coming into the room. The first thing she'd done after the paramedics had given her the all-clear was to get on the phone to anyone in the surrounding area who might have spare stalls in their stables so she could provide shelter for her beloved horses. 'I'm sorry, I should have given you the details. I was just so desperate to get the smell of smoke off me.'

'I understand,' he said.

Betsy was already scribbling names down on a sheet of scrap paper in her small precise script. She passed it to the policeman and put a reassuring hand on Micky's shoulder. 'Now, if that's all, we'd appreciate a little peace and quiet,' she said, charming but firm. When they were alone, she cradled Micky's head against her breasts, loose inside her eminently respectable tartan dressing gown. 'I don't want another evening like this in a hurry,' she said.

'Me neither,' Micky sighed. 'I can't believe he tried to kill the horses. What's that about?'

'It's about hurting us, I think,' Betsy said sensibly. She let Micky go and went to pour herself a Scotch. 'Do you want one?'

Micky shook her head. 'If that's the case, I'm glad he chose the horses to go after rather than you.'

'Oh, honey, don't say that. It cost Johnny his life, don't forget. And those poor horses. They must have died in utter fear and total agony. It makes me furious. Poor old Midnight Dancer and Trotters Bar. Innocent animals. There's not much I would have put past Jacko, but harming those glorious, innocent animals is lower than I thought he could sink.'

Micky shook her head. 'There's nothing Jacko wouldn't do if it served his ambitions. We should have realised that before we tied our lives to his.'

Betsy curled up on the chair opposite Micky. 'We had no way of knowing what his secret life was.'

'Maybe not. But we always knew he had one.' Micky fiddled with her hair, winding a strand round her finger. 'I'm so glad you're safe.'

Betsy chuckled. 'Me too. There was a terrible moment when I thought, "That's it, Betsy. Curtains for you." And then Johnny came to the rescue.' Her face grew solemn.

Micky shivered. 'Let's not talk about it.' As she spoke, they heard voices in the hall. What they were saying was indistinct, but it sounded like a man and a woman.

The door opened and a woman walked in. She looked familiar – short blonde hair cut thick and textured, medium height, grey-blue eyes, good looks worn down by tiredness and time – but Micky couldn't quite place her. The clothes were no clue either – navy suit, decent cut but not extravagant, pale blue open-necked shirt, lightweight leather jacket that brushed the top of her thighs. She could have been anything from a lawyer to a journalist. Her mouth tightened as she looked at Micky and Betsy, apparently relaxed in their farmhouse kitchen. 'You don't remember me, do you?' she said, giving them both a cold stare.

'I do,' Betsy said. 'You're the police officer who arrested Jacko. I remember you giving evidence at the Old Bailey.'

'Jacko, is it? The man tries to burn down your livelihood and he's still Jacko to you?'

Micky looked to Betsy for a lead. Her lover's expression hardened and a new watchfulness crept into her eyes. 'He was Jacko to us for years. It's habit, that's all.'

'Is it? Is it really all? Or does it betray your real attitude, Ms Thorne?' The woman's voice sounded strangled, as if it was a struggle to control herself.

'You have the advantage of us. I'm sorry, I don't remember your name.'

'You should. It's been in the news enough this week. It's Jordan. Carol Jordan. Detective Chief Inspector Carol Jordan. Sister of Michael Jordan.'

The silence that followed Carol's words seemed to swell till it filled the space between the three women. Finally, it was Betsy who broke it. 'I'm very sorry. What happened to your brother and his wife was unforgivable.'

'Partner. Lucy was his partner. Not his wife. They never married. And now, thanks to your ex –' She tipped a nod to Micky '– they never will.'

'I can't tell you how sorry I am,' Micky said.

'You could try,' Carol said, eyes blazing.

'We're victims too, you know,' Micky said. 'Betsy could have died in that burning stable block.'

'But she didn't, did she? She had a miraculous escape.' Carol threw her shoulder bag down on the kitchen table. 'In my line of work, miraculous escapes are suspicious things, not hallelujah, praise the Lord things. You see, often the miraculous escapes are set-ups. They're set up to divert suspicion.' She kept her eyes moving between the two of them, watching their reactions, looking for the tells she'd learned to spot after years at Tony Hill's side.

'That's a pretty outrageous thing to say. An employee of ours died this evening while saving my life,' Betsy said, her outward show of calm unruffled. Micky knew better, though. She knew that under the surface, Betsy had a temper that would see off the likes of Carol Jordan.

'Is it really that outrageous? I'm looking at the scale of Vance's revenge. Tony Hill's home was burned to the ground. The one place in the world he's ever felt at home. But all that happens to you is a little fire in a stable block. My brother and his partner were brutally murdered. I've never seen so much blood at a crime scene. But all that happens to you is that two horses die. And a stable lad whose name you don't even bother with. Does that seem proportionate to you?'

'It was meant to be much worse than that,' Betsy said. 'The fire brigade said if we hadn't had the stable block timbers treated with anti-inflammatory chemicals, the whole roof would have come down. Ja— Vance obviously couldn't have known that.'

Carol shrugged. 'Not unless you told him.' She turned her stare on Micky.

'Why on earth would we do that? Why would we help him? It's not as if he's been a great help to us over the years. His actions destroyed Micky's TV career.' Betsy was clipping her syllables tight now, clamping down on her anger.

'Which suited you just fine, didn't it? Let's face it, Betsy, TV was never your world, was it? This is much more like it. Country tweeds and horses. Pukka accents and polo chukkas. Vance's disgrace did you a favour, I'd say.'

'That's not how it was,' Micky said, her expression pleading. 'We were pariahs, it's taken years to rebuild our lives.'

'You were his enabler, his mask. Practically his accomplice. He hid behind you for years while he kidnapped and tortured teenage girls. You must have known there was something he was hiding all that time. Why should I believe you're not still facilitating him? Somebody's helped him set all this up. Why not you? You cared about him once.'

'This is outrageous,' Betsy said, her tone a blade that cut through Carol's tirade.

'Is it? How does it work, Betsy? I don't have a big house or a string of horses to care about so I have to lose my brother?' All at once, Carol sank into the nearest chair. 'My brother.' The words came out as a sob. She buried her face in her hands and for the first time since Blake had broken the news, she cried properly. She cried as if she had never cried before in her life and was determined to run through every available variation on the theme. Her whole body convulsed in sobs.

Micky gave Betsy a 'what do we do now?' look, but she was too late. Already Betsy was halfway across the room. She pulled up another chair and held Carol close, as if she was her child. Betsy stroked her head and made inarticulate sounds of comfort as Carol cried herself out. At a loss, Micky went to the cupboard and poured three large whiskies. She put them on the table then fetched the kitchen roll.

At last, Carol stopped weeping. She raised her head, gave a hiccuping gulp and swiped her face with the back of her hand. Micky tore off a few sheets of kitchen roll and handed them to her. Carol sniffed and blew and wiped then spotted the whisky. She emptied one of the glasses in a single shuddering swallow then took a deep breath. She looked wrecked, Micky thought. Literally and figuratively. 'I'm not sorry for what I said,' she said.

Betsy gave her an admiring smile. 'Of course you're not. I rather think you're a woman after my own heart, Chief

Inspector Jordan. But please believe me. It might not look like it from where you're standing, but we're Jacko Vance's victims too. The only difference between us is that you've only just joined the club.'

48

After Carol's whirlwind departure from the barge, Alvin had gone back to HQ. Usually, Tony was glad when people left him to his own devices. Even the people he liked. But right now, every time Carol walked out on him, he was gripped with a fear that it might be for the last time. Her visit to the barge had not been a reconciliation, he knew that. She'd come because she needed something from him and that need had transcended her desire not to have him in her sight. What would happen when all of this was over? The prospect filled him with gloom.

When he hated his own company like this, the only cure he knew was work. And so he turned back to his laptop and tried to put Carol Jordan from his mind. But it wasn't that easy. He kept coming back to his awareness of her pain. He hated to see her suffer, especially when that suffering could be laid, at least in part, at his door. Worst of all, she'd stormed off. He didn't know where she was or how to help her.

Tony tried to concentrate, but it wasn't working. It didn't help that the saloon smelled of the remains of the fish and chips he hadn't managed to eat. He pulled the bag out of the bin under the sink and tied it in a knot. Then he climbed out on to the stern and walked up the pontoon to the nearest bin, leaving the doors open so the cool evening air could freshen the interior of the boat. 'If this was a thriller,' he said aloud, 'the bad guy would be sneaking aboard right now and hiding in the cabin.' He turned back, noting that the boat was motionless. 'No such luck.'

Back at the boat, he leaned against the stern rail and looked out across the marina. The roofs of the boats looked like black beetles, lined up in rows. A few boats were lit up, their soft yellow light spilling in pools on the black water. In the distance a man was walking a pair of Westies. The voices of a group of young men leaving the pub carried across the marina in a jumble of sound. In the old warehouses, now converted to apartments with views of the canal basin, squares and oblongs of light split up the dark facades in random patterns.

'Motive,' he said to a passing mallard. 'That's what separates psychologists and police officers. We can't do without it. But they're really not that bothered. Just the facts, ma'am. That's what they want. Forensic evidence, witnesses, stuff they think you can't fake. But I'm really not all that bothered about the facts. Because facts are like views. They all depend on where you're standing.'

The duck stopped paddling away from him and came back for more. 'I need a motive for these murders,' Tony said. 'People don't just kill for the hell of it, no matter what some of them say. In their heads, what they're doing makes sense. So we've got a killer who's murdering sex workers but it's not about having sex with them. And it's not about being turned on by the killing because he's doing that differently every time. People who are turned on by murder have very specific triggers. What pushes my hot button does not push yours.' He sighed and the duck lost interest. 'I don't blame you, mate. I bore myself sometimes.'

He stood up and jumped back on to the pontoon. Finally

he'd found a place to pace. Head down, he walked to the end then turned back and walked the full length again, his limp easing a little as his limbs loosened up along with his brain. 'So if you're not doing it for the gratification of the killing, what are you getting out of it? What are you trying to achieve? I don't believe it's notoriety. When you want notoriety and you don't get it, you start sending emails to the likes of Penny Burgess. If there's someone you want to impress, they're already in a position to get the message.' He turned back and walked down the pontoon again, more slowly this time.

'Let's think about the victims. One way or another, it's about the victims. Sex workers. You're not a religious nutter trying to cleanse the streets. A man with a mission, he's not going to bother with all this elaborate TV series stuff. It's the cleansing that matters, not some arcane message.'

'What's the effect of what you're doing? What does it achieve?' He stopped abruptly, possible light dawning. 'You're trying to scare them off the streets? Is that it?' He felt very close to something revelatory, something that would make sense of the information he'd been studying. 'Not them. Her,' he said slowly. 'You need her to stop. You need her to come off the streets. To come home.'

He spun round on the balls of his feet and ran back to *Steeler*. It felt like he was in pursuit of an idea that might slip away if he didn't share it. Back on board, he grabbed his phone and speed-dialled Paula. As soon as she answered, he said, 'He's trying to scare someone.'

'Is that you, Tony?'

'It's me, Paula. Your killer – he's trying to scare someone.'

'He's scaring a lot of people, Tony.' She sounded exasperated. He imagined it had been a long day without Carol at the helm to steer them straight.

'I realise that. But there's one person in particular he's trying to scare. He's trying to make her too frightened to work the streets. He wants her to come home. You can see it in the escalation. He started with the lowest of the low then he worked his way upwards. He's saying, "It doesn't matter what rung of the ladder you stand on, the bad thing can still get you." He wants her to understand that, whatever she's running from, it's better than what she's run to.'

'Makes sense.' Paula sighed. 'But how does that help me?'

'I don't know. What about Vice? Do they keep track of the new girls on the block? At least they'd know where to go to ask around. You're looking for someone who's not been on the streets for long. She'll probably have showed up in the weeks before the first murder. See what you can find out. Names, background details, as much as you can nail down. Once you find her, you'll find him. The man who wants her back.'

'Why doesn't he just take her back? He's been taking these other women off the streets.'

'He needs to kid himself that she's come back of her own free will. Remember, Paula, he doesn't look at the world the way we do. Imagine normal motives, then give them a twist. I think this is all about scaring her home so he can tell himself he's the one she wants to be with.'

'I worry about you sometimes, you know,' Paula said. 'The way you figure out the twists and turns inside their heads.'

'I worry myself. Did Stacey get anywhere with the *Maze Man* website, by the way?'

'Sort of. There's no regular frequenter of the site from the UK, but she found an email from a bloke trying to contact anyone in the UK with a full set of videos. He's using a hotmail address, so it's hard to get any reliable data. But Stacey's done one of her magic tricks and established that most of the emails sent from that address have been sent from the Bradfield area. She's also been running the number plate recognition data and she's narrowed down his base of operations to an area in Skenby. The high flats and a few surrounding streets.'

'That's another step in the right direction. Good luck with it all. Let me know how you get on with the Vice.'

'Will do. Have you been in touch with the chief?'

Tony closed his eyes momentarily. 'I saw her earlier. She turned up out of the blue and found me working on your case.'

'Oh shit,' Paula said.

'She's got bigger things to worry about right now. She's running away from her emotions. When they finally catch up with her, it's not going to be pretty.'

'At least she's got you in her corner.'

Tony felt the prickle of tears in his throat. 'Yeah. For what it's worth. Anyway, you need to get on. Keep me posted.'

He ended the call and turned back to the computer. When all else fails, talk to the machine.

Stacey stared intently at her monitor, occasionally tapping a few keys or clicking her mouse. Ambrose, whose desk was behind hers, looked over from his screen and watched her covertly, admiring the absolute focus she brought to her task. He wished they had an officer like her on their team instead of having to rely on the unreliable Gary Harcup. Gary was good enough, but he wasn't always around when he was needed, and he certainly couldn't pull off stuff like this woman could. He wasn't sure whether all her burrowing was entirely legal, but he didn't care as long as she came up with the goods and a cover story that would satisfy the CPS and the courts.

As he watched, she pushed back from the screen and turned round, catching him in the act. 'Result,' she said, showing none of the triumphalism that normally went with that claim.

'Really?' Ambrose got up and went across, peering into her screen. 'Vinton Woods? What's that?'

'An exclusive community within ideal commuting range of Bradfield and Leeds,' Stacey said. 'It's in West Yorkshire, so I guess it's either part of DCI Franklin's patch or close to it. I got a fragment of the name from the partially deleted material on Terry Gates's hard drive and did a universal search of properties that have changed owner at the Land Registry in the past six months. There were a couple of matches, but this is the only one that fits the profile of what would suit Vance.' She clicked and typed and estate agent's details of a substantial mock-Victorian house appeared on the screen. 'This was bought by a company registered in Kazakhstan. The payment came from a Liechtenstein trust who bank in the Cayman Islands. Unravelling all that will take weeks. But it's exactly the sort of set-up Vance would use to hide behind.'

'If you say so,' Ambrose said. 'It makes my head hurt just thinking about it.'

Stacey shrugged. 'Well, we know that Vance shipped all his cash offshore after he was arrested, and that there was a lot of it. A house like this would be the perfect base. Even if he's only here for a matter of weeks, he's got total control of his bolthole and he's got an asset he can dispose of when he doesn't need it any more.'

'Oh, I believe you,' Ambrose said. 'I just can't get my head round the mind of someone who can be arsed to go to these lengths just for revenge.'

Stacey turned and gave him an indulgent smile. 'That's probably quite healthy, skip.'

'I need to get up there,' he said.

'Shouldn't we get the local lads to keep a discreet eye on it? It's going to take you at least two hours to get there, even blues-and-twos.'

Ambrose shook his head. 'This is our pursuit. From what your guv'nor said about Franklin, I don't trust him not to go in mob-handed like a glory-hunter. This needs careful handling and I think we've earned the right to lead it. I'm going up there with a hand-picked team. We'll call on local support once we know what we're dealing with.' He patted her on the shoulder. 'You've done a great job. I'll make sure my boss knows who's responsible for this breakthrough. Just don't speak to Franklin about this. Or any other West Yorkshire detectives.'

Paula hoped someone would be on duty in the Vice squad's office this late on a Saturday. She expected most of them would be doing whatever it was that off-duty cops got up to on a Saturday night. Anybody working would probably be out on the street on the busiest night of the week for the sex trade. But her luck was in, even if the cop who answered the phone sounded as if he was down to his last shredded nerve. 'DC Bryant. What do you want?'

Paula identified herself and her unit. 'I need some info,' she finished up.

'Paula McIntyre? You're the one who got nailed in that undercover that went tits-up a while back, aren't you?' His tone was accusing, as if it was somehow her fault that her colleagues' cock-up had nearly cost her her life. Even thinking about it made the back of her neck sweat.

'And you're the division who supplied the detective who caused the problem, but I'm not going to hold that against you,' she snapped back at him.

'There's no need to be like that,' he grumbled. 'So what do you need to know?'

'Does anybody keep intel on new girls on the street?' she asked.

'What kind of intel?'

'Names. Background, that sort of thing. How long they've been on the game. Or at least, how long you've known about them.'

He sniffed loudly. 'We're not fucking social workers, you know.'

'Believe me, that never crossed my mind. Do you have any intel like that or not?'

'The sarge keeps a file. But she's off duty tonight.' There was an air of finality in his voice.

'Can you get hold of her? It's really important.'

'It always is, with you MIT lot.'

'It's four fucking murders so far, DC Bryant. I really can't be arsed bothering my chief with your snotty attitude, but if that's what it takes to get a bit of action going round here, I will do it. Now, do you want to phone your sergeant and ask her, or do you want my guv'nor to do it?'

'You need to take a chill pill, detective,' he said. She could hear the laugh under his voice. 'I'll call her. But don't hold your breath.' The phone clattered down at his end.

'Bastard,' said Paula. She wondered if there was a way to circumvent Vice, but she couldn't think of one. Not on a Saturday night with all her social services contacts tucked up in front of the telly with a takeaway curry and *Casualty*. She'd just have to wait for DC Bryant to get his finger out. Bastard, right enough.

Stacey watched Ambrose get into a huddle with DI Patterson. She was uneasy about his proposed angle of attack on Vance's putative bolthole. She understood his desire to be the one to recapture Vance. They'd done all the groundwork, after all. It was only fair that they should get to front up the news reports, let their kids see them on the telly and be proud. What wouldn't be so good would be if their way meant Vance slipped through the net. If that happened, Stacey had a funny feeling it might end up being her fault.

She picked up her phone and called her boss's number. Even in her present state of mind, Carol was a better judge of operational matters than these very nice men who, with the best will in the world, hardly ever dealt with the level of stuff

Bradfield's MIT handled all the time. When Carol answered the phone, her voice sounded odd. Like she had a cold or something.

'Hi, Stacey. Any news?'

Stacey reported her discovery of the Vinton Woods address, and what Ambrose was proposing. Carol listened without interrupting, then said, 'I don't trust Franklin either. He was completely sceptical about the idea that it might be our friend in the first place. Rather than have him go at it half-hearted, I think we should leave him right out of the loop for now.' She paused for a moment. 'I'm going up there. If I leave right now, I should make it ahead of the posse. I can figure out the lie of the land and see what the options are. Thanks for letting me know, Stacey.'

And she was gone. Stacey stared at the phone, not feeling in the least reassured. This was starting to feel like something that was headed full-speed ahead for disaster. And with Jacko Vance in the driving seat, the only guarantee was that there would be nothing half-hearted in what happened next.

49

When Stacey's call had come through, Carol was almost back in command of herself. Exhausted and mortified though she was, she knew a weight inside her had shifted. She could pick herself off the floor and get a grip on the task in hand. Which was to stop Jacko Vance causing any more damage.

She'd stood up and stepped away from Betsy to speak to Stacey. So she'd already begun the process of separating herself from the two women. One thing she knew for sure was that she didn't want them to know her plans just in case she'd been right about their loyalties. Carol ended the call and said, 'I have to go.'

'I don't think you're in a fit state to go anywhere,' Betsy said, kindly rather than bossily.

'I appreciate your concern,' Carol said. 'But I'm needed elsewhere. I have a team in Bradfield who need their commander. Your ex-husband isn't the only person intent on destruction right now.' She picked up her bag and ran a hand through her hair, feeling sweat on her forehead. She supposed she was feverish. It was hardly surprising after that outburst. 'I can see myself out.'

She wasn't sorry to get out of the room. Betsy had showed her the sort of kindness that disarms. And yet she'd been very cool about the human victim of Vance's attack. Thinking about that offset the kindness, which suited her because Carol did not want to be disarmed, especially not where Micky Morgan was concerned. She remained unconvinced the woman was truly free of Vance. It didn't matter whether it was charisma or fear that held her in thrall, Carol believed there was still something unresolved between them.

Outside, she sat in her car for a moment, gathering her thoughts. She was going to bring Vance down. His capture had her name on it. Nobody had more right to that moment than her. If Ambrose was putting a team together, he wouldn't have left Worcester yet. She could beat him to it. She bet he wouldn't drive all the way from Worcester to Vinton Woods with flashing lights and sirens. Neither Ambrose nor Patterson was gung-ho enough. She pulled the blue light out of her glove box and slapped it on the roof of her car and set it going, spitting gravel from her wheels as she took off.

She'd take Vance down tonight or die trying.

Tony wondered how Paula was getting on with the Vice team. They'd always been a law unto themselves, straddling the twilight zone between the respectable and the disreputable. Unless they developed a rapport with at least one segment of the group they policed, they couldn't do their jobs. That rapport had always gone hand in hand with the easy, sleazy promises of corruption. And historically, a lot of Vice cops had gone to the bad, though not always in the predictable ways. Because they dealt with a perverted reality, their crimes had an unhealthy knack of being less than straightforward.

And Paula had history with them. He wondered whether guilt made them more inclined to help her, or if she reminded them of a period in their history they'd rather forget.

His phone rang, the screen saying 'blocked'. He wondered whether it might be Vance, calling to gloat. But then he'd never been one of those who had to boast about their crimes. He didn't kill because he craved attention. He did almost everything else in his life for that reason, but not the killing.

There was only one way to find out. Tony pressed a button and waited. 'Dr Hill? Is that you?' It was a woman's voice, familiar but too tinny for him to identify.

'Who is this?'

'It's Stacey Chen, Dr Hill.'

Well, that made sense. She was probably using some electronic scrambler to disguise her voice. That would fit with her general suspicion about the world around her. 'How can I help you, Stacey? Well done on that Oklahoma website, by the way.'

'It was just number crunching,' she said dismissively. 'Anyone could have done it with the right software.'

'How are you getting on with tracing Kerry Fletcher? Has he shown up yet?'

'I'll be honest, it's frustrating and I don't like to be frustrated by computer systems. He's not on the electoral roll or the council tax register. He's not claiming benefit and I can't find a fit in the right age group in medical records. Whoever he is, he's been living under the radar.'

'I can see how that would frustrate you.'

'I'll get there. Doctor, I'm not sure I should be ringing you. But I'm a bit worried and you're the only person who can help, I think.'

Tony gave a little laugh. 'You sure about that? These days when I'm the answer it's usually because somebody is asking the wrong question.'

'I think I've found where Vance is hiding when he's not committing his crimes.'

'That's great. Where is it?'

'It's called Vinton Woods. It's between Leeds and Bradfield. The last bit of woodland before you hit the Dales.'

'Does that mean it's on Franklin's patch?'

'It's in the West Yorkshire force area.'

'Have you called Franklin?'

'That's the problem. DS Ambrose was there when I found it, so I told him. He's determined that West Mercia should make the arrest and he ordered me not to tell Franklin or any of the other West Yorkshire detectives.'

'I can see that would be awkward for you,' Tony said, still not clear why Stacey was involving him.

'Just a bit. So I thought I'd speak to DCI Jordan and let her make the call.'

'Only, she won't call Franklin either, am I right?'

'Exactly. She's heading there now. I don't know where she's heading there from, but the chances are she's going to get there ahead of West Mercia. And I'm afraid she'll bite off more than she can chew. He's a very dangerous man, Dr Hill.'

'You're not wrong, Stacey.' Even as he spoke, he was reaching for his coat and groping in the pockets for his car keys. He got one arm in a sleeve then juggled the phone to his other ear. 'You did the right thing, calling me. Leave it with me.'

'Thanks.' Stacey made an odd sound, as if she was about to speak but thought better of it. Then said in a rush, 'Take care of her.' And the line went dead.

As he stuffed the other arm in its sleeve and hustled up the steps and padlocked the boat, Tony thought that those four words from Stacey were the equivalent of anyone else in MIT grabbing him by the throat and shouting, 'If you let anything happen to her, I will kill you.'

'I'll take care of her, Stacey,' he said to the night as he ran up the pontoon and sprinted down the marina to the car park. He didn't stop to think until he was joining the motorway and realised that he didn't actually know where he was going. Nor did he have Stacey's number. 'You numbskull,' he shouted at himself. 'You fuckwit numbskull.'

The only thing he could think of was to call Paula. Her phone went straight to voicemail and he swore all the way through the outgoing message. After the beep, he said, 'This is really important, Paula. I don't have Stacey's number and I need her to text me the directions to the place she's just told me about. And please don't ask either of us what this is all about or I will have to cry.'

It wasn't an idle threat either. In spite of his determination to keep his emotions at arm's length, Tony was starting to feel fraught, as if the threads that held him together were fraying. It was easy to take for granted how important Carol was to him when she was there in the background of his life. He'd grown accustomed to their companionship, he was used to the lift in his spirits when their encounters were unexpected, he had come to rely on her presence as a constant steadying force.

Growing up, he'd never learned the building blocks of love and friendship. His mother Vanessa was cold, her every gesture and comment calculated and calibrated to get precisely what she wanted from any situation. This was the woman who had taken a knife to Eddie Blythe, her fiancé, when it had seemed the most profitable thing to do. Luckily for Tony, she hadn't managed to kill him. Just scare him off for ever.

When Tony had been a kid, Vanessa had been too busy constructing her business career to be bothered with the shackles of motherhood and she'd mostly abandoned him to his grandmother, who was equally lacking in warmth. His grandmother had resented him occupying the space she thought ought to be occupied by an unfettered old age and she let him know it. Neither Vanessa nor his grandmother brought their social lives home with them, so Tony never had much chance to watch people interact in normal, routine ways.

When he looked at his childhood, he saw the perfect

template for one of the damaged lives he ended up treating as a clinician or hunting as a profiler. Unloved, unwanted, harshly punished for normal childhood mischief or obliviousness, estranged from the normal interactions that allowed for growth and development. The absent father and the aggressive mother. When he interviewed the psychopaths that became his patients, he heard so many echoes of his own empty childhood. It was, he thought, the reason he was so good at what he did. He understood them because he had come within a hair's breadth of being them.

What had saved him, what had given him the priceless gift of empathy, had been the only thing that ever saved anyone like him – love. And it had come from the most unexpected of places.

He hadn't been an attractive child. He remembered knowing it was true because that's what he was always told. He didn't have much objective evidence. There were almost no photographs. A couple of class photos when the teacher had actually managed to shame Vanessa into ordering a copy, and that was that. He only knew which one was him because his grandmother had pointed it out to him. Usually accompanied by, 'Anybody looking at this photograph would know which one was the most worthless bastard of the lot.' Then she'd stab the photograph with her knobbly arthritic finger.

Little bastard Tony Hill. Short trousers that were just a bit too short, a bit too tight, revealing skinny thighs and bumpy knees. Shoulders hunched, holding himself together with arms ramrod straight by his side. Narrow face under a tousle of wavy hair that looked like it hadn't ever seen anything as poncey as a stylist. The wary expression of a kid who's not sure where the next slap is coming from, but knows it's coming. Even then, even there, his eyes had commanded attention. Their blue sparkle was undimmed by everything else. They were the clue to a spirit that hadn't entirely given in. Yet.

He was picked on endlessly at school; Vanessa and her mother had invested him with the air of the trained victim and there were plenty willing to take advantage of his unprotected status. You could batter Tony Hill and know his mother wouldn't be up at school next morning bellowing at the Head like a Grimsby fishwife. Last to be chosen for team sports, first to be jeered at for anything, he'd stumbled through school in a state of misery.

He was always last in the dinner line. He'd learned that was the only way to get any dinner at all. If he let all the big kids get well ahead of him, he could hang on to his tray without having his crumble and custard 'accidentally' dumped in his stew and dumplings. None of the little kids was interested in tripping him up or spitting on his chips.

He'd never paid much attention to the dinner ladies. Tony was used to keeping his head down and hoping the adults wouldn't notice him. So he was taken aback one day when one of the dinner ladies spoke as he approached the hot table. 'What's matter wi' thee?' the woman said, her strong local accent making the question a challenge.

He'd looked over his shoulder, panicked that one of the bullies had crept up behind him. Then startled, he'd realised she was looking at him. 'Aye, thee, tha big daft lad.'

He shook his head, his upper lip rising in fear, showing his teeth like a nervous terrier. 'Nothing,' he said.

'You're a liar,' she said, ladling an extra-large portion of macaroni cheese on to his plate. 'Come round the back here.' She gestured with her head to the side passage that led to the serving kitchen.

Truly terrified by now, Tony made sure nobody was looking and slid sideways into the passage. Clutching his tray to his chest like a horizontal shield he stood in the kitchen entrance. The woman came towards him, then led him round the corner to the back kitchen where the real work happened. Four women were washing huge pots in deep sinks amid clouds of steam. A fifth was leaning against the back-door jamb, smoking. 'Sit thysel' down and eat,' the woman said, pointing to a high stool by a counter.

'Another bloody rescue pup, Joan?' the smoking woman said.

Tony's hunger overcame his anxiety and he shovelled his food into his mouth. The woman, Joan, watched him with satisfaction, her arms folded across her chest. 'You're always last in the queue,' she said, her voice kindly. 'They pick on you, don't they?'

He'd felt tears well up in his eyes and nearly choked on the slippery macaroni. He looked down at his plate and said nothing.

'I keep dogs,' she said. 'I could do with a hand walking them after school. Would that be something you might fancy?'

He didn't fancy the dogs. He just wanted to be with somebody who spoke to him the way Joan did. He nodded, still not looking up.

'That's settled, then. I'll see you at the back gate when the bell goes. Do you need to let them know at home?'

Tony shook his head. 'My nan won't mind,' he said. 'And my mum never gets back before seven.'

And that had been the start of it. Joan never asked him about his home life. She listened once he understood he could trust her, but she never probed, never judged. She had five dogs, each with a distinct personality, and while he never came to care for the dogs the way Joan did, he learned how to fake it. Not in a disrespectful way, but because he didn't want to let Joan down. She didn't try to be a mother to him or to bribe him into investing her with more significance in his life. She was a kind, childless woman who had been drawn by his pain in the same way that she'd been drawn to her dogs down at the animal rescue. 'I always know the ones with the good

345

temperaments,' she would boast to him and to the other dog walkers she'd stop and chat to.

And she encouraged him. Joan wasn't a clever woman herself, but she recognised intelligence when she saw it. She told him the way to escape whatever ailed him was to educate himself so that he had choices. She hugged him when he passed his exams and told him he could do it when he grew discouraged. He was sixteen when she told him he had to stop coming round.

They'd been sitting in her kitchen at the formica-topped table, drinking tea. 'I can't have you coming round any more,' she said. 'I've got cancer, Tony lad. Apparently I'm bloody riddled with it. They say I've only a matter of weeks to live. I'm taking the dogs to the vet tomorrow to have them put down. They're all too old to adapt to some other bugger, and I doubt your nan would give them houseroom.' She'd patted his hand. 'I want you to remember me as I am. As I have been. So we'll say our goodbyes now.'

He'd been horrified. He'd protested at her decision, declaring his willingness to be by her side till the end. But she'd been adamant. 'It's all arranged, lad. I'm putting everything in order then I'm taking myself off to the hospice. I hear they couldn't be nicer in there.'

Then they'd both cried. It had been hard, but he'd respected her wishes. Five weeks later, one of the dinner ladies had called him over and told him Joan had died. 'Very peaceful, it were,' she said. 'But she's left a bloody big hole round here.'

He'd nodded, not trusting himself to speak. But he'd already discovered that Joan had taught him how to negotiate that bloody big hole for himself. He wasn't the same boy she'd befriended.

It was years later, when he was doing postgraduate work on personality disorders and psychopathic behaviour, that he understood the power of what Joan had done for him. It wasn't overstating the case to say that Joan had saved him from what lay in prospect when she had snatched him out of the dinner line. She'd been the first person to show him love. A brusque, unsentimental love, it was true. But it had been love and even though he'd had no experience of it, he'd recognised it.

In spite of Joan's intervention, though, he'd never quite mastered the art of making easy connections with others. He'd learned to pretend – 'passing for human', he called it. He didn't have a raft of mates like most of the men he'd worked with. He didn't have a backlist of girlfriends and lovers like them. So the few people he cared about were all the more valuable to him. And the thought of losing Carol Jordan gave him a physical pain in his chest. Was this what the precursor to a heart attack felt like?

There was more than one way to lose her. There was the obvious – the fact that she'd made it clear that she didn't care if she never saw him again. But there was always hope that he could change her mind. Other ways were more final. In the state she was in, she would place little value on her life. He could imagine her deciding to go it alone against Vance, and he feared that would only have one outcome.

Then it dawned on him that he might not be the only person capable of saving Carol from herself. He reached for his phone and called Alvin Ambrose. 'I'm a bit busy just now,' the sergeant said when he answered.

'I'll keep it brief, then,' Tony said. 'Carol Jordan's on her way to confront Jacko Vance.'

50

Paula looked at her watch, feeling glum. She was inches away from giving up on Vice and going home. Right now, she should have been sitting in her kitchen, drinking red wine and watching Dr Elinor Blessing applying her surgical skills to carving a leg of lamb. She hoped there would be some left over after their dinner guests had eaten their fill. She yawned and laid her head on her folded arms on the desk. She'd give them five more minutes, then to hell with it.

She woke with a start because someone was standing next to her. Blinded by the pool of light from her desk lamp, Paula could only see the outline of a figure against the dimly lit squad room. She jerked upright and pushed back in her chair, scrambling to her feet. A low laugh came from what she could now see was a woman. Middle-aged, middle-height and middle-weight. Dark hair in a neat bob. Face a bit like a garden gnome, complete with button nose and rosebud mouth. 'Sorry to disturb your nap,' she said. 'I'm Sergeant Dean. From Vice.'

Paula nodded, pushing her hair back from her face. 'Hi. Sorry. I'm DC McIntyre. I just put my head down for five minutes ...'

'I know who you are, pet.' The accent was from the North

East, the cadences blunted from years spent elsewhere. 'No need to apologise. I know what it's like when you're in the thick of it. Some weeks, you wonder if your bed was only a dream.'

'Thanks for coming in. I didn't expect you to give up your Saturday night.'

'I thought it was easier to come in. And besides, my husband and my two lads are off to Sunderland for the late kick-off game, they'll not be back till gone eleven by the time they've had their post-match curry. So all you're keeping me from is crap telly. What Bryant had to say sounded a lot more interesting. Care to fill in the blanks?' DS Dean settled herself comfortably in Chris Devine's desk chair and propped her boot heels on the bin. Paula tried not to mind.

Slightly wary of the Vice cop's obvious interest, Paula explained Tony's theory as best she could then smiled apologetically. 'The thing with Dr Hill is that his ideas can sound . . .'

'Stark staring mad?'

Paula chuckled. 'Pretty much. But I've worked with him for long enough now to know that it's kind of spooky how often he gets things right on the money.'

'I've heard he's good,' Dean said. 'They say that's part of the reason Carol Jordan has such a great success rate.'

Paula bristled. 'Don't underestimate the chief. She's a helluva detective.'

'I'm sure she is. But we can all use a bit of help now and again. And that's the reason I'm here. Whenever other detectives are interested in my turf, it's time to take a personal interest. None of us wants our carefully cultivated contacts rubbed up the wrong way.'

Now that Dean had laid out her stall, Paula felt more comfortable in her presence. 'Naturally,' she said. 'So, can you help me?'

Dean dug into the pocket of her jeans and took out a

memory stick. 'I'll share what I can. Bryant said you were interested in new lasses?'

'That's right. I hear there are more new faces because of the recession.'

'That's true, but a lot of them are inside workers, not on the street. How new are you interested in?'

'A month before the killings began?'

'I like to keep my ear to the ground,' Dean said, digging into the pocket of her jeans and coming out with a smartphone. 'I also don't like putting anything on the computer that doesn't have to be there. Especially when it comes to vulnerable young women.' She fiddled with the phone then gave a grunt of satisfaction.

'There's no hard and fast way of dealing with the crap out on the streets,' Dean said, thumbing through a list. 'It's all a bit ad hoc, you might say. When new faces show up, we try and get alongside them. Sometimes a little bit of leaning is all it takes, you know? Especially with the more or less respectable ones. A mention of how a criminal record will fuck up everything from their childcare to their credit rating and you can see the wheels going round. But that's a tiny minority. Once they've got as far as walking down that street, there's mostly no going back. So what I'm looking for there is to develop sources. And just to keep an eye out, you know?'

'Nobody wants bodies turning up.'

'Aye, well, I like to think we mostly manage to step in before it gets that far. My bonny lads tell me I'm living in cloud cuckoo land. But at least I try to get their names and a bit of background so we know what to put on the toe-tag, if it comes to it.'

'So what are we looking at here?'

'Forty-four square miles of BMP force area. Nine hundred thousand population, give or take. At any given time, there's somewhere around a hundred and fifty women working as prostitutes. When you think that about fifty per cent of men admit to having paid for sex, them lasses are working bloody hard for a living.'

'Not much of a living, either,' Paula said.

'Enough to keep them in drugs so they don't care what they're doing to earn the money for the next fix.' Dean shook her head. 'I bloody hope I've brought my lads up with a better attitude to women, that's all I can say.' She took her feet off the bin and sat up straight. 'The time frame you're looking at, I've got three names for you.'

'I'm just glad it's not more than that.'

'We're getting into summer time. The nights are lighter and the punters are more wary of being recognised when they're kerb crawling.'

'I never thought of prostitution as being seasonal.'

'Just the street stuff, pet. Indoors goes like a fair all year round. If you were interested in indoor, this list would be more like a dozen. So here we go. Tiffany Sedgwick, Lateesha Marlow and Kerry Fletcher.'

Paula couldn't believe her luck. 'Did you say Kerry Fletcher?' she said, excitement quickening in her.

'Does that ring a bell?'

'Kerry Fletcher's female?'

Dean looked at her as if she'd lost the plot. 'Of course she's female. You didn't ask me about rent boys. Why? Does the name mean something?'

'It came up earlier in a different part of the inquiry. Given the context, we thought it was a bloke. Kerry, it could be a bloke's name.' She frowned. 'That makes no sense.'

Dean smiled. 'You can check it out for yourself. You'll find her most nights down the bottom end of Campion Way. Near the roundabout.'

'Do you know anything about her?' Paula scribbled the name in her notebook, opening up her email program and starting to type a note to Stacey.

'I know what she told me about herself. How much truth there is, who knows? They all make stuff up. Good stuff and bad stuff. Whatever they need to feel all right about themselves.'

'So what did Kerry tell you?' Paula liked a bit of job-related chit-chat as much as anyone, but right now the only thing she was interested in was Kerry Fletcher.

'Well, she's a local lass. I suspect that bit's true, because she's got a broad Bradfield accent. She was born in Toxteth Road, round the back of the high flats in Skenby.'

Paula nodded. She knew Toxteth Road. What the local cops said was that even the dogs went round mob-handed down there. It was also in the area Stacey had identified from the number plates. 'Desolation Row,' she said.

'Bang on. Then when she was five or six, they moved to a sixteenth-floor flat. And that was that for her mother. She never left the flat from the day they moved in. Kerry's not sure if it was claustrophobia or agoraphobia or fear of Eric – that's the dad. But whatever it was, she became a prisoner in her own home.' The sergeant paused for dramatic effect. It was clear that she relished her stories.

'And that made her the perfect bargaining chip for Eric Fletcher,' Dean continued. 'He began sexually abusing Kerry when she was about eight. If she didn't do exactly as she was told, Eric took it out on her mother. He'd batter her, or push her out on the balcony and leave her there till she was a gibbering wreck. And little Kerry loved her mum.'

Paula sighed. She'd heard variations on this tale so many times, but every time had the force of the first time. She couldn't help imagining what it must have been like to feel so powerless. To endure a poverty of experience that meant this was a child's only exemplar of love. When that was all you knew, how could you believe anything else was achievable? The relationships you saw on TV shows must have felt as fantastical as Hogwarts. 'Of course she did,' she said. 'Why wouldn't she? Until she learned to despise her.'

Dean looked slightly pissed off. This was her story, after all. 'And so it went on. Even after she left school and started working at the petrol station on Skenby Road. She had no life of her own. Eric saw to that.' She gave Paula a shrewd look. 'It's what your Tony Hill would say. People become complicit in their own victimhood.'

'You know a lot about Kerry Fletcher.'

Dean gave her a wary glance. 'I make it my business to know as much as I can about all of them. A cup of coffee and a motherly attitude goes a very long way on the shit side of the street, Paula.'

'So what happened?'

'The mother died. About four months ago, as far as I can make out. It took a few weeks for it to dawn on Kerry that she was free at last.'

'So she went on the streets? What happened to the job at the garage?'

'When the scales fell from Kerry's eyes, they made a right clatter on the pavement. She didn't just want to be free, she wanted to rub Eric Fletcher's nose in it. He wasn't getting her for free any more, and she was making other men pay for what had been his.'

Paula whistled. 'And how did Eric take that?'

'Not well,' Dean said drily. 'He kept turning up where she was working and begging her to come home. Kerry refused point-blank. She said it was safer on the streets than in his house. We warned him off a couple of times, he was making a scene in the street and it was shaping up to turn nasty. Since then, he's kept a low profile, as far as I'm aware.'

'She said it was safer on the streets than in his house,' Paula repeated. 'That sounds like the perfect fit for what Tony was talking about. And he must have used her email address. Of course he did.' Energised now, she was tapping on the computer keys, composing an urgent message to Stacey to look for an Eric Fletcher in the Skenby flats, probably the sixteenth floor.

As she sent it, she noticed a message had arrived from Dr Grisha Shatalov. 'Bear with me a second,' she said, momentarily abstracted. *Paula,* it read, *We've got a torn piece of fingernail embedded in the exposed flesh of the latest body. It doesn't match the victim's fingers. It's almost certainly that of the killer and we should be able to get DNA – enough certainly for identification via STR and Mitochondrial DNA. Hope that cheers up your Saturday night. Give my condolences to Carol if you see her before I do. Dr Grisha.*

Sometimes a case reached a point that was like turning a key in a complicated lock. One tumbler would fall, then another, then it felt like an inevitable matching of pins and key, and the door would swing open. Here, now, late on a Saturday evening, Paula knew it was only a matter of time before MIT would be able to point to their last case with pride in the result. Carol could walk out with her head high, knowing she'd created something, whereas Blake could only destroy.

It would be a moment to relish.

Ambrose's voice had risen to a bellow. 'She's what? Who the fuck told Jordan where Vance is hiding?'

'Stacey, of course,' Tony said, sounding far more patient and reasonable than he felt.

'What the fuck was she thinking? That's operational information.'

'And Carol Jordan is her boss, not you. She turned her expertise to this problem for Carol, not for you. You shouldn't be surprised that she is loyal to the person who gave her the chance to shine.'

'You need to stop Jordan,' Ambrose said, his voice hard and rough. 'I don't want her blundering into this. He's too dangerous to confront single-handed. You need to stop her before something terrible happens.'

'That's exactly why I'm hammering up the motorway right now,' Tony said, keeping his tone level to try and take the heat out of the situation. 'When are you leaving?'

'Within the next five minutes. When did she take off?'

'Stacey spoke to her directly after she spoke to you. And then she spoke to me. And I left about fifteen minutes ago.'

'Fuck. This is a nightmare.'

'There's one thing you could do,' Tony said, moving over into the fast lane.

'What?'

'You could call Franklin and ask him to intercept her.'

Ambrose snorted. 'That's your idea of a solution? We'll end up with a Mexican stand-off between Jordan and Franklin while Vance hightails it out the back door, over the hills and far away.'

'Please yourself,' Tony snapped. 'I'm just trying to save her life, that's all.' He ended the call and coaxed another five miles an hour out of his protesting engine. 'Oh, Carol,' he groaned. 'Please don't do anything brave. Or noble. Just sit tight. Please.'

Sam Evans had never lost his appetite for getting out on the street and talking to people. He didn't have Paula's skills in the interview room, but he was good at drawing people into conversation then sussing out when to charm and when to lean. He could slip straight back into his working-class accent, and that helped when you were dealing with people at the bottom of the heap. Sam opened his mouth and they imagined someone who wasn't condescending or judging.

When Paula had passed on the background she'd got

from the sergeant in Vice, the obvious next step had been to find Kerry Fletcher and bring her in, out of harm's way. Paula needed to stay in the office, pulling together any information that might give them a lead on where to find Eric Fletcher. Meanwhile, Sam would do his best to find Fletcher's daughter.

Temple Fields on a Saturday night was thronged with people. Drag queens, beautiful boys, striking baby dykes with their tattoos and piercings, and Lady Gaga wannabes were the eye candy, but there were plenty of more conventional-looking people out for a good time in the gay bars and restaurants that lined the streets. The area had shifted from hardcore red-light zone to gay village back in the nineties, but the new century had made it more eclectic, with the hippest of the straight young people happy to hang out in what they perceived as the cool clubs and bars. Now, it was a heaving mix, an anything-goes part of town. And there was still a thriving kerbside sex trade, if you knew where to look.

Sam weaved his way through the crowds, alert for female and male prostitutes. Sometimes they saw him coming, smelled 'cop' on him and melted away into the anonymous crowds before he could speak to them. But he'd managed to talk to half a dozen of the women. A couple of them had completely blanked him, refusing to engage in conversation at all. Sam suspected they knew their pimps were watching.

Two of the others denied any knowledge of Kerry Fletcher. A fifth said she knew Kerry though she hadn't seen her for a day or two, but that was probably because Kerry usually worked Campion Way, not the main drag. So Sam had moved down towards the boulevard that separated Temple Fields from the rest of the city centre. There he'd found a more informative source.

The woman was leaning against the wall in the mouth of an alley, smoking and sipping on a coffee. 'Christ, can't I have ten fucking minutes to myself?' she said as Sam approached. 'I don't give freebies to the Bill.'

'I'm looking for Kerry Fletcher,' Sam said.

'You're not the only one,' the woman said sourly. 'I've not seen her tonight, but her old man was round looking for her last night.'

'I thought he'd been warned off?'

'Maybe so. He's turned the volume down, that's for sure. But he still hangs around, watching her every move. She turned on him last night, though. Told him to fuck right off.'

'How did he take that?'

'He didn't have much choice, she went off with a punter.'

'So what was he saying to her to wind her up?'

'I wasn't paying a lot of attention. I was trying to earn a fucking living. He was going on at her about how it's not safe on the streets. That somebody's killing whores like us and she should come home. She said she'd rather take her chances out on the street than with him. And he said he'd do anything she wanted if she'd just give up selling herself on the streets. And she said, "I just want you to stop this. Now fuck off." Then she walked away and got in this bloke's car.'

'Have you seen them go at it like that before?'

The woman shrugged. 'He's been trying to freak her out about there being a serial killer out there.' She curled her lip in disdain. 'Like we don't know there are bastards out there who get off on hurting us. You don't do this job if you're worried about health and fucking safety. We all know it, all the time. We just try not to fucking think about it.'

'What did he do then, her dad?'

She tossed her cigarette end on the pavement and ground it out. 'He did what he was told. He fucked off. Now I'd like you to do the same.' She waved her fingers at Sam in a shooing motion. 'Go on, you're ruining my trade.'

Sam backed away and watched the woman totter to the

kerbside on insanely high heels. What he'd learned didn't take them much further forward. But it was corroboration. And when you were building a case, sometimes that was the best you could hope for.

51

There was something blissful about the way the blue light carved a line through the traffic. Cars and vans scuttled sideways like crabs when they spotted her. Carol especially loved the ones who were pulverising the speed limit till they saw her in their rear-view. Suddenly they'd brake and slew into the middle lane with an air of, 'Who, me, guv?' When she passed them seconds later, they'd always be staring resolutely straight ahead, their vain pretence glaringly obvious.

Sometimes people genuinely didn't see her. They were lost in music or Radio 4 or some football phone-in on Talk Sport. She'd get right up behind them then give them a blare on the horn. She could actually see one or two of them jump. Then they'd jerk the wheel and she'd be past them, so close she imagined them swearing.

It was exhilarating, this feeling of finally taking action. It felt like forever since she'd stood in the barn looking down at Michael and Lucy's bodies, a viscous sea of time that dragged at her feet and stopped her making any progress. She wanted to move forward, to bury the horror. But she couldn't even start while Jacko Vance walked free. At liberty, he was an affront to her sense of justice.

It wasn't death that Carol wanted to mete out. She knew a lot of people in her shoes would be satisfied with nothing less. But she didn't believe in capital punishment, or even private vengeance that ended up with bodies on the floor. She and Vance were oddly at one on this point. She wanted him to live with the consequences of what he had done. Every day, she wanted him to know he was never going to look at an unfettered sky again.

And she wanted him to know who had put him back behind bars. Every day, she wanted him to hate her more.

Vance couldn't remember the last time he'd been in Halifax. It must have been back when he was making his hit series, *Vance's Visits*. He knew he must have been there before, because he clearly recalled the spectacular road curving down from the motorway round one side of the bowl of hills that cradled the town itself. Tonight it was a basin of lights, sparkling and twinkling below. It must have been hellish in Halifax after the Industrial Revolution. All those wool mills, spewing out smuts of smoke and clots of coal dust, filling the air with noxious fumes and filth, and nowhere for it to escape to, held tight in the embrace of the hills. He could understand the working man's attraction to getting out to the dales and the moors to breathe clean air, to feel like a human being and not just a part in the vast machine.

He swept down from the high motorway into the valley below, keeping an eye out for a possible temporary base. He needed somewhere with wi-fi, so that he could check that his target was where he hoped she would be. It was too late for coffee shops, always supposing Halifax had anything so cool. And he didn't want an Internet café, where people could peer over your shoulder and wonder why you were looking at CCTV pictures of a woman in her living room when she was clearly well past the age of sexual fantasy.

As he rounded a bend, he saw the golden arches of a McDonald's. He remembered Terry telling him that, when all else failed, you could always count on McDonald's. 'Coffee, grub, or the Internet, you can get it there.' Vance shuddered at the thought. Even when he'd pretended to have the common touch, he'd drawn the line at McDonald's. But maybe for once he could make an exception. There must be a quiet corner where he could drink coffee and get online.

At the last minute he swung into the entrance and parked the car. He grabbed his laptop bag and went inside. The restaurant was surprisingly busy, mostly with teenagers who were fractionally too young to persuade even the most short-sighted bartenders that they were old enough for alcohol. Their desperate need to feel cool had driven them out from houses where *Match of the Day* was the natural late-night Saturday fare into the unforgiving glare of McDonald's lighting. They slouched around the place with their milkshakes and colas, the boys with baseball caps at any angle except the conventional, the girls with an astonishing amount of flesh on display. Vance, who considered himself a connoisseur of teenage girls, felt faintly queasy at the sight. He had no interest in girls who had no sense of dignity. What was there to break down when the girls had already given everything away?

Vance bought a cup of coffee and found a table for two in the furthest corner. Although it was near the toilets, he could angle his screen away from prying eyes. Ignoring his drink, he quickly booted up and ran through his camera sites. Nothing at all at Tony Hill's house, though the gateway had been boarded up and 'Danger! Keep Out!' signs had been posted. From the other camera shots, he could see why. The building was gutted. No roof, no windows, just a partially collapsed shell.

The third scene was the one that made him want to shout abuse at the screen. But Vance knew he had to maintain the appearance of calm. The last thing he wanted was to draw attention to himself. Teenagers were notoriously solipsistic, but even so, it only needed one sharp-eyed observer to create all sorts of problems. Still, seeing the stable block still standing filled him with rage. While he watched, Betsy herself came into shot with an armed policeman, a pair of spaniels at her heels. She was gesturing to various aspects of the relatively undamaged stable block as they walked, clearly having an animated conversation. She didn't seem to be suffering at all, the bitch. He wanted her on her knees, weeping and tearing her hair out, locked into painful mourning. Maybe next time he should do the dogs. Cut their throats and leave them on Micky and Betsy's beds. That would show them who had the power. Or maybe he should just do Betsy.

He took a deep breath and clicked on to the last set of active camera feeds. Clockwise, it showed the driveway and frontage of a detached stone-built villa that looked somehow unmistakably Northern. It wasn't a big house – it looked like three reception rooms and three bedrooms, but it was solid and well maintained. In the driveway, outside a detached wooden garage, was a two-seater Mercedes.

Next was a modern kitchen that had the pristine air of somewhere that's only ever used to reheat meals supplied by Waitrose or Marks and Spencer. The lights under the wall cabinets were on, casting a cold glow on pale wood worktops. Beyond the kitchen the ribs of a conservatory loomed pale through the darkness.

In the third view, a camera with a fish-eye lens had obviously been mounted in a corner of the half-landing on the stairs. It was possible to see up to the head of the stairs and through an open door that led to a bedroom, and also down the stairs to the front door, whose stained glass glowed faintly, backlit by the street lights outside.

The fourth feed showed a living room that looked as if not

much living went on there. There was no clutter; no books or magazines, just an alcove lined with DVDs. A long, deep sofa almost as big as a bed and piled with cushions was at the heart of the room. In front of it, an elaborately carved wooden coffee table that held a trio of remote controls, a wine bottle and a single half-full glass of red. An open briefcase sat on the floor at one end of the table. On the opposite wall was an ornate Victorian fireplace. Where one might have expected a complicated overmantel, there was instead a plasma screen TV that filled the whole chimney breast. The room resembled the most private of cinemas, a sad screening room for one. As he watched, a woman walked into the room wearing a loose kaftan, golden brown hair in a shoulder-length bob tucked behind her ears. The definition wasn't good enough for much detail, but Vance was surprised to see that the woman neither looked nor moved like someone on the downward slope of her sixties. She picked up two of the remotes and curled into the sofa, adjusting cushions and pillows so that she was comfortable. The screen sprang into life. The angle made it impossible for Vance to identify what she was watching but she seemed intent on it.

Which was all he needed to know. He wasn't planning on finesse. An elderly woman in the house alone wasn't exactly a challenging target. Especially since there were no obvious weapons in the room – no convenient fire irons or hefty bronze statues. He'd take his chances with a wine bottle.

He watched for a couple of minutes more, then folded his laptop shut and walked out, throwing his untouched coffee in the bin. Nobody paid any attention. Once that would have pissed him off. But Jacko Vance was slowly coming to appreciate the beauty of anonymity.

Tony did not believe in omens. Just because he was hammering up the motorway well over the speed limit and he hadn't had any encounters with the traffic police didn't mean the heavens were aligning in his favour. At one point, a flashing blue light had appeared in his rear-view mirror, but he'd pulled over and the liveried police car had thundered past without a second glance. Clearly someone else was behaving with even less regard for the law than he was. It still didn't mean the gods were on his side.

Besides, he'd completely failed in his attempts to get Carol to talk to him. He'd been trying her number every few minutes, but it kept going straight to voicemail. At first, he'd hoped she was in one of the few remaining black holes for phone reception, but he couldn't sustain that optimism for much longer. To begin with he'd left messages, but he'd stopped doing that. There were only so many times you could caution someone against recklessness without them feeling fatally insulted.

The only thing left that he could think of was to try and shock her into inaction. So, at the next service area, he pulled off the motorway and wrote a text. 'I love you. Don't do ANY-THING before I get to you.' He'd never said it before. It might not be the most romantic of occasions, but it should, he thought, freak her out enough to stop her in her tracks. As soon as she turned on her phone, she would see it. Before he could pause to consider the wisdom of his words, he sent it.

Tony got back on the road, wondering how Ambrose was doing. Maybe that had been his team that had hammered past in the outside lane a while ago. He wasn't sure whether to be happy or anxious about that possibility. He considered calling Ambrose, but before he could do anything about it, Paula rang. 'Can you talk?' she said.

'I'm driving but I'm hands free,' he said.

'I think you were right,' Paula said, filling him in on Sergeant Dean's information. 'I'm just waiting for Stacey to come back with an address for me. She'd done the preliminary checks, only with the wrong gender. Now she's gone back to try again. So far, Fletcher's name's not coming up on any of the Skenby flats.'

'Try his wife's maiden name,' Tony said.

'You think? They've lived there for at least ten years, according to Sergeant Dean.'

'With some people, covering your tracks is second nature. They do it just because they can, not because there's any specific reason for doing it.'

'I'll get Stacey on to it.'

'Good. I could do with something working out tonight.'

'Having a bad time?'

'I'm kind of scared, Paula. I think Carol's on a collision course with disaster and I don't know if I can stop her.'

'That sounds a bit melodramatic, Tony,' Paula said gently. 'And the chief doesn't really do melodrama.'

'I think tonight might be the exception.'

'Is there anything I can do?'

'No, and I don't even want you to try. You need to bring Eric Fletcher in.'

'He can wait.'

Tony sighed. 'Actually, Paula, I'm not convinced about that. He's escalating both in terms of the gaps between his killings and the risk-taking involved in choosing his victims. He's close to the tipping point. If Kerry doesn't give in to his demands soon, he's going to run out of options.'

'Then what? He'll kill himself? Good luck to him, if he does,' she said contemptuously. Paula cared a lot less about keeping the bad guys alive than Carol did. She'd always thought it was because she'd lost more than her boss. But maybe that wasn't true. Maybe they just differed on that fundamental point of principle.

'If he can't scare her home, he'll bring her home,' Tony said.

There was a long silence while Paula digested what Tony

meant. 'Then I'd better chase Stacey up for that address,' she said quietly.

'Do that. I'd like to get through tonight without any more bloodshed.'

Carol hit the speed bump so fast her suspension squealed and she had to wrestle the wheel to keep moving in a straight line. If anyone was watching the CCTV whose camera lights glowed red above her, they'd hit the panic button. People who lived in secluded estates like Vinton Woods paid for security because they didn't want the kind of toerags who hit speed bumps at fifty miles an hour tooling round their streets. Carol tapped the brakes and tried to drive more in keeping with her *Stepford Wives* surroundings.

As she passed the mock Queen Anne houses, Carol noticed no signs of life. Yes, there were lit windows and cars in drives. But the only thing with a pulse that she saw was a sheepish fox who skulked out of her headlights as she rounded a bend. She had to acknowledge Vance had made a smart move. The kind of people who craved this sort of soulless existence simply wouldn't notice if a serial-killing jailbreaker moved in next door, as long as he drove a nice car and didn't come knocking on their door because he'd run out of milk.

She pulled over to the kerb and consulted the map she'd loaded on to her smartphone. Vinton Woods was too new to appear on her car's GPS system, but she'd found the developer's map on their website. She worked out where she was in relation to Vance's house and set off again. Within minutes, she was driving into the cul-de-sac where his house was situated. She tried to make it look like she'd taken a wrong turning, reversing in a neighbour's gateway and heading straight back down to the feeder road.

In her fleeting glimpse, there had been no obvious sign of presence. Carol drove to the end of the street and considered her options. She wanted to take a closer look at the house, but there was no easy way to do it. There was no casual footfall on these pavements. Nobody walked anywhere, because there was nowhere to walk to. No cars were parked on the street because everyone had driveways and garages enough for all the cars their households could possibly support.

She cruised back along the feeder street slowly, noticing that the house opposite the entrance to the cul-de-sac was in darkness. There were no cars in the drive either. Carol decided it was worth taking a chance, so she reversed into the drive and parked in front of a garage door. She had a clear line of sight past Vance's neighbours to his house. It was the perfect spot for a stake-out.

It didn't resolve the problem of getting a closer look at the house. But maybe she didn't need to get up close and personal with the bricks and mortar. As far as she could see, none of the windows facing down the cul-de-sac was curtained. There was no light visible within the house. Unless Vance was in the dark in a room at the back of the house, the chances were that the house was empty. And if he was asleep in a back bedroom, Carol would be best advised to stay put. Who knew what motion sensors and cameras he had in place around the perimeter to alert him to intruders. Everything he'd done so far had been well considered and well planned. The house would be the same.

On the other hand, if she stayed put, she would see him as soon as he left the house. She could shoot out of the driveway here and either ram him, block him or follow him. It made sense from a policing point of view.

It just didn't make much sense from a Carol Jordan perspective. The longer she waited, the more likely it was that Ambrose would turn up mob-handed and fuck up the whole thing. There was only one road in and out of Vinton Woods. If Vance got a sniff that the police were interested, he'd just carry on driving and disappear again. She'd have to try to persuade Ambrose to let her be point man on the operation. They'd have to stay well back, out of sight of anyone driving on to the estate, and trust her to alert them as soon as he showed up. Ambrose had worked under her command before and Carol thought she could probably persuade him that she was to be trusted in that role.

The question was whether she could persuade herself.

The suggestion Tony had passed on via Paula had infuriated Stacey. Not because she thought it was a waste of time, but because she should have got there by herself. She didn't approve of making excuses for herself – her mother had inculcated her in a culture of taking responsibility equally for success and failure – but she did think that if she'd been sitting at her usual workstation, covering the bases would have been much more like second nature. Trying to run two major operations on a laptop and a West Mercia desktop that had a processor with all the speed of a crippled tortoise had proved trying, to say the least.

Finding the details of Kerry Fletcher's mother's death was the work of a couple of minutes. Once she had the woman's maiden name, running those details against the council tenancy list she'd been accessing earlier that evening was something Stacey could have done with her hands tied behind her back.

Within ten minutes of taking Paula's call, Stacey was back on the line. 'You were right about the sixteenth floor. Pendle House, 16C. Sorry, I should have thought it through.'

'No harm done, we've got there now.'

Stacey screwed her face up as if she had a bad taste in her mouth. 'I know, and I don't mind when Dr Hill comes up with stuff that's outside our area of competence. But we're supposed to be detectives, we should have come up with that ourselves.'

'The chief would have,' Paula said, glum in spite of the result.

'I know. I'm not sure I want to carry on being a cop if Blake assigns me to routine CID work.'

'That would be crazy,' Paula said. 'Everybody knows you're a complete geek. Why would Blake not want to make the most of your skills?'

'My parents have relatives whose lives were trashed in the Cultural Revolution. I understand that sometimes people get punished for being too skilled.' Stacey had never spoken so freely to one of her colleagues before. It was ironic that it was the imminent disbanding of their unit that had liberated her tongue.

'Blake's not Chairman Mao,' Paula said. 'He's too ambitious not to exploit you to the full. More likely you'll be chained to a bank of monitors and only allowed daylight once a month. Trust me, Stacey, nobody's going to unplug you. All the scut work, that'll be down to the likes of me and Sam, as per usual. And speaking of Sam – don't you think it's about time you said something to him?'

'What are you talking about?'

'Don't come the innocent with me, Stacey. I am the best interrogator on this squad, nothing gets past me. Ask him out. Life's too short. We're not going to be working together for much longer. You might not see him again from one month's end to the next. Let him know how you feel.'

'You're out of order, Paula,' Stacey said weakly.

'No, I'm not. I'm your mate. And I nearly missed out on Elinor because I had my head too far up my arse with work. Then she gave me half a chance, and I grabbed it. And it changed my life. You need to do the same, Stacey. Or he's going to be gone and you're going to regret it. He's a shit and he doesn't deserve you, but apparently he's what you want, so do something about it.'

'Don't you have an arrest to be making?' Stacey said, recovering some of her spirit.

'Thanks for the info.'

Stacey replaced the phone and stared at the laptop screen. Then she stood up and walked across to the window, looking down at the parking yard below, turning over Paula's words in her head. Apparently there were some things you couldn't figure out by staring into a screen.

Who knew?

52

Vanessa Hill stretched out and refilled her glass, then settled back on her sofa pillows. She loved this sofa with its textured tapestry upholstery, its deep cushions and its high sides. Lounging on it made her feel like a pasha, whatever that was, or a Roman at a feast. She loved to snuggle among the pillows and throws, nibbling at delicate little snacks and sipping wine. She was well aware that the staff at her recruitment agency indulged in lurid water-cooler speculation about her private life. The truth was that what her success and her money had bought her was the right to please her bloody self. And this was what pleased her – her own company, bloody good red wine, satellite TV and an extensive collection of DVDs. It wasn't as if she got the chance to cosset herself that often. A couple of nights a week, at the most. The rest was devoted to building her empire. She might have a bus pass, but Vanessa was a long way from retirement.

The episode of *Mad Men* faded to black and the titles rolled. She considered whether to watch another episode, then decided she'd watch the news and come back to the drama. She switched away from the DVD player and came in at the tail end of yet another bulletin about unrest in the Middle

371

East. Vanessa harrumphed. She'd soon bloody sort them out. None of those men had balls enough to say what they meant. She'd thought it would revolutionise things to have Hillary Clinton running American foreign policy, but mostly it had just been more of the bloody same. Even the newsreaders were looking weary of it all. The only person who seemed to thrive on it was that miserable woman on the BBC who only ever turned up when everything had gone to pot. Vanessa gave a tight little smile that showed precisely where the botox had been injected. You'd run for the hills if you ever saw her coming down your street with a camera crew.

'Former TV presenter Micky Morgan's racing stud was the scene of a vicious attack earlier this evening,' the newsreader said, showing a little animation now. Behind him, a split screen showed an apparently idyllic farmhouse and stable block, and a shot of Micky Morgan at her most glamorous, those famously lovely legs crossed and angled across the front of the sofa she was sitting on. Not a patch on Anne Bancroft, Vanessa thought. 'A stable lad and two horses died in a shocking arson attack at her Herefordshire home. Only the quick response of her staff saved the lives of the remaining valuable racehorses that are boarded at the farm for stud purposes. Another of the stable lads was taken to hospital with smoke inhalation. He's said to be in no danger.'

The screen behind changed to show a live shot of a young reporter standing at the end of a driveway with police officers in the background, the wind whipping her hair into wild strands round her head. She had the faintly startled air of a woman who's been rousted out from watching the *X-Factor*. She waited patiently for the anchor to bring her in but he still had script to work through. 'Micky Morgan used to host the flagship lunchtime show *Midday with Morgan*. She abandoned her TV career after her then husband, fellow TV presenter and former champion athlete Jacko Vance, was revealed as a serial killer of teenage girls. Vance himself made a sensational jail-break earlier this week when he escaped from Oakworth prison, a mere forty-five miles from his ex-wife's farm. Over now to Kirsty Oliver at the scene. Kirsty, are the police connecting this attack to Vance?'

'Will, they're not saying anything officially yet. But I understand there has been an armed police presence here at the farm since news of Jacko Vance's escape became public two days ago. In spite of that, someone managed to infiltrate the stable yard and set a fire in a hay barn behind the main stable block, which you can see in the background.' She waved vaguely over one shoulder. 'The farm remains closed off to visitors and we've seen no sign of Micky herself or her partner Betsy Thorne, though we have been told that they are in residence.'

'Nice of you to let Vance know they're at home,' Vanessa muttered.

'Thanks, Kirsty. We'll come back to you if there's any breaking news from your location.' Sincere, concerned face. 'Police have indicated that they wish to question Jacko Vance in relation to two other incidents – the double murder in Yorkshire yesterday morning and another arson attack in Worcester yesterday evening.' Photographs of two good-looking thirty-somethings appeared behind the newsreader. 'In a new development, police have identified the murder victims as Michael Jordan, a games software developer, and his partner, criminal barrister Lucy Bannerman. Michael Jordan's sister is a detective with Bradfield police, and she's believed to be the officer who arrested Jacko Vance for murder.' Vanessa hastily put her glass down and pushed herself upright. 'Carol Jordan,' she spat, her face as twisted with distaste as it could get these days.

Few people had ever thwarted Vanessa. Even fewer had got away with it. Carol Jordan was one of that tiny band. She was one of the pieces of grit in the oyster of Vanessa's life. She could almost bring herself grudgingly to respect the Jordan woman – she had power and was willing to use it, she was ruthless, and she could clearly be single-minded in pursuit of her goal. These were qualities Vanessa herself possessed in overwhelming amounts and she valued them in others. She also suspected that Jordan shared her ability to assess people's strengths and weaknesses. Where Vanessa used that trait to her own advantage to build her reputation as a shrewd headhunter, Jordan seemed to apply it to bringing criminals to justice. Vanessa couldn't see the point. Where was the profit in that? It wasn't that she minded the existence of the police. Somebody had to keep the scum in their place. But it wasn't the sort of career for anyone who had something about them. And that was why, ultimately, she couldn't respect Carol Jordan.

Before she could wander too far down the path of her feelings towards Carol Jordan, the bulletin caught her attention again and this time it transfixed her. The newsreader had done with the murder and was moving along. 'Vance is also wanted for questioning in another arson attack. Last night in Worcester, this house was razed to the ground.' A photograph of a smoking ruin appeared on the screen. 'Luckily, nobody was home when the fire started. Police have not released the name of the householder, but neighbours said the previous owner, Arthur Blythe, died last year and the new owner has spent very little time here.'

Arthur Blythe. The name Eddie had chosen to live under after he'd recovered enough to walk away from her. As if he'd wanted to lose himself. She'd deserved that house after what she'd had to go through. But he'd left it to the bastard. Why anybody would leave anything to Tony was beyond her. She certainly wasn't going to. She was going to get through the lot before she shuffled off this mortal coil. In a year or two, once the economy started to pick up its heels, she'd flog the business she'd spent a lifetime building up. And then she would rack up all the experiences in her bucket list – all four tennis grand slams in the best seats, safaris to see all the great beasts of Africa, an up-close-and-personal cruise in the Galapagos, the Cannes film festival, the Northern Lights and a dozen more besides. By the time she was done, there wouldn't be two halfpennies for Tony.

The newsreader had moved on to football, but the image of the ruined house was still sharp in Vanessa's head. It was a funny thing to go for if you were trying to hurt somebody. But Jacko Vance was somebody else Vanessa had a grudging respect for. He was another one who'd made his mind up and gone for it. Never mind that what he wanted was illegal and immoral and half a dozen other glib condemnations that the media would deliver at the drop of a dead body. He was determined to achieve his goals, and if it hadn't been for Carol Jordan and, presumably, Tony trotting along in her wake like a pet dog, he'd still be doing what he was best at. No wonder he wanted to get his own back. In his shoes, she'd have felt exactly the same.

Vanessa gave a dark chuckle. If she ever spoke honestly out loud, the water-cooler crowd would wet themselves. If you wanted to get on in this world, you had to be mealy-mouthed. She'd have to admit, Jacko Vance had been impressive on that front too. With all his charity work and his supposed support for the dying, he'd got them all convinced that he was little short of a saint.

He hadn't convinced Jordan, though. And it looked like Vance held Tony responsible too. But burning his house down? It said all you needed to know about what a useless waste of space her bastard son was. At least Jordan had people in her life that it would grieve her to lose. All Tony had was a house. And if you thought Tony was the sort of person who would be bothered by losing a physical possession, your research wasn't as thorough as it should have been.

Even as that thought flitted into her head, Vanessa felt a cold trickle down the back of her neck. What if the house was just the start? What if Vance's research had been really shoddy? Carol Jordan had lost her brother. What if Tony was scheduled to lose a blood relative too?

Tony had just joined the Manchester orbital motorway when his phone rang. He was so shocked to see Carol's name on the screen he almost swerved into the central reservation, his tyres rattling over the studs on the road's edge like automatic weapon fire. Thoroughly discombobulated, he stabbed at the phone's answer button and shouted, 'It's me, I'm here. Are you OK?'

'I'd be better if you didn't leave stupid attention-seeking messages on my phone,' she said. There was nothing friendly in her voice. 'Where's Vance?'

'I've no idea,' he said.

'Not much of a profiler, are you?'

He ignored the insult. He thought she was just trying to wind him up. He hoped, anyway. 'Where are you?'

'I'm at Vinton Woods. I'm staking out the house, but I don't think he's there. Where's Ambrose?'

'Same as me. On his way to where you are.'

'I tried to call him but he's not answering. There's only one road in and out of this development. I think they should hold position away from the estate. If Vance gets a sniff of them, he won't even turn off the main road and we'll have lost him. And this time there won't be some convenient clue on Terry Gates's hard drive.'

'That makes sense,' Tony said.

'I know it makes sense, but I can't communicate that to Ambrose. I don't know if he's blocking my calls, but I can't raise him. You need to call him and tell him. He'll listen to you. He thinks you've got a handle on what's going on.'

She was losing it, he thought. She was losing it and he was still too far away. 'Even if I can get through to him, he won't listen to me. I'm not a cop. I don't have any operational command here. You need to talk to Patterson. Or go further up the chain of command. This isn't something I can do, Carol.'

'You don't *want* to do it, you mean,' she said, her voice low and bitter. 'You can't help yourself, can you? Because you fucked up, now you're overcompensating. Somehow you've got to protect me. You'd rather let Vance escape than have me confront him, because you think I'll fuck up and get killed. Well, you're wrong, Tony. I know what I'm doing. If you won't help, fuck you.'

The line went dead. Tony smacked his fist on the steering wheel. 'Masterful,' he shouted. 'Fucking masterful.' His self-disgust plumbed new depths as his rage simmered down. The one good thing was that Vance hadn't been there when Carol had arrived. The confrontation might only be postponed, but at least it hadn't happened yet.

He drove on, his mind racing over what he knew and what the possibilities might be. Why had Vance not returned to his base camp? He'd been on the road a long time. He'd need to rest properly, not in a hotel room where he had no control of his environment. He'd need to change his appearance somewhere nobody would notice that he looked different going out from coming in. The instinct of the predator was always to return to his lair. So why was Vance not in Vinton Woods? Where could he be? And why?

Tony chewed on the problem as he skirted Manchester and Stockport, Ashton and Oldham and shot out on to the M62. In a few miles, he'd hit the motorway link for Bradfield. He was getting close to Vinton Woods now. He could argue the toss with Carol on the ground.

But still the question of Vance's whereabouts nagged him. 'You want us to live with the pain,' he said. 'Most people would think Carol's the only one who's had that kind of pain so far. It's like she got the full dose, but me and Micky, we've just got our starters.' He gripped the wheel so tightly his knuckles hurt.

'Even if you meant it to be enough, it all went pear-shaped at Micky's. Two horses and a stable lad dead, that's sad, but it's not really a tragedy, even for Betsy, who loves the horses. You're not going to be able to let that rest. But not tonight. Not while the place is crawling with cops. You're going to have to wait.' He sighed in exasperation. 'So all the more reason for you to go back to your hole in the ground, the place you think you're safe. Rest. Regroup. Plan. Then do something to Micky that she'll carry like a scar for the rest of her life.' It felt right. It had the shape of Vance's thinking. It had taken Tony a while to crawl back inside Vance's mind. But now he was sure. He didn't just know with his head. He empathised. He understood what made Vance tick, what he needed and what would satisfy him.

'You thought this was going to be quick and dirty. You'd gallop through your list, and you'd feel vindicated. But now you know it's not that easy. The suffering needs to be very particular . . . ' His voice tailed off.

If the horses weren't enough, the house wasn't enough. In Tony's world, it was as shattering and disruptive as a bereavement. However, that wouldn't be how others saw it. Vance might have got it, if he'd been doing the watching and the deciding himself. If he'd seen Tony in the house with his own eyes, he'd have known precisely what he was achieving. But he hadn't. He'd had to rely on the reports of others. Others who couldn't creep about inside strangers' heads with any degree of insight.

In those circumstances, the house couldn't be enough. Carol would be the obvious person to take from him. That would rip his heart out, no doubt about it. But Vance couldn't kill Carol,

378

because her ongoing pain was integral to his satisfaction. And what had happened to Chris, not Carol, would that have been enough? Maybe. But if a disfigured and damaged Carol wasn't enough, that didn't leave many options. Tony's life was not overburdened with friendships. There were plenty of acquaintances, colleagues, former students. There were a handful of people he thought of as friends, but they weren't close in the way that Vance would need. Besides, from the outside, they probably didn't appear to be more than workmates. If he went for a drink with Ambrose or Paula, it would look like colleagues having a couple of beers after work. No big deal. Only someone who knew Tony a damn sight better than Vance possibly could would have grasped the importance of those connections. When it came to revenge, they didn't even register.

And if revenge was to be worth anything, it had to matter deep down. Tony understood the atavistic importance of getting your own back in the right way. All through his life, his mother had used him as an emotional punchbag. She'd belittled him, criticised him, made fun of him. She'd made sure he grew up without a father, without a refuge, without love. She hadn't cared whether he succeeded or failed. And he'd grown into an emotionally limited, dysfunctional man, saved from ruin only by fragments of other people's love and the gift of empathy.

When he'd first found out the full scope of Vanessa's treachery and lies, he'd sworn he never wanted to speak to her again. But the more he'd grown into the idea of changing his life and accepting the hand Arthur Blythe had offered from beyond the grave, the more he'd wanted her to know that, in spite of her best efforts, he was not destroyed. That the man she'd driven from his life had found a different kind of strength, one that could circumvent Vanessa's confrontational negativity. And that had healed some vital part of Tony's spirit.

He couldn't think of anything that would piss her off more than knowing that.

So he'd driven over to Halifax one afternoon and waited for her to come home. She'd been surprised to see him, but she'd asked him in. He'd said what he had to say, raising his voice and talking over her when she tried to undercut him. Eventually, she'd shut up, settling for an expression of amused contempt. But he could read her body language, and he knew she was raging with impotent fury. 'I'm never going to enter this house again,' he said. 'I'm never going to see you again. You better make your funeral arrangements in advance, Vanessa. Because I'm not even going to be there to bury you.'

And he'd left, a lightness in his heart that was completely alien to him. Getting your own back was a wonderful thing. He understood exactly the sense of release that Vance was looking for.

Then it hit him. He'd visited his mother's house. A watcher would have had no idea why he was there or what had gone on inside. He'd just have seen a dutiful son visiting his mother and coming out of the house with a smile on his face and a spring in his step. The watcher had made his report and Vance had leapt to the wrong conclusion.

All at once, Tony knew exactly where Jacko Vance was.

53

Paula bounced from foot to foot, dragging incessantly on her cigarette. 'Where the fuck are they?' she demanded, scanning the approaches to the dingy grey concrete tower where they were waiting. Above their heads were twenty-one floors of egg-box flats, all thin walls and cheap paint and peeling laminate covering cold damp concrete floors. More stolen TVs than hot dinners. Skenby Flats. Bradfield's answer to *Blade Runner*.

'They're always late. It's their way of showing how important they are,' Kevin grumbled, trying to find a spot under the block of flats that didn't feel like the working end of a wind tunnel. 'Where's Sam?'

'He's gone out to Temple Fields to see if he can pick up Kerry. You never know, she might be ready to grass him up for all those years of misery.' Paula exhaled a long sigh of smoke. It seemed to dissolve straight into the concrete. 'I just don't get how you keep your mouth shut when a man starts abusing your child.' Kevin opened his mouth to say something, then shut up, seeing her minatory shake of the head. 'I know all the feminist arguments about being beaten down and victimised. But you have got to know that there is nothing more wrong

381

than this. Nothing worse than this. Frankly, I don't understand why they don't all top themselves.'

'That's a bit harsh for you, Paula,' Kevin said, once he was sure she'd finished. The lift doors groaned as they opened. A couple of lads in hoodies and low-slung sweat pants slouched past them in a waft of cannabis and sweet wine.

'What would you do if you found out someone had been abusing your kids, and your wife had known and done nothing about it?'

Kevin's face went into an awkward lopsided expression. 'It's a stupid question, Paula, because it wouldn't happen that way in our house. But I get what you're saying. You've got to know in your head there's a huge yawning gulf between loving the very bones of them and abusing them. I'm glad I'm not Tony Hill and I don't have to let that kind of shit contaminate the inside of my head. And speaking of Tony, has anybody heard how he's doing? With the house and all that?'

Paula shrugged. 'I don't think he's in a good place. As much because of the chief as the house. And of course, he's upset about Chris.'

'Any news on that front?'

'Elinor texted me a while back. Nothing's changed, and apparently the longer it stays that way, the better her chances of avoiding major lung damage.'

Neither of them spoke for a few moments. Then, his voice soft, Kevin said, 'When she gets to the far side of this, I don't know that she'll thank them for saving her.'

It was no more than Paula had already considered. 'Don't,' she said. 'Don't go there. Imagine what it's going to be like for the chief.'

'Where is she, anyway?'

'I have no idea. Frankly, I feel like we're well out of it. And here we go,' she said, pointing down the walkway to a group of half a dozen officers jogging towards them in tactical support gear. Stab vests and forage caps, door ram and a couple of semi-automatic weapons. Paula turned to Kevin. 'Did you ask for firearms?'

'Nope,' he said. 'That'll be Pete Reekie, grandstanding.'

The black-clad officers reached them and milled around, jaws up, trying for hard. None of them was displaying numbers or rank on their jumpers. They made Paula feel nervous.

'My operation,' Kevin said. 'We're going to do this the old-fashioned way. I'm going to knock on the door and see if Eric Fletcher is at home and whether he'll invite us in. If he doesn't, you can do the knock,' he said, tapping the door ram with his knuckles. 'Let's go.' He pressed the lift button.

'We should use the stairs,' the apparent leader said.

'Please yourself,' Paula said. 'I'm on twenty a day and Eric's on the sixteenth floor. See you there,' she added, stepping through the opening doors, followed by Kevin. 'At some point in history, I signed up for what was nominally the same job as them. Doesn't that feel scary to you?'

Kevin laughed. 'They're just boys. They're more scared than the villains are. We just need to keep them well away from the action.'

They waited by the lifts for the elite squad to make it up the stairs. Paula used the time to smoke another cigarette. 'I'm nervous,' she said, catching Kevin's disapproval.

At last the tactical group arrived and were deployed around the landing. A swirl of rain blew into their faces as Kevin and Paula walked along the gallery. The door of 16C had been badly painted so many times it looked like an entry for the Turner Prize with its array of drips and blisters and scuffs of different colours. Now it was mostly royal blue with dirty white plastic numbers.

Kevin knocked at the door and at once they heard the shuffling scuffle of feet in the hallway. The door was opened in under a minute, bringing a waft of bacon and cigarettes with it.

The man who stood there wouldn't attract much attention at first glance. He was a couple of inches taller than Paula, with fine mousy hair that reminded her of a child's. He wore jeans and a T-shirt that revealed pale, doughy arms. His face was pudgier than his body, and there was nothing remarkable about his pale blue eyes. But there was an intensity in his manner that was instantly obvious. If they were right about him being the killer, Paula was surprised that he managed to get prostitutes to come along with him so willingly. In her experience, most of the street women had a pretty good instinct for a punter who was a bit off. And Eric Fletcher screamed 'off' to her.

They identified themselves and Kevin asked if they could come in. 'Why do you want to do that?' Fletcher said. His voice was dull and grating. He cocked his head at an angle, his stare challenging without being defiant.

'We need to talk to you about your daughter,' Paula said.

He folded his arms across his chest. 'I've got nothing to say about my daughter. She doesn't live here no more.'

'We're concerned about her well-being,' Kevin said.

Fletcher raised one corner of his top lip in a sneer. 'Well, I'm not, ginger.'

'Do you drive a car, Mr Fletcher?' Paula asked, hoping a change of tack would unsettle him.

'What's it to you? First it's my daughter, now it's my car. Make your mind up, love. Oh, but wait. You can't, can you? You being a woman, and all.' He made a move to shut the door, but Kevin's arm shot out and stopped it.

'We can do this inside or we can do this down the station,' Kevin said. 'What's it going to be?'

'I know my rights. If you want me to come down the station, you can arrest me. Otherwise you can fuck off.' Fletcher smirked, catching the look between Kevin and Paula. It was as if he knew how little evidence they had and he wanted to taunt them.

Part of Paula wanted to arrest him on suspicion of murder. Her years of experience told her he had something he wanted to keep hidden. But if she did that, the clock would start ticking and they'd only have thirty-six hours to question him before they had to charge him or let him go. 'I think you should invite us in,' Paula said in her toughest voice.

'I don't think so,' Fletcher said. There was a determination in those four words that provoked Paula beyond bearing. She knew they were right and she wasn't going to let him slip through their fingers.

Paula put her hand to her ear and tilted her head towards the hallway. 'Can you hear that, Sarge? Somebody shouting for help?' She moved forward till her leading elbow was touching Fletcher's chest.

Now Fletcher showed some edginess. 'It's not shouting for help. It's *Match of the Day*, you stupid bint. It's football supporters.'

'I think you're right, detective,' Kevin said, moving in behind her. Fletcher was going to have to yield or be pushed aside. He spread his legs and stood his ground. Kevin turned and shouted down the landing, 'We've got someone in here shouting for help.'

And then it was all a blur of noise and movement and black. Paula flattened herself against the wall as the tactical squad batted Fletcher to the ground and cuffed him. They poured into the living room at the end of the hall like they expected Osama bin Laden's ghost to be hunched over the gas fire. Two of them slipped back into the hall and busted into the first room. Paula saw the corner of a bathroom before the two men backed out and slammed open the door opposite. They stopped on the threshold and one said, 'Oh, fuck.'

Paula pushed past them and looked in. The only thing it was possible to take in was on the double bed. The remains of a woman's body appeared to float on a sea of red. She had been slashed to ribbons, her flesh flayed from the bones in places. Just as Tony had predicted, the only intact part of her was her head. Splashes and drips of blood dotted the walls like a modern art installation. Paula turned away, an overwhelming sense of waste choking her. Tony had been right about something else too. There had been an issue of urgency. And they hadn't been nearly urgent enough.

Kevin was reciting the words of the caution over Fletcher's prone body. One of the tactical squad was on his radio calling for a full crime-scene technical team, another was on the phone to Superintendent Reekie reporting on what they'd found. If this was a blaze of glory, you could stick it up your arse, Paula thought.

The two cops by the bedroom door backed into the living room. Paula followed them into the dusty disarray and gave the TV an empty glance. 'It was *Match of the Day*, after all,' she said wearily. 'My mistake.' Next to the TV, a framed photo had pride of place. A few years younger, it was true, but there was no doubt that the woman on the bed was Kerry Fletcher.

'She should have come home,' Fletcher shouted. 'None of this would have happened if she'd just come home.'

Tony shot up the exit ramp, his tyres squealing as he hit the roundabout and dragged the car round till he was tearing back on to the motorway in the opposite direction. As soon as he could prise a hand off the wheel, he reached for his phone and hit the redial to speak to Ambrose. And went straight to voicemail. The same thing that had happened to Carol.

'Please, no,' he wailed. 'This is crap.' The phone beeped. 'Alvin, this is Tony. I know where Vance is. Please, call me back as soon as you can.'

Another five miles back to the M62, then a few more miles to the Halifax turn. What if he was too late? How easy would that be to live with?

His phone rang, shaking him out of his introspection. The voice was crackly and remote. 'Dr Hill? This is DC Singh. I'm dealing with DS Ambrose's phone because he's driving and doesn't want to be distracted. You say you know where Vance is?'

'Put Alvin on. This is important, I don't have time to explain it from scratch.'

There was a crackly confusion of speech. Then Ambrose's voice boomed out. 'What the fuck, doc? I thought Vinton Woods was a definite.'

'That's where he's based, not where he is right now.'

'So where is he right now?'

'I think he's at my mother's house,' Tony said. 'He wants blood, Alvin. Bricks and mortar's just a start. And the only blood I've got is my mother.'

'I've got a whole team on their way to Vinton Woods. How can you be sure he's not there?'

'Because Carol Jordan is and she says the house is empty.'

'Can you trust her?'

'Yes.' Tony didn't even have to think about that one. She might not want to be in the same room as him, but that didn't mean she'd start lying to him about the important stuff.

'And you think he's at your mother's house? Have you got any evidence to back that up, doc?'

'No,' Tony said. 'Just a lifetime of experience dealing with fucked-up heads like Vance. I'm telling you, he wants blood on his hands. He killed Carol's brother and my mother is the logical next move.' There wasn't any point in trying to explain Vance's likely misunderstanding of the relationship between Tony and Vanessa. 'I'm on my way there now. I'm probably about fifteen minutes away.'

There was a long interval of static, then Ambrose said, 'Give DC Singh the bloody address, then. And don't do anything stupid.'

Tony did the first part of what he'd been told. 'How far away are you?' he asked DC Singh.

'We're on the M62, a couple of miles before the Bradfield exit.'

He was still ahead of them, but only just. And Vance was a long way ahead of all of them.

54

There were a few cars parked on the quiet Halifax street. Not all of the houses had drives that could accommodate all their vehicles, especially on a Saturday night when people came round to eat dinner and complain about the government. That suited Vance. Nobody would notice one extra parked among the locals. He slotted in between a Volvo and a BMW three houses down from Vanessa Hill and opened up a window on his smartphone that showed the live camera feed from her living room. The image was small and lacked resolution at that size, but it was clear enough to let him see she was still curled up on her regal sofa watching TV.

It was hard to imagine Tony Hill at ease in that room, focused as it was on meeting the needs of one person alone. Where did he sit when he visited? Did they camp out in that sterile kitchen, or was the conservatory the place where Vanessa gave some consideration to the comfort of her guests? Or was it more that her son had inherited his lack of casual social skills from her? Over the years, Vance had replayed his encounters with the strange little man who'd chased him down based on instinct and insight rather than robust forensic evidence. He'd often wondered if Hill was autistic, so awkward was he in social encounters that were not based exclusively on drawing information from the other person. But maybe it was less interesting than that. Maybe he'd grown up with a mother who had no interest in social encounters in the home, so Hill hadn't learned how to do it at an early enough age for it ever to have become second nature.

Whatever the dynamic here, it wasn't going to exist for much longer.

Vance gave a last look round to check there was nobody about, then he got out of the car and took a holdall from the boot. He walked briskly up the street and turned in at Vanessa's gate as if he lived there. He walked past the Mercedes, his rubber-soled shoes silent on the block-paved driveway. There was a gap between the 1930s wooden garage and the house, barely wide enough for an adult turned sideways. Vance slipped into the space and sidestepped his way to the back garden. He hadn't had a chance to scout out the back of the house; he didn't even know whether there were security lights. But for once, he was willing to take the risk. It wasn't as if his target was much of a challenge. An old woman with a bottle of wine inside her wasn't exactly going to be on full alert if her back garden lights suddenly came on. Even if she noticed, she'd write it off as a cat or a fox.

But as he emerged, no light flooded the patio. All was still, silent but for the distant hum of traffic. He put down his holdall and squatted beside it. He took out a paper overall like the ones worn by the CSI teams and struggled into it, almost falling over as he tried to get his prosthetic arm inside without dislodging any crucial connections. Plastic bootees over his shoes, blue nitrile gloves on his hands. He wasn't trying to avoid leaving forensic traces. He didn't care about that. But he wanted a quick getaway and he didn't want to be soaked in blood on the short drive back to Vinton Woods. That would be the kind of carelessness that deserved to be punished by a random road accident.

Vance stood up, rolling his shoulders and flexing his spine to make the overall settle on his body. He hefted the crowbar in his hand and set the knife down on the sill of the window by the back door. He took a good look at the door, assessing its strengths and weaknesses, and smiled. Someone had replaced the original solid wood door with a modern one whose glass panels rendered it a lot weaker. Luckily, they'd gone for wood rather than UPVC. Contemporary wooden doors were made of soft wood that splintered and broke relatively easily. This was not going to be much of a challenge.

He pushed against the top and bottom of the door to test whether there were any bolts, but apparently Hill hadn't invited his good friend DCI Jordan round to sort out his mother's security. It seemed that the door was only secured by the mortice lock and the door catch.

Vance pushed the point of the crowbar into the spot where the door met the jamb. It was a tight fit, but he was strong enough to force it in, denting the soft wood of the door-frame in the process. He pushed harder, trying to put more stress on the lock before he began the serious business of forcing it.

Once he was satisfied he had the leverage right, Vance leaned into the crowbar, using his weight as well as his strength against the wood and metal holding the door closed. At first, his only reward was a faint creak of wood. He put more effort into it, grunting softly like a pianissimo tennis player on the serve. This time, he felt something give. He paused to realign the crowbar's bite and put everything into shifting the lock body out of the box keep. This time, there was a scream of metal and a splintering of wood as the door burst open.

Vance stood panting on the threshold, feeling very pleased with himself. He shifted the crowbar into his prosthetic hand, checking his grip was secure. It was amazing how well this worked. He could actually 'feel' that he was holding something and he could judge how much pressure he needed to apply to keep hold of it. And those bastards had wanted to deny him access to this technology. He shook his head, smiling at the memory of his delight at their defeat in the European Court. But this was no time for basking in past victories. He had work to do. Vance reached for the knife with the seven-inch blade that he'd left on the window sill and stepped inside the kitchen.

To his surprise, there was no sign of Vanessa Hill. He hadn't made a lot of noise, it was true, but most people were attuned to the sounds of their home at an unconscious level, particularly when they were home alone. Anything out of the ordinary would bring them to their feet to investigate. Apparently Vanessa Hill was either hard of hearing or so engrossed in whatever crap she was watching on TV that she hadn't heard him break in. Admittedly, the door into the hallway was closed, which might have made the difference between hearing and not.

Vance moved across the kitchen as quietly as he could, lifting his feet high to avoid the shuffle of his bootees on the tiled floor. He inched the door open and wasn't surprised to hear American voices talking and laughing. He walked down the hall, his movements loose and relaxed now he was so close to accomplishing his goal. First he'd taken Tony Hill's home from him. Now he was going to rob him of his only relative, his beloved mother. Vance's one regret was that he wouldn't be sticking around to see the suffering at first hand.

Two steps away from the threshold of the living room he paused, straightening his spine and squaring his shoulders. The flickering TV light reflected on the shining steel of his blade.

Then he was through the door and round the sofa and brandishing his weapons at the woman sitting upright among the cushions. Her response was not what he expected. Instead of screaming panic, Vanessa Hill was simply looking at him with mild curiosity.

'Hello, Jacko,' she said. 'What kept you?'

55

Tony assumed the blue flashing lights that were gaining on him all the way up the main drag belonged to Ambrose. He turned into the side street leading to his mother's road just ahead of them and managed to stop them overtaking him before they all took a hard left into her street.

Tony abandoned his car in the road, making no attempt at parking. He ran for the front door, but before he got there, a young Asian man grabbed him in a bear hug and slammed him into the side of the house. 'No, you don't,' he said. Then Ambrose was in front of him, struggling into a stab vest the size of a car door.

'Take it easy, Tony,' he said softly. 'You don't go in first. Have you got a key?'

Tony snorted. 'No. And no, I don't know if any of the neighbours has one. I'd doubt it, though. She's a very private person, my mother.'

A couple of other officers were hanging back near the gate. 'We could just ring the bell,' one of them said.

'We don't want a hostage situation,' Ambrose said.

'You're not going to get a hostage situation,' Tony said. 'He's here for a reason. He'll kill then leave. If he's still in there, it's only because he's in the process of leaving.' He gestured with his head towards the narrow passage by the garage. 'You might want to send one of your lads down there in case Vance is going out the back door.'

Ambrose pointed to one of the officers then stabbed his thumb at the gap. 'Take a look.' He gave Tony a perplexed look. 'Let's ring the bell, then.' He pointed a finger at Tony. 'But you stay behind us. Whatever happens, you stay behind us.'

They walked up to the door, surprisingly quietly for such big men. Tony found enough space between Singh and Ambrose to see what was going on. Ambrose rang the bell then stepped back so he was out of reach of anyone swinging a punch from the doorway.

Tony felt his stomach clench. He was convinced he was closer to Vance than he'd been at any time in the past twelve years. Whether the killer was in the house already or on his way here, this was the place where they'd find him. What the cost of that confrontation might be, Tony didn't want to consider right now. What he wanted was to see Vance caged again and caged for good. No question about it, he was one of the ones who should never have any kind of freedom. It went against the grain of Tony's heartfelt conviction that rehabilitation should always be the goal of the judicial process, but every now and again, he was forced to accept that someone was beyond help. Unredeemable. Vance was a walking exemplar whose very existence felt like a rebuke. He and his kind reminded Tony that the system's failures generally created more fallout than its successes.

A light snapped on behind the glass and they could hear a key turning in the lock. The door inched open and Vanessa's face appeared in the gap, her hair disarranged as if she'd been roused from a nap. Ambrose and Singh held out their ID and garbled their names and ranks. Tony gave a thin smile and waved at her. 'Hello, Mum,' he said, sounding as weary as he suddenly felt.

'That was fast,' Vanessa said, opening the door wider to reveal a scarlet stain spreading across her kaftan from chest to mid-thigh. 'I've only just rung 999. You'd better come in.'

Ambrose turned and looked at Tony, wide-eyed with shock. Feeling light-headed, Tony pushed past the cops and stepped inside as Vanessa pulled the door back and invited them in.

She pointed to the barely ajar living-room door and said in a matter-of-fact way, 'You won't want to go in there. It's what you lot call a crime scene. But we can go into the dining room. He didn't go in there at all, so there's nothing to contaminate.' She led the way down the hall to another door and swung it open. 'Don't just stand there, come through.'

Ambrose took a step forward and nudged the living-room door further open. Tony edged round so he could see past him. A man was sprawled on the floor like a marionette, legs askew, arms out to the side, a blonde wig adrift above his head. 'It's Vance,' Tony said. 'I recognise him.' Vance's overall was ripped open. His abdomen was bright red and blood had flowed on to the carpet around him. His chest was motionless. Tony didn't know much about emergency medicine, but he reckoned the paramedics would be wasted on Jacko Vance.

'She killed him?' Ambrose said, incredulous.

'Looks that way,' Tony said.

'You don't seem surprised.'

Tony felt as if he might burst into tears. 'Nothing about Vanessa has ever surprised me. Let's go and see what she has to say for herself before the local plods arrive.'

They followed Singh and the other officer into the dining room, where Vanessa had settled herself at the head of the table. When they came in, she said, 'Tony, fetch me a brandy. There's a bottle and glasses in the sideboard.'

'I don't think you should drink,' Ambrose said. 'You're in shock.'

Vanessa gave him the contemptuous look her staff had

learned to fear. 'In shock, be blowed,' she said, sounding eerily like Patricia Routledge channelling Hyacinth Bouquet. 'This is my house and my brandy and I won't be bossed around by the likes of you.'

'Believe me, it's easier to go with the flow,' Tony said, opening the sideboard and fixing his mother a drink. He took it to her and said, 'What happened?'

'He came in through the back door armed with a crowbar and a knife and walked into my living room, bold as brass. Of course, I recognised him.' She took a sip of brandy and pursed her lips. For the first time since they'd arrived, the mask slipped, revealing age and tiredness normally held at bay by cosmetics and willpower. 'I'd been expecting him, truth be told.'

'Expecting him?' Ambrose sounded as gobsmacked as Tony felt.

'I do watch the news, Sergeant. And aren't you a little bit low down the totem pole to be dealing with a murder?'

'Sergeant Ambrose isn't here in response to your phone call. He's here because we have been trying to catch Vance.'

Vanessa gave a dry little laugh. 'Should have been here earlier then, shouldn't you.' She shook her head in exasperation. 'I saw the news and I recognised that house Eddie left you down in Worcester. I'd already heard about your girlfriend's brother.'

Ambrose gave Tony a startled glance.

Tony sighed. 'She is not my girlfriend. How many times?'

Vanessa waved a dismissive hand at him and drank more brandy. 'Then his attack on the ex-wife. I thought to myself, he started on a high with murder, now he's on a downward spiral and he's not going to be impressed with himself over two racehorses and a stable lad who didn't even merit a name check. So I reckoned he might be daft enough to think that killing me would cause that one some grief.' She tipped her head towards Tony. 'Stupid bugger.' It wasn't at all clear whether she meant Tony or Vance. 'So I thought, better safe than sorry. I got a knife out of the kitchen drawer and tucked it down the side of the sofa. I didn't hear him break in at all. The first I knew about it, he was standing in my living room like he owned the place.' She gave a shiver. Tony thought it was entirely calculated.

'He came at me with the knife. I grabbed my own weapon and struck out at him. I took him by surprise. He fell on top of me and it took all my strength to push him away. That's when I got covered.' She swept her hand from her chin to her knees. 'It was him or me.'

'I understand,' Ambrose said.

'Shouldn't somebody caution her?' Tony couldn't quite believe that Ambrose seemed to be falling under his mother's monstrous spell.

'Caution me? When all I've done is defend myself against a convicted murderer attacking me in my own home?' Vanessa went for pitiful rather than outraged.

'It's for your own protection,' Ambrose said. 'And Tony's right. We should say that you do not have to say anything but it may harm your defence if you do not mention now something you later rely on in court. Anything you say may be given in evidence.'

Vanessa gave Tony one of her indefinable looks. He'd learned the hard way that it meant he would pay for it later. It was one of the pleasures of having her out of his life that these days there could be no later. 'Thank you, Sergeant,' she said, giving him a frail smile.

Before anyone could say anything more, there were voices in the hall. Ambrose went out and returned moments later with a couple of local uniformed officers. 'I've told these officers they need to contact DCI Franklin in the first instance,' he said to Tony. 'They'll need a statement from you at some point. But right now, I think you need to get off.'

Tony looked puzzled for a moment. 'You don't need me to stay?'

Ambrose gave him the hard stare of a man trying to communicate a meaning beyond his words. 'The colleague we spoke to earlier? At the marina? I think you need to liaise.'

Now Tony understood. He turned to Vanessa. 'You'll be all right?'

'Of course. These lovely men will take care of me.' Vanessa stood and walked into the hall behind him.

When they were out of earshot, he said bitterly, 'You've always been handy with a knife, Mother.'

'You must have realised I was a target. You should have warned me,' Vanessa fired straight back at him. With her back to everyone, she could show her true face: vindictive, hateful and unforgiving.

Tony looked her up and down, appalled at the thought sneaking around in the darkness at the back of his mind. He believed this really might be the last time he would ever willingly be in the same room with her. 'Why?' he said as he walked away.

56

It was midnight when Tony drove wearily on to the Vinton Woods estate. There were few lights visible as he tried to find his way round the development. He made a couple of wrong turns before he finally found himself on the right street. He crawled along, looking from side to side, trying to spot Carol's car.

Then he saw her, tucked away in someone's driveway, opposite the mouth of a cul-de-sac. He parked on the street and laid his head on the steering wheel for a moment. He'd reached that point of exhaustion where his very bones seemed to hurt. He dragged himself out of the driver's seat and walked back towards Carol's car, barely capable of maintaining a straight line.

Tony reached the gate and stood there, occupying the middle of the drive. The way things were, he didn't feel he could presume to open the passenger door and get in beside her. It felt too much like invading her space.

A long time seemed to pass but finally the driver's door opened and Carol emerged. She looked haggard, wired, beyond his reach. 'You'll scare him off, standing there,' she hissed at him. 'For Christ's sake. Get in the car.'

Tony shook his head. 'He's not coming, Carol.'

A flare of hope livened her eyes. 'He's been taken?'

'He's been killed.'

She stared wordlessly at him for what felt like minutes, the small muscles in her face shifting between joy and pain. 'What happened?' she said at last, her lips barely moving.

Tony stuck his hands in his trouser pockets and shrugged like an awkward teenager. 'It's ridiculous.'

'Tell me what happened.'

'Vanessa . . . she stabbed him.'

'Vanessa? Your mother, Vanessa?'

Incredulity, Tony thought. He was going to have to get used to that. *Yes, it was my mother who killed the notorious serial killer Jacko Vance.* That was going to provoke a lot of very odd looks. For now, he had to get through the only explanation that counted. 'He broke into her house. To kill her. But she'd figured it out. Can you believe that? The woman with the empathy bypass figured out what none of us with all our training could work out. That she was on his list.' He could hear the bitterness and anger in his voice, but he didn't care. 'So she had a knife tucked down the side of the bloody sofa.'

'She went for him?'

He shifted his weight from one foot to the other. 'She says he went for her and she caught him unawares. Whatever happened, that'll be the official version.'

Carol giggled, a strangled hysterical sound. 'Vanessa killed him? She stabbed him?'

'She's got better at it since the last time.'

'How do you feel about that, Doctor Hill?' There was a harsh sarcastic edge to Carol's question.

'I'm not sorry Vance is dead.' He raised his chin and looked Carol straight in the eye. 'But if things had gone the other way, I wouldn't have been sorry about that either. That's the hard one I'm going to have to live with.'

'Still a bloody sight easier than the one I'm going to have to live with.'

He spread his hands out in a gesture of helplessness. 'I'm sorry.'

'I know you are. That doesn't make it any easier.'

'But at least he's dead now. The damage goes no further. It's over.'

Carol's expression mixed sorrow and pity. 'It's not all that's over, Tony.' She turned away and got back into the car. The engine burst into life and the headlights blinded him. He jumped to one side and watched her drive away, not sure whether it was the sudden brightness of the lights or the bone-weary exhaustion that had brought the tears to his eyes.